DISCOVERING Sophie

A Novel

DISCOVERING

A Novel

by
Cindy Roland Anderson

**WINSOME
PRESS**
PUBLISHING

Discovering Sophie
Cindy Roland Anderson
©2013 Cindy Roland Anderson
Published by Winsome Press Publishing

Published by Winsome Press Publishing, Farmington, UT

LIBRARY OF CONGRESS CATALOGING-IN-PUBLICATION
DATA
LCCN: 2013952357

1. Fiction. 2. Women's. 3. Romance
ISBN- 13: 978-0615901992
ISBN-10: 0615901999

Editor: Sadie L. Anderson
Typeset Sadie L. Anderson
Cover Design by Harbertson Design
Cover Photography by Tomi Kennedy

For my parents Mitch and Reva Roland—thank you for always supporting me and for making me believe I could do anything I set my mind to. I love you both so much.

Chapter One

It was love at first sight. Those baby blue eyes captured Sophie Kendrick's heart the minute she looked into them. "Hey, sweetheart," she said running her fingers through soft brown curls. "Don't you look handsome today."

The only reply she received was a firm tug on the stethoscope that hung around her neck, bringing her face close to skin scented with one of Sophie's favorite smells—baby lotion.

Sophie smiled at the little boy and gently reclaimed her stethoscope, only to have chubby fingers grasp onto dark brown strands of her chin-length hair. Laughing, Sophie freed her hair and passed the child back to his mother. "He's beautiful and perfectly healthy."

"Thanks, Dr. Kendrick. I wasn't sure if you'd remember us or not."

"You're welcome, and I do remember you." Sophie caressed the little boy's cheek. "I just can't believe how much he's grown."

"Me either." The mother cuddled the little boy close. "Well, we just wanted to stop and say hello."

"I'm glad you did."

Sophie watched mother and child leave the Denver Children's Hospital multipurpose room, grateful that a mere six months ago her steady hands had successfully repaired the baby's defective small intestine a few days after his birth.

As a pediatric surgeon, she didn't often get to see the kids she'd helped once they were healed. However, today the hospital was celebrating the opening of a new wing by throwing an open house for the public.

It gave Sophie an opportunity to see some of the children she'd provided medical care for since she'd come to Colorado almost two years earlier.

Sophie surveyed the gathered crowd, noticing other doctors, hospital administrators, and a few notable donors among the community of patrons and former patients. She caught sight of her boyfriend, Peter Elliot, standing in the corner. He'd arrived an hour ago, greeted her briefly, and then excused himself to take a business call. She'd seen very little of him since that time.

As always, whenever she looked at Peter, she couldn't help thinking how incredibly handsome he was. Dark wavy hair styled to perfection and a strong jaw line made him stand out in any crowd. Given the way his shoulders filled out his Armani suit, Peter fit the image of the successful attorney that he was.

Most of their acquaintances thought they were the perfect couple—a doctor and an attorney—and since both of them had dark hair and brown eyes, they were bound to have beautiful, dark-haired, intelligent children.

If only it were that simple.

While Sophie loved Peter, she wasn't *in love* with him. It was crazy. Sophie longed to get married and start a family, and although Peter was a very sought after bachelor, she hadn't been able to give him an answer when he'd asked her to marry him a couple of weeks ago.

The familiar pang of unease lodged in her chest as she continued to watch him. Peter had said he'd give her time, especially with everything that was going on in her life, but how long would he wait?

Before she looked away, Peter met her gaze and gave her an impatient look, then gestured toward his watch. He had wanted to leave thirty minutes ago.

Knowing she'd made him wait long enough, she nodded her head and stooped down to pick up her purse.

A wave of dizziness made her start to lose her balance. As she straightened back up, Sophie drew in a long, cleansing breath and waited for the dizzy spell to pass. The weeks of sleepless nights were finally getting to her.

The nightmares had started a month ago. At first they only came once or twice a week. Now, each night when Sophie closed her eyes, the recurring dream would awaken her, remind her that her father was still missing and that she had no idea what had happened to him.

Sophie crossed the room, hoping she didn't look as bad as she suddenly felt. She finger-combed the wispy layers in her hair, hoping it helped restore some of its style. Reaching inside her purse, she pulled out her tinted lip gloss. What she really needed was a shower, but she didn't want to miss having dinner with the Elliot family.

As she approached Peter, a twinge of guilt pricked her conscience. She might not be madly in love with him, but she was completely in love with his family. His parents were wonderful people who loved being surrounded by their children and grandchildren.

The fact that she loved Peter more for his family than for him troubled her. But at the same time, while Peter had said he loved her, Sophie had a feeling his affection had more to do with her looks and her chosen profession. He had often said that dating a beautiful doctor was good for his image and that he loved having a girlfriend men envied him for.

Meeting Peter's gaze, she could see his brown eyes no longer held irritation. Now he watched her with concern. "Are you okay?"

"Just a little dizzy." She gave him what she hoped was a confident smile. "It's been a long day."

He reached out and took her hand in his. "Mom delayed dinner. I'm sure you'll feel much better once you can sit down and eat."

"She didn't need to do that, but I appreciate it." Mrs. Elliot's consideration warmed Sophie's heart.

Sophie leaned into Peter's shoulder as they stepped onto the elevator. Maybe she did love him enough to marry him. He made her feel safe and protected.

She'd already been in a long-term relationship where passion had been the pervading element. That had ended four years ago when Sophie had finally realized David, her boyfriend at that time, never had any intention of marrying her. She'd given everything to David, much more than just her heart. In the process she'd distanced herself from God by letting go of her Christian faith and the values she'd always adhered to in her youth. When she had reaffirmed her faith and resumed attending church again, David hadn't liked the changes in her—or their relationship. He had walked away without looking back.

How ironic for her to now be dating a great guy who shared her faith and wanted to marry her, yet she was the one who couldn't commit. It didn't make sense. She was an only child, and after her mother died when Sophie was eight years old, it was just her and her father. That's why she loved being with Peter's family. He had his parents, two sisters and two brothers—all of which were married—and nearly a dozen nieces and nephews. She wanted that for herself.

The first time Peter had taken her to a family dinner at his parents' house, Sophie had been awestruck. She'd felt like Lucy—the Sandra Bullock character in *While You Were Sleeping*—when she had celebrated Christmas with her pretend fiancé's family.

Like Lucy, Sophie had taken everything in that day, loving the family interaction between the adults and children, the laughter and the incredible food. Peter's parents and siblings had welcomed her with open arms, expressing how glad they were that he was dating someone like Sophie.

If she didn't marry him, what were the chances she would find another guy with an amazing family who loved and accepted her like she belonged? She was so conflicted inside and desperately wanted to fall head-over-heels in love with Peter. Part of her believed those feelings would come if she stayed with him long enough.

For the time being, she told herself that she could hold off on her answer to Peter since her father seemed to be missing somewhere in the Costa Rican jungle. Although she and her father hadn't been close, she'd made more of an effort to stay in touch with him over the last couple of years. Even so, it wasn't unusual for her to not hear from him for two or even three months while he was doing research. She'd only begun to worry when four months had passed with still no word from him.

Concerned, Sophie had contacted the university and discovered they hadn't heard from her father either. The department head had assured her they would look into it, and Sophie tried not to worry. Then, the nightmares had started, and Sophie sensed something had happened to him.

The bad dream was virtually the same almost every night and felt like some sort of omen. Sophie ran frantically through the jungle, calling out for her father. She would always catch a glimpse of him right before someone grabbed Sophie around the throat and pressed a hand against her mouth. Her terror filled scream would awaken her, leaving her shaking and unable to fall asleep again.

Peter tugged on her hand as the elevator door slid open. They reached the main lobby and exited to the parking garage. Sophie pulled her keys out of her purse. "I'll just follow you in case I get a call for an emergency."

"I thought you weren't on call?" Peter's voice had an edge to it, letting her know he didn't like the way she ran her practice.

Sophie was one of the few doctors who wanted to be notified if there was an emergency with one of her patients. They always called her first, and she would then decide whether or not she deemed it necessary to follow up herself or allow the on-call doctor to take care of it.

"I'm not, but you know I like to be available if a child needs me."

He let out a deep sigh as he continued to lead her toward his car. "If you really need to return to the hospital before our evening is done, I'll bring you back."

"Thank you." She glanced up at him. "Sorry I made us late for dinner. Every time I started to leave, another mother or father would stop me."

Peter didn't look at her or make a reply until they had made it to his black Mercedes. Instead of opening her door, he leaned her against the car and kissed her. She kissed him back, wanting to feel something beyond contentment and security.

Ending the kiss, Peter pulled back and stared at her. His dark eyes blazed with passion, making Sophie feel even guiltier for not feeling the same way.

"If you agree to marry me, we'll have more time together and I won't mind how much you work."

She bristled at his comment. He worked more hours than she did, but since her job required her to be on call, a lot of their time in the evenings or on weekends was cut short.

"You could've stayed by my side tonight and met some of my patients, instead of hiding in the corner with your phone." It wasn't like Sophie to be so sharp-tongued, and she almost apologized. Then she thought about how irritated Peter would get if they were at a social gathering and she would have to take a call.

He took several seconds to respond to her terse comment. Finally, he nodded his head. "You're right. While I did have some pressing issues with the Van Buren case, I shouldn't have used the added time I had to wait for you to conduct business. I apologize for not being more considerate." He leaned down and gave her another lingering kiss. "Forgive me?" he whispered against her mouth.

She'd been with him long enough to note his apology was couched by pointing out that *he* had been waiting for her, but she was too tired to say anything about it right now.

"Of course," she said, turning her head so his lips brushed against her cheek. He gave her a brief hug before he stepped back and opened her door.

Sophie caught the scent of his expensive cologne as she slid into the immaculate car. He climbed in behind the wheel and started the engine. Deciding to touch up her makeup, she pulled down the visor and almost gasped at how bad she looked. While Peter was always put together, she frequently looked like she had been wearing a scrub cap all day long. It didn't matter that she actually *did* wear a scrub cap all day long—or at least part of the day—she should have done something with her hair before going to the open house.

She used her fingers to comb her hair, and then dabbed a small amount of concealer under each eye, hoping to hide the dark circles that had recently appeared. After applying some lip gloss, she flipped up the visor, knowing the only thing that could help her look better was a good night's sleep.

"You look tired, Sophie," Peter said. "Have you heard anything about your father?"

"No." Her voice quivered as the constant worry she felt bubbled to the surface. "The man I hired to find him changed his email address and his phone number once I sent him more money."

"You should've asked me before you issued additional funds. I could've advised you to never send anyone more money until you have some kind of results from the first payout."

Sophie held back another biting reply. Lashing out at Peter wouldn't help anything. "Probably," she said, glancing out the passenger window.

"So, now what happens?" he asked, reaching over and taking her hand.

"I need to decide what I should do next." Something she planned to do once she heard back from her friend Camille.

"If I have time this week, maybe I can do a little research and find someone else to search for your father." He gave her fingers a gentle squeeze before releasing them. "Someone a little more reputable, like a private investigator."

Sophie *had* hired a private investigator. Peter must have forgotten that little tidbit. Sometimes it seemed like he never listened to anything she said.

"That's not necessary, Peter. I'll figure something out."

"But I want—" Peter's words were cut off when his phone beeped an incoming call. "I need to get this." He didn't wait for her to respond before answering the call with his Bluetooth earpiece.

While Peter was deep into his conversation with one of his clients, Sophie leaned her head against the back of the seat and closed her eyes. She didn't need to hire another private investigator.

What she needed to do was go to Costa Rica and look for her father herself. A plan she had already set in motion. A plan she knew Peter would never support. So, Sophie had simply decided not to tell him. Yet.

She had already requested the time off for the end of the month and was just awaiting the contact information for the guide she hoped to hire.

Sophie recalled the telephone conversation she'd had with her best friend, Camille Campbell, two weeks ago.

"I have a brilliant idea!" Camille said, her voice bubbling with excitement. "I can't believe I didn't think of it earlier."

Sophie had just finished with a four hour surgery and she desperately hoped Camille's idea involved chocolate. "What is it?"

"Did I ever tell you about Jack Mathison?"

"No," Sophie said, pulling off her scrub cap. "Who is he?"

Camille went on to explain that when she was in high school, her older brother Tyson had just graduated from college and had gone on a youth service mission trip with their church to Central America. He lived in Costa Rica for four months, and Jack Mathison, another volunteer, had been one of his roommates.

"I had the wildest crush on the guy," Camille said on a sigh. "He came home with Tyson and stayed with us for a week and then burst my seventeen-year-old fantasy bubble when he introduced me to his fiancée."

"Okay," Sophie said, glancing at the clock. She had an hour break before she needed to get to her office to see patients. "But how does this all amount to a brilliant idea?"

"I'm getting there. Anyway, the twins were taking a nap this morning, so I decided to watch TV while I folded laundry. The first channel I turned to was that movie *Dragonfly* with Kevin Costner.

He plays the part of a doctor who goes into the Amazon jungle to the place where his wife died. I totally got sucked into it when all of the sudden it reminded me of Jack!"

Sophie rubbed her eyes, wondering where Camille was going with this. "Jack looks like Kevin Costner?"

"No. Jack was way better looking."

"Camille, you have totally lost me."

"That's because you won't let me finish." Camille blew out a big breath. "Anyway, Tyson and Jack had lost contact with one another, but about eight years ago, Tyson had run into one of the other guys who had also gone on the mission trip. He told Tyson that Jack had never married and had permanently relocated to Costa Rica. The last he'd heard, Jack took medical outreach groups deep into the Costa Rica jungle so they can provide medical services for the natives in some of the remote villages."

A spark of interest ignited in Sophie as she finally got what Camille might be trying to say. If this Jack Mathison still did that, it would be the perfect setup. Sophie could search for her father while doing humanitarian work.

"You could go look for your father while at the same time be doing your doctor stuff, and Jack can be your guide!" Camille said, confirming they were on the same page.

Sophie sat down on a chair, her mind going a million miles an hour. The logistics of her traveling to Costa Rica seemed insurmountable, but the warmth inside her chest confirmed that this was exactly what she was supposed to do.

"Sophie, you still there?" Camille asked.

"Yes. It *is* a brilliant idea."

"I know, right!"

Camille's enthusiasm made Sophie smile. "Does your brother know how I can get a hold of Mr. Mathison?"

"I'm not sure. Tyson and his wife just left for a Caribbean cruise. I've emailed him, but I have no idea when he'll get the message, or what he can do until he comes back."

A chime alerted Sophie of an incoming text, bringing her back to the present. Peter was still engrossed in his conversation, and she hoped the text wasn't the hospital calling her in for an emergency. He wouldn't be very happy about turning around and taking her back right now.

Reaching down to get her purse, she slipped her phone from the outside pocket. A tiny smile curved her lips when she read the message from Camille.

Houston, we are go for launch. Call me ASAP.

Before Sophie could reply, Camille sent her another text. This one made Sophie want to roll her eyes at her friend's impertinence.

FYI: JM is still single!

Chapter Two

A few weeks later, Camille invited Sophie inside her house, holding a finger to her lips to quiet her. "I just got the twins down for their nap." She raised her eyebrows mischievously. "We have the whole house to ourselves, and a fresh pan of brownies."

Slipping off her shoes, Sophie followed her friend into the kitchen. She loved Camille like a sister, even though they looked nothing alike and were polar opposite in coloring and build. Camille's blue eyes, blonde hair and fair skin testified of her Swedish descent. Compared to Sophie's five three petite stature, her friend towered over her by five inches. While she and Camille were both thirty-two, her friend had been married for eleven years and had four children: A fact that always set Sophie's biological clock ticking very loudly.

Inhaling the tantalizing aroma of warm brownies, Sophie slid onto one of the bar stools. She needed a friend's advice, as well as the chocolate. "How did you know I needed this?"

Camille grinned. "You sounded pretty stressed this morning."

"I am." Sophie sighed dramatically, resting her elbow on the bar and cupping her chin with her palm. "I can't believe I'm leaving at the end of the week. That gives me three days to finalize everything and pack."

Taking a spatula, Camille sliced the brownies into thick squares. "And only three days to get ready to meet Jack." An impish smile wiggled her lips. "This morning I rummaged around in my box of things from high school and found a picture of him. Wanna see?"

Sophie narrowed her eyes. Camille loved teasing her about how handsome Jack had been. "I really don't care what he looks like," Sophie said, reaching for a brownie.

Laughing, Camille opened a drawer and pulled out a photograph. "Okay, but I just thought you might want to prepare yourself, you know, so you don't fall for him or anything."

Her curiosity piqued, Sophie pretended not to be interested. "I already promised not to be taken in by his good looks."

Camille studied the picture. "Yep, he was definitely hot. Not as hot as my husband, but he's a close second." Her blue eyes twinkled as she looked at Sophie. "I wonder if he's aged well?"

When Sophie didn't respond, Camille pulled the drawer back open and put the picture down inside. Sophie couldn't stand it any longer. "Oh, just give me the picture already."

Grinning, Camille handed over the photograph. "He's the one on the left."

Sophie studied the two younger men. Tyson looked almost exactly like he had when she'd met him for the first time this past summer. Jack's face wasn't very visible. He had his head turned to the side, pointing a finger to his flexed muscle bulging under the short sleeve of his tee. Sophie could see from his profile that Jack Mathison *was* a good-looking guy.

She handed the picture back, feeling somewhat interested. "From what I can tell, he looks pretty average to me."

"You are such a liar. But if you need more proof, I'm sure Tyson has a better shot of him."

"No thanks." Sophie lifted the brownie and took a small bite. "Besides, there's nothing to worry about. I'm not looking for romance, and from what your brother said, I gather neither is Mr. Mathison."

She started to take another bite before she quickly added, "And I'm dating Peter."

Camille rolled her eyes, knowing the ambivalent feelings Sophie struggled with. "Speaking of Peter, how does he feel about all of this?"

Lowering her head, Sophie mumbled an answer, "I haven't told him yet."

Coming around the bar, Camille took a seat beside her. "I know you're confused about how you feel right now…but, Sophie, don't you think you should at least tell him you're going out of town?"

"Yes." Sophie took a deep breath. "I'm making him dinner when he comes back from his business trip on Thursday. I'll tell him then."

Camille clicked her tongue against her teeth. "Girl, that's the night before you leave."

"I know." Sophie took another bite of her treat. It wasn't very mature to have kept it from him, but she knew he would try to prevent her from leaving. "I have to do this by myself and I know Peter isn't going to be happy about it."

"Good luck." Camille patted her on the shoulder sympathetically. "And I suggest you make him his favorite meal. Methinks you're gonna need it."

Sophie groaned and put her hands over her face. "Oh, what is wrong with me?"

"Nothing. You're not engaged to—" Camille pulled Sophie's hands away from her face. "You're not engaged, right?"

Sophie thought about the diamond ring sitting in her jewelry box. Before leaving on his business trip, Peter had insisted on her taking the ring, asking her to hold on to it until she found out what happened to her father.

Poor Peter believed that was the only thing holding her back and probably thought having the ring in her possession would sway her. She felt even worse for not being completely honest with him.

"No. You know I would never get engaged and not tell you."

"That's what I thought." Camille spun Sophie's barstool around so they were facing each other. "Now, let's talk about your trip. What's going to happen when you show up and Jack finds out Dr. Kendrick is a woman?"

Sophie bit her bottom lip. "I hope he'll consider my situation and help me find my father."

Unable to look Camille in the eye, Sophie dropped her chin. It's not like she had lied to Mr. Mathison. She just hadn't made it clear she was a woman. Besides, according to Tyson, it wasn't an enforced regulation but rather an off-hand comment Jack had made that he would never again take another woman into the jungle.

Tyson hadn't given her many details about Jack's broken engagement, but explained it had left Jack a little bitter and untrusting of women. More recently, a woman Jack had met while guiding a team of doctors and nurses into the jungle had betrayed him. They had only gone out a few times, but Jack had caught her cheating with a married doctor. Then she had threatened to sue Jack for sexual harassment if he said anything to the doctor's wife, who had usually accompanied her husband on other expeditions.

Legally, Jack couldn't expressly forbid women on his tours, but he could personally decline his services to anyone. Tyson had hinted that it might be a good idea for Sophie to not disclose her gender to Mr. Mathison until she was in Costa Rica. Once she was there, Tyson didn't think Jack would refuse her.

Sophie had agreed and justified her deception by telling herself her mission was to find her missing father. And of course she wasn't romantically interested in Jack Mathison. Even after seeing his picture, Sophie knew she wouldn't develop any kind of feelings for her guide. She already had her hands full with Peter and her father's disappearance. So when Sophie had exchanged emails with the man, she had always signed them simply as Dr. S. Kendrick.

"I'm sure it won't be a big deal, Sophie." Camille laughed. "In fact, after Tyson talked to Jack, he thinks you'll be good for the guy and can help him overcome the low opinion he has of women right now."

"How can I help?" Sophie asked in bewilderment.

"Well, according to Tyson, you're one of the nicest people he has ever met."

"He just thinks that since I stitched the cut on his hand for free and gave him pain pills."

Camille smiled. "Tyson also said Jack isn't involved with church anymore. He's hoping you can light a fire in Jack's faith." One of her eyebrows rose. "Personally, I hope he lights a fire in you."

"Stop it. He's going to be my guide. Nothing more."

"Oh, I wish I could go with you," Camille said, letting out a squeal that sounded like some of the teenage girls in the youth group Sophie mentored each week when they were talking about boys. "Once you meet Jack, you have to promise to text or email me what happens." Camille reached out and snagged a brownie for herself. "While I'm home chasing four kids under ten years old, you'll be roughing it with some tortured hot guy in the Costa Rica jungle."

"Hopefully I'll also find my father."

Camille's enthusiasm tapered off and her eyes sobered. "I'm sorry, Sophie. I shouldn't be making light of this trip. I pray you will find your dad alive and well."

"Me too," Sophie whispered. "Me too."

* * *

The timer on the oven buzzed and Sophie glanced nervously at the clock. Peter would arrive any minute now. Opening the oven door, she grabbed a couple of hot pads and pulled out the homemade chicken pot pie, placing it on top of the stove. It was his favorite meal, and she hoped it would help soften the news of her departure for Costa Rica tomorrow.

Peter had been very busy the past couple of weeks, going on several business trips. Sophie probably could have found an opportunity to tell him during that time, but she honestly didn't want to have to defend her reasons for going to Costa Rica and then have Peter use his attorney skills to try and talk her out of it. The trip had miraculously come together quickly and she couldn't afford to lose the window of opportunity.

She had also decided to give Peter back his ring. It wasn't fair to make him believe she would accept his proposal anytime soon, not when she didn't love him the way she wanted to. Besides, she couldn't make such a serious decision until she had resolved her father's whereabouts.

The doorbell chimed, and Sophie's stomach twisted with apprehension. She drew in a deep breath and crossed the living room floor. Praying Peter would understand, she opened the door. He looked impeccable, wearing a pair of tan chinos and a fitted polo. He held out a dozen red, long-stem roses.

"Oh," she said, accepting the flowers. "They're lovely. Thank you so much."

"You're welcome." He leaned in and gave her a soft kiss. "Mmm, you're wearing the strawberry stuff, right?"

On occasion, Peter would try to guess what lip gloss flavor she had on, but he had never once gotten it right. "It's actually watermelon," Sophie said, unable to look him in the eye. She held up the roses and took a step back. "Let me get a vase for these."

She went into the kitchen to look for a vase. There were quite a few to choose from since Peter frequently gifted her with flowers.

"Boy, something sure smells good," Peter said, coming in behind her.

"I made chicken pot pie." She filled the vase with water and arranged the flowers in it.

After she placed the roses in the center of the dining room table, Peter pulled her in for a hug. "Thank you for making me dinner." Then he kissed her again.

Sophie tried to lose herself in the kiss, but all she could think about was getting dinner on the table and giving him her news. No matter how hard she tried, she didn't feel that stop-your-heart-can't-breathe kind of love.

She had planned on telling him after dinner, but the way Peter gazed at her, she had to tell him now. Sophie didn't like hurting people. As a doctor, she'd tapped into her natural tendency to nurture and heal. Hurting him was the last thing she wanted to do. Yet, continuing to date him, knowing how she felt for him, was anything but nurturing.

Anxiety looped a knot in her stomach as they sat down at the table. "Before we eat… there's something I need to talk to you about."

His eyes dipped down as he reached for her left hand, running his thumb over her bare finger. "What is it?" he asked, bringing his gaze back to hers.

"I need to find out what happened to my father. I can't sit around any longer, hoping to hear something."

His eyebrows drew together with concern. "What do you have in mind?"

"I want to visit the village he was last living in."

"Wow." He let go of her hand and sat back. "Sophie, I don't think that would be wise. It would be like looking for a needle in a haystack. I told you I would find a private investigator." He pulled his phone out of his pocket. "I'm sorry I didn't get right on it, but I'll text my assistant to start looking for someone right now."

His objection was something she had expected, but whether or not Peter agreed with her, she was going to Costa Rica. She also knew it was the right thing to do.

"I can't wait that long. I know I should've talked with you earlier, and I'm sorry that I didn't, but I've already made arrangements, and I'm leaving..." She paused. "I'm leaving in the morning."

Shock registered on his face. His eyes flashed with anger as he abruptly scraped his chair back and stood up. "You're leaving tomorrow and this is the first time you've bothered to mention it?"

While his anger was understandable, it still made her feel defensive. Rising from her seat, she moved behind the chair and gripped the top of it. "I said I'm sorry, Peter, but I don't need your permission to go."

He pressed his mouth into a tight line and took a couple of deep breaths. "I know you don't need my permission." His voice was clipped, as if he could barely contain his ire. "I do, however, think you could've been more considerate of my feelings and talked it over with me."

She winced, knowing he had a point. "I'm sorry. I agree that I should've talked to you."

"Yes, and if you had, I could've told how futile your trip will be."

Ah. There was the Peter she knew and tried to love.

"And that's exactly why I didn't tell you. I don't need to hear how hopeless you think it might be. It's not your father who's missing." Her bottom lip quivered and tears stung her eyes. "Mine is, and he's all the family I've got. I'm all alone."

Peter's jaw tightened. "You're not alone. You have me."

"But I don't have my dad." A lone tear rolled down her cheek. She and her father had been at odds as far back as she could remember. They had clashed over everything from what language she was learning in school to what kind of doctor she had wanted to become. Still, despite their differences, she loved him.

"I know." He ran a hand through his hair. "So, what *is* your plan?" He shook his head and gave a short derisive laugh. "How are you even going to find him?"

"The university gave me the GPS coordinates for the last village he was known to be living at."

"Sophie, this is crazy! How are you even going to do this? The jungle is a dangerous place."

"I've hired a guide."

He looked down at her through narrowed eyes. "Like the man you paid to find your dad? What if this guy takes the money and leaves you stranded somewhere in the jungle?"

"He won't. He's a..." *Believer?* She couldn't truthfully say that, not after what Tyson had said. "...good guy, and Camille's brother knows him from college when they both served a youth service mission in Costa Rica."

"Surely," he said in a condescending tone, "you aren't naïve enough to believe that will make him an upstanding citizen."

His sarcasm was uncaring and belittling. "Peter, I'm tired, and I have to get up very early in the morning. I've made my decision, and any argument you have won't change my mind."

For several seconds, he stood there watching her, his chest rising and falling with slow, deep breaths. Finally he said, "I'm not happy about this, and I still think you'd be better off hiring more investigators, but, like you said, anything I say won't change your mind."

Sophie briefly closed her eyes, relieved their argument was over, and glad she was leaving in the morning so Peter wouldn't have a chance to start the dispute all over again.

Knowing she had one more thing to address—his marriage proposal—Sophie met his gaze. She had wrestled with her decision all week, but knew that marrying Peter primarily to inherit his incredible family wasn't fair to him, or to her, for that matter. Peter deserved to have a wife who was passionately in love with him. Likewise, Sophie wanted to be passionately in love with her husband. Besides, now that she was going to church again, wouldn't her chances of finding a faithful man with the same type of close-knit family Peter had go up considerably?

"Peter, there's one more thing we need to talk about." She swallowed, and forced the words out. "I care for you, but I don't love you—at least not in the way you want me to." She ignored the shocked look on his face and withdrew the black velvet ring pouch from her pocket. "And not in the way that I can accept this. I'm sorry I waited so long, but with everything that has been going on with my father, I haven't been able to think clearly."

His eyes flickered down to the velvet pouch, then back up to her. "That's just it, Sophie. You haven't been able to think clearly, and I should've realized that before asking you to marry me."

Before she could say anything, he came around the table, pulled her to him and hugged her tight. He edged back just enough to lower his head and kiss her.

"I love you," he said, pulling back to gaze into her eyes. "And I think you love me too. We're good together, but I understand why you can't give me an answer right now." He took the velvet pouch from her. "I'll hang onto this for now. When you come home and you've had a chance to sort everything out, let's see where we stand. Christmas is coming soon, and I'd like to announce our engagement."

Her head was spinning with confusion. This was not at all the response she had been expecting. Sophie nodded her head, not even sure what she was agreeing to. When she returned from her trip, she hoped to have answers about her father's whereabouts and, in turn, an answer for Peter. Time away from him would give her an opportunity to analyze her feelings more thoroughly.

The rest of the evening was subdued, and she hardly slept that night. By the time the sun crested the eastern mountains, Sophie had boarded the plane for Costa Rica.

Chapter Three

The air, thick with humidity, dampened Jack Mathison's shirt as he carried a large duffle bag and placed it with the rest of the gear that was waiting to be loaded into his Jeep. "Hey, Hector. I need to take a shower. Would you please go to the airport and pick up Dr. Kendrick?" Jack tossed his friend the keys.

Hector Garcia, dressed in camouflage pants and an army green tee, caught the keys. "*Sí*, but how will I know what this gringo looks like?"

While the excursion into the jungle had come together quickly, Jack wasn't sure how he'd failed to find out what the man looked like or how to identify him. He shrugged. "I have no idea. Just look for an American that's about my age."

Hector glared at him. "Are you *loco?* The airport will be crawling with Americans."

Laughing, Jack said, "I'm kidding. Hang on a second and I'll make you a sign." He went back inside his house and hastily drew the doctor's name on a white piece of paper.

"Does this gringo speak Spanish?" Hector asked, taking the paper.

"Honestly, I never asked. You speak English, so I guess it doesn't really matter."

"True." Hector grinned. "But maybe I'll keep my bilingual skills to myself. I always enjoy hearing Americans say things they don't think I can understand."

Jack chuckled and waved goodbye to his friend. Being fluent in two languages, combined with a teasing personality, Hector got a kick out of playing that game with the tourists.

Returning inside the house, Jack peeled off his T-shirt and tossed it in a laundry basket. He hurried upstairs to take a shower. It would be the last hot shower for at least a couple of weeks.

As he lingered under the spray of warm water, he thought about the only lead he had on Dr. Kendrick's missing father—the GPS coordinates of his last known location. Jack mentally plotted out the trail and knew it would take them through *Por El Río*, Manuel Carrero's village. It also meant he would see Manuel's daughter, Elaina. Jack knew from past experiences that Elaina would create some kind of drama.

Jack had known Manuel for years. They had become friends over a decade ago when Jack had first started guiding people through the jungle. He'd watched Manuel's daughter grow from an awkward thirteen year old into a beautiful woman. During that time, Elaina had developed a crush on Jack.

It was a harmless flirtation, at least on his part. He'd found out differently when one of his visits two years ago had almost turned disastrous for Jack, his business, and the well-being of the female nurse who had spent more time flirting with him than offering humanitarian aid. Elaina had turned a little psycho on him and had taken a machete to the woman's clothing in a fit of jealousy. Manuel had made up excuses for his daughter, blaming PMS for her bad behavior.

Jack had been back to *Por El Río* a couple of times since that incident—without any young, single women in the party—and had smoothed things over with Manuel. Elaina had still flirted with Jack, but on his last visit four months earlier, she had gotten herself a boyfriend. If he was lucky, Elaina might be blissfully married by now. If not, at least their small party would only consist of men.

Drying off, Jack donned a pair of khaki nylon cargo pants and pulled a navy blue T-shirt over his head. Vainly, he flexed in the mirror, satisfied his hard work had paid off. Although he lifted weights every day, he had stepped up his workout the past few months. He hadn't been this fit in years. Being in shape was necessary, especially with the increasing amount of doctors and dentists he took into the jungle. Plus, Jack was only three years away from turning forty, and he was determined to never become one of those guys with a protruding gut.

Turning off the bathroom light, he walked into his room and removed the backpack from his bed. Sort of a neat freak, he smoothed the quilt and straightened a pillow. Before leaving, he noticed the pamphlet on his dresser and picked up the brochure, studying the smiling youthful faces on the cover.

At one time, Jack had been just like these young adults: happy and eager to share his faith with those less fortunate, while at the same time, working hard with other missionaries to improve living conditions for the villagers. He'd been doing God's work and what had he gotten in return? Nothing but heartache.

Jack tossed the pamphlet back on the dresser, wondering why he had ever agreed to look over the program in the first place. Ben, one of the dentists Jack had taken into the jungle a couple of months back, was active with the youth in his church and wanted to bring some of the college kids over with him the next time he came. Once he found out Jack had actually done something similar when he was younger, the man had been relentless about having Jack agree to participate as a guide and a counselor.

Immediately, Jack had made it clear he wasn't going to be anyone's counselor. Especially a spiritual counselor.

Ben had only grinned and reassured Jack he didn't have to do anything he wasn't comfortable with. He had promised to send him some information about the program and would touch basis with him by email.

Making his way downstairs, Jack passed by his computer and paused. There were a couple of messages from Ben sitting in his inbox. He had yet to open them, let alone make a reply. Part of him just wanted to delete the messages altogether. The last thing Jack wanted to do was lead a bunch of overzealous college kids on a missionary trip.

Grumbling a few words that would make Ben frown, Jack continued on to the kitchen and pulled open the fridge to get a protein drink. He popped the tab and took a long drink, relishing the cold liquid. One disadvantage about going deep into the jungle was the lack of refrigeration. Still, Jack couldn't wait to start the journey. Traveling with such a small party this time was going to be great, and the tour should go much smoother.

His eyes landed on a yellow notepad sitting on the countertop with Tyson Andrews' phone number and email address written on it. The call from his former friend a few weeks ago had disturbed Jack's peace of mind even more than the request from Ben.

When he and Tyson had parted ways nearly fifteen years earlier, Jack had assumed he would see his friend a few months later at his own wedding. However, in only a matter of weeks, Jack's life had fallen apart. While he had been off serving God and the Costa Rican people, his fiancée Heather had been cheating on him with his older brother Adam.

After their betrayal, Jack had let the bitterness seep into every part of his being, driving him away from his family, his friends, and eventually his faith.

Jack hadn't been able to stomach attending church services week after week, listening to the pastor preach about forgiving others, even if the offending party never sought your forgiveness. He had left Colorado without giving anyone his forwarding address. Tyson must have found him via the Internet.

Jack took another long swallow, and finished the drink. The conversation with Tyson had been fun until his friend had asked about Jack's marital status. The bitterness and dislike he felt toward the female populace had oozed out and opened up old wounds that had never completely healed. The mild expletives he had used to describe what he thought of matrimony had not offended Tyson, but instead had made him laugh.

Later, when Tyson had good-naturedly tried to probe into Jack's spiritual life, Jack had been honest and said that he and God didn't see eye to eye about a few issues right now. Then he had moved onto a new subject, focusing on the reason behind Tyson's call, which was to help find Dr. Kendrick's missing father.

The problem was that long after the phone call had ended, Jack had been thinking about his jaded relationship with God. It wasn't that he didn't believe in God. He did. He just didn't believe God cared about him or his life. To be honest, Jack found it was much easier to keep things the way they were. He wasn't interested in changing, but somewhere deep down inside, Jack got the feeling that God had different ideas.

* * *

Sophie made her way through customs, excited about being in Costa Rica, but nervous about meeting Jack Mathison. With one bag over her shoulder, she pulled along two other heavy bags that were mostly filled with medical supplies.

Moving out of the flow of traffic, she paused and placed a hand over her stomach, trying to quell the butterflies dancing around her middle.

Her eyes scanned the airport, looking for Jack, or at least a good-looking American man that resembled the picture Camille had shown her. Not wanting to ask her friend for an updated picture, Sophie had tried Facebook stalking Jack Mathison, but none of the profiles she had found fit his age group or his location. There had been a few links to his website that talked about his credentials and showed scenic pictures of the region, as well as a few images of the medical personnel and their endorsement of Mr. Mathison. Unfortunately, there hadn't been one picture of the guide.

She looked around the busy airport and noted several men holding up signs with names written on them. She squinted to see if one was for her. So far, nothing. Part of her was relieved to have a few more minutes to brace herself for the meeting. How upset would he be when he found out she was a woman? But, then again, it seemed stupid to even worry about that kind of thing. She *was* Dr. Kendrick, and she wanted to find her father. Besides, if he had a problem with her being a woman, it was too late—his fee had been paid, and she was in Costa Rica.

Pulling her luggage behind her, she moved with the crowd, continuing to search for her ride and probably looking as lost as she felt. Several locals approached her, asking her if she needed a taxi. She shook her head, holding tight to her luggage.

Turning around, Sophie noticed a nice looking Hispanic man holding a piece of paper with her name on it. Relieved, she made her way toward him. "Hello, I'm Dr. Kendrick," she said, smiling at the man.

Both eyebrows shot up, his brown eyes registering surprise. If he didn't speak English, he probably had no idea why she was even talking to him.

Sophie said one of the few things she knew in his language. "*No hablo español.*"

He grinned and pointed at her and then the sign. "*¿Doctor?*"

"Yes…*sí*, I'm Dr. Kendrick."

"*Sí, doctor.*" He flashed his white teeth and stuck out his hand. "*Hector.*"

The tension she'd been feeling disappeared, leaving her with a huge smile on her face. She shook his hand firmly. "It's nice to meet you. I'm sorry that I don't speak your language."

Hector's dark brown eyes were still lit with humor as he reached for her luggage. He motioned for her to follow him, and she trailed after him as they silently made their way outside.

The large airport, with all the taxi cabs lined up in front, reminded her of a typical international airport in the United States. A lump formed in her throat as she watched a little girl and her father get into a waiting cab. The few times she'd visited her dad while he was on location in Central America, he'd rarely made it a point to pick her up from the airport. Usually, it was one of his research assistants. Sophie had learned not to let it bother her too much, but she still had hopes that one day she might have that special kind of father-daughter relationship other girls had with their fathers. Now she wondered if it was too late.

Hector looked over his shoulder and paused to wait for her. She quickly pushed the negative thoughts out of her mind and smiled as she caught up to him.

When they made it to his Jeep, Hector held open the passenger door for her. "*Gracias,*" Sophie said, wishing she knew more than just a few Spanish words.

The skin around Hector's eyes crinkled. "*De nada.*"

He closed the door and loaded her luggage in the back.

With all the windows down, Sophie felt the tropical air tease her hair. The warm sun felt wonderful, and the cloudless, blue sky made it hard to believe October was almost over. Back home, the weather had already turned chilly. Halloween was in two days, and the forecast had called for snow.

Sophie reached inside her purse and pulled out her lip gloss and a small mirror. Studying her reflection, she was pleased to see the dark circles under her eyes had faded. The preparation for this trip had invigorated her, and the past two weeks she'd only had the nightmare a couple of times, allowing her to catch up on sleep.

As she applied a thin layer of lip gloss, Hector stopped at an intersection to allow a group of school children to cross the street. He looked at her sidelong and grinned when he caught her primping. Sophie was glad he didn't seem to be bothered that she was a woman instead of a man. In fact, she got the feeling he found it amusing. Hopefully his boss felt the same way.

"Let's hope your friend Jack has a sense of humor."

Hector raised an eyebrow, almost like he understood her. "¿Señorita?"

"I'm sorry. I wish I knew more Spanish," Sophie said. "I know I should've corrected Mr. Mathison's assumption that I was a man, but Tyson assured me it won't be a big deal. I just hope that's true."

Hector's smile widened at her speech, and he shrugged his shoulders. Sophie must really be nervous if she was carrying on a one-sided conversation in English with someone who couldn't understand her.

The car behind them honked, and Hector jerked his focus back to the road to find the intersection clear.

They resumed their journey, and Sophie decided not to talk anymore. She would find out soon enough how Jack was going to react.

Once they left the city limits, Sophie rested her head back against the seat and closed her eyes. Weary from the days travel, the heat from the warm sun relaxed her body. The delicious haze of sleep settled over her, and she told herself she would only close her eyes for a few minutes.

She wasn't sure how long she'd slept when Hector gently shook her arm. "*Señorita.*"

Sophie startled awake, blinking her eyes against the bright sun. At least she hadn't had a nightmare. Maybe she wouldn't now that she was here.

Hector smiled and pointed in front of him. Across the street stood a beautiful Spanish styled home with white stucco and a red tiled roof. Tropical plants and trees adorned the property, the bright colored blossoms vibrant against the white exterior of the home.

Sophie's stomach twisted with apprehension as Hector pulled into the circular driveway and came to a stop. He jumped out of the Jeep and came around to open her door. "*Un momento, por favor,*" he said with a wink. Then he jogged toward the house, leaving her standing by the vehicle.

She straightened her top and smoothed a hand down her jeans as she waited to meet Mr. Mathison. Hector stuck his head in the door and yelled something in Spanish. Then Jack stepped out, and Hector spoke to him in low tones.

Sophie swallowed, trying to get control of her thoughts. The guy was more than devastatingly handsome; he was probably the most beautiful man she had ever seen. His light-brown hair was cropped short, almost like he belonged in the military. His chiseled face, tan from the Costa Rican sun, was covered with a dark shadow of whiskers.

He looked like he could grace the cover of any magazine. The T-shirt he wore molded to solid muscles, his biceps bulging against the short sleeves.

Alarmed by her reaction to his appearance, Sophie drew in a deep breath. This man was going to take her into the jungle, not out on a date. Her pounding heart and weak knees had more to do with all the hype surrounding Jack Mathison and the fact that she was now going to have to own up to letting him assume she was a man.

Jack raised his face and pale, ice-blue eyes met her gaze. Immediately, Sophie knew she was in trouble. He did not look happy.

Sophie waved and forced her quivering mouth into a smile. Her knees shook as he purposely strode toward her. He stopped a few feet away, and she noticed how tall he was, guessing he was probably a foot taller than her five three frame. Even though she wore four inch heels, he still towered over her.

"Hello." She offered him a trembling hand. "I'm Dr. Kendrick."

He ignored her hand, narrowing his eyes. "You're a woman."

Uh-oh. "Yes," she said, dropping her hand. "Is that a problem?" Her tone was uncharacteristically defiant.

"Not mine." He crossed his arms in front of him, drawing her eyes to his impressive biceps. "*You*, on the other hand, need to find yourself another guide."

She raised her chin a notch. "Why?" *Because she was a woman?*

His blue eyes were hard, and his square jaw was clenched tight with irritation. "Look, lady, I don't have to defend my reasons, but let's just say I've had enough experience to know there is no way I'm spending the next two weeks in the jungle with someone who looks like you."

"What's that supposed to mean?"

"It means I don't need the headache and trouble a beautiful woman will cause me. Besides, the jungle is hard terrain, and I'm not pampering someone who has probably never even slept in a tent."

Sophie ignored his back-handed compliment about her looks and took a step forward. "I'll have you know I'm an avid hiker and I've slept in plenty of tents, as well as under the stars." She tilted her chin up a little higher. "I've paid you your fee, and I'm not leaving."

The muscle in his jaw jumped. "You'll get a full refund. I'm not taking you."

He seemed totally serious, but she didn't want a refund. All her bravado seeped away as her chest seized in panic and her eyes burned with emotion. This couldn't be happening.

Hector moved behind Jack, his gaze filled with concern. It triggered the tears welling in her eyes, making them spill over.

"Oh, brother," Jack said in exasperation. "Don't cry."

Her tears were genuine, but he clearly saw them as some feminine ploy. How could she make him change his mind? "Please, Mr. Mathison," she said, reaching out and laying her hand on his corded forearm. "I need to find my father."

* * *

Jack flinched as he felt a shock of heat from her fingertips when she touched him. "Look, I'm sorry about your missing father." He pulled his arm away. "But I'm not taking you."

"Please, Mr. Mathison," she begged softly as another tear slipped down her cheek.

If it was meant to make him change his mind—it wasn't working. An emotional woman wouldn't last a day in the jungle, and one this pretty would definitely cause problems with Elaina and others they might encounter.

Not to mention the fact he was single and she was single, and after the fiasco last month and the false accusations, Jack did not want to be alone with another female, especially a dishonest one. If his attorney found out, he would probably have a stroke.

"The answer is still no." He moved to his vehicle. "Now please get back in the Jeep, and I'll take you to a hotel."

She didn't move, but stood stock-still staring at him.

Jack held his ground. Yeah, he was being a little harsh, but she had intentionally been deceitful. With his past, lying was something he didn't tolerate.

He met her gaze and the despair in her eyes made his stomach tighten with guilt. *Ah, man. Why'd she have to be so pretty?*

He watched her despair turn to anger as she wiped away the tears with the back of her hand. "Fine. Do you have any recommendations for another guide?"

Another guide? He hadn't been serious—but she sure seemed to be, or maybe she didn't value her life or her virtue. "No. My suggestion is for you to find someone to locate your father for you. In fact, I'll do it. I know I can find him. And," he said, looking at her pointedly, "I've already been paid."

"If you'll do it then why can't I go with you?"

"Lady, I already told you why." Her persistence was annoying.

Defiance flickered in her eyes. "You said you didn't want to pamper me. Well, you won't have to. I've already told you I'm an avid hiker and I'm in excellent shape."

Jack's eyes skimmed over her white fitted shirt and dark skinny jeans that accentuated her well-toned legs and looked great with a pair of sexy, but very unpractical, turquoise colored high heels. Yes—she was definitely in excellent shape.

His appreciation abruptly came to a halt when he met her gaze. *Shoot.* He'd been caught checking her out.

She narrowed her pretty brown eyes. "I know about the incident that happened last month with one of the women in your group. I'm not here for any reason other than to find my father, and believe me, you have no need to worry about me being attracted to you." She moistened her lips. "Because I'm not."

Oh yeah? Well, then he wasn't attracted to her either. "Fantastic. I'm still not taking you."

She briefly closed her eyes and drew in a deep breath. "I'm sorry for deceiving you, Mr. Mathison. I know it was wrong."

He felt his heart harden with the apology. He hated when people apologized for lying, especially since being dishonest was an intentional decision and expressing their regret was only meant to make themselves feel better.

"But," she said with more strength. "I need your assistance in locating my father. When I was young, I spent many weeks in different jungles. I'm not afraid, and I won't complain."

Yeah, but someone who looked like her could cause more problems than he wanted to deal with. On the off chance Elaina had broken up with her boyfriend, Jack didn't want to have to deal with her jealous obsession. Avoiding *Por El Río* wasn't an option. It was the best route to where he believed Dr. Kendrick's father was, and he had no choice but to pass through.

"Look, I said no, okay? If you want me to find your father, I'll do it." He pointed his finger at her. "But without you."

She met his stare, and he read the defeat in her eyes. Good. He'd won. Jack loaded her luggage back inside the Jeep as she slowly made her way around the vehicle and climbed into the front passenger seat.

Chapter Four

I gnoring the twinge of remorse, Jack slid behind the wheel. "So," he said, turning toward her, "do you want me to find your dad or what?"

She looked down at her hands. "I don't know. I...well, I really felt like this was what I was supposed to do. I need time to think and pray about it."

He stared at her for a few seconds and was tempted to call her out as a hypocrite. Despite having purposely deceived him, it appeared as if she had no problem praying for guidance. Before he said something he'd regret, he started the Jeep. "Yeah, well when you get an answer, just let me know."

Hector glowered at Jack as he pulled away, obviously mad at him for refusing to take the doctor. He'd have to smooth that over with him when he returned.

Winding his way through the city, Jack's passenger remained quiet, looking straight ahead. When he pulled up in front of a reputable hotel, she turned to look at him. That glint of anger was back in her eyes.

Jack couldn't help smiling. For such a tiny little thing, she sure was spirited. Her gaze narrowed when she saw his smile, and she jerked her door open. Grabbing her carry-on bag, she hefted it to the ground.

While she worked on getting one of the heavier bags out, Jack exited the Jeep and snatched her other piece of luggage before she could refuse his help. He circled around the vehicle and placed the bag next to her feet. He retrieved a business card from his wallet and handed it to her. "Call when you decide if you want me to go look for your father."

Her slender fingers grasped the card, frustration and disappointment written on her face. "Thank you."

"If not, I'll refund the money and have Hector take you to the airport. It's about two hours away and taking a cab that far would be expensive and risky."

Her eyes flickered up to meet his. For a brief moment, both of them hesitated as they held one another's gaze. Despite his anger, he felt a spark of awareness pass between them. It made him almost recant his decision not to take her, but his pride kept him rooted in place when she slipped the strap of the carry-on piece over her shoulder, pulled the other two bags behind her and entered the hotel lobby.

The scent of her perfume drifted on the breeze as the hotel doors closed. Jack let out a big breath and climbed into his Jeep. As he pulled away from the hotel, he tried to erase Dr. Kendrick's stricken face. He growled as he gripped the steering wheel hard. Man, he hated feeling guilty.

When he arrived home, he saw Hector sitting by their gear, making his guilt even worse.

"Way to go, *amigo*," Hector said sarcastically. "You just turned down a beautiful *señorita* and her money."

Climbing out of the Jeep, Jack leaned back against the frame. "I have a feeling Dr. Kendrick is still going to want our services."

Hector sighed. "Jack, what is wrong with you? You have the chance to take a woman who looks like that into the jungle and you said no?"

Jack narrowed his gaze and laughed dryly. "You know how I feel about women right now, and I'm not looking for a fling or a wife. Besides, you're married, and I saw the way you were looking at the doctor."

Hector chuckled. "I might be married, and I love my wife, but I can still look at a beautiful *señorita* when I see one, *¿no?*"

Jack grunted and started toward his house. "Beautiful or not, I'm not taking her." He paused and looked over his shoulder. "Hopefully she'll let me know tomorrow if she still wants us to look for her father."

* * *

Early the next morning, sunlight filtered through the blinds and Jack woke up feeling even more disturbed by Dr. Kendrick. He'd done something he rarely did: he had dreamed, and what's more, he had dreamed about the doctor.

Sitting up, he rubbed his hands over his face and recalled how vivid the dream had been. Dr. Kendrick ran through the jungle, calling for her father. Jack could see a dark figure chasing her and knew he had to help her. He had awakened before he could reach her.

Climbing out of bed, Jack pulled on a shirt and a pair of cargo shorts. After making his bed, he went downstairs and opened the shutters, allowing bright sunlight to penetrate the kitchen. He needed a caffeine boost, and since he wasn't a fan of coffee, he opened the fridge and grabbed an energy drink.

Jack stepped out on the veranda, cradling the cold can and wondering if he would hear from the doctor today. Her image materialized in his mind, reminding him of her flawless skin and those expressive, dark eyes.

He took a sip of his drink and frowned. He was thinking entirely too much about the woman.

Maybe he should just contact her and get it over with. He'd called Tyson last night to chew him out, but the guy had been laughing too hard to listen to any of Jack's complaints. It was futile to stay mad at him, and Tyson had taken the blame for giving the doctor bad advice about keeping her gender a secret. He had also pointed out that while she may have not corrected Jack's assumption she was male, she had done it to find her father, not to trick him.

Now Jack had her cell phone number programed in his phone. He just had to decide what he was going to do with it. At the very least, he should apologize for his rude behavior.

Scowling, he took another sip of his drink, and tried to tell himself he didn't want to see her again, but he'd never been good at self-deception. The truth was that he did want to help her find her missing father and that he had been attracted to her. That part bothered him.

As he thought about how pleased the doctor would be with him if he called her, he felt his heart rate accelerate. Yeah, maybe he would wait another day to contact her. By tomorrow, his hormones might be restored to normal and he could think more clearly about what he wanted to do.

* * *

Sophie climbed out of the taxi, smoothing a hand over her pants. She had almost dressed in her khakis, T-shirt and hiking boots, but didn't want to be too presumptuous. "*Gracias*," she said as the driver helped her with her bags.

"*De nada*." He grinned widely, revealing several missing teeth. "*Muchas gracias*," he said when she tipped him generously.

Standing in front of Jack Mathison's house, Sophie was determined to get him to take her. She had prayed about having him go alone, but she felt like she was supposed to go—like somebody needed her help. The only problem was she needed to convince Jack.

As she drew close to his front door, she tried suppressing the trepidation dancing in her stomach. Today had to go better than yesterday. He had been rude, but he'd also been angry with her for not being upfront with him about her gender. Maybe, after a good-night's sleep, he'd reconsider and offer to be her guide.

Camille had said her brother thought it was worth asking him again.

She pushed the doorbell, her foot tapping with apprehension. After waiting for a minute, she knocked softly. If the man wasn't an early riser, this might not go the way she wanted.

Please say yes, she thought as she heard the lock being turned. Jack opened the door, barefoot and wearing a tight T-shirt and brown cargo shorts. The shadow on his jaw had darkened, making him look a little dangerous—well, dangerously handsome and unquestionably irritated.

"What're you doing here?" he grumbled. "Isn't your phone working?"

Hmm. Maybe she should've waited a little longer. Gathering her courage, she met his gaze only to have her breath hitch. Those pale blue eyes made something deep within her stomach tighten. "I was going to call, but I felt like I needed to see you again." She inwardly winced at the breathy tone of her voice.

One of his eyebrows rose. "Oh?"

She cleared her throat. "May I come in, Mr. Mathison?"

He studied her for a few seconds then stepped back and motioned with his arm for her to enter. "Of course, Dr. Kendrick."

Relieved he hadn't shut the door in her face, Sophie stepped inside and marveled at the beauty of his spacious home with its high vaulted ceilings. To the left sat a pristine off-white leather couch and loveseat with an array of colorful pillows. The taupe walls were decorated with Spanish and Indian artifacts and paintings. She hadn't expected a bachelor pad to look like this. Not a thing was out of place. "Your house is very beautiful."

Jack smiled, but his eyes said he didn't want any polite small talk. "Thanks." He folded his arms across his chest. "Now, what did you need?"

Obviously, he wasn't going to invite her to sit down. "I prayed about what I should do. I want you to find my father, but…I want to come with you."

His eyes narrowed, and he frowned. "I thought we already had this conversation, Dr. Kendrick."

"I know." She drew in a fortifying breath. "But I feel like I am supposed to go—like somebody needs me to go." She met his gaze, wishing she could somehow make him understand. Although he had lost his faith, couldn't he remember what inspiration felt like? "Please, Mr. Mathison. I don't know who else to turn to."

He continued studying her with his intense gaze, his face unreadable. Silently, she prayed for him to change his mind. After what seemed like minutes, he drew in a deep breath and slowly shook his head.

She felt her hopes fall. His answer was no.

"Okay," he said reluctantly.

Okay?

He scowled and pointed his finger at her. "But if you so much as complain or slow me down, I'll make Hector take you back. Understand?"

A tiny squeal of excitement accompanied the smile she gave him. "Thank you, Mr. Mathison." She had the craziest urge to hug him and had to force herself to stand still. "I promise not to cause you any trouble."

He gave her an exasperated look. "You've already caused me trouble." Abruptly, he turned and stalked down the hallway.

Sophie stared at his retreating back and thought she heard him mumble, "I have a feeling it isn't going to stop."

The urge to hug him fled as rapidly as the aggravating man had.

A tiny part of her wanted to march after him and make Jack explain why he was so irritated with her, but Sophie decided it would be best not to do anything that might make him change his mind.

Instead, she closed her eyes and thanked God for answering her prayers. Now all she had to do was find her father.

* * *

"I can't believe I said yes," Jack murmured to himself. He could have just as easily apologized for being a jerk and then reasoned with her about why he should go alone. Instead, he'd agreed to let her come along without taking the time to think about it.

Hector patted Jack on the back. "I'm happy you changed your mind, *amigo*." He grinned knowingly, wiggling his eyebrows. "You could not resist her, *¿no?*"

Jack wasn't exactly sure what had happened. He looked at his house and sighed loudly. "Apparently not."

Chuckling, Hector loaded a couple of bags in the Jeep before wandering off to answer a phone call from his wife.

Jack packed a few more supplies in the back of the vehicle, keeping an eye out for Dr. Kendrick. Right now, she was in his house changing her clothes. After showing her to the bathroom on the main floor, Jack had hurried back outside. Having a pretty girl inside his house, especially one who made his pulse jump erratically, left him feeling vulnerable.

When she came outside a few minutes later, Jack suppressed his response of male appreciation for the attractive doctor.

She wore a pair of tan cargo pants and a fitted lime-green tee.

"Are you ready?" he asked gruffly, frustrated with how she made him feel.

"Yes. Thank you for allowing me to leave the rest of my stuff at your house."

Yeah, like I had a choice. He cut her an annoyed glance but kept his mouth shut.

"What can I do to help?" Her chipper voice grated on his already taut nerves.

You got yourself into this Mathison. "Just make sure you have everything." He walked away from her but then stopped and pivoted back around. "By the way, you're carrying your own pack, Dr. Kendrick."

She narrowed her eyes a fraction, but kept her smile in place. "I planned on it. I'm not some helpless female. And my name is Sophie."

Jack held her gaze for a few seconds, wishing she wouldn't have reminded him about her name. Addressing her as a doctor kept her at a professional distance. The crazy attraction he felt toward her demanded he keep as much space between them as possible.

"I don't think you're helpless, Dr. Kendrick, just incredibly naïve and optimistic."

This time her smile faded, and her eyes reflected disappointment rather than defiance. He swallowed back the desire to soften his answer and call her by her first name. Instead, he turned away to heft another bag into the back of the Jeep.

Hector ended his call and walked back over toward Dr. Kendrick. "*Señorita,*" he said, holding out his hand.

Jack turned and watched Dr. Kendrick take Hector's hand. The genuine smile she offered him was nothing like the tight-lipped smile she had just given Jack.

"Hello...I mean...*hola.*"

Hector's eyes flashed with merriment. "It is a pleasure to see you again, Dr. Kendrick."

The woman's eyebrows shot up. "You...you speak English?"

Hector chuckled sheepishly. "*Sí.*" Lifting her hand, he brought it to his mouth and kissed her knuckles.

Pink colored her cheeks as she pulled her hand away. "I hope I didn't say anything to offend you yesterday." Her eyes skittered over to Jack. "I'm not exactly sure what I said."

"Nothing to offend me, I assure you." Hector glanced at Jack and chortled. "Nothing at all."

So what had she said about him? Jack was dying to know but wasn't about to give Hector the satisfaction by asking him.

"If you're done flirting with the doctor, do you think we can leave?"

Hector continued to laugh. "*Sí. Sí.*"

Dr. Kendrick slipped the backpack from her shoulders. Before she could put it in the Jeep, Hector raced to her assistance. "*Señorita*, let me get that for you."

"Thank you, and please call me Sophie."

Hector grinned and helped her into the back of the Jeep. "All right. Sophie it is."

Jack climbed in behind the wheel and adjusted the seat. Hector took shotgun and said, "Let's go."

As Jack pulled away, a cell phone jingled an unfamiliar ringtone that was silenced when the doctor answered. Curious, Jack listened to her end of the conversation.

"Yes, Peter, I'm safe." She sighed. "I'm sorry I didn't call last night. The guide couldn't take me...until this morning."

Who is Peter? A boyfriend?

"I know. I…I miss you too. I'll call as soon as I can, probably not for a couple of weeks."

Jack made a stop at an intersection; in the quiet of the car, he could hear Peter's voice tell Sophie how much he loved her.

She let out another deep breath. "I know you do."

As Jack pressed on the gas pedal, he let it sink in that Sophie hadn't reciprocated the declaration of love. In fact, she didn't sound like a woman who missed her boyfriend all that much. Why did that make him feel better?

He ground his teeth together and downshifted hard, not liking where his thoughts were taking him. Being attracted was one thing. Acting on that attraction was something else entirely.

* * *

Sophie ended the call with Peter and caught Jack's reflection in the rearview mirror. His lips were pulled tight as if he were angry again, his gorgeous eyes focused on the road ahead.

Turning her gaze away from the driver, Sophie felt guilty for comparing the color of his eyes to the azure sky overhead. Here Peter had just expressed his love and concern for her and all she could think about was the way Jack Mathison made her feel.

Why would she be attracted to a guy like him? Sure, he was extremely handsome, but his personality left a lot to be desired. No wonder the grouchy male was still single.

She lifted her phone, needing to text Camille that she was really on her way before she lost cell phone service. As she pushed send, Jack rounded a corner sharply, tipping her pack over and making Sophie hold onto the door to keep upright. "Hey."

Jack's eyes flickered to the rearview mirror, his lips lifted at the corners. "Sorry, the roads from here on out are very much like the jungle will be. Unpredictable and sometimes dangerous."

Sophie got his message and wanted to wipe the smirk off his face. She barely refrained from sticking out her tongue.

"I appreciate your reminder of the risks I'll face, but I assure you I'm prepared."

"I hope so," he muttered as the Jeep hit a big rut in the road that made them all bounce.

Hector turned around, flashing a white-toothed smile. "Don't let Jack scare you. We'll both make sure you will be safe."

Jack shot the man a contemptuous glare. *For what? Being nice?*

"Thank you, Hector," Sophie said sincerely.

As they ascended higher into the mountains, Jack shifted into a lower gear, and Sophie watched the muscles in his arm harden with the movement. Her mouth went dry, and she averted her eyes, trying to concentrate on something other than his biceps, the expanse of his well-built shoulders, or how blue his eyes looked against his tan skin. *Stop it!* What was wrong with her? She did not like Jack Mathison.

Squirming uncomfortably in her seat, she focused on the view. Costa Rica's landscape was absolutely breathtaking. The green trees were large and majestic, surrounded by colorful flora. She squinted, trying to penetrate the thickness of the tropical forest. Was her father out there somewhere?

She stared at the passing scenery until her eyelids felt heavy. Unable to fight it any longer, she relaxed her head against the seat and closed her eyes.

Sometime later, she felt someone shaking her. "Wake up, Doc."

She didn't want to wake up and shook her head, burying her face into her arm.

"C'mon. We need to get going."

"Five more minutes," she mumbled, wanting the person to leave her alone.

"Look, lady," a voice said sharply, "if you don't wake up, I'm leaving you."

Chapter Five

The voice registered in Sophie's brain and suddenly she remembered where she was. Instantly, she shot up and slammed into something hard. She cried out in pain and heard a muffled moan from the person she had hit.

Now wide awake, she stared into the steely gaze of Jack Mathison. He held a palm to his forehead. She rubbed her own head, feeling a small lump forming as she climbed out of the Jeep. "I'm sorry. Did I hurt you?"

Jack dropped his hand and eyed her warily. "I think I'll live."

Hector snickered under his breath as he unloaded the Jeep.

Sophie lightly pressed her fingers on the sore spot and gave Jack a pointed look. "You have a hard head."

Hector's snickers turned into uncontrollable laughter.

"Me?" Jack snorted and looked at her incredulously. "I don't think I'm the only one who can claim the title. That, Dr. Kendrick, belongs to you, too."

He had yet to call her by her first name, but given the fact that she'd just slammed her head into his, she decided to let it alone. As she turned around to retrieve her backpack, her knees started to buckle. Just how hard had she hit her head? She felt woozy and started to pitch forward.

Jack's arms shot out and caught her. "Don't tell me you're going to faint." The annoyed tone of his voice was edged with concern.

He kept a hold of her, his muscular chest solid under her cheek. *Oh, my.* He smelled really good. The masculine citrusy scent probably affected her more than the bump on her head.

"I'm not going to faint." She straightened and stepped out of his arms. "I just felt a little dizzy, but I'm okay now."

It was stupid to have fallen asleep. What if she'd had her nightmare? Then she would feel obligated to warn him it might happen again, and that would be just the excuse Jack needed to not take her along.

She chanced a look his way and found him watching her quite intently. His expression was unreadable, but she could feel tension radiating from his entire body. She had no idea what he was thinking but she prayed he wasn't going to rescind his decision about letting her go with him.

Her eyes zeroed in on the spot where she had accidentally hit him. "Your forehead is red and swollen." Instinctively she stepped close to him and lightly brushed her fingers over his brow just under the marred skin. "I really am sorry."

"It's okay," he said gruffly and backed away to break the contact. "This is where we start our journey, so if you need to use the restroom, you better do it now."

"Um-hmm," she said absentmindedly, still focused on Jack's face. The doctor in her wanted to apply a cold pack to the injured area and medicate him with ibuprofen. Her gaze dropped to his mouth. The woman in her…well, she didn't want to think about that part.

"So, do you need to use the restroom or what?"

She blinked, embarrassed by the direction of her thoughts. "Uh, yes."

He pointed a finger behind her. "It's over that way."

Grateful for a chance to get her feelings under control, she turned away and started for the restrooms. She had only taken a few steps when she paused and looked back at him over her shoulder. He was still watching her.

"You aren't going to leave me here, are you?"

The look that crossed his face said he'd been
contemplating doing exactly that. Seconds ticked by before
one corner of his mouth lifted. "I won't leave you, Dr.
Kendrick."

Relief washed over her, and she smiled. "Okay. I'll be
right back."

She faced forward and resumed her trek to the
bathroom. It was difficult not to look back to see whether or
not his eyes still followed her. She resisted the temptation,
though, because it shouldn't matter either way—at least
that's what she told herself.

* * *

Jack waited until the doctor was out of his view before
he groaned in frustration. He had made a lot of mistakes in
his life, but agreeing to take this woman into the jungle had
to be the worst. The pull he felt toward her was like free-
falling from a cliff before plunging into the water.

Hector sauntered up next to Jack and grinned. "She is a
very beautiful woman, ¿no?"

Shooting a warning glance Hector's way, Jack refused
to be baited in to commenting on the undeniable statement.
"I'm going to see if the canoes are ready." He moved toward
the river. "Are you coming with me?" he called over his
shoulder.

Hector laughed. "*Sí*, I'm right behind you."

Five minutes later, Jack and Hector began to load all of
their supplies into a canoe tethered to the one they would be
traveling in.

Jack hefted Sophie's heavy pack onboard, and caught
the scent of her perfume. His reaction to the tantalizing
fragrance was ridiculous. Immediately he remembered how
good it had felt to have her in his arms, even if it had only
lasted for a few seconds. He crouched down, scooting her
pack over to allow room for more of their gear.

Glancing up, he caught sight of Sophie walking toward him, applying lip gloss to her full lips. Yeah, she was beautiful and looked more like a college student than a medical doctor. His heart thumped erratically as she drew closer. Jack needed to get a grip on these wild emotions she evoked. He reminded himself that this woman was no different from any other and could not be trusted. Hadn't she already lied to him in order to get her own way?

She stopped beside him and slipped the tube of gloss into her pocket. "We're traveling by canoe?"

"Yep."

Hector jumped into one of the vessels, and it almost toppled over. Her eyes widened. "I've never been in a canoe. Are they safe?"

"For the most part, yes." Jack stood up, his six two frame towering over her. "Do you know how to swim?"

Surprise flitted across her face. "You want me to swim in the river?"

"Preferably, no. I just need to know if something happens that I won't have to rescue you. You know like CPR and mouth to mouth. That kind of thing."

She narrowed her gaze. "I can swim, Mr. Mathison. And I'm very familiar with cardio pulmonary resuscitation."

Getting her angry with him was one way to take control of the situation. He felt better already.

"Just checking, Dr. Kendrick." He met her gaze, and for a few heartbeats, they stood there staring at one another.

Hector coughed, bringing their staring match to an end. "We're all set to go."

As they boarded the craft, Jack instructed Sophie to sit in the middle. For some twisted reason, he half hoped she would require a little help. She didn't, expertly taking a seat in front of him without so much as rocking the boat.

Hector looked back over his shoulder. "Ready?"

"Yep," Jack said, digging the paddle in the water.

It took a few minutes for him and Hector to get into a rhythm. Soon they were smoothly flowing along with the current as they traveled deeper into the rainforest. Jack drew in a deep breath of the humid air, realizing how much he loved being here.

After a while, Jack's muscles burned and perspiration beaded across his forehead. He switched sides with the paddle as Sophie turned, viewing the passing foliage of the tropical forest. She tucked a piece of hair behind her ear, revealing the curve of her cheek and part of her slender neck.

Jack's pulse tripped as attraction rocketed through him. Okay, so he found her appealing. It didn't mean anything, right? Maybe if he stopped fighting these feelings, his fascination with her would fade. Besides, she had a boyfriend who was in love with her. Jack might as well relax and enjoy the scenery. All of it.

She leaned to the side, skimming her hand across the water. Hopefully there wasn't something under there that was hungry. "I wouldn't do that if I were you," Jack said. "I would think as a doctor you might need your hand."

She abruptly snatched her hand back. "What's in there?" She turned to look at him for an answer.

"Quite a few things that bite."

"Oh. Thank you for warning me." Her lips curved up into a smile. "I guess I should've known that."

Yeah, she should have. How much time had she really spent in the jungle? "You need to be a little more cautious, Dr. Kendrick. You said you've been to Central and South America before. I hope you weren't *lying* about that."

Her smile faded and two little lines creased between her eyebrows. "I didn't lie," she said, turning around to face him.

Jack raised a skeptical brow.

She cleared her throat. "Look, I don't typically try to deceive people. I'm sorry about letting you assume I was a man. Could we please start over?"

Her apology seemed sincere, and the tension in his shoulders was messing with his rhythm. It was time to face the facts and move on. She was here. He had agreed to take her with him. He was attracted to her, and he wasn't looking to act on that attraction. She had a serious boyfriend. Simple.

Some of the tension eased. "Okay."

She studied him for a few seconds, and then slowly her mouth lifted into a soft smile. "Thank you, Jack."

Oh, man. Swallowing, Jack gave her a curt nod and looked away. It was a good thing she was off-limits. The last thing Jack would ever do was steal another man's girlfriend away. After all, he knew what that felt like.

* * *

Sophie turned back around to face forward, relieved Jack had accepted her apology. She was confused and very intrigued with her handsome guide. She wasn't sure what to think about him. Arrogant, yes. But underneath his gruffness, she sensed there might be a softer side to him.

Trying to drive the puzzling thoughts away, Sophie gazed at the gorgeous scenery. Huge trees lined the bank of the river, some of their branches dipping into the water. The noises coming from within the trees sounded similar to some of the tropical exhibits at the Denver Zoo.

It also reminded her of the few times, so long ago, she had spent in the rainforest with her father. Flashes of memories bombarded her mind as they slowly floated down the river. She remembered her father showing her a beautiful Red Macaw with its yellow and blue tipped wings.

Sophie had wanted to take one home, but her father had always been very adamant about keeping birds in their natural habitat.

Then there were the times when he had taken her swimming in one of the many pools at the base of waterfalls generated during the rainy season. Maybe she would get a chance to swim in one again, but doubted there would be as many as she remembered. The rainy season was winding down, and she had read reports predicting November would be drier than normal.

Hector ended her musings by pointing out a couple of monkeys swinging in the trees. They brought back memories as well, and Sophie wanted to get a picture of the playful monkeys to show Camille's children when she returned home. Reaching into one of her pockets, she pulled out her digital camera and took a number of pictures before the monkeys were out of sight.

She took several more shots as she panned the tropical surroundings. Out of the corner of her eye, she caught sight of Jack's shoulder. If she turned just a little more, she'd be able to capture his image, and she needed at least one picture of her guide, right? Besides, Camille would want to see how Jack had aged. Which, incidentally, he'd done quite well.

Straddling the seat, she pulled the camera down and turned toward him. "Do you mind if I take a picture of you?" She kept her voice neutral and tried to keep her eyes from drifting down. Her peripheral vision took in the way Jack's muscles flexed as he paddled the canoe effortlessly.

His lips curled up slightly. *Darn.* Her eyes had only strayed for a second. The smug look he gave her made her almost change her mind.

"I don't mind," he said, that arrogant little smirk back on his face.

"It's not for me, Mr. Mathison. Camille and her brother will want to see you." She winced at the mild deception. While her friend would like to see Jack, the picture was really more for her benefit.

He flashed her a smile. "Of course."

Did she really want a picture of him?

Swallowing her pride, she raised the camera up, and centered him on the screen. Those eyes of his glittered with amusement, his teeth white against tanned skin as she depressed the button. "Thanks," she said, turning around to discreetly review the digital image. The man was gorgeous and very photogenic. A deep chuckle sounded behind her and she almost pushed the delete button.

Almost.

To make it not look so obvious, she asked Hector to turn around for a picture. He lowered his paddle and posed. Then he held out his hand. "Let me get one of you, *Señorita.*"

She handed him the camera and smiled, while simultaneously wondering if Jack would show up in the background.

Hector took several shots until Jack interrupted him. "Hey, Hector?" he asked with sarcasm. "Do you think we can wait on this *Hallmark* moment and keep paddling?"

A wry grin tipped Hector's mouth. "*Sí*, Jack." He handed Sophie her camera, his lips spreading into a grin.

Looking over her shoulder, Sophie cast Jack an annoyed look. He shrugged and gave her a lopsided smile. "We're almost there, Dr. Kendrick. You might want to turn around."

Sophie whirled around and saw men near the water's edge. Returning the camera to her pocket, she felt excitement bubble up at the prospect of really starting their journey. The canoe scraped along the bottom as Jack maneuvered it to the shore.

Sophie stood up just as Hector jumped out to bank the watercraft. The movement rocked the boat and she started to lose her balance, her arms flailing backward.

"Careful," Jack said, his hands settling on her waist.

"Thank you." The gentle pressure from his hands rendered her motionless. What was it about him that made her so responsive to his touch?

"Hang on a second." Jack jumped out of the canoe and held out his hand for her. Good manners made her accept his help. She tried to ignore the jolt of awareness that zinged as their palms connected.

A muscle twitched in Jack's jaw as he lowered his eyes to their joined hands. As soon as she touched the ground, he released his grip and turned away from her.

Jack spoke to the men in Spanish, and they immediately started to unload the canoe. When one of the men lifted Sophie's backpack, Jack said something to the man in Spanish and pointed at Sophie. The man grinned and set the pack down in front of her.

She met Jack's gaze and read the challenge in his eyes. He was just waiting for her to complain. Clamping down her irritation, she picked up the heavy, full frame backpack and slipped the straps over her shoulders. Jack's lips curved up ever so slightly before he slung a pack over his shoulder and picked up a couple of tents.

"Follow me," he demanded, walking past her.

She quickened her pace and matched his step evenly. She wasn't following him just because he commanded her to.

"Are you hiring those men to carry everything else?" she asked, struggling with the burden of her pack.

"Yes."

Unbelievable. He *was* trying to prove a point.

Full of righteous indignation, she stomped next to Jack, determined to carry her own weight.

A group of children ran alongside of them, their high pitched giggles conveying their delight at the visitors. Sophie's heart softened at the sight of the brown skinned, dark-eyed children. One little girl lagged behind the group of older kids, running as fast as she could with bare feet. Suddenly, the little girl tripped on a branch and tumbled to the ground. With all the chaos their arrival created, no one seemed to hear the child's cry for help.

Sophie stopped and shrugged the heavy pack from her shoulders. The child looked at her with big brown eyes. She couldn't be more than four years old. "Let me take a look, honey," Sophie said, kneeling down next to her.

The child's cries subsided as she watched Sophie with curiosity. Gently, Sophie examined the small knee, imbedded with dirt and tree bark. As she wiped the dirt away, she saw nothing had broken through the tender skin. "You're going to be okay, sweetie." Sophie patted the little girl on the head and gave her a soft smile. The child might not understand English, but hopefully the tone of Sophie's voice would reassure her.

A shy smile appeared on the little girl's face as she got to her feet and raced toward the other children. Sophie smiled and turned to get her pack when her gaze collided with Jack's. His lips were lifted slightly, and his pale blue eyes held hers with warmth she'd never seen before. He studied her for a few heartbeats before he lifted her backpack and strode away without saying anything to her.

Sophie followed him, thinking maybe he wasn't such a jerk after all. She scratched that idea as she stopped and stared at the donkey Hector and the other men were loading down with most of their supplies.

Jack had failed to mention this to her. "Didn't you just tell me you hired those men to carry the supplies?"

"Yes. And, if I'm correct—" He gazed at her with a hint of mirth in his eyes. "—they did carry our supplies."

"I thought I would be carrying my own pack?"

He held up a frameless daypack. "You still will. Transfer whatever you want to have with you all the time." He pointed to the donkey. "Fred will carry the rest."

He held out the pack, and looked very pleased with himself for not telling her about the donkey. She detected a tiny note of victory in his eyes. The man was completely exasperating.

"Thank you," she murmured, reaching for the pack. Inadvertently, she grabbed Jack's hand. Disturbed by the spark of energy she felt, Sophie quickly jerked her hand back, pulling the backpack to her chest.

Jack's blue eyes reflected awareness from the contact. He didn't look happy about it. "When you're done," he said tersely, "bring it back to me, and I'll tie your tent to it."

She didn't want this electrifying attraction any more than he did, and he sounded so put out. "I can do it myself," she said sharply. "I'm not a novice."

"Fine, *Dr. Kendrick*. I was just trying to help."

She closed her eyes briefly, drawing in a deep breath. Being rude was not in her nature. "I'm sorry I snapped at you."

The muscle in his jaw tensed. "Don't worry about it." He handed her the small tent.

"Thank you." She took the tent, careful not to touch him.

An uncomfortable lapse of time ensued before he turned away from her. "We need to get going."

Watching him walk away, Sophie felt a stab of disappointment. Why wouldn't he call her by her first name? Kneeling down, she quickly transferred her things into the daypack, making sure to include a basic first-aid kit.

After she tied the tent to her backpack, Hector came over and picked up the full framed pack. "You have what you need?" he asked, offering her his hand to help her stand.

"I think so." She pointed to Fred the donkey. "Does Mr. Mathison have any other surprises?"

Hector grinned. "Not that I know of." He shrugged. "But with Jack, you never know."

They both watched as Jack laughed at something one of the little native children said to him. He ruffled the boy's hair, and then glanced over at her and Hector. Flashing his white teeth, he said, "We're wasting daylight. Let's go."

Chapter Six

Jack took the rear, leading the donkey behind him. Hector had the lead, slicing his machete to make a path for them, and Sophie was in the middle.

Sophie. He was being immature and stupid to avoid using her first name. What he wanted to avoid was her. Period. That was a little hard to do with her directly in front of him. He hated to admit that he enjoyed the view.

She was a natural beauty and didn't wear much make-up. He noticed, however, that she frequently applied lip gloss to her perfectly shaped lips. Every time she did, he wondered what her lips would taste like. Then he would mentally yell at himself for even entertaining such a stupid thought.

After some time, she stopped and turned around. Her face glistened with moisture, making her even more attractive. "How much further until we reach the village?" she asked, wiping the back of her hand across her forehead.

"You're not already complaining, are you?"

A tiny spark of irritation flashed in her eyes. "I wasn't complaining. I simply asked a question."

"Okay," he said, unable to resist teasing her. "But if you want, it's not too late for me to take you back."

"You'd like that, wouldn't you?" she said, her gaze narrowing a fraction.

Jack curbed the desire to smile at her snarky reply. "We'll make camp in a few hours. The village is still two days out."

"Thank you."

"Any time."

Their eyes held for a few seconds before she gave him a shy smile. Turning around, she started to walk again and then started humming. *Humming?* Jack followed behind, trying to place the soft melody. Was this girl for real? Despite her initial deception, Sophie seemed to be a genuinely nice person. So unlike the girl he'd planned on marrying who had crushed his dreams faster than Hector cut a path through the jungle foliage with his machete.

A few minutes later, they passed under a natural archway covered in green moss and bright orange and pink blossoms. Sophie stopped, looking back over her shoulder. "This is so beautiful, Jack."

Hearing her call him by his first name did something to his gut, and, for the first time, Jack detected a slight Southern accent. Curiosity burned inside, and he had to force himself not to ask about where she had been raised.

She held out her camera. "Do you mind taking a picture of me under the archway?"

Normally he would mind, but like the lackey he'd turned into this morning, he took the camera. Holding it up, he centered her on the screen, watching in fascination as she applied more lip gloss. Wanting to get this over with, he said, "Say cheese."

She laughed, and he took the shot. He stared down at the screen. She was incredibly beautiful.

"Is it okay?" she questioned. "Or are my eyes closed?"

He swallowed and glanced back up at her. "Nope. It's good." He held out the camera to her.

"Thank you." She reached for the camera and tipped her head back to look into the canopy of trees. "Can you believe how gorgeous it is here?"

Jack felt a little tongue-tied. The scenery wasn't the only thing he found gorgeous. "Breathtaking."

She looked at him curiously, as if trying to determine if his words held a double meaning. Jack wasn't about to let her inside his head. "We better get going. There are plenty of other photo ops as we go along."

Giving him one last long look, she swiveled around and started after Hector. Jack followed her the rest of the day. His respect for her grew with each passing hour. She remained cheerful and continued to exclaim how beautiful everything was. She was a nice person, and it bothered him that he liked that. It bothered him that he wanted to get to know her better; it bothered him that he wanted her to like him as well.

By the time they stopped to make camp, Jack was aggravated with himself. It wasn't like him to be so smitten by someone, especially in such a short time. He needed to be in control—that way he could never be the one who got hurt.

* * *

Sophie took off her daypack and rolled her shoulders back. She was tired, sick of the bugs, and hungry. At the same time, she was exhilarated with the knowledge that she was one step closer to finding her father.

Swatting at a bug, she turned and saw the men were busy setting up camp. Hector assembled a small propane cooking stove and started making dinner. Jack removed supplies from off the donkey, and she wondered if he needed her to do anything.

"Can I help?" she asked, standing next to Jack.

His muscles strained as he untied the canvas bag, and his blue eyes flickered to her own. "You can go ahead and get your tent set up."

"Okay. Where do you want me to set it up?"

Jack let out a big breath and peered over her head.

"Hector, will you please show the doctor where to put her tent."

"*Sí*," Hector said happily, motioning for her to bring her tent over to him.

"Thank you," Sophie said, moving toward Hector. At least *he* was consistently kind.

Rolling out her tent, she stared at the pieces for a few seconds, familiarizing herself with the equipment.

Jack sauntered next to her with his own tent. "Need some help?"

She eyed him dubiously. Was he being nice or arrogant? "No, thank you." She reached for one of the poles.

He chuckled. "Okay, but remember I offered."

The cynical way he said it let her know he thought her incapable of setting up her own tent. Too bad for him she happened to have basically the same model back at her condo. When she set up her tent without a hitch, she noticed Jack still trying to assemble his own.

"Need some help?" she asked smugly.

He cast his steely eyes to her and answered tightly, "No."

"Okay, but remember I offered." She heard him emit a low growl, and she tried not to laugh. This was totally unlike her, and she blamed Jack for her deviant behavior.

She left him to his tent and wandered over next to Hector. "I'm starving. Can I help you with anything?"

Hector grinned and held up one of the freeze dried meal packages. "Not much to it, *chica*." He motioned to a camping chair. "Go and sit. You've had a long day."

Jack said something under his breath that sounded like, "Haven't we all."

Ignoring his moody behavior, she reached inside her pack and pulled out her journal. Sophie had discovered years ago that writing about her day was a good way to get things off her mind.

The small waterproof journal had been purchased for this trip so she could record her thoughts as she searched for her father. Since meeting Jack, however, she needed to unload.

She wrote about him, scribbling down how he made her feel—and she felt a lot of things when she was around him—including attraction. Which didn't make sense. He was definitely not her type.

So caught up in her writing, Sophie didn't notice Jack standing over her with a bowl of food.

"I thought you were hungry," he said, startling her.

She slammed her journal closed, praying he hadn't read his name. "I am. Thank you." She took the plate and looked around him, speaking to Hector. "*Muchas gracias*. This looks good."

"*De nada*," Hector replied with a smile.

Jack took a seat next to her. "And you said you didn't know how to speak Spanish."

Was he teasing her? She eyed him a little warily. "Yeah, I think you've heard all the words I know."

Jack chuckled and took a bite of his food. Sophie tasted her meal and was pleasantly surprised by how good it was. "Mmm, this is really good."

Hector winked at her. "I'm glad you like it. You might not feel the same way after a week, though."

"I'm not picky." She took another mouthful and glanced Jack's way, only to catch him watching her. He was the first one to look away, and the two of them continued to eat their meal in silence.

After a few minutes had passed, Jack said, "*Sooo*, Sophie, what were you...ten when you graduated from high school?"

Hearing him call her by her name made her look back up at him.

She stared into pools of blue and forgot the question. "What?"

His lips twisted upward, giving her the first genuine smile since she'd met him. It transformed his chiseled face into something much more likeable. "I asked how old you were when you graduated from high school."

"I was sixteen." She didn't tell him that she'd only been sixteen for a few weeks. It tended to intimidate people. "Why?"

"Well…" His eyes briefly scanned her face. "You look like you're barely twenty right now. I just wondered how you could possibly be a doctor."

She felt her face heat, pretty sure there was a compliment somewhere in that statement. "I just turned thirty-two a few months ago."

The corner of his mouth twitched as he continued to study her. He wouldn't be the first person to comment on her youthful appearance. In high school and college, it had driven her crazy. Even now, her colleagues didn't give her the same respect they seemed to give other physicians strictly because of how young she appeared.

"You can't be that much older than me."

He shrugged. "I'll be thirty-eight in January."

Jack took a drink of water and then resumed eating his meal, allowing Sophie to study his profile. Laugh lines creased the tanned skin around his eyes, and the perpetual five O'clock shadow on his jaw gave him a rugged, outdoor look that was very appealing.

He and Peter were only a few months apart in age, but the two men couldn't be more opposite. Peter spent most of his days inside an office, leaving his complexion pale in comparison to Jack.

Suddenly, Jack turned and met her gaze.

Sophie couldn't bring herself to look away. His light blue colored irises mesmerized her, and warmth flooded her chest. A twinge of guilt pricked her conscience. Never once had gazing into Peter's brown eyes caused this kind of reaction.

Hector severed the connection when he walked past them. "I'm going to get water for washing." He held up a collapsed plastic container. "I'll be back soon."

"Do you need help?" Sophie asked, feeling guilty for allowing him to do all the work.

He shook his head and winked. "I can manage."

"Okay, but I want to do the dishes."

He smiled. "*Muchas gracias, señorita.*"

"You're welcome. *De nada.*"

Hector sauntered off, whistling a jaunty tune. Sophie glanced toward Jack just as he shifted his gaze from Hector to her.

"I'm curious," he said, giving her another great smile. "For someone as smart as you are, and with a father who spends a lot of time in Central and South America, why don't you speak Spanish?"

She bit her lip and considered her answer. Finally, she settled on the truth. "It sounds silly, but it was the only way I could rebel."

Jack's eyebrow rose. "Not learning Spanish was rebelling?"

She wasn't sure if it made any sense, but at the time it was the only thing she could do. "My mother died when I was six. After her death, my dad poured himself into researching different eco-systems in Central and South America. I was left alone a lot."

"You're dad left a six-year-old kid alone?"

She smiled. "No. I always had a housekeeper or nanny to look after me.

I guess since my dad is the only living relative I have, it felt like I was alone when he was gone so much." She shifted in her seat, not entirely sure if she wanted to share any more with him.

He looked at her expectantly. "Go on. I'm dying to see when the rebellious child came out."

"Are you making fun of me?"

"Yes," he said, his eyes crinkling at the corners.

The man could definitely be charming when he wanted to. She rendered him a small smile, liking this side of him so much better.

"I started taking Spanish at a young age in order to please my father. But as I got older..." She lifted one shoulder in a shrug. "I resented the time he spent away, and decided that learning his preferred language wasn't going to keep him around." Looking away from Jack, she continued to explain. "While other teenagers rebelled with drugs, sex, and alcohol, I refused to speak Spanish and focused on school. Much to my father's dismay, I studied French and became a doctor. Just not the kind he wanted me to be."

* * *

Jack studied Sophie as she painted a picture of herself in her youth. She was opening up to him, and now he wasn't sure that's what he wanted. However, it was sort of cute to think she considered not speaking Spanish as rebellious.

"Not a party girl, huh?"

"Nope." She gave him a soft smile. "To be honest, getting wasted wasn't my idea of fun. Besides," she said, looking down at the ground, "I wasn't invited to very many parties, so it wasn't really an issue."

He laughed, making her look at him. "Come on, someone as pretty as you are had to be popular."

"I wasn't very popular, especially with the guys."

Color stained her cheeks. "I was a nerd, so nobody ever wanted me anyway."

Now that was hard to believe. She was probably one of the most beautiful women he'd ever seen. "So you never had any boyfriends?"

"Well, yes, and I was with someone all during med school."

For some reason, Jack felt a pang of jealousy. "What happened to him?"

She paused, as if pondering whether or not to answer him honestly. "David didn't like the change in our relationship when I returned to my faith." She moistened her lips, and looked down into her bowl of food. "He was angry when I made the ultimatum to either marry me or move out."

A surge of emotions coiled in Jack's gut. David sounded like a jerk. Despite his own skewed views on marriage, Jack wanted to track this guy down and pummel him for hurting Sophie. He tried to tamp down the irritation he felt about her living with the guy.

"Sounds like you made a good decision."

She lifted her lashes and gave him a soft smile. "Thank you."

He knew she was seeing someone now. Peter something. From what little he had gathered, she didn't seem that into him. Jack wasn't sure why, but he wanted to probe further. "So I guess the guy you're dating now shares your faith?"

"Yes. Peter is a good man, and he has the most wonderful family." Her eyes lit up. "Every Sunday after church, we gather at his parents' house for dinner. All four of his siblings are married and have a couple of children each so you can't imagine how crazy and noisy it is, but I love every second of it."

Given his estrangement with his parents and brother, her enthusiasm for Peter's large family rubbed Jack the wrong way. She continued to talk about the family get-togethers, extolling each event and tossing out a few names of her favorite nieces and nephews. For a woman who hadn't returned her boyfriend's declaration of love earlier today, she seemed pretty tight with his extended family.

"Wow, it sounds like you might like Peter's family more than you like him," he said sardonically.

The light in Sophie's eyes dimmed, and color seeped out of her face. "You know, I don't feel very good." She stood up abruptly. "Please tell Hector I'll do the dishes another night."

Before Jack could say another word, she dashed off to her tent and slipped inside. He wasn't sure why his remark had upset her so much. Unless it was true.

He glanced toward her tent and wondered if he should try to find out if she really didn't feel good or if his comment had bothered her. For several seconds Jack debated about what to do. A blue butterfly flitted in front of him and then hovered over the seat Sophie had vacated. The blue wings edged with black fluttered effortlessly before coming to rest atop a brown book. Sophie's journal.

Chapter Seven

Jack moved toward the book, and the butterfly darted away. The journal lay there innocently, the pen marking the page where he had read his name at least three times. What had Sophie been writing about him?

Tentatively, he picked up the small volume and rubbed his thumb over the smooth surface. It would be so easy to flip to the page of her last entry, but reading her journal would be a major violation of her privacy. As much as he wanted to see what she had written about him, he couldn't bring himself to look. But he was tempted.

It would be better to hand it over to Sophie before he gave in to his curiosity. Maybe he should apologize to her while he was at it. Hector would be back any moment and wouldn't be happy about Sophie holed up in her tent. The only problem was Jack wasn't exactly sure what he was apologizing for. He had a feeling if he asked, it would only make matters worse.

Jack slowly walked toward her tent, wondering what he should say. Part of him just wanted to place the journal at the tent's door and leave it alone, but he knew it would probably rain during the night and he didn't want her journal ruined.

Before he could alert her of his presence, she asked, "What do you want, Mr. Mathison?"

"How did you know it was me?" Sophie remained inside, and the tent window and door were zipped shut.

"A lucky guess."

He bit back a smile at her sarcasm and waited for her to come out. She didn't, nor did she say anything else. Jack shifted on his feet as the seconds ticked by. Still nothing.

Was he supposed to wait here all night?

"I have your journal," he stated flatly.

She let out a gasp and unzipped the tent door faster than he'd thought possible. She was kneeling on her sleeping bag, looking up at him with those big brown eyes. Jack crouched down so he was at eye level with her. Silently, he handed her the book.

"Did you read it?" Her voice was whisper soft.

Boy was he glad he could answer her honestly. "I was very tempted. But, no, I didn't read it."

"Thank you." Her eyes softened with appreciation.

"Sure." He held her gaze, acutely aware of their close proximity. If Jack didn't leave soon, he might do something stupid. Right now she looked very kissable. "Well, good night."

Her lips curved up slowly, drawing his eyes to her mouth. "Good night, Jack."

He left while he had the chance.

That night, Jack had trouble falling asleep. He laid in his tent, listening to the rain pattering softly, his thoughts fixated on the woman a few feet away from him. He liked Sophie—more than he wanted to. She was kind and wholesome and everything a good Christian boy could want. If he was being honest with himself, part of him wanted her.

But he wasn't a good Christian boy anymore. He was a cynical man, and he could never be worthy to have someone like Sophie. The resentment he harbored against God and his family had a hold of him as tightly as a Boa Constrictor squeezing its prey.

Unwilling to continue his train of thought, he turned on his side and closed his eyes. He needed to sleep, or he would be worthless in the morning.

Just as he drifted off, he heard a blood curdling scream coming from Sophie.

His heart pounded fiercely as he tried to get out of his tent. He could hear her crying. Who or what was hurting her? When he finally scrambled outside, Hector emerged from his own tent.

Sophie screamed again, and Jack nearly ripped open the canvas door. She thrashed around on top of her sleeping bag. *All this from a nightmare?* He knelt down beside her. "Sophie," he said, shaking her gently.

Her eyes flew open. Then she threw her arms around his neck, clutching the back of his shirt. Instinctively, Jack gathered her small body close to him. She buried her face into his shoulder and continued to cry. Gently, Jack patted her back in an effort to comfort her. "Hey, it's okay," he whispered against her hair. "You're safe."

She tightened her hold on him, pressing closer, and he caught the scent of something sweet and tropical. His pulse, already spiked by adrenalin, accelerated to an erratic rhythm. *Oh, man.* Maybe comforting her hadn't been the best idea.

All at once, she pushed him away and covered her face with her hands. "I'm sorry," she mumbled through her fingers.

* * *

Sophie didn't want to remove her hands from her face. She felt so stupid about her reaction to Jack. Why on earth had she hugged him?

Jack grasped each of her wrists and took her hands away from her face. "There's nothing to be sorry about. It's not like you can control your dreams."

Her nightmare wasn't what she had apologized about. It had more to do with her throwing herself at him and sobbing like an idiot.

Hector patted Jack on the back and mumbled something before going back inside his tent.

The moon cast its pale light, allowing Sophie to see the fine mist of rain dampening Jack's head, water running in tiny rivulets down his forehead and cheeks. He seemed oblivious to the moisture as he continued to hold onto her hands, his eyes warm with concern. The man was a quandary to her. One minute he was a sarcastic jerk, and then the next, he was a soft-spoken gentleman.

She pulled her hands back into her lap. "I'm sorry. I didn't mean to wake you up."

His eyes crinkled. "I think you woke up the entire jungle."

She heard the noises surrounding them, and suddenly the frogs and cicadas sounded sinister instead of comforting. The occasional cry of a monkey pierced the air, sending a chill down her back. "You can go back to sleep now. I usually don't have the dream again in the same night."

He frowned. "You've had the dream before?"

"Almost every night." Then she realized what she had just confessed. "I should've said something. Warned you. That way you wouldn't have rushed in to help me."

He wiped the water from his brow. "If you scream like that every night, I can guarantee I'll come rushing in."

She felt bad, knowing there was a very good chance it would happen again tomorrow night and possibly each night throughout the entire excursion.

The lines in his face deepened. "What else haven't you told me?"

"I...I didn't withhold it on purpose." *No, Sophie. That's a lie.* She had made a conscious decision not to tell him. "That's not true. I decided not to mention it because I didn't want you to use it as an excuse to leave me behind."

The intense look he gave her made her want to crawl inside her sleeping bag and hide.

She really wasn't a liar, but he'd never believe that. Her only defense was her desperation to end her nightmares and find out what had happened to her father.

"I'm sorry, Jack."

The muscle in his jaw tightened, but he didn't say a word. Feeling like a horrible person, she scooted down in her bag and turned her back to him. "Good night, Mr. Mathison."

She heard him let out a long breath. "Good night, Dr. Kendrick."

* * *

Sophie awoke early the next morning and quickly dressed for the day. While she rolled up her sleeping bag, she listened to hear if the men were awake. Just thinking about facing Jack this morning made her stomach twist with apprehension. She was embarrassed about being caught in another lie, even if it was by omission. Would it do any good to try and explain her reasons?

Of course that wasn't the only reason she was nervous. The memory of him holding her close and tenderly quieting her fears had plagued her most of the night. If she were being honest—something she was clearly having difficulty with lately—she had liked being in his arms. He had made her feel safe. He had also evoked other emotions she wasn't ready to acknowledge.

Stop it, Sophie. He was just being a nice guy. Good grief. If she wasn't careful, she was going to turn into one of the many female admirers Jack seemed to attract.

Frustrated with her line of thinking, she finished getting ready and applied sunscreen and insect repellant. Outside, she heard the donkey bray and Hector speaking in Spanish. She had no idea if he was talking to Jack or the donkey.

Knowing she couldn't hide any longer, she finger-combed her hair, applied a little lip gloss, and dropped the tube into one of her pockets. Her hand shook slightly as she unzipped the canvas door and stepped out.

Sunlight peaked through the trees, warming the wet ground. The heavy air, scented from the musty foliage, filled her nostrils, as did the pungent smell of ground coffee beans. She saw Jack sitting on a log, slicing a mango into a bowl. He wore tan cargo pants and another tight fitting T-shirt which, she realized when he glanced up and locked his gaze on her, was the same color of blue as his eyes.

Sophie's step faltered, and she quickly looked around for any sign of Hector. The man was just disappearing beyond a copse of trees, the donkey ambling slowly beside him. If she'd come out sooner, she could've accompanied him to get water.

Nervously, her focus returned to Jack. "Good morning." She hoped her voice didn't sound as shaky as she felt inside. "Can I help?"

She waited for his answer, trying to determine if he was still angry with her. Although he'd been a little more civil toward her, he was still moody.

"There's not much to do," he said, and pointed to an aluminum thermos sitting on top of the small butane stove. "Coffee's hot, if you want to help yourself."

"Is there a chance it's decaf?"

"Nope." He laughed. "You remember you're in Costa Rica, right? World renowned coffee and all that?"

High up in the canopy of trees, Sophie heard the chatter from a group of monkeys. She tipped her head back and watched as a few of the acrobatic animals swung from branch to branch. "I remember where I am," she said, smiling at their antics.

Sensing Jack watching her, she returned her gaze to him. "Caffeine makes me jittery, and I have a hard time falling asleep."

At the mention of sleep, one of his eyebrows rose. "Which would be a problem if you truly have nightmares every night."

"Yes." She sensed he was still bothered by her not telling him about the recurring bad dream. "I really am sorry, Jack. Like I said, I know I should've told you about my nightmares."

His eyes pierced her as he measured her words. "You don't have any more secrets to reveal, then?"

Her eyes drifted down to his bulging biceps, bringing back the memory of being held within those impressive arms. Yeah, she had another secret. She was hopelessly— against her wishes—attracted to this man.

"I'm a girl. Of course I have secrets." She made herself look directly at him. "But I can assure you those secrets won't have any impact on you." Because neither she or Jack were looking for a relationship, especially not with each other.

Besides, after ending things with David, she had vowed to never again date anyone who didn't believe in God. This pull she felt toward Jack was nothing more than a school girl's crush. It could never be anything more.

* * *

Sweat trickled down the middle of Sophie's back. She wiped her brow with the back of her hand, wondering if a woman should perspire this much. Discreetly, she checked to see if she had any sweat rings under her armpits.

The next thing she knew her steps halted abruptly as she smacked into something solid. The weight of her backpack made her lose her balance, and Sophie yelped as she felt herself topple backwards.

She realized the solid mass she had run into was Jack and, in desperation to keep from falling down, she reached out and grabbed onto the straps of his pack. "Oh no," she said just before she tumbled on her backside. Then Jack flattened her when he landed on top of her.

The weight of Jack's body and his forty pound pack compressed all the air in Sophie's chest, rendering her unable to breathe or scream for help. Even after Jack quickly rolled off of her, Sophie still couldn't draw in any air.

"What happened?" Jack said, shrugging off his backpack. "Are you okay?"

All Sophie could do was gasp while she waited for her diaphragm to start working again. She closed her eyes and tried not to panic, concentrating on the simple task of taking a slow deep breath.

"Sophie," Jack said, jostling her shoulder. "Hey, talk to me."

Unable to answer him, Sophie opened her eyes to find Jack's face hovering near her own. The dark stubble covering his jaw was so close she could almost feel the prickly whiskers against her skin. His light blue eyes were filled with worry as they held hers.

Finally, she was able to take a full breath. "Ouch," she said in a soft voice. "That hurt."

The corner of his mouth twitched. "You scared me. For a minute there I thought I was going to have to give you CPR or something."

"It wouldn't have helped." *Although the mouth to mouth would have been interesting.* "You knocked the wind out of me."

His lips parted into a full grin. "*Hmm.*" He inched back, his gaze still holding hers. "All I did was stop to look at my GPS, and then, wham, I got knocked off my feet."

"Well, maybe you should warn me when you're stopping."

"Maybe *you* should pay closer attention."

"Maybe I should."

Amusement lit his eyes as he eased away and held out his hand to help her up. She did her best not to react to the flash of heat when she placed her palm in his and climbed to her feet. She winced when a muscle in her back protested as she straightened. "Thank you."

Jack was slow to let go of her hand, his forehead lined with concern. "You sure you're okay?"

Not really. Her back was killing her, and her heart beat erratically merely from touching him. "Yes. Just a little sore." She pulled her hand away.

Jack eyed her for a few more seconds before he leaned over to get his pack. "Looks like you dropped something," he said, kneeling down to pick up two tubes of lip gloss that must have come out of her pocket when she'd hit the ground.

Sophie held out her hand, but instead of giving the items back to her, Jack read the names on the tubes. "Whipped Vanilla and Frozen Daiquiri. That sounds…" He paused, and gave her a wry grin. "…refreshing."

Her mouth went dry when his gaze drifted down to her lips. She felt her lungs squeeze together and her pulse race even faster. A flicker of mirth crossed Jack's features, and Sophie knew he was aware of the effect he had on her.

Swallowing, she reached out to snatch both tubes of gloss from his fingers. "I guess you'll never know."

He gave her a lazy smile. "You're probably right."

For some reason the implied declaration that he would never taste-test her lip gloss disappointed her. Flustered, Sophie stepped away from him and glanced over to see Hector watching both of them, clearly amused.

"Since we're stopped," Hector said, handing her a bottle of water. "It would be a good time to rest, ¿*no*?"

"*Gracias.*" Sophie accepted the bottle of water. "But I'm okay to keep going." She didn't dare look at Jack and was relieved when he said they could rest for a few minutes.

Sophie shrugged off her backpack and sat down, using the pack as a seat. Jack talked to Hector about what was ahead of them and where they'd make camp tonight. He didn't once look her way and acted as if nothing had happened between them.

What *had* happened between them? Or, rather, what had happened to her? Her feelings made no sense because half the time she didn't even like Jack. She twisted the lid off of her bottle and took a long drink of water.

Forcing thoughts of Jack out of her mind, she focused on her dad and wondered where he might be. Hopefully she would find him doing what he loved best—studying and finding ways to preserve the ecosystem, especially inside the rainforest. She prayed the reason she hadn't heard from him was because he was too busy and had lost track of time.

Tipping her head back, Sophie looked up into the canopy of trees, her eyes searching for the monkeys she could hear. She loved watching them, just as she had as a child. The lush green leaves fluttered from movement of the jungle life as flashes of colorful birds hopped from one branch to another. It was so incredibly beautiful here—completely different from her childhood home in Texas.

No wonder her dad had spent most of his life living in this setting. Had she not graduated so early from high school, she probably would've ended up accompanying him on some of his trips again. But once she had started college, the loneliness she had known most of her life had dissipated with a variety of roommates and the campus social life.

So deep in thought, Sophie hadn't heard Jack talking to her. "I'm sorry, what did you ask me?"

He sat all alone, watching her with one eyebrow raised. "I asked if you're okay? You were kind of spacing off." One corner of his mouth edged up. "You didn't jar your brain when you landed on your butt, did you?"

Sophie couldn't suppress a laugh. "I'm fine. I was just thinking about my dad and how much he loves the rainforest. Being here again, and seeing it through adult eyes, I think I can understand how he feels. I would love to come back here and do humanitarian work alongside my dad."

He gave her a soft smile. "I'll bet he would really like that."

Sophie was grateful Jack talked like there was hope her father was still out there healthy and alive. It occurred to her she knew nothing about his family. "What about you? Have any of your family members ever come over here to take a tour with you?"

Jack's lips pressed together tightly, and Sophie thought she saw a hint of sadness in his eyes before they hardened. "No. They never have." He got to his feet. "Well, if you're okay, we really need to get moving."

"Sure." Sophie stood up and slipped on her backpack. It seemed obvious Jack didn't want to talk about his family. Although she was curious, she didn't feel comfortable asking him about it. She avoided looking at his face as she walked away from him.

"Sophie! Stop!" Jack shouted, making her heart miss a beat.

Chapter Eight

The panicked tone of Jack's voice made Sophie stop in her tracks. She sucked in a frightened breath when he swiftly moved in front of her, and swiped his machete to cut off the head of a colorful snake coiled just inches from her feet. Generally, she wasn't afraid of snakes, but she knew enough about a coral snake to know its venom is deadly.

Putting a hand over her chest, she watched Jack use the toe of his boot to toss the lifeless body away from her. He crouched down and wiped the blood off the blade of his machete in the grass.

"Thank you. I…I didn't see it."

Jack tilted his head up. "I'm impressed how quickly you listened to me, Dr. Kendrick. If you had taken one more step, I would most likely be hauling your body back to the States."

"I'll be more careful from now on."

His eyes remained locked on hers as he stood up. "Yes. Being careful is always a good idea." He continued to hold her gaze. "Nobody wants to get hurt."

Sophie didn't try analyzing whether or not his words had a double meaning because the look she read in Jack's eyes was something she couldn't quite decipher. *Admiration?* Or was it something more? For some reason, it made her happy she had somehow pleased him.

He regarded her a moment longer before motioning her forward. "After you."

As Sophie trailed behind Hector, she looked forward to making camp tonight, and hoped to spend some time talking with Jack. She wanted to get to know him better—the real guy under all the sarcasm and jokes.

They had at least ten more days to spend together, and it would be nice if they could become friends. She told herself that a friend was all she wanted to be, but deep down she suspected she might like it to be more than that.

They hiked for a couple of hours longer, and then stopped just before the sun went down. Sophie slid the backpack from her shoulders and stretched her neck from side to side.

"We better hurry and get the tents up," Jack said, dropping his pack to the ground. "It's going to rain."

"*Sí*," Hector said, handing each of them a protein bar. "This will have to be your supper."

Sophie tucked the peanut butter bar into her pocket and picked a spot to set up her shelter. While Jack and Hector unloaded the donkey, Sophie retrieved their tents and laid them out on either side of hers as they had instructed the night before.

She set up her own tent first and then went to work on Hector's. As she connected the poles together, Jack knelt down and started on his own shelter. Building a friendship with the man was her goal, but he was so focused on getting his tent up that he hadn't even looked her way.

He worked quickly as if he expected a downpour any second. Not wanting to get caught in the rain, Sophie decided she better pick up the pace. Jack cursed under his breath when one of the poles wouldn't fit together. This morning he'd had the opposite problem and had struggled pulling the poles apart. A little petroleum jelly would help solve the problem, but he seemed touchy about setting up and taking down his tent, so she kept silent and continued to work.

"*Gracias*," Hector said when Sophie completed the task. "Maybe you can help Jack now." His voice held a hint of laughter.

At the suggestion, Jack shot the man a fierce look. "I got it."

Sensing Jack's rising frustration, Sophie wisely didn't say anything. They'd had a relatively good day together, and she didn't want to do anything to put him in a bad mood again. It was her hope that their rocky start was in the past.

Fat drops of rain began to fall just as Jack finished. The rain was coming, and she was disappointed they wouldn't have a few minutes to talk.

Their eyes met briefly, and Jack gave her a quick nod of his head. "See you in the morning."

"Okay." She smiled and then hurried inside her sleeping quarters. Tomorrow would be soon enough to get to know Jack a little better. She quickly changed into her cut-off sweats and T-shirt and crawled into her sleeping bag.

Exhausted from the miles they'd covered, she could barely keep her eyes open. After saying her prayers, she felt her muscles relax as sleep overtook her. She was hopeful her nightmare wouldn't come tonight, especially since her mind kept replaying Jack's teasing laugh and the tender look he'd given her after saving her from the snake.

Another smile tugged at her lips, and she looked forward to the morning.

* * *

Jack rubbed his eyes, feeling a little grumpy about how poorly he'd slept his second night into their trip, and it wasn't only because Sophie had had another nightmare. Just like the night before, he'd bolted from his tent to rush to her aid. But instead of getting a hug, this time he had found her fully alert and assuring him she was okay.

Well, he wasn't okay.

He had dreamed about her again, but this time it was about something much more disturbing than him trying to rescue her.

In it, he wore a tuxedo and stood inside a church, waiting for her to join him as she made her way down a long aisle wearing a shimmering white wedding dress.

He hadn't been able to go back to sleep. Why on earth would he dream about a wedding—no, their wedding? It was absurd, and this growing fascination he felt for her needed to be dealt with. Getting involved with a woman who already had a serious boyfriend was wrong. Besides, how could he really trust someone who had purposely deceived him twice?

He cradled his tin mug of coffee and stared at Sophie's tent. She was awake. He could hear her moving around and softly humming. Glancing around, Jack wondered what was taking Hector so long. He'd gone to use the latrine twenty minutes ago. For some reason, Jack didn't feel like being alone with her.

Taking a sip of the hot brew, he heard the tent door unzip and the humming stop as she stepped out.

He swallowed the bitter liquid and studied her through half-lidded eyes. She wore tan cargo pants and a fitted brown tee. Like yesterday, she had on very little makeup. She looked good. A little too good.

When their eyes met, Jack's chest tightened with conflicting emotions. Fighting the hold she had on him, he scowled at her. Her chin rose, and she returned the glare—a challenge in her eyes.

"Don't you ever look homely?" he finally asked.

"Is that a rhetorical question?"

He tried not to laugh. "I just figured after you kept me up most of the night, it should only be fair that you look as bad as I feel."

"I'm sorry about the bad dream." She bit her bottom lip. "Maybe I should put my tent somewhere else."

"Yeah," he snorted, "like maybe back where you came from."

A flash of anger darkened her eyes. "Do you have a split personality?"

"What?"

She stalked over and stood right in front of him. "I asked you if you have a split personality. You know, dramatic mood swings."

What is she insinuating? Slowly, he stood up and leaned down close to her face. "Maybe I do."

"Oh," she said, delicately lifting one eyebrow.

His answer dispelled some of her anger. But, to be honest, since he'd met her, yes, he'd say he had a split personality. Heck, he couldn't keep up with his mood swings. He was a man—he shouldn't be having mood swings!

Acutely aware of how close they stood, Jack clenched his hands, fighting the urge to pull her to him. Her glossy lips looked inviting. How could he be so annoyed by her one minute and then have the desire to kiss her senseless the next? So maybe he was nuts.

"You're the doctor. Why don't you tell me what's wrong with me."

Her lips slowly curved up. "You admit there's something wrong with you?"

Maybe. "I—" The sweet scent of her lip gloss drew his attention back to her mouth, and he could swear she just inched a little closer. *She* was the one driving him crazy.

"What flavor are you wearing today?" Jack asked in a low voice.

Sophie's brown eyes grew large. "What?"

"Your lips, Doctor."

He felt a stab of disappointment when she took a step backward. "It's…uh." She withdrew the product from her pocket and looked down. "Watermelon Sorbet."

Having effectively changed the subject of his sanity, Jack didn't make a comment about how delicious the ridiculous name of her lip gloss sounded. She really would think he was *loco*.

They needed to break camp and get moving. The sooner he found her father—the sooner he could get rid of her.

Jack stomped over to his tent and started removing the rain fly. "We need to get the tents down and packed."

Hector, who had been watching the whole thing, sauntered past, chuckling under his breath. "When the two of you are done, breakfast will be ready."

Jack saw Sophie cast Hector a sweet smile. "*Muchas gracias*," she said, moving next to her tent. "This won't take me long."

Jack took that as a challenge. Today he was determined to take his tent down first.

Sophie hummed while she worked. Jack picked up his speed, working as fast as possible, but the new tent poles had to be defective because they were wedged again. Then he realized Sophie was no longer humming. She sat back on her heels, staring at him.

"What?" he snapped.

She smiled at him knowingly. "Nothing, Jack. You must be very hungry."

He watched her finish rolling up her tent and accepted defeat—Sophie had beat him again.

* * *

A few hours later they stopped for a break. Feeling hot and muggy, Jack shrugged off his heavy pack. He looked longingly at the clear blue pool of water they'd stopped by, imagining how good it would feel to dive in. A waterfall tumbled down one side, flowing between luscious green foliage and bright colored flowers.

Sophie sat on her pack, one hand stroking the donkey. "Poor Fred. He looks exhausted."

Jack held back an eye roll. He was still in a foul mood, and for the past three hours, he'd listened to Sophie's nonstop chatter. *Oh, Jack, look how beautiful. Jack, look how darling that monkey is.* It was like going camping with Merry Little Sunshine. She wasn't bothered by the rain, the bugs, or even the snakes. What was wrong with this woman?

Nothing. And that was the whole problem.

"Jack?" Sophie said, standing in front of him with a bright smile. "This is beautiful. Can we swim in it?"

Well, now that she suggested it, he wanted to say no. "Sophie, we don't have leisure time. Remember we're trying to locate your father."

The smile on her face disappeared. "I know why we're here. I just wanted to—" She turned away from him and mumbled, "It doesn't matter."

Hector shot him a reproachful look. "*Amigo*, what could it hurt?"

"It's okay," Sophie said flatly. "Jack's right—we don't have the time."

Jack dropped his eyes, avoiding both Hector and Sophie's condemning looks. Ripping open a granola bar, he bit off a chunk. It tasted like sawdust. He finished his snack and turned to find a bottle of water. He caught sight of Sophie as she tipped her head back, drinking from a water bottle. Helplessly, he stared at her slender throat. When she finished and pulled out her tube of lip gloss, Jack gave up.

Emitting a low growl, he stalked over to where Sophie sat. Standing in front of her, Jack waited for her to acknowledge him. Without looking at him, Sophie slipped the lip gloss back in her pocket and then studied her hiking boots intently.

Great. He was going to have to grovel. He hoped this wasn't going to be a pattern. "Sophie, I didn't mean to snap at you. I think it's a good idea to go swimming."

She lifted her lashes, still reluctant to talk to him. He held out his hand and offered her a smile. "It'll be a nice break."

* * *

Sophie lowered her eyes to Jack's open palm. If she put her hand in his, she knew exactly what would happen to her. Against everything inside of her, she found herself attracted to this cynical man. Despite the apology, Sophie wasn't going to fall for his nice mood this time. She ignored his outstretched hand. "We don't have to on my account."

He took a deep breath. "Come on, it'll be fun."

She almost snorted. Jack clearly didn't know what *fun* was. But the temptation to relive one of her fondest memories of going swimming underneath a waterfall with her father was too great.

"Fine." She stood up and started marching toward the waterfall. He grabbed her arm, making her halt. "What, Jack?"

His eyebrows drew together. "You just can't go off walking by yourself. Snakes like to be around water."

"Whatever," she said, sounding more like a teenager than a thirty-two-year-old doctor.

He started to laugh. "Sophie, don't be mad at me."

Huh? She wanted to wipe that silly grin right off his handsome face. "I don't even know why you would care." She jerked his hand off of her arm. "I irritate you, and I don't even know what it is I've done."

"I don't think I know what it is exactly, either." He blew out a long breath. "Look, I'm...sor...I'll try not to snap at you anymore."

She gave him a dubious look. "Okay. But in the future, if you're going to get mad at me, can you at least let me know why?"

He looked totally exasperated. "I'll do my best."

Satisfied, she gave him a small smile and stuck out her hand. "Truce?"

Jack took her hand, and immediately she regretted her actions. "Truce," he said as he slowly wrapped his large fingers around her hand, stealing her breath.

Tugging back, she tried to distance herself from him. Jack held fast and pulled her with him to the water's edge. It was hard not to respond to the warmth radiating up her arm. His hand felt good, and Sophie hated to admit how much she liked holding it.

"Hector, are you coming?" she questioned as they walked away.

"*Sí.* I'll be there in a minute."

The crystal blue water looked inviting. Her hair felt matted and sticky and she fantasized what it would feel like to swim under the small waterfall. "So this is safe to swim in, right?" she asked, looking for any signs of something lethal.

Jack sat on a rock to remove his boots. "It's safe."

Taking a seat on the same rock, Sophie removed her shoes and socks. She wiggled her toes in the cool, moist grass, glancing down to check for snakes. Jack had his back to her, and it was as if she could feel the heat radiating from his body, making her painfully aware of him.

She pulled her lip gloss out of her pocket and put it inside her shoe. Unclasping her watch, she added it to the pile. The pants she wore could be unzipped at the knee, converting them into shorts.

Finished, she stood up to find Jack assessing her with his cool blue eyes. "Are you one of those women who won't get their hair wet?"

Sophie didn't answer him. Instead, she made a shallow dive into the clear water. It felt so refreshing, and instantly her bad mood disappeared. She surfaced, blinking the water out of her eyes. Jack still stood on the edge. "Jack, it feels so wonderful. Are you coming in?"

The minute she asked the question, Sophie knew she had made a mistake. She hadn't thought it through very carefully, but she should've known he would take off his shirt.

Before she could think of something to discourage him, he tugged on the hem of his tee and pulled it over his head. Sophie caught a glimpse of his washboard stomach and immediately turned around. The rest of his upper body would look just as good and she didn't need another reason to feel attracted to him.

She heard the splash as he entered, the water rippling around her. Maybe swimming wasn't such a good idea after all, and where in the world was Hector?

Surfacing next to her, Jack's eyes glistened with mischief. "Wanna race to the waterfall?"

He sure seemed to have a competitive streak in him. She was beginning to think he didn't like that she could put up her tent faster than him. "Sure. On the count of three."

They both counted to three and then took off. Sophie wasn't a great swimmer, and she could never compete with someone taller and stronger than she was. Jack was already under the falls when she came to a stop.

"You win," she conceded.

He grinned. "What took you so long, Kendrick?"

She flicked water at him. "You're a poor winner."

Shaking the water off, he laughed and said, "I am not."
Then he splashed her back. "You're just a poor loser."

"It wasn't a fair race," she said petulantly. Then she slid
her hand along the water and propelled a large wave right in
his face.

Jack sputtered, then his blue eyes narrowed, and he
moved a little closer. "Wanna race again? I'll give you a
head start."

"No," Sophie said with a laugh.

"Chicken."

This time she gave into her childish side and stuck out
her tongue. Jack smiled and clasped his hands in front of him
and managed to shoot a stream of water directly at her.

"Would you stop that?" she said, moving out of the line
of fire.

"Only if you don't start up again."

So, as long as Jack was the last one to splash water in
her face, they could quit? He had probably not been any fun
to play tag with when he was a kid. The game would've
never ended because Jack would always have to be the last
one to tag someone.

She leaned her head back to float on the water, letting
him think she was done. When she came up, she used both
of her hands to shove as much water as she could, then she
took off, knowing he would come after her.

She tried swimming as fast as possible, but within a few
strides she felt him grab her leg. Screaming, she giggled as
he pulled her back toward him. "Stop!" she shrieked as he
prepared to launch her into the water.

Deep laughter rumbled behind her as Jack's hands
circled her waist. "This will teach you, little girl." He lifted
her fairly high and then tossed her away from him.

When she surfaced again, Jack stood right in front of
her.

Rising up on her tippy toes, the depth of the water allowed Sophie's head to be above the surface, her shoulders barely peeking above the water. Jack's browned shoulders and chest were well above the water. She moved her hands, ready to launch another assault. It was either that or openly stare at the bronzed Adonis in front of her.

Before she splashed him, Jack grabbed both of her wrists. "I wouldn't if I were you." Droplets of water clung to his eyelashes, and the blue of his eyes matched the water surrounding them. His mouth tilted up in a crooked smile, and his teeth appeared even whiter against the dark stubble covering his jaw.

Mercy, the man is gorgeous. Her pulse tripped, and Sophie purposely kept her eyes focused on his face. However, her peripheral vision noted every detail of Jack's muscular and tan body.

"Okay. You win. You can let go now," Sophie said a little breathlessly. Pulling on her hands, she struggled to escape the hold he had on her—both figuratively and literally.

He shook his head, keeping a tight grip. "What if I don't want to let go?"

He drew her toward him, making Sophie dizzy at the close proximity. His eyes lowered to her mouth, and, against her will, she found herself wondering what it would feel like if Jack kissed her. Even more distressing was the fact that she wanted him to.

"I think you want me to kiss you," Jack said smugly.

What? How did he know? "I certainly do not."

A wry smile tipped his mouth. "Yes, you do."

Maybe she had, but not now. The arrogant look in his eyes doused her desires as effectively as dumping water onto a fire.

More than likely he was toying with her, probably waiting for her to throw herself at him just so he could rebuff her.

Sophie jerked her wrists free and pushed his solid chest away from her. "I think I'm done."

Chapter Nine

Jack let Sophie swim away, feeling annoyed at how much he had wanted to kiss her. When she climbed out of the water, he hollered, "You just don't want to admit it."

He tried not to laugh at the incensed look on her face. She put her hands on her hips, her brown T-shirt clinging to her form. "Just so you know, kissing you was the last thing on my mind."

"If you say so," he said, making his way to the shore.

Her gaze narrowed. "I mean it, Jack."

"I'm sure you do." He climbed out and saw her eyes briefly scan him, causing a pink blush to spread across her cheeks. Abruptly, she turned around and sat down on the rock. Sophie was attracted to him. Somehow knowing that made him feel a little more in control.

"But I really have to say that you looked like—"

She whirled around and cut off his sentence. "I don't care what it looked like. I do not want to kiss you."

Obviously not now—which was his plan. But he would bet money that she had wanted that kiss as much as he had.

He reached for a hand towel Hector must have dropped off. He probably saw all the flirting going on and didn't want to interrupt them. "All I was going to say is you looked like you…were enjoying yourself."

She ignored him and dried off her feet, then proceeded to put her socks and shoes on. Jack pulled on his shirt, and then sat beside her to dry off his own feet and put on his socks. While he put on his boots, he cut a sly glance toward Sophie and watched as she finger-combed her hair.

Pretty, even with wet hair.

She looked his way and caught him staring at her. The instant their eyes met, the spark of awareness flared between them again. The intensity was alarming to Jack, and he was glad he hadn't kissed her.

He ducked his head and finished lacing his boots. It scared him to think how easy it would be to put aside his fears and give in to the emotions she evoked. She was dangerous to him, and he needed to put a barrier in place.

"Hey, I'm only teasing you." He stood up and grinned. "I wouldn't want your boyfriend to hunt me down after you go home."

"Peter isn't the violent type, so I think you're safe," she said, standing beside him.

"That's good to know." He glanced at her and winked. "Good Christian men are hard to find. You better hang on to him."

An emotion he couldn't define flickered across her face. Slowly, she gave him a soft, almost sad-like smile. "I think you're right." Then she turned away and walked back toward their gear. Jack followed behind her, keeping a safe distance between them.

Her reaction was exactly what he had wanted. If he made it clear how wrong he was for her, both of them could ignore the chemistry between them. Besides, Jack didn't plan on getting involved with a woman who could potentially hurt him even more than Heather had.

He refused to analyze why Sophie could do more damage than his former fiancée. Deep down, he just knew that she could.

They found Hector leaning against his pack, taking a *siesta*. Jack's nylon pants were already drying, but he encouraged Sophie to change out of her wet clothes.

She went behind a big tree while he and Hector turned their backs. Once she was changed, they continued on their journey. If all went well, they should make it to *Por El Río* by dusk.

* * *

Rain soaked Sophie's clothes, making her wonder why she'd even bothered changing out of her wet clothes from swimming. Not for the first time, she replayed the events of that swim over and over. Especially the almost kiss.

It was stupid, and she kept telling herself how much she *didn't* like Jack Mathison—she kept telling herself that repeatedly. But every time she thought about his tanned, muscled body, or his blue eyes and that mischievous grin, she felt a warm, fluttery feeling inside her chest.

What an absurd reaction. Jack might be nice to look at, but he was not a nice person. Something he had made sure to point out to her with his reference to Peter and hanging onto a "good Christian" man.

She was so confused. While Peter had his faults, he truly was a good guy, and he did share her faith. He enjoyed being involved in church and made generous weekly donations to further demonstrate his commitment. So why couldn't she feel the same intense feelings for him that she had for Jack?

She gripped the straps of her backpack tight as if holding onto to them could keep her from giving up and sitting down. She squinted against the pouring rain, hoping to see the village they would be staying at tonight.

Part of her wanted to turn around and ask Jack how much further they had to go, but he would probably think she was complaining. Besides, she wasn't talking to him. It was easier to be mad at him rather than deal with her stupid feelings.

Hector paused in front of her. He grinned and pointed his finger at a thatched roof coming into view. Finally, they'd made it to *Por El Rio*. She knew there wouldn't be a hotel, but hopefully someone had a generator and enough warm water for a bath. Earlier, Sophie had slipped on the wet grass, and her pants were covered in mud and grass stains.

Jack came up beside her, and she instantly felt the tingle of awareness that only seemed to get stronger each time she was around him. She didn't dare look at him right now, afraid he might see how he affected her.

She almost jumped out of her skin when he lightly touched her back. "Easy," he said, laughter evident in his voice. "I didn't mean to startle you."

Taking a fortifying breath, she turned and looked at him. Rivulets of rain poured off his hat, his eyes partially hidden by the bill of his ball cap. "What did you want?" Her question came out with a little more bite to it than she had intended.

Jack noticed and, of course, found her irritation funny, marked by the sardonic grin he gave her. "I just wanted to let you know we'll only be staying one night. Manuel is a friend of mine, and he has a hut you can stay in so you won't have to worry about setting a tent up in the rain."

"And where will you and Hector be sleeping?"

"Hector will stay with you. I'll figure something out."

Either the hut was very small or Jack had another reason for bunking somewhere else tonight. Despite her curiosity, she wasn't about to ask him for clarification.

"Great. Let's go."

She started forward, but he held her back with a gentle hand to her arm. The heat of his palm seared her wet skin. She paused, trying to understand her confusing feelings toward Jack.

Of all the men she'd ever been acquainted with, why did she have to pick *this* one to be so attracted to?

"What now?" she asked, feeling frustrated, wet and tired.

"Manuel will want you to stay longer. I'm sure they haven't seen a real doctor since the last group I brought through here six months ago."

"Okay." Unable to think clearly, she took a step away from him, forcing his hand to fall away.

He gave her a questioning look but only said, "I just want you to be prepared for any demands the people will make on you and remind you that we don't have time to linger more than a day. Out of courtesy, we'll help all we can but only for a few hours in the morning."

"Got it. Can we go now?" Thoroughly soaked, her hat was completely useless at this point. All she wanted was to be dry again.

He gave her another one of his lazy smiles before turning her around and giving her a little push forward.

In the fifteen minutes it took them to get to the village, the rain had finally dissipated to a fine drizzle. *Por El Río* looked primitive, but the locals were dressed in modern clothes. They talked excitedly with each other and, once again, Sophie wished she could speak the language.

Following Jack and Hector to the center of the village, she scanned the faces, wishing her father was among them. She knew he wouldn't be, but she longed to find him. Her life had been in such an upheaval since he'd gone missing. For a girl who claimed she didn't need a father around all the time, she had quickly found out how wrong she'd been. Families were important, and she vowed that from here on out, nothing would keep her from having a relationship with her father.

It might just be the two of them, but it didn't mean they couldn't have the same close-knit relationship Peter's family had. She only prayed it wasn't too late.

Under a large thatch-covered pavilion, a nice looking man smiled at them and motioned them toward him. His dark hair had just a touch of gray at the sides, and Sophie guessed he was probably in his mid-fifties.

"Jack, *mi amigo*." He reached out and embraced Jack, patting him on the back.

He had to be Manuel. But who was the beautiful woman standing next to him? His wife? She looked to be half his age, dressed in a pair of jeans and a tight V-necked tee, emphasizing her curvaceous body. Her sleek, black hair hung nearly to her waist. It was beautiful and shiny, making Sophie keenly aware of her own matted hair underneath the sopping wet hat.

The dark-haired beauty openly admired Jack, making Sophie's stomach tighten with an uneasy feeling of annoyance. You would think with her husband standing next to her and the villagers looking on, the woman would at least pretend not to be so interested in Jack.

"Elaina," Jack said, leaning in and kissing her on the cheek.

Elaina wrapped her slender arms around Jack and murmured something in his ear. Jack chuckled and pulled back, his face turning red. *Jack Mathison blushed?*

Turning around, Jack motioned toward Sophie. "Dr. Kendrick, this is Manuel Carrero and his daughter, Elaina."

His daughter. Not his wife. But judging by the way Elaina's dark brown eyes devoured Jack, she must be single.

Fingers of jealousy gripped Sophie's middle as she contemplated whether or not Elaina was the reason Jack would be staying somewhere else tonight.

Jack pointed out Hector, who greeted Manuel with a wave, while simultaneously keeping a hold on the donkey. Some of the children were interested in Fred and were trying to pet him. Hector was doing his best to keep them in front of the animal instead of behind where they could get hurt.

"Hello," Sophie said, holding out her hand to Manuel.

"*Hola*, Doctor." The older man bypassed the handshake and pulled her in for an exuberant hug, kissing her on the cheek. "Welcome, welcome," he said in heavily accented English.

Sophie turned to greet Elaina. The girl ignored her outstretched hand, and took her time skimming her eyes over Sophie's bedraggled look. Her perfectly sculpted lips lifted into a smile that was anything but friendly. Elaina's gaze flickered to Jack, and then she said something to him in Spanish.

Whatever she'd said made all of them look at Sophie. Manuel looked concerned. Elaina looked smug, and Jack looked amused, although his eyes also held sympathy. It was obvious Elaina had just made some derogatory comment about Sophie's appearance.

It didn't bother Sophie—much. Truthfully, if she could've heard what Elaina had said, she probably would agree with her. Obviously, Sophie needed a bath and a change of clothes. She just needed to know where she should go.

Manuel spoke to Jack in a lowered voice and several times gestured toward Sophie. She had no idea what they were saying, but wondered if it involved Elaina and Jack with Sophie as the third wheel.

Jack shook the older man's hand and then Hector and Manuel walked off together with Fred in tow. Manuel looked back and yelled, "Elaina, *vamos!*"

Elaina pressed her body close to Jack and whispered in his ear, making him laugh again. She cast a triumphant smile at Sophie before turning to follow her father.

Sophie watched Jack as *he* watched Elaina walk away. A knot twisted her gut, and it felt like a vice squeezed her chest. Jack seemed to forget she was even here. She cleared her throat. "Excuse me, but I would very much like to change my clothes, and I have no idea where to go."

At the sound of her voice, Jack turned toward her. "I'll show you. Elaina is getting some warm water ready for each of us now, but I'm afraid you won't have too much time to clean up. Manuel is anxious for your help right away."

So, while Sophie was off being a doctor, what was Jack going to be doing? Spending time with Elaina?

"Are you going to offer your services as well?" *Oh, shoot.* She really hadn't meant to say that out loud.

A look of amusement crossed his face, and the corner of his mouth lifted. "Just what services are you talking about, Dr. Kendrick?"

"I don't know." She lifted one shoulder uncomfortably. "What do you usually do?"

Jack grinned. "Not what you're thinking."

Sophie put her hands on her hips. "Just what is it you think I'm thinking?" She hoped he wouldn't actually tell her.

"I think—" The sudden reappearance of Elaina cut off Jack's words. "I *think* we need to finish this conversation later," he said in a low whisper.

Not if Sophie could help it.

An old woman was walking slightly behind Elaina. She approached them and spoke directly to Sophie. "*Doctor, mi nieto necesita ayuda, por favor.*"

"What did she say?" Sophie asked, turning to Jack.

Jack didn't answer right away. Elaina had already entwined her arm through his.

She leaned in and whispered in his ear. It seemed the girl took every opportunity to speak to him in such an intimate manner. This time Jack didn't blush or chuckle. Instead, he spoke to the old woman and offered her a genuine smile.

Then he looked at Sophie. "This is Elaina's great-aunt Guadalupe. Her grandson is sick, and she wants to know if you can help him."

Immediately, all the petty feelings Sophie was struggling with evaporated like the rain when the sun came out. Caring for the sick, especially innocent children, was her calling in life. Sophie gazed into the wrinkled face and smiled. "*Sí*. I will help." She glanced at Jack. "Tell her I'll come as soon as I change my clothes."

Jack translated to the old woman. When Guadalupe spoke back to him in rapid Spanish, Jack laughed out loud. Elaina just cast Sophie a self-satisfied smile.

"Guadalupe is very pleased you will help her grandson," Jack said. "But she first insists you need a bath. She is concerned that your…well, how do I say it? Your unclean appearance will not be beneficial for Mario." Jack winked at her. "That's her grandson's name."

Sophie looked down at her mud-soaked pants and then at her dirty hands. She wasn't the least bit offended and smiled at the older woman. Cleanliness was something she whole heartily approved of. "Tell her I'll hurry but be very thorough." At least the rain had finally stopped. So, when she did get into dry clothes they would stay that way.

After Jack translated again, the old woman closed her eyes and made the sign of the cross. Sophie said a prayer of her own that she would be able to help this woman and her grandson.

Elaina whispered something to Jack and only once did her eyes dart over to Sophie. Then, giving Jack one last sultry look, she escorted Guadalupe back the way she had come. Sophie tried not to let the girl's attitude bother her. What was the deal with her and Jack anyway? Maybe Elaina was yet one more reason Jack no longer liked to take women on his tours—because he didn't want to make her jealous.

A group of children playing in a clearing next to the pavilion came running toward them, kicking a soccer ball. One particular move sent the black and white sphere straight for Sophie. Jack blocked the ball and softly kicked it back to a little girl who was trailing behind the group. The child's face lit up, and she kicked it back to him.

Jack scooped the ball up, and all of the kids clamored around him, chanting in Spanish. Sophie suspected they were begging him to play with them. He shook his head and tossed the ball in the air. When he caught it again, he dropped kicked it back into the clearing. The other children ran after it, all except the same little girl he'd kicked the ball to earlier. She was holding his hand and looking up at him with admiration on her brown face. It would seem females of all ages were drawn to Jack.

Sophie felt her breath catch when Jack knelt down in front of the little girl and talked with her eye to eye. The gentle smile he offered the child revealed yet another side to Jack Mathison. Patting the little girl on the head, he stood up and watched her run to catch up with the others.

Before Sophie had a chance to look away, he turned around and caught her watching him. As he walked toward her, she forced herself to relax. "Giving out free soccer advice?" she said, pleased with the light tone of her voice.

He grinned. "Just telling her not to let the big kids leave her out. She's small, but fast, and if she's brave enough to go after the ball, she could leave all those boys in the dust."

Warmth spread through Sophie at his kindness. He clearly had a soft spot for children. Something they both had in common. Another burst of laughter came from the group of kids, reminding Sophie about the little boy who needed medical attention. Both Manuel and Guadalupe were anxious for a doctor to see the child, and she didn't want to delay finding out what the problem was.

"Could you please show me where I can clean up? I really want to see Guadalupe's grandson as soon as possible."

Jack nodded. "Sure. Let's go."

Relieved he hadn't brought up their conversation from a few minutes ago, Sophie walked by his side in silence. Jack led her through a cluster of huts, most of which had cooking fires burning within and women tending to what looked like dinner preparation. Smoke curled out of each roof, and Sophie was assaulted by a number of interesting smells, some good and some less than appetizing. Hopefully Hector was planning on cooking their meal.

She saw the donkey tied next to a good sized hut. Hector came out of the doorway and waved. "Sophie, I have bath water waiting for you in the bedroom. The door latches, and there are curtains covering the windows." He hefted her bag from the ground next to Fred. "I'll just put your things in there for you."

"*Gracias*," Sophie said, removing her daypack from her back.

"*No problemo*." Hector smiled and picked up her pack and carried it with her other bag inside the shelter.

As soon as Hector disappeared inside, Sophie turned to Jack. "I won't take very long. Will you be able to show me where Guadalupe lives?"

He studied her for a few seconds and rubbed a hand across the stubble on his jaw. Jack took the time each morning using a solar powered razor to keep his whiskers trimmed to the perfect five O'clock shadow most Hollywood heartthrobs sported. She had to admit it looked good on him, but at the same time, she wondered how much his appearance would change if he were clean shaven.

"Yeah," he said. "I'll need to change first. I'll be back here in thirty minutes."

"Okay." That little niggling voice of jealousy wanted to rear its head again and ask where he was going to change his clothes, but she managed to refrain. "I'll see you then."

Jack nodded and took a step backward, then turned and walked away. Sophie battled once more with her conflicting feelings for him. She shouldn't care where he was going. She shouldn't—but she did.

Chapter Ten

Jack hated playing head games, especially when it came to women. Yet the minute Elaina had greeted him so warmly and he'd felt the possessive tension radiating from Sophie, he had gone ahead and flirted back.

He groaned as he applied underarm deodorant. Not only was it stupid, it could also be dangerous. Elaina might have a boyfriend, but it hadn't seemed to lessen her interest in Jack. The derogatory comments she'd made about Sophie should have been a warning to Jack, but when he'd seen the jealous look on Sophie's face, he hadn't been able to resist teasing her.

Yeah, he had been stupid, and he only had his ego to blame. First of all, he knew Elaina would probably be jealous when she saw he was traveling with Sophie. His plan had been simple: treat Elaina cordially, not let his attraction for Sophie be obvious, and leave early the next morning.

At least he could count on the last part of his plan, which meant he only had to make it through tonight.

Taking a crumpled T-shirt out from his bag, he pulled it over his head, grateful to be clean and dry again. While he put on his boots, he heard Elaina giggle. *Great.* She must be waiting for him to come outside. Morning couldn't come soon enough.

His stomach rumbled from hunger, and he hoped Hector was cooking up something other than an MRE. Usually when they stayed in the different villages, his friend would purchase fresh produce and meat to prepare their meal.

Grabbing his bag, Jack made his way through the Carrero house to the front door.

Manuel had offered a room to him, but Jack had made the decision to camp outside the hut where Sophie was staying. Hector would do the same, giving Sophie a little privacy.

Jack believed that between the two of them, they could keep Sophie safe from any unwanted visitors. While the village was relatively crime free, there were still plenty of problems created from too much drinking. Sophie was a beautiful woman, and the men here would be very interested in her.

Another one of Elaina's giggles made his muscles go rigid. However, when he stepped out the door, Jack saw who was making Elaina laugh. She was wrapped up in her boyfriend's arms and seemed oblivious to his presence. The relief he felt made the knot in his shoulders loosen.

Taking a path that made a wide berth around the couple, Jack slipped away unnoticed. He avoided a puddle left over from the downpour earlier and hurried to get Sophie. He was a few minutes past the thirty minutes he'd given her, but figured she wouldn't mind the extra time. Most women usually needed at least an hour to get ready.

He rounded the corner and found her sitting outside, talking to Hector as he chopped up some vegetables. Her dark hair, still damp from her recent bath, had a slight wave to it, and Jack knew if he got close enough he'd pick up the subtle coconut scent he found so appealing.

She glanced his way and held his gaze for a few seconds, her eyes guarded and pensive, before she lowered her lashes.

"*Amigo*," Hector said with a huge grin. "You are just in time to help me with dinner." He pointed to a box sitting on the ground.

Jack walked over and looked inside to see a live chicken. He'd helped Hector before by catching and cleaning fish, but killing a chicken and then plucking its feathers wasn't something he liked to do. Neither did Hector.

"Come on, I just changed my clothes," Jack said. "You know how messy this will be."

Hector rolled his eyes. "I'll find you an apron."

Sophie leaned over and peered into the box, a frown marring her smooth skin. "He's so…alive." She looked up at Hector with those big brown eyes and said, "Can't we just let him go?"

The incredulous look on Hector's face made Jack smile.

"What?" Hector asked. "Do you know how hard it was for me to catch it?"

"Poor thing," she cooed, looking back into the box. "Being chased by the big, bad man."

Jack snorted a laugh, and Hector threw up his hands. "Would you two just leave and let me get on with dinner."

"Sure," Jack said. "That's why I'm here." He turned to Sophie. "You ready to go?"

"Yes." She patted Hector on the shoulder. "I'm just kidding—sort of. I guess I really don't think about where chicken comes from and that it doesn't just magically appear in the store." She leaned in and kissed Hector on the cheek. "Thank you for preparing all the meals."

Even from where Jack stood, he could see the rising flush on Hector's brown skin. "For you, *señorita*, I will chase many chickens."

Jack had to admit that he might even consider chasing a few chickens in order to win a kiss from Sophie.

Waving goodbye to Hector, she reached down and picked up the heavy medical backpack Fred had been carrying.

Jack stepped in front of her and took the pack from her. "I've got this."

"Thank you." Her eyes had lost their wariness and now were soft with gratitude. "Will you be able to stay and translate for me?"

"Sure." He had already planned on staying with her, but it was nice to be asked.

They said goodbye to Hector, and Jack pointed out the direction they were heading. Neither of them spoke as they walked side by side toward the outskirts of the village where Guadalupe lived. They passed a cluster of young men, passing a bottle of liquor from one to another. When a couple of them whistled at Sophie, Jack placed a protective hand on her lower back.

She stumbled and Jack moved his hand to her waist to steady her. "We're almost there," he said, very much aware of his palm against the curve of her hip.

Sophie lifted her face toward him, and his chest constricted at the swirl of conflicting emotions reflected in her deep brown eyes. Emotions that mirrored his own. He wasn't the only one battling against the undeniable chemistry between the two of them.

He was the first to look away as he guided her to their destination, but his fingers tightened at her waist to keep her from moving away from him.

What did that mean? Was he making the choice to stop fighting his feelings?

A few feet ahead of them, Jack noticed the wood-carved statue of the Virgin Mary in front of the small hut. According to the directions he'd gotten from Manuel, he was sure they had arrived at the correct place.

"I think this is it," he said as they followed a path toward the entrance.

The door opened and Guadalupe motioned for them to come inside. Sophie hesitated for just a second before she stepped away from him and followed the older woman inside.

Jack entered the humble dwelling, and almost vomited from the smell. It was a good thing his stomach was empty. Holding his breath, Jack looked around for the source of the foul scent.

In the corner, Sophie knelt on the dirt floor next to a small, dark-haired child. She turned to Jack. "Could you ask his grandmother what happened?" Gently, she felt the little boy's forehead. "Oh, he's burning up."

The child opened his eyes, unable to even move. Jack asked his grandmother what had happened and swallowed back the bile when Sophie lifted the blanket off the boy's leg, exposing an inflamed wound about four inches in length.

Sophie didn't flinch and even leaned in closer to inspect the deep laceration, swollen and oozing with puss. "Sweetie, what happened?" Sophie questioned the boy in a soft, caressing voice.

Jack looked away from the wound, relaying what the boy's grandmother told him. "Last week while playing in the water, he fell on some rocks and sliced his leg."

Sophie opened her medical bag and started pulling supplies out. "First off, little guy, we need to help get that fever down." She held up a bottle of liquid Tylenol, uncapping it and pouring the desired amount in a little cup. "Can you ask how old he is?"

He asked Guadalupe and relayed the information to Sophie. "He's seven." Jack started breathing through his mouth, unable to bear the putrid smell any longer. He told the little boy he needed to take the medicine to get better. The poor little kid was too weak to protest.

Sophie pulled out more medical supplies and asked Jack to repeat everything she said. "I need to clean the wound. It is going to hurt him, but we need to get all the infection and necrotic tissue out."

She put on a pair of gloves and then went to work on the ugly gash. With gentle efficiency, she worked on the injury all the while talking softly to the boy. Occasionally, the child let out a small whimper, but other than that, he lay as still as a stone. The kid must be pretty bad off to not offer any kind of resistance.

When she finished, Sophie stood up, removing the soiled gloves. "Jack, I need to give him antibiotics. He's dehydrated, and I'd like to start an IV and give him some fluids along with some ampicillin."

Needles. Jack hated needles. "What do you need me to do?"

"I have what I need for now, but I'll have to get more supplies in order to stay here for the night." She pulled a syringe out of her bag and a small vial. "Right now I'll give him a shot of Penicillin, and then IV fluids through the night with a dose of antibiotics."

She uncapped the needle, and Jack internally shuddered at the sight. He felt lightheaded and a little queasy as she drew up the medication. It was ridiculous for a grown man to be afraid of a little needle.

Holding up the syringe in front of her, she flicked the side of it with her finger until an air bubble appeared at the top. "Can you explain to them what I need to do?" she said, pushing the air out of the needle.

Jack broke out in a cold sweat, his head whirling. He pulled his eyes away from the syringe. He didn't like the idea of Sophie staying the night here. What if she had another nightmare?

"Are you sure you need to stay here all night?"

She leaned in and whispered, "This little boy is very sick, Jack. He needs me."

Not given much of a choice, Jack translated Sophie's treatment plan. The old woman smiled serenely, then closed her eyes and made the sign of the cross as she prayed.

"Tell me what she said," Sophie asked, placing her hand on Jack's arm. "Did she give me permission?"

"Yes." Jack gazed into Sophie's somber eyes. "She also said that God sent you."

As he relayed the message, Jack had the strongest impression that God had also sent Sophie for him. Instead of rejecting the idea, he allowed the thought to take root. Maybe it was time for him to discover why Sophie had come into his life.

He watched her mouth lift into a soft smile. "He did send me."

Right then, Jack wished he was worthy of someone like Sophie. But how could he ever hope to be when he still harbored so much animosity for his family? He knew that withholding his forgiveness was the stumbling block that kept him from fully recommitting himself back to his faith. He wasn't sure he could do it, but for the first time in years, he was willing to try.

* * *

Sophie tied the rubber tourniquet just above Mario's elbow. His skin was hot and dry to the touch, the fever still raging inside the small body. She adjusted the headlamp light so it shone on the child's forearm and palpated the skin with her fingertips until she felt the vein that was barely visible. Praying her IV skills were as good as they'd been in med school, she tore open an alcohol wipe and thoroughly cleansed the area.

Putting on a clean pair of disposable gloves, she picked up the pediatric sized IV catheter and removed the plastic cap. Mario didn't even flinch as Sophie pierced the skin and pushed the tip of the needle in at an angle, probing gently. She felt the tiny pop as the needle entered the vein. Slowly, she advanced it forward until she saw the flashback of dark red blood at the hub. She pulled the needle out while simultaneously threading the catheter into the vein.

"Good boy," Sophie said to Mario, removing the tourniquet and attaching the tubing to the IV. Jack stood next to her, holding the bag of fluids. She opened up the roller clamp, allowing the fluid to drip freely, and taped the IV securely.

"Wow," Jack said with awe, "the kid didn't even move."

"I know." The child hadn't even opened his eyes. "That's what worries me." She glanced around the hut trying to decide how best to hang the bag. She noticed a nail protruding out of the wall behind the child's pallet. "Do you think you could string the bag up to that nail?" she asked Jack.

"Sure."

While Jack jury-rigged the bag, Sophie mixed up the antibiotics, wanting to get the first dose of ampicillin in as soon as possible. Over the next three minutes, she slowly pushed the antibiotic through the IV port.

After she finished, Sophie cleaned up her mess and then documented the time and dosage of the antibiotic in the small notebook she kept with her medical supplies. She then adjusted the roller clamp so the IV fluids dripped at a therapeutic pace. Mario still hadn't stirred, and Sophie hoped that with hydration and the medication he would start to perk up.

She placed her hand on the boy's forehead, pleased to find it cooler. She brushed back a few locks of hair from Mario's brow as he slept peacefully. A soft snore came from his grandmother who had fallen asleep in the rocking chair while Sophie attended to Mario.

Guadalupe was exhausted and probably hadn't slept well since her grandson had become ill. By letting herself fall asleep, Sophie knew the older woman must trust her. She continued to pray for direction about how to help Mario get better.

Satisfied, Sophie stood and stretched, her knees protesting after staying in one position for so long. Needing some fresh air, she turned to quietly sneak outside. Jack stood by the door, watching her with his intense, blue eyes. Her heart thudded, and she gave him a tentative smile. "He's doing a little better."

His gaze continued to penetrate her, and she wondered what was going through his head this time. With Jack, she could never be sure.

"You're a good doctor," he said softly.

She lowered her lashes, feeling her face go warm. How did he do that? It caught her off guard when he spoke so tenderly and made fighting the attraction pointless. "Thank you." She ran a hand through her disheveled hair. "I need to get my tent and sleeping bag, and then I'll come back to stay the night."

Jack's eyes darkened, and he frowned. "Why do you have to stay here? Can't you just come back in the morning?"

She wondered why he would care. Wasn't he planning on being somewhere else tonight? Sighing, she whispered, "Let's go outside to work out the details."

He opened the door, and they both stepped out into refreshing night air.

The ordinary nocturnal sounds of the jungle were replaced by music and the laughter of humans. One raucous group was not too far away from Guadalupe's hut. Flames from the campfire flickered in the night, illuminating images of individuals dancing to Latin music.

Sophie guessed this was why Jack was worried. She'd been so intent with Mario's care she hadn't even heard the lively party going on.

Jack crossed his arms in front of his chest, taking the stance of a man who wouldn't take no for an answer. "It's not safe for you to set up your tent here."

He was probably right. As uncomfortable as she might be in the small space, her only option was to sleep inside the hut. "If I'm inside with Mario I'll be okay."

"You won't get any sleep. How are we supposed to travel tomorrow if you're wiped out?"

As much as Sophie wanted to keep on their journey to find her father, she couldn't leave Mario when he was this sick. "I know what you said, but we can't leave tomorrow. Mario needs me."

The muscle in his jaw tightened. "What if he's better?"

"Jack, another day or two and Mario would've died. I have no idea why he isn't septic now. I have to be here to administer the antibiotics and keep him on IV fluids until he can start taking in water and food orally."

Jack scrubbed his hands over his face in frustration. "That means I need to make camp out here."

He sounded put out, and she realized he must be angry that his plans for tonight would have to be canceled. "I don't need you to babysit me."

His eyes sparked with irritation. "You're a woman, and I'm responsible for you. Leaving you alone and unprotected would be stupid."

"I'm not helpless. Go do whatever it was you were going to do."

"I'm going to be sleeping. Out here." He leaned in close to her. "Don't argue with me about this."

The nearness of his face momentarily distracted her, but she could take care of herself. "I'm not arguing. I'm just stating a fact."

The corner of his mouth lifted. "Hey, Doctor. This is one of those times when you're making me mad."

Was he being charming? His moods were so hard to read. "Well, this time I was actually trying to make you mad."

He started to chuckle and took her hand, entwining their fingers. "Come on, Sophie. Whether you like it or not, I'm sleeping near you."

She didn't know how to respond to this even-tempered Jack, so she let him lead her back to their supplies. When they were within a few yards of the hut, she saw Elaina standing outside. Even from this distance, Sophie could see the girl's dark eyes were filled with hostility. The second Jack noticed, he dropped Sophie's hand.

"What's the matter, Jack?" Sophie hissed. "Don't want to make your girlfriend upset?"

He spoke low, clearly as annoyed as Sophie was. "No, I'm just trying to keep you safe for the night. Let's just say when it comes to me, she can be a little obsessive."

More envious feelings rocketed through her. "So are you trying to provoke her? Correct me if I'm wrong, but if you're sleeping with me, she won't be too happy."

Jack swung his head around, his eyes opened wide with astonishment. Then he spoke through gritted teeth. "Boy am I glad she can't hear us. And just for clarification, Sophie…I'm sleeping *near* you, not *with* you."

Heat flooded her face. "I know that...I didn't mean—"
She threw her arms up and stomped away. "You are driving
me crazy."

Chapter Eleven

Yeah? *Well, welcome to the club.* Jack thought sourly as Sophie disappeared inside the hut. He had pretty much lost all sense of mental balance when it came to Sophie.

He eyed Elaina warily, wondering why she wasn't out with her boyfriend. He wasn't exactly sure how to handle this whole situation. Forcing his lips into a smile, he lifted a hand and waved. "*Hola,* Elaina."

Her dark eyes narrowed, and she asked him where he had been.

Jack explained his role in helping Mario get better. The way he worded it made it sound like Sophie would be incompetent without him. It wasn't the truth, but he hoped it would placate Elaina.

A smile crossed her face, and she threw her arms around his neck. Startled, Jack turned his head just as her lips grazed his cheek instead of his mouth. This was getting out of hand, and he was to blame. Even more unfortunate was the delay in their departure.

Hector suddenly appeared, leading the donkey by a rope. His arrival allowed Jack to untangle Elaina's arms from around his neck. The timing couldn't have been more perfect. The kid who had been kissing Elaina earlier, stormed across the yard toward his girlfriend. Fear entered Elaina's eyes for just a moment before she coolly thanked Jack for giving her an update on her cousin.

Taking the young man by the hand, Elaina led him away and said something to make her boyfriend laugh while putting his arm around her shoulders.

Jack watched them disappear and hoped Elaina wouldn't try anything else tonight.

Hector gave a low whistle as he tied the donkey to a tree branch. "The sooner we leave the better, ¿*no*?"

"That had been my plan." Jack laughed humorlessly. "Sophie won't leave the little boy, though. He's too sick."

A look of concern entered Hector's eyes. "He is bad, then?"

"Yeah." He glanced at the hut. "She's going to sleep there tonight."

"What will you do about Elaina?" Hector asked, knowing all about the girl's obsessive tendencies.

"I guess I'll have to set up my tent by Guadalupe's."

One of Hector's bushy eyebrows lifted. "*Amigo*, would you like me to do it instead?"

"Yes, Jack," Sophie said, coming outside. "You should let Hector come. That way your night will be free to spend with Elaina."

Sophie seemed jealous and very angry with him. Jack really needed to set the record straight about Elaina so Sophie would know he wasn't interested in the girl. For now, he said, "Thanks for the offer, but Hector will stay with Fred and I'll go with you."

Sophie's nostrils flared, and Hector stifled a laugh before picking up Jack's gear and handing it to him. "*Buena suerte esta noche.*"

Jack grinned. He'd need more than luck to make it through their visit without any more problems. His stomach gurgled loudly, and he remembered they hadn't eaten dinner.

"Do you think we could take some food with us?" He glanced around but didn't see any evidence of the meal Hector had been working on.

For the second time that day, Hector's face colored.

"Someone stole the chicken when I wasn't looking." His eyes narrowed. "They even took the vegetables."

"I was going to say the chicken got lucky, but it sounds like he's still on the menu."

"I would've started something else, but I've been searching for the culprit." Hector gave an apologetic shrug. "I'll go ahead and get started now."

"Hector," Sophie said, stepping in front of him. "Don't worry about it. A protein bar will be fine with me."

When Hector looked like he was going to protest, Jack moved next to Sophie. "I agree with Sophie. Besides, I know she wants to get back to the little boy right away."

He thought he'd score some points with her, but she didn't even acknowledge him as Hector turned and grabbed a couple of the meal replacement bars. "Thank you, Hector. Have a good night," Sophie said, marching past Jack without a backward glance.

"*Buenas noches, señorita*," Hector said to her retreating back.

Jack watched Sophie making tracks before he hollered, "Hey, Sophie." He waited until she turned to look at him. "You're going the wrong way." He pointed out the correct direction and tried not to laugh when she spun on her heel and stomped the other way.

The two of them made pretty good time. Jack didn't try to talk—he was smart enough to know now was not the time to bring up Elaina.

When they arrived at Guadalupe's small home, Sophie continued to ignore him and headed for the front door. Jack put a hand on her shoulder and stopped her. "Hang on a minute, would you?"

She let out a long breath. "What do you want?"

What did he want? He eyed her contemplatively, wishing he had more time to analyze such a loaded question.

"Jack," she said impatiently. "I would like to go in and see Mario."

"Are you actually going to sleep in there?"

She glowered at him defiantly. "Yes."

"Okay." There was no use arguing with her. "I'll set my tent up right outside the door."

Her chin shot up. "I told you that isn't necessary."

"And I told you it is." He peered into her eyes and softened his voice. "I really am just trying to look out for you, Sophie."

That did the trick. In the glow of the setting sun, Jack saw her lips curve up into a smile. "I know," she said. "Hopefully Elaina will forgive you."

He tried not to grin. Sophie didn't stay angry very long, and she was still jealous. "What if you have a nightmare?"

She frowned. "I had almost forgotten about that. I'll try not to sleep, and then tomorrow I'll catch a nap while you're off spending time with Elaina."

Despite his earlier conviction, he found it funny how she kept bringing up Elaina and Jack couldn't resist teasing her. "Thanks, after how angry I made her, I'll need a little alone time."

Sophie wasn't very good at hiding her feelings. Her eyes clouded, and her perky little mouth turned down into another frown. "Good. I'm happy for you."

She didn't look happy.

"You don't mind?"

There went her chin again. "Why would I mind?"

Jack's mouth quirked up at the corners. "I don't know. You just seem bugged."

"Not every woman you meet falls for your good looks."

He folded his arms across his chest and raised an eyebrow. "So you think I look good?"

"I didn't say that!"

He started to chuckle. "Sophie, you said, and I quote, 'Not every woman you meet falls for your good looks.'"

She looked at him totally annoyed. "Okay, Jack. You look good. Are you happy?"

He smiled smugly. "Yes."

She stormed inside the hut, leaving Jack with a huge grin on his face.

It was time to face reality. The lovely Dr. Kendrick had gotten under his skin. Her sunny disposition wasn't as maddening as it had been at first. In fact, he liked knowing that his surly attitude didn't seem to affect her. Well, at least not for very long. She was a good person, and had left a comfortable home, a thriving medical career and a devoted boyfriend in order to locate her father.

Jack's mood darkened at the thought of Peter Elliot. Sophie had been dating him for a long time, and he knew how much she loved his family. The real question was: how much did she love Peter?

He dropped his tent and backpack to the ground. Whether or not Sophie had a boyfriend, Jack was certain she felt something for him. He'd seen it reflected in her eyes.

Still, there was one question that haunted him: Would he be just like his brother if he pursued another man's girlfriend?

* * *

Sophie opened her eyes, surprised to find it was morning. The rising sun bathed the one room hut in soft tones of pink and orange. In the early light, she saw Mario staring at her. His eyes appeared more alert than before, encouraging Sophie about his recovery.

He moved his head to the side and scanned the room, probably looking for his *abuela*. Guadalupe was not around and must have gone outside.

Sophie got to her feet and smiled at Mario. The child looked a little panicked. Either he couldn't remember Guadalupe introducing Sophie to him, or she guessed that after nearly two liters of IV fluids, he needed to use the bathroom.

"*Un momento*," she said, and then pointed to the door. "I'll go find your *abuela*."

Knowing he only understood a few of her words, Sophie hurried out the door. She looked all about the yard, but Guadalupe was nowhere in sight.

Sophie's gaze landed on Jack's tent, and she knew she had no choice but to ask him for help. She closed her eyes and drew in a deep breath. She'd made a fool out of herself last night and didn't want to see him just yet. Unfortunately, she was going to have to face him one way or another.

Approaching his tent, she mentally prepared herself for the inevitable meeting. "Jack," she said, hoping he was awake. She listened carefully, but didn't hear anything stirring. She tried again, this time a little louder. "Jack."

When he still didn't respond, Sophie reached out and unzipped the tent door. It sounded extremely loud to her, but when she peeked inside the tent, Jack was sleeping soundly.

Taking a moment, Sophie stared at him. His chiseled face, darkened by another day's growth of whiskers, appeared relaxed and soft. Her gaze traveled over his powerful arms, crossed over an equally impressive chest. The man really was quite attractive.

She moistened her lips and then whispered loudly, "Jack. Wake up. Mario needs your help."

Nothing. He still slept on, his chest rising and falling evenly. Not sure what to do next, Sophie scooted on her knees a little further into the tent. Just as she reached out to jostle his arm, her gaze connected with his.

"Need something, Sophie?" he asked, sitting up and stretching.

Her mouth went dry. He wore a white T-shirt that molded to his muscles. "Uh, yes." She just couldn't remember what it was.

His mouth edged up into a smug smile, and Sophie felt her cheeks flush with embarrassment. "Um, Mario is awake. His grandma isn't here, and I wondered if you could come in and translate for me?"

"Sure." He pushed back the sleeping bag. "Is he doing better?"

"Yes. His fever broke, and he is much more alert than before."

"That's great." Jack held her gaze and slowly moved toward her. The tent seemed to shrink and Sophie couldn't move—couldn't breathe. She sat perched on her knees, remaining frozen in place with Jack now only inches away. Her heart thrummed rapidly inside her chest and her head felt dizzy, as if she'd spun around and around in a circle. Time stood still, and heat completely infused her body. *Kiss me.* She thought recklessly.

His eyes skimmed over her face, reflecting the same longing she felt inside. Then he leaned in close, and Sophie braced herself for the rollercoaster ride that was sure to come with his kiss. She lowered her lashes and waited.

"Sophie," Jack said, instead of kissing her.

She opened her eyes to find him only a breath away.

"Yes," she barely managed to whisper.

"You're in my way."

Her spinning head came to a screeching halt. *She was in his way?* Blinking, she sat back on her heels and stared at him. The teasing light in his eyes masked the desire she'd seen only seconds ago.

She was so addled she didn't know if she should slap him or grasp the front of his shirt, pull him to her and kiss him anyway.

He couldn't have read her mind, but for a moment the mask slipped and a flame of desire flickered in his eyes again. *The rat!* He deserved a slap, but since she wasn't the violent type, she quickly turned around and exited his tent.

Without waiting to see if he would follow her, she slipped back inside the hut. Mario looked like he was about to cry and his *abuela* was still missing. Sophie felt horrible and wanted to blame Jack. But the culpability was all hers. Well, at least it was her wacky brain's fault. What was it about this man that made her act so crazy?

Jack entered the hut and went over to Mario. He crouched down and spoke to him. The boy answered in rapid Spanish. Jack said something else and gave the child a reassuring pat on the head. Rising, he looked over at Sophie. "The poor kid needs to use the bathroom." He lifted one brow. "Any ideas how he can do that?"

"He can either use a urinal or you could help him outside and hold the IV bag."

Jack looked at her incredulously. "What am I? Your nurse?"

"No. You're a man."

He grinned. "I'm glad we got that straight."

Like there had ever been a question. "Jack, he's a boy and so are you. I don't have a problem helping him, but he might be uncomfortable since I'm a woman."

Just then Guadalupe returned. Mario started speaking frantically to her, gesturing to his IV bag. Jack spoke again, and Guadalupe nodded and then went over to some shelves that held a variety of things, including a half gallon sized glass bottle that probably had once contained milk.

Jack spoke to Mario, showing him the bottle. Sophie could see Jack trying not to laugh out loud when the boy pointed to the container. His grandmother handed it to him and, without blinking an eye, the seven year old filled it in front of everyone present. Apparently, modesty wasn't an issue.

* * *

While Guadalupe took the bottle outside to empty it, Jack hovered behind Sophie as she removed Mario's bandage. The putrid smell was gone, but from what Jack could see, the wound still looked nasty. He wondered how long Sophie would insist on staying.

"It looks a little better," he said, amazed at the bravery Mario showed as Sophie cleaned the wound. The child had his eyes closed, his teeth clenched tight together. It was much better than yesterday when he hadn't even flinched from Sophie's ministrations.

"Mmm-hmm," Sophie murmured, without looking over at him.

But that didn't stop Jack from watching her. Her forehead was creased in concentration as she quietly and quickly worked on the damaged tissue. A beam of sunlight shot through the window, and Jack noticed a hint of deep reddish brown highlights in her dark hair. She was beautiful, and he found himself regretting not kissing her when he'd had the chance.

His gut tightened at the thought, knowing as difficult as it had been, he'd made the right choice. After retiring to his tent the night before, Jack had thought long and hard about Sophie. In the end, he had decided he couldn't do what Adam had done to him—steal another man's girlfriend behind his back.

But then Sophie had come inside his tent to awaken him and all of his reasoning from the night before didn't seem so reasonable. She had wanted him to kiss her, and oh how he'd wanted to comply. It had taken every bit of self-restraint to use humor to extinguish his desires—and hers.

The only way he would consider further exploring the electrifying chemistry between Sophie and him was to find out where she stood with Peter. Hopefully they would have the opportunity to talk as soon as she finished with Mario.

Jack knew at some point today Elaina would try to find him, and he guessed by now the villagers would be aware that a doctor was in their midst and would seek Sophie's help. Plus, Manuel had invited them to attend the villages *fiesta* tonight, leaving them very little time to talk.

Moving away from the child, Sophie stood up and briefly glanced at Jack. "His leg is responding to the antibiotics." She adjusted the roller clamp on the IV and asked Jack to explain to Mario that if his leg continued to improve and he could drink enough water, she would discontinue the IV tomorrow and start him on oral antibiotics.

The little boy gave them a weak smile and closed his eyes to sleep. Guadalupe came back inside, and Jack repeated the information to the older woman about possibly removing the IV and switching the antibiotics. She nodded in understanding, then turned toward Sophie and took her by the hand. Guadalupe thanked her over and over for saving her grandson's life. He figured he didn't need to translate for Sophie this time and watched her pretty face light up with joy as she gave the older woman a hug.

A knock sounded at the door and Hector stuck his head inside. "Is there a doctor in the house?" he asked.

Sophie immediately walked toward him. "Are you hurt? Do you need me?"

Hector grinned and shook his head. "Not me, *señorita*." He pointed behind him. "Them."

Sophie peered out the door, and Jack was right behind her. There was a large crowd of villagers gathering in the yard.

"What's going on?" Sophie whispered.

"I think your free clinic is just about to get underway." Jack leaned in close to her. "Let me guess, you want me to play nurse again?"

She met his gaze, and the smile she gave him made his insides melt. "Yes, that would be great."

"Just remember I don't do bedpans."

She laughed. "I'll keep that in mind."

They probably would've stayed like that, staring into each other's eyes and making small talk if Hector hadn't interrupted them by clearing his throat. "We can work out the duties later. Right now, you both need breakfast and a place to see all these people."

Jack suggested using the covered pavilion in the center of the village for the clinic. Hector agreed and told the people the doctor needed to get her supplies and where she would meet them. As the crowd dispersed, Sophie retrieved her medical backpack from Guadalupe's hut.

Before turning to help her, Jack caught sight of Elaina at the edge of the property. She was close enough for him to see the resentment in her dark eyes. Not wanting to make her any angrier, he lifted a hand and waved at her. Elaina made no effort to return the greeting. Instead, she stared at him for a few uncomfortable seconds, then slowly turned around and walked away.

A knot of dread twisted in Jack's empty stomach.

Elaina was a wild card, and her involvement with a boyfriend hadn't lessened her ongoing crush on Jack. Of course his idiotic decision to make Sophie jealous by flirting with Elaina hadn't helped matters. He just prayed Mario would be well enough for them to leave the next day.

* * *

It turned out there were quite a few people who were sick enough to need Sophie's skills. The only regret Jack had for agreeing to help Sophie was when she had to give someone a shot, which seemed to happen often. Like now.

A little girl, with a deep rattling cough, sat shivering on the table as Sophie drew up another dose of Penicillin. "*Medicina*," Sophie said, showing the syringe to the mother.

Jack tried not to react to the sight of the needle, but just like before, he felt lightheaded.

"Can you please explain to the mother about the shot?" Sophie said as she held the syringe in front of her, flicked the side of it with her finger, then pushed the tiny air bubbles out of the needle.

Feeling unsteady, Jack pulled his eyes away from the needle and explained to the mother how the antibiotic would help heal her daughter.

Not wanting to see the injection, Jack turned around to see how many more people were left waiting to see the doctor. Thankfully, an older gentleman was the only one left waiting in line. Finally, he and Sophie would get a break.

"*Buena niña*," Sophie said, stroking the child's head. As the day progressed, Sophie had picked up on a few more Spanish words. The little girl smiled brightly when Sophie offered her a sucker.

"*Muchas gracias*," the mother said, wrapping her arm around her daughter and guiding her away.

Sophie greeted the old man as he moved to stand in front of her. Before Jack could ask him what he needed the doctor for, the man pulled a full set of dentures out of his mouth and held them in his palm.

Both Sophie and Jack stared at the teeth while the man pointed to a molar that was cracked in the middle. Jack quickly explained that Sophie was not a dentist and wouldn't be able to fix his teeth. With a shrug, the older man plopped the teeth back in his mouth, turned around and walked away.

"Poor man," Sophie whispered. "I hope he didn't stand in line all morning, only to find out I was the wrong kind of doctor."

"He didn't seem that put out." Jack nudged her in the shoulder with his arm. "You ready to call it a day?"

Sophie never got a chance to reply as two young men burst through the trees, shouting for help. Jack saw they were carrying a man who didn't look too good. They drew closer and Jack noted the man was unconscious and had dried blood crusted in his hair.

Before he could offer his assistance, Elaina came barreling toward him and launched herself into his arms. She was crying hysterically, and that's when Jack noticed that the injured man was Elaina's boyfriend.

Chapter Twelve

Sophie cleared the table and motioned for the boys to place their friend there. The young man looked to be in his mid-twenties, and right away she noticed the gash on the side of his temple and the dried blood matted in his hair. The injury wasn't new, and Sophie wondered how long he had been unconscious.

Elaina had her face buried in Jack's shoulder, crying inconsolably. "This is Elaina's boyfriend," Jack said, looking a little bewildered by the hysterical female clinging to him.

Putting on a pair of latex gloves, Sophie focused on her patient. She asked Jack to find out if anyone knew what had happened and how long ago it had occurred. While he spoke in rapid Spanish with the young men, she placed her fingers at the man's neck and felt a slow, but steady pulse. She observed his chest at the same time, relieved to see it rise and fall within normal limits.

She continued to assess her patient's neurological status, waiting for an answer from Jack. Testing for pain response, Sophie pinched the skin under his upper arm. Her patient didn't moan, but he did try to pull his arm away, which was a good sign.

"They don't know what happened," Jack said as Sophie used the light from her otoscope to check the man's pupils, finding them equal and reactive to light. "They all had been drinking last night and don't remember much. Elaina is the one who found him lying outside the back of his bungalow."

Sophie wondered if drinking was all they had done. She wished she could get a tox screen to see what other substances she might find in his system.

"What's his name?" she asked, running her fingers over his head to see if he had any bumps or gashes she couldn't see. She discovered a pretty good sized goose egg behind his ear. The likely scenario was that he didn't quite make it home and fell and hit his head.

"Andre," Jack said, making Elaina wail even louder at the sound of her boyfriend's name. "How is he?"

"I'm not sure," she said as she doused a clean 4x4 gauze pad with hydrogen peroxide. "His vitals are stable, but the fact that he hasn't woken up has me worried. There's a nasty bump behind his ear, but without a CT scan, I have no idea how serious it is." She used the gauze pad to gently clean the gash on his temple and noted it wasn't deep enough to require sutures. "He doesn't need stitches, so really there's nothing more to do other than wait and see."

A crowd of villagers had gathered around the pavilion. She hoped someone had seen something and might come forward with more information.

She looked at Jack, feeling a twinge of irritation that he still held Elaina. "Does he have any family?"

Jack asked Elaina and the girl nodded her head. Just then, a large woman pushed through the crowd. "That's his mother," he said as the woman took one look at her son and broke down into tears.

"*Mi hijo*." She clasped her son's hand in hers, and Sophie was pleased when the young man moaned. Maybe he would come around sooner than she thought.

With anger etched on her face, Andre's mother glared at her sons friends. "*¿Qué pasó?*"

While the mother held what sounded like a heated conversation with the boys, Manuel emerged through the crowd. He assessed the situation and spoke to Elaina, in a tone that sounded like he was reprimanding her.

Elaina let go of Jack and snapped back at her father. Jack winced as he eased back from Elaina and came around the table to stand next to Sophie.

"This is all giving me a headache," he said, rubbing one of his temples with the tips of his fingers.

Sophie's own head was pounding, and she was exhausted after seeing so many people over the past four hours. "Would you like a couple of Tylenol?"

"Yeah, and some food, peace and quiet, and a bed."

"You have the celebration dinner to look forward to."

He glanced at her sidelong. "Have you ever heard a live Mariachi band?"

It sounded kind of fun to Sophie. "Take some Tylenol, go have Hector feed you, and lay down for a couple of hours. You'll be as good as new."

"And what will you do?"

"I'm a doctor. I'm used to getting no sleep and not eating for hours." She tried to hide her disappointment about missing the party. "Besides, between taking care of Andre and Mario, I'll have my hands full."

"Andre has a mother," Jack said. "And Mario's *abuela* is perfectly capable of taking care of him for a couple of hours. The fiesta is for all of us. Come with us tonight, Sophie. You need the break."

Sophie's empty tummy filled up with butterflies at the thought of spending the evening with Jack. It almost felt like a date, except Hector would be there. She just wished she had something to wear other than khaki's and T-shirts. "I don't know." She ran a hand through her hair. "I really need a bath."

"That can be arranged. I need one too." Jack rubbed his palm across his jaw. "I also need to shave."

Her desire to be with Jack, even for only a few hours, outweighed her good sense. "Okay. I'll go."

The butterflies in her stomach stirred again as she watched his mouth edge up into a sexy smile. "It's a date, then."

Was it? Or was it just a figure of speech?

Andre's mother stopped shouting at her son's friends and turned to speak to Sophie.

"She wants to know if we can move Andre to their house," Jack interpreted.

Sophie checked the wound she'd cleaned up and didn't see any fresh bleeding. "*Sí*," she said, offering a reassuring smile to the woman." She looked at Jack. "Just make sure they move him slowly and stabilize his head and neck."

Several men in the crowd helped to transport Andre. Sophie and Jack followed along to make sure her patient remained stable. Andre moaned again with the movement, and Sophie hoped he would regain consciousness by tonight.

After they had him settled, Sophie looked around for Jack. She found him outside with Elaina hanging all over him, the two of them talking quietly. It annoyed her how Jack seemed to placate the girl, encouraging her behavior.

Sophie spotted Hector, and when he waved at her, she left Jack with Elaina and asked Hector to accompany her back to their bungalow. On the way, Sophie saw many of the villagers getting ready for the *fiesta*. Hector pointed out a group of teenage girls wearing beautiful colored costumes, and said they would be performing tonight.

"Will everyone be dressed up?" Sophie asked, wishing she had something to wear other than her khaki's and a T-shirt.

"Probably, but do not worry." Hector winked at her. "You look beautiful in whatever you are wearing."

Sophie thanked him, but she wasn't as confident. Chances were Elaina wasn't going to be sitting vigilantly by her boyfriend's side tonight, but instead would be hovering over Jack and looking beautiful in a dress similar to the dancer's costumes.

By the time Sophie finally got her bath, Jack still hadn't come back to the bungalow. He was probably still consoling Elaina. As Sophie sunk down in the warm water, she told herself it was better this way. She just needed to focus on her goal of finding her father. She believed Mario would be well enough for them to leave some time tomorrow. Once she found her father, she could figure out what she was going to do about Peter.

Not Jack. Jack didn't seem like the type of guy to make any commitments. She just needed to remember that the next time she saw him.

* * *

Outside their bungalow, Jack finished shaving, leaving his beard reduced to the shadow he liked to wear. He pulled on a clean shirt and glanced around to make sure Elaina hadn't tracked him down yet. He wasn't sure how much longer he could take her advances.

While her boyfriend lay unconscious, Elaina had pulled him aside and giddily informed him she would be able to go with him to the *fiesta* tonight. Jack pointed out that Andre would probably like to have her there when he woke up. Elaina didn't seem to care about that. By the time he'd finally given up trying to convince her otherwise, Sophie had disappeared with Hector.

When Jack had returned to the hut, Sophie had been taking a bath. He and Hector had discussed the situation about Elaina and had both agreed in light of her past behavior, it would be best if Jack escorted Elaina and Hector took Sophie.

He hoped Sophie would understand, and wanted to have the chance to tell her that in person.

Kneeling down, he tied the laces on his boots, frustrated with the whole situation. Tonight would've been the perfect opportunity to talk to Sophie about her relationship with Peter. That discussion would definitely need to wait until they were gone from *Por El Rio*.

Glancing at his watch, Jack stood and wondered how much longer Sophie would be, and if she had found the gift he'd left for her. Since he wouldn't be taking her to the festivities tonight, Hector had suggested Jack should do something nice for Sophie and gave him the idea of buying her something pretty to wear to the party. So Jack had purchased an authentic Costa Rican dress for her as well as some simple sandals made by one of the natives. He knew most of the women would be dressed up tonight, and he didn't want her to feel left out.

Just as he was about to knock on the door to see if she was okay, Sophie emerged from the hut. Jack's chest tightened as he admired the new dress on her. The bright, multicolored skirt was full and hung just above her ankles, showing off the delicate sandals. The simple white top had a round neck with tiny red, blue and yellow flowers embroidered at the neckline. A bright red sash, tied around her waist, completed the ensemble.

When she noticed Jack watching her, a frown creased her brow. "Where's Hector?"

"He's getting cleaned up." He took a step toward her. "You look beautiful."

"Thanks." She smiled and smoothed her hands down the soft material of her skirt. "I wanted to thank him for getting me the dress. It was sweet of him since I told him I was sick of wearing pants and T-shirts."

Now he knew where Hector had gotten the idea. "Uh, that's what he told me, so I bought the dress for you." He smiled at the incredulous look on her face. "I'm glad you like it."

"Oh." Her dark eyes softened. "Thank you. You look nice too." She looked him over, scrutinizing him a little closer. "I thought you said you were going to shave?"

Jack ran a hand across his whiskers. "I did." Maybe she didn't like the bad-boy-Hollywood look he'd kept for the past couple of years. "You don't like it?"

She tilted her head. "Are you fishing for a compliment?"

"Yes."

A giggle escaped. "Okay. You look extremely handsome."

"Extremely?"

She pushed his arm. "Yes, Jack. Extremely. Now are we done with the flattery?"

"Not if there's more."

Hector came around the corner and whistled when he saw Sophie. "*Muy bonita*. Jack did well, *¿no?*"

"Yes—*sí*." Her eyes flickered to Jack's. "Jack did well."

Suddenly, the light in her eyes dimmed as she stared at something over Jack's shoulder. He turned and saw Elaina walking toward him. He swallowed hard and knew he was in trouble. Elaina wore a similar dress to Sophie's, only the top looked like it was a size too small and came off her shoulders.

He averted his gaze to her face and hoped the heat crawling up his neck wasn't visible. This was bad. Why couldn't she have waited a few more minutes before showing up unannounced?

He'd never had the chance to explain things to Sophie.

A wicked smile parted Elaina's red lips. She sidled up close to him and wrapped her fingers around his bicep. He didn't dare look down, so he kept his gaze straight ahead.

"Ready?" Elaina said in perfectly accented English.

Sophie stood there staring at him, as if she couldn't quite wrap her mind around what was happening. Hector was right beside her, his gaze transfixed on Elaina's top. He snapped out of his trance when Sophie took a hold of his arm. "You two have a good night." She yanked on Hector's arm. "We'll see you later."

Jack blew out a long breath, watching as Sophie practically had Hector jogging to keep up with her. His only hope at redemption was for Hector to explain why Jack was escorting Elaina.

Not left with much of a choice, Jack and Elaina followed the same path as Sophie and Hector. Jack asked about Andre, but Elaina said he had still not awakened. He continued to ask Elaina questions about her and Andre until Elaina finally snapped at him, telling him she didn't like Andre and had intended on breaking things off with him.

It seemed awfully convenient that her boyfriend was laid up, leaving Elaina free for the night.

By the time they reached the party, Jack's headache was back. The first chance he got, he was going to leave. And, no matter what, he was going to have that talk with Sophie.

It looked as if the entire village had turned out for the celebration. It was so crowded that Jack lost sight of Hector and Sophie. Elaina tried to get him to dance with her, but he adamantly shook his head and told her he needed to get something to eat. Despite how upset he felt, he was hungry, and the tantalizing aroma of slow-roasted pig made his mouth water.

Elaina guided him to sit at her father's table. Manuel sat next to a pretty woman Jack didn't recognize. Since Manuel's wife had passed away several years ago, he seemed to like playing the field rather than finding another woman to settle down with.

"*Mi amigo*," Manuel shouted over the noisy gathering and raised his glass up in acknowledgement of Jack.

Jack smiled and sat down next to Elaina and tried his best to ignore how close she was to him. He scanned the crowded courtyard and found where Sophie was sitting. He wasn't surprised she already held a small child on her lap. She was beautiful, laughing and playing with the little girl. Jack longed to be the one sitting next to her instead of Hector.

Elaina pressed her body close, placing her hand on Jack's thigh. The exotic scent of her perfume made his eyes water. Had she used the entire bottle? Schooling his emotions, he removed her hand. "Please pass the rice," he asked, trying to distract her.

"*Sí, mi amor.*" She reached for the steaming bowl, her arm brushing against his. Jack wished Manuel would do something about his daughter, but he was too enamored by the woman he was with to pay any attention to Elaina's antics.

Once again, Jack looked across the expanse to watch Sophie. More children had surrounded her and clamored for her attention. He loved the smile on her face as she interacted with the kids.

As if she sensed him watching, her eyes lifted and their gazes connected. Even from this distance, she made his pulse leap, and he couldn't look away. Her mouth curved up into an alluring smile, the angry look no longer marring her features. Hector must have done a very good job of explaining things.

"Jack," Elaina said, taking his face with her hand and turning him toward her. She held a piece of fresh pineapple, dripping with sweet juice. Without giving him a chance to say no, she thrust the fruit between his lips. Elaina used her thumb to wipe away the excess juice around his mouth, then placed her thumb between her own lips, eyeing him seductively.

Jack nearly choked on the piece of fruit and knew he needed to call it a night. They were leaving tomorrow, and he was tired of playing this game. Elaina picked up another piece of pineapple, ready to repeat the intimate gesture. Jack held up his hands to ward her off and reached for his Coke to chase down the fruit.

His eyes automatically sought out Sophie again. The smile had completely vanished, her lips now tightly pressed together. Dropping her gaze, she turned away and touched Hector on the arm. Jack watched helplessly as Sophie handed the baby to the mother and walked away with Hector.

Frustrated with the whole situation, Jack tried to come up with something that would allow him to leave while Elaina stayed at the party. When he was eleven he had faked a stomach ache so he could stay home from church to watch the World Cup final match. He had gone as far as making himself throw up so his parents would believe him. If it would get rid of Elaina, he wasn't afraid to go there.

Everyone at the table was saved from his plan when a group of girls came to get Elaina for a dance they would be performing as part of the program. Jack couldn't believe it had been that easy. He stayed in his seat for at least two minutes, just to make sure Elaina really wasn't coming back right away.

In order to not offend Manuel, Jack stood up and held a hand to his gut. He apologized for having to leave such a wonderful party early, but something at dinner hadn't agreed with his stomach. It was all true, just not the whole truth. Given the situation, Jack could now sympathize with Sophie and the reason she hadn't corrected his assumption that she was a man in the first place. He would have to tell her, that is if she would even talk to him.

Jack made his way toward Guadalupe's hut. He knew he'd find Sophie there and hoped she wasn't too mad at him.

The Latin music faded with each step he took. As he approached the humble dwelling, he could hear Sophie humming. He peeked inside, finding her hunched over, changing Mario's dressing.

The boy's grandmother smiled widely and waved him inside. "*Entras, Señor* Jack."

Sophie's hands froze and she stopped humming. Her gaze flitted over to him, and he saw his coming here had surprised her. Jack started to smile but stopped when a flash of anger darkened her eyes.

Shoot. He had a lot of groveling to do.

Chapter Thirteen

Sophie wanted to ask why Jack was here and not back at the party with Elaina, but she was not in the mood to talk to him. Plus, she didn't want to hear him try to justify his actions by saying he was protecting her. She knew flirting when she saw it.

Turning back around, she tried her best to ignore him as she finished with Mario's dressing. Jack crouched down next to her to talk to Mario. His voice was soft and Mario listened to each word with wide, alert eyes. With Jack so close, she caught the scent of his spicy deodorant. Despite being so mad at him, her body betrayed her and reacted to his nearness. She took a slow and steady breath, trying to decrease her racing pulse rate.

"*Sí*," Mario said to Jack as a grin spread across the little boy's face.

Jack patted the child on his head before rising up. The distance allowed Sophie to concentrate on her task. She was pleased with how well the wound and infection had responded to the medication. The child's appetite had returned, and he was taking in adequate fluids for the IV to be removed after the next dose of antibiotics. Her supply of ampicillin was running low anyway, so it would be good for him to switch over to oral antibiotics. She had a limited supply of those as well, and she hoped she wouldn't encounter anyone else who needed them as much as Mario had.

Sophie stood up and cut a sideway glance at Jack. "Can you tell Mario I'll remove his IV in the morning?"

Jack relayed the message, and Mario grinned at the news.

Guadalupe nodded her head, a pleased smile on her wrinkled face. She spoke, looking directly at Sophie. Jack translated for her, and the words of gratitude from the older woman warmed Sophie's heart.

With nothing more to do for Mario, Sophie wanted to check on Elaina's boyfriend. Since she needed Jack to go along with her, she reluctantly met his blue eyes. "I'd like to check on Andre. If you're not busy, would you mind coming with me?"

He studied her for a few seconds before his mouth lifted up into a crooked grin. "I don't mind, but we'll have to be on the lookout for Elaina."

Sophie's stomach curdled. "Sure." She averted her gaze and hurried outside. Jack followed close behind her, and she whirled around, deciding she didn't want his help after all. "I can find Hector to help me. That way you can go find Elaina and enjoy the rest of your evening."

Jack's eyes sparked with amusement. "I told you we need to be on the lookout for Elaina so I can avoid her." He grinned. "Right now Manuel thinks I had to leave early for…digestive problems. My symptoms came on suddenly when Elaina left the table to go perform a dance as part of the evening's entertainment."

Comprehension of his words slowly disrupted the jealous thoughts she was fighting. "Oh." She fumbled in her pocket for her lip gloss, trying to reconcile what he was saying with what she had witnessed—Elaina feeding him intimately. "That's too bad you're sick," she said sarcastically. "From what I could see, it looked as if you were enjoying the food."

One of Jack's brows lifted. "What you saw was Elaina attempting to woo me."

"Did it work?"

"No, having someone shove food in my mouth just doesn't do it for me."

She was so tempted to ask him what did work, but kept her mouth shut as she applied her daiquiri flavored gloss to her lips.

A slow smile spread across his handsome face. "Aren't you going to ask me what does work?"

"Why would I?"

He shrugged. "I just figured if you're ever interested, you might want to know what I like."

"Thanks." She rolled her eyes. "*If* I'm ever interested, I'll be sure to ask you."

"Ouch."

Sophie laughed and realized Jack had managed to use his sense of humor to dispel her anger. She liked that about him.

"I'm sorry about tonight," he said softly. The sincerity in his voice drew her gaze to his eyes. "I didn't want to be with Elaina."

Sophie wanted to believe him. Hector had given her the history of Elaina's fatal-like attraction for Jack and told her that he'd only been trying to protect Sophie by escorting Elaina to the party. But a tiny part of her knew there were times when Jack had purposely flirted with the girl.

She stared into his incredibly blue eyes, and the honesty she saw reflected in them made her give him the benefit of the doubt. "That's what Hector told me."

"Hector's a great guy," Jack said with a smile. "With him as your date, I hope you at least had some fun tonight."

She thought about the pretty dress she still had on and how she had hoped the evening would go. "It was nice." She sighed. "I really do wish I would've learned Spanish, though."

"Yeah," he said dryly. "Our teenage rebellious moments do have a way of coming back and biting us in the butt, don't they?"

"I knew I should've never told you that story."

"I swear never to tell anybody else," Jack said, holding up his fingers in the Boy Scout promise.

She gave a light laugh. "Somehow I don't believe you."

Jack feigned a wounded look as he flattened his palm against his chest. "That hurt."

"You are so annoying."

"So I've been told."

They both were smiling now, the feelings between them much more amicable. Jack nodded his head to his left. "We better go check on Andre before the party ends."

"Oh, that's right," she said as they started walking in the right direction. "You're trying to avoid your date."

"Very funny," he muttered. "Since Mario is doing so much better, please tell me we can leave tomorrow."

"Yes. I believe we can."

The path narrowed, and their arms touched as they continued side by side. "Good. We have another three days to travel before we reach the village your father was last living in."

Her stomach clenched, and she felt guilty for not focusing on the reason she was here in the first place. Flirting with Jack wasn't supposed to be a part of the plan.

"I didn't realize we were so close. I hope the information the university gave me was accurate. Peter seemed to think it wasn't a good sign when the private investigator I hired couldn't come up with anything else."

She felt Jack's gaze on her, and she briefly glanced up at him. His eyes were filled with an emotion she couldn't quite define.

"I've been meaning to ask you something about Peter."

"Yes." She halted when Jack stopped walking.

"Are you planning on marrying him?"

The tone of his voice was so intense, and it occurred to her that he might be…jealous? Warmth slipped over her, making her feel as if she had just immersed herself in a hot bubble bath. Still, she wasn't sure how to answer him. "It's complicated."

He looked away and then started to walk again. She took a few quick steps to catch up with him. "Peter asked me to marry him. I just haven't been able to give him an answer."

"Can I ask why?" he said, glancing over at her again.

Because I've never felt anything for him like I do when I'm around you. She let out a big breath. "Like I said, it's complicated."

Jack was quiet, and Sophie wasn't inclined to say anymore at the moment. Andre's house was only a few feet ahead of them. The sounds of the fiesta were loud here, and the music playing had changed, sounding more like a Calypso band.

Jack knocked on the door and announced their arrival. Andre's mother swung open the door and motioned them inside. There was a young teenage girl sitting by the unconscious man, but Elaina was conspicuously absent.

Andre's mother spoke to Jack, gesticulating with her hands. Jack turned and translated her words. "He opened his eyes a little while ago but wouldn't talk. When Mom here tried to make him wake up again, he groaned and swatted at her hand."

"That's good," Sophie said. "He'll probably come around soon, and when he does, I suspect he'll have a headache that will be more than just a hangover."

She placed her fingers on the inside of Andre's wrist, feeling a steady and strong pulse. His skin was warm and dry, and he didn't appear to be in any kind of distress. "Tell Mom to make sure he drinks plenty of water when he awakens, and I'll be by in the morning before we leave to see how he's doing."

After Jack relayed the information, they headed over to their bungalow where Sophie wanted to change out of her dress. She had no idea if she would ever have a place to wear the clothing again, but she wanted to take them home with her.

"So," Jack said. "Until Mario's IV comes out, I guess you'll be sleeping in the hut again?"

"Yes." She glanced at her watch. "The last dose of antibiotics is due in a few hours. After I give it, the fluids should be about up, and I can DC the IV then."

"Do you want me to set up your tent so you can get a few hours of sleep?"

"No thank you. I'd feel more comfortable sleeping inside in case Mario needs me." She fingered the red sash around her waist. "I just need to change my clothes." She glanced at him. "Thank you again for the dress. I hope I can find room to pack it so I can take it home."

"We'll find room for it." It was his turn to look at her. "I already said it, but you look beautiful."

"Well," she said, feeling her cheeks heat up. "In a few minutes it will be back to T-shirts and khaki's."

"Yeah, that doesn't change anything."

She paused and looked up at him. "Are you being charming again?"

His lips twitched, then he smiled. "Yes, ma'am. I believe I am."

A delicious feeling of satisfaction unfurled inside her, leaving her to hope that she was actually starting to see the real Jack Mathison for the first time.

* * *

Although he tried, Jack couldn't sleep. He couldn't stop thinking about Sophie. After more than an hour had passed, he decided to see if she was still awake. Peeking inside the hut, he found her writing in her journal by a small LED lantern.

He watched her for a minute before her gaze lifted, making a connection with his eyes. The little boy and his grandmother were fast asleep. Sophie put her fingers to her lips, signaling him to be quiet, even though the grandmother was snoring so loudly he doubted any sound he or Sophie made would awaken her. Then she motioned for him to join her.

Jack only hesitated a second before he quietly moved over and sat down next to her on the pallet. Their shoulders touched, and he was instantly aware of the contact. He caught a whiff of her coconut scented shampoo and had the intense yearning to bury his face in her hair and hold her close.

"Hi," he whispered.

"Hi." She gave him a soft smile. "What are you doing up?"

"I couldn't sleep." He nudged her in the shoulder. "What are you doing up?"

"I just gave Mario his last dose of antibiotics and thought I'd write in my journal until I get sleepy."

"Anything good?" He leaned over to try and sneak a look, although the pages were shadowed and he couldn't make out any words.

She closed the book and nudged him back. "That's for me to know and you never to find out."

"I don't get it. If no one can read it, then what's the point in writing it down?"

"I'm not writing it for someone else to read, silly." She hugged the book close to her chest. "At least not yet. I'm sure someday I'll want to share parts of it with my children."

"What about your husband?"

Sophie looked up at him through her thick lashes, and a shy smile parted her lips. "I don't know. I guess I'll share it with him too."

Jack had the wildest impulse to snatch it from her and declare he wanted a preview and that eventually, as her husband, he'd read it thoroughly. It was a crazy thought. First, he had pretty much written off marriage. He never wanted to be that vulnerable again. Second, Sophie was practically engaged to another man.

He needed to get his mind on something else. Nobody was more surprised than he was when he asked, "How many kids do you want?"

She looked at him curiously. He just smiled. For some dumb reason, he really wanted to know.

"A lot. As many as I can talk my husband into."

"Really?" he asked, feeling slightly alarmed by the potentially large number. Jack was pretty sure any man married to this woman would have a hard time saying no. "What if he only wants, like two or three?"

Jack had only one brother. One cheating, fiancée-stealing brother. If he'd had at least one other sibling, maybe he wouldn't be estranged from his parents right now.

"I guess we'd have to work it out, but before we married, I would make sure he knew I want a big family. I want my kids and their spouses and their children to come over for Sunday dinner.

I want big family get-togethers for all the holidays. I want to be close to my husband's family, too. I want to share his parents, or at least his mother."

The muscles in Jack's stomach tensed. She would have that with Peter. Truthfully, from what she'd already told him, she did have that with Peter's family. What would Jack have to offer her? Certainly not a big fun-loving family. Heck, if he and Adam were ever in the same room again, Jack was pretty sure he wouldn't be giving him a brotherly hug.

He tried to picture being an uncle to Heather and Adam's first kid. He wasn't even sure what her name was. He knew it was a girl. His mother had sent him a birth announcement, and the only thing Jack could remember was it was all pink.

"Wow, I hope you have a big house, then. With all the partying you plan to do, you'll need it."

"Not too big. I want my home to be cozy—a place where my family will feel comfortable. Not some showcase."

He slanted her a glance. "What woman doesn't dream about owning the biggest, nicest house?"

"Me."

Jack studied her for a few seconds. He believed her. His muscles tensed again. He also wanted her.

Could she be happy with someone like him? He'd be faithful to her. He'd even take her to church each week. How could he be mad at God anymore if he ended up with Sophie? As far as children, he'd do his best to give her as many as she wanted. He just couldn't give her in-laws. At least not now. Maybe never.

Then she asked him the one question he didn't want to have to answer.

"Jack, what about your family? Do you have any brothers and sisters?"

"Yeah, one brother." The familiar anger twisted his insides. "We're not close."

"Oh." Her voice was small. Jack couldn't bring himself to look at her, knowing the disappointment in her eyes would be too much for him to take in right now. "Well, what about your parents?"

His fingers curled into fists, and he swallowed hard. In order to explain the rift between him and his family, he'd have to tell her what Heather had done to him. He just couldn't go there yet.

"They live in Fort Collins, but I haven't been home for a while, now." The truth was he had no idea if they still lived in the same home he'd grown up in. Shoot, he didn't even know if they were both still alive. All at once, the desire to see his parents hit him so hard he felt like his chest was being crushed, and he could barely take a breath.

How was he supposed to go about contacting his family? Would he write a letter or give them a call? He thought about the upcoming holidays. How would his family feel if he showed up for Thanksgiving dinner?

Struggling with the overwhelming feelings, he gently cleared his throat. Guadalupe snorted in her sleep and both Jack and Sophie looked toward the dark corner where she slept. They both visibly relaxed when the loud, rhythmic snoring started up again.

Jack glanced down into Sophie's eyes, dark and questioning, as if she knew the inner turmoil he was dealing with. "After listening to you talk about family, I realize it's time I make a visit home." He felt some of the incredible burden he'd carried for so long lift.

He still had no idea how he'd face Adam and Heather, but it was time to seek out his mom and dad. "Thanks for sharing all of that with me."

Her mouth curved up, and he caught the telltale scent of her lip gloss. Before he would ever let himself taste what flavor it was, he needed to clear a few things up. "Tell me about Peter? What is he like?"

Surprised flitted across her face. "Um, well, he's an attorney. Actually, he was just made a partner at his firm. He's into running and has run several marathons for charity. His whole family has even done a two-day relay race to raise money for our church." She smiled wistfully. "Like I said before, I'm an only child, and being with Peter's family is so magical."

Jack noticed Peter's family seemed to be the biggest selling point for her.

"So you love his family. What about him?"

"I told you it's complicated." Her smile faded, and she glanced down at the journal she held in her lap. "I'm so confused. I…love him, but I don't think I love him enough to marry him."

Jack's gut twisted with envy at her admission of love. It eased a bit when she followed up with the caveat to her feelings. "Hmm. Does he expect an answer when you get home?"

She nodded her head and smoothed her fingers over the leather cover of the small book. "That's what I told him."

Every fiber of his being wanted to do everything in his power to ensure her answer would be *no*. So what did that mean? Realistically, how could he even contemplate getting involved in a serious relationship with a woman who lived in Colorado, not Costa Rica?

"What about you?" she asked. "Have you ever wanted to get married?"

Jack shifted on his seat. It was a fair question and deserved an honest answer. Whereas only a few minutes ago he hadn't been ready to share his past about Heather, now seemed like the right time.

"I was engaged once." He rubbed his palms across the fabric of his pants. "But my fiancée married my brother instead of me."

He licked his lips and nervously turned to look at Sophie. She watched him with wide eyes, concern written on her face.

"We were supposed to get married soon after I returned from my service mission here in Costa Rica. While I was serving God, she was busy planning our wedding. At least that's what I had thought." The familiar ache inside his chest pressed on his heart when he thought about what Heather had really been doing.

Jack had to look away, unable to look at Sophie. "A couple of weeks before the wedding date, Heather announced she was three months pregnant...and my brother Adam was the father."

Sophie drew in a sharp breath. "Oh, Jack. I'm so sorry."

Bitterness filled his mouth, and he fought back the anger rising inside. He couldn't tell her how his parents had sided with Adam, chastising Jack for being so angry. Just when he thought he could let it all go and forgive them, the feelings of betrayal and hatred extinguished his noble quest for absolution.

"The best part was Heather still wanted me to marry her." He stifled a derisive laugh. "I declined and let Adam have her."

His hands were clenched into a fist, and he felt wound up tighter than a piano string. He almost flinched when

Sophie placed her warm hand on top of one of his fists.

His throat constricted with emotion, and he felt the sting of tears prick his eyes.

Oh man, he couldn't cry now. Not when he hadn't shed one tear over Heather and Adam's betrayal before.

Sophie gently pried his hand open and pressed her palm against his, threading their fingers together. He savored the warmth of her hand, amazed at how well they fit. Her goodness seeped into his soul, calming him like the Valium a doctor had once given him before he'd had laser eye surgery.

She adjusted her weight and leaned close to him. "That's the reason you haven't been home for a while," she said as if she truly comprehended his feelings. "I don't blame you."

He expelled the breath trapped in his chest, loosening the tension in his shoulders. She understood and didn't blame him. Her words were something he'd needed to hear for a long time. She hadn't judged or condemned him, nor had she extoled the virtues of forgiveness and why he shouldn't hold grudges. Instead, she had acknowledged his pain and offered him sympathy. It seemed a very Christian thing to do, and once again, he could see the possibilities of reconnecting with his parents.

Thankfully, Sophie didn't ask any more questions about Heather and Adam, their child or his parents. She just sat close to him, holding his hand. In the quiet of the hut, he ran his thumb across her soft skin. "Thanks for listening."

"You're welcome."

He glanced down and she turned her face, their eyes meeting. He wanted to kiss her, but Guadalupe's loud snores reminded him they were not alone. "Good night, Sophie."

"Good night," she whispered back, lowering her head to his shoulder.

Chapter Fourteen

Sophie tipped her head to the side and rubbed at the sore spot along the back of her neck with her fingertips. She'd slept against Jack's shoulder for most of the night, and her stiff upper body let her know it hadn't been as pleasant as she remembered.

She sneaked a look at Jack as he helped Hector load their gear. He looked good this morning. Happier. Something had changed between the two of them, and she felt closer to him after he'd shared his painful past. She wished they could've talked more, but she figured they would get the chance when they made camp tonight. Somewhere far away from Elaina.

He turned and caught her staring at him. A slow smile parted his lips as he walked toward her. "Hey, I'm going to tell Manuel goodbye."

Despite their new found friendship, her stomach knotted as she stood up to meet him. Why did he want to go alone? "I can come with you."

He shook his head. "I'd like to get on the trail as soon as possible. While I'm gone, Hector will take you to see Andre. I'll swing by and get you and we can leave."

She wanted to argue, but what if Jack wanted one last chance to see Elaina again? She tucked her fingertips inside the front of her pockets. "Be sure and thank Manuel for me."

"I will," Jack said, turning to go. "I won't be long."

Before she thought about it, Sophie stopped him. "Jack?"

He paused and looked back over his shoulder, that cocky grin still on his face. "Yes?"

"Tell Elaina good-bye for me, too."

The smile vanished, and his blue eyes narrowed a fraction. "Sure. Anything else?"

Now she felt stupid. Sophie shook her head and looked down at her shoes. Why had she brought up Elaina? Jack had already explained the situation, and she had believed him.

Her eyes darted back up to apologize, but he'd already walked away. Her apology would have to wait until he returned. She just hoped her insecurity and lack of trust hadn't ruined the change in their relationship.

After last night, she sensed Jack might be developing feelings for her that went beyond friendship. She knew her feelings were changing. Many times she'd asked herself if Jack would want to see her again after they found her father? Is that what she wanted?

She watched him disappear around the corner and smiled. She *did* want to see Jack again. Hope for something more fluttered inside her chest like the wings of the butterfly flitting above her head. It would be very easy to fall in love with Jack Mathison.

The donkey brayed loudly, snapping Sophie out of her musings. She glanced over to see Hector watching her with a knowing grin. "He's coming back. I promise."

A nervous giggle bubbled out of her. "I know." The donkey stamped his foot as if protesting the load on his back. "Fred doesn't seem very happy."

Hector shrugged. "I interrupted his siesta, and he's a little grumpy this morning." He winked. "Usually it's Jack who is the grumpy one, but he seems awfully happy this morning, ¿*no*?"

Sophie tried not to smile too brightly. "Hmm. I guess that's because we're leaving."

Hector laughed. "Yes, *señorita,* I'm sure that is part of the reason."

He clicked his tongue against his teeth and tugged on Fred's lead rope. "Let's go see your patient so we really can be on our way."

She would feel better if Andre was fully awake before continuing on their journey, but at least Mario was doing better. After discontinuing his IV early this morning, Sophie left the oral medication with Guadalupe to finish giving her grandson. The child's miraculous recovery was a testament to the wonders of modern medicine. Sophie was glad she was here at the right place and at the right time.

They reached the hut, and Sophie knocked on the door. Andre's mother looked relieved to see a doctor. She spoke to Sophie with frantic gestures of her hands again, and Hector interpreted for her. Apparently, Andre had awoken and sipped a little bit of water but then refused to drink anymore. The fact that he'd kept the water down was another good indication he would probably be okay.

She went inside to assess Andre, and Hector said he would wait outside with Fred. The donkey was very ill-tempered today, and Hector was afraid he might run off. Sophie had brought her stethoscope with her and listened to Andre's heart and lungs. She moved down and listened to his belly, hearing loud rumbling bowel sounds that signaled Andre would also be hungry when he awoke.

She took her penlight and lifted one of his eyelids to test his pupils. Andre moaned and shook his head. She started to check the other pupil when he sat up, his eyes wide open.

His mother clapped her hands and started talking to her son. Andre closed his eyes and put a hand to his head and moaned again. Then his eyes popped opened, and he started talking loudly to his mother, trying to get off the bed. Whatever he had said made his mother angry, and she started shouting back.

Sophie had no idea what was going on and hoped Hector would hear the commotion and come inside. While Andre's mother struggled to push her son back down on the mattress, Sophie ran outside to seek Hector's help. He was nowhere to be found. Fred was missing, and Sophie hoped the donkey hadn't run off too far with their supplies.

Both Andre and his mother continued to yell at each other, but Sophie had no idea what it was all about. At least a little familiar with her surroundings, she knew Manuel's house wasn't too far from here. Deciding there was a good chance Jack would intercept her, she quickly walked toward the Carrero's home.

Sophie hadn't gone very far when she heard the low tones of a man talking. It sounded like Jack. The hair on the back of her neck stood on end when she heard the soft voice of a woman, followed by a giggle. Sophie pressed a hand to her stomach and crept quietly, peering behind a vacant hut.

Shock jolted through her when Elaina threw her arms around Jack's neck and kissed him full on the mouth. A stunned gasp escaped her mouth, and Jack jerked away from Elaina and glanced over just as Sophie lost her balance and stumbled backward. Regaining her equilibrium, she bolted back the way she had come.

"Sophie!" Jack called.

Like she was going to stop. Why had she gone looking for him? It was none of her business who Jack Mathison kissed. He probably had a girl in every port—or in this case—village.

She heard his footsteps behind her. *Rats!* He was a fast runner. He caught her before she made it all the way back. "It's not what you think," he said breathlessly.

She wrenched her arm out of his hand. "I'm pretty sure it is."

"No. It's not. I didn't kiss her."

She gave a harsh laugh. "Jack, don't lie. I know what I saw."

He stepped forward, an intense look on his face. "What you saw was Elaina kissing me. I didn't kiss her back."

Was he serious? "I don't see how there is any difference."

He cast a steely gaze at her, placing both of his hands on her upper arms. "Oh, there's a difference all right. Would you like me to demonstrate?"

"No." Her eyes strayed to his mouth, and she cursed the part of her that wanted a demonstration. "No," she said again, taking a step backward.

Just then, Elaina came up behind Jack, and Sophie wanted to wipe the know-it-all smile from the girl's face. Whirling around, Sophie only made it a few steps before Andre came stomping down the path with his mother chasing behind him. From what Sophie could tell, they were still having the same argument.

Andre's dark eyes locked on Elaina, and he started shouting even louder. Sophie watched the color drain out of Elaina's face. Both of Jack's eyebrows shot up as he looked from Elaina to Andre. When Elaina started fighting back, Jack slowly edged away from the couple. He eased around the crowd that was gathering and came to stand by Sophie.

She was still angry with him, but she wanted to know what was going on. "What is Andre so mad about?" she asked.

Jack crossed his arms over his chest and gave a low whistle. "It would seem that Andre wasn't that drunk, and he remembers Elaina coming at him with a tree branch. She hit him in the back of the head, and that's the last thing he remembers."

"That would explain the lump behind his ear. He must have cracked his forehead open when he went down."

"Elaina claims he was drunk and trying to hurt her."

Andre pointed a finger at Jack, as he continued to yell at Elaina. His face was so red Sophie hoped he didn't pop a blood vessel.

Jack dropped his hands to his side and shook his head. "I knew the girl was obsessed but not crazy. Well, at least not this crazy." He glanced down at Sophie, his forehead creased with concern. "Andre said Elaina was trying to get rid of him so she would be free to be with me."

Her eyes narrowed suspiciously, clearly remembering the kiss Elaina had just planted on him.

Jack reached down for Sophie's hand and led her away from the growing crowd. "I think it's time for us to make our exit."

They walked quickly away, then broke into a jog. After going a couple of yards, Sophie pulled her hand out of Jack's. She was still peeved with him. Yes, Elaina was stalking him, but despite what Jack claimed, Sophie had seen the two of them kissing.

As they came to the rendezvous place they had met at earlier, they stopped and looked around for Hector. He was coming down another path, yanking on Fred's rope, the donkey resisting all the way.

His face was flushed, and he was speaking in his native tongue, his voice low and angry. When he saw Sophie, he immediately stopped. "Pardon me, *chica*. But this donkey is making me *loco*."

Jack grabbed Sophie's daypack and handed it to her, then he strapped on his own backpack. "It's a good thing Sophie doesn't understand Spanish, because you were making my ears burn, and after what I just heard—that's saying something."

Hector raised one dark eyebrow. "What is it you heard?"

"A lot of cursing." Jack tugged on the donkey's rope, and Hector glowered again when Fred started to walk without any resistance. "Let's go, and I'll tell you on the way," Jack said. "But say goodbye to *Por El Rio,* because we are not coming back. Ever."

If this declaration was for her benefit, Sophie wasn't in the mood to acknowledge it. Elaina might have initiated the kiss, but Jack hadn't been in any hurry to end it. In fact, if she hadn't gasped so loudly, she wondered if he would've broken it off at all.

* * *

Jack rolled his shoulders back, thinking it was time to find a good place to set up camp for the night. The trek had been slow and boring, and he was ready to call it a day. He'd been following behind Sophie for hours and she had basically ignored him the entire time. Sophie was still mad at him. Even though Jack had apologized and explained that he had not kissed Elaina, Sophie refused to listen. If he asked her questions, she kept her answers short and wouldn't look him in the eye.

Although she was pretty mad at him, her jealous reaction made him smile because it meant her feelings for him were deeper than he'd thought. That both thrilled and terrified Jack. If he decided to pursue Sophie, it needed to be with the intent of marrying her. He might be selfish, but he wasn't that big of a jerk to lure her away from Peter and his extraordinary family just to have a brief relationship with her to satisfy his male ego.

There was also his faith, or lack of faith, to consider. After their talk last night, and her non-judgmental attitude toward him, he felt a desire stirring deep within him to reconnect with his faith.

"Oh, look," Sophie said, and Jack snapped his eyes to her, hoping his exile was over.

It wasn't.

She was standing next to Hector, pointing at a large Scarlet Macaw that sat on a low hanging branch. Jack started to approach the pair, prepared to wow Sophie with his knowledge of the colorful bird. But Fred, which Jack had been leading throughout today's journey, had other ideas. The donkey stopped and jerked Jack, nearly knocking him down on his backside.

"Come on," he said, tugging on the rope. "Let's go."

Fred blinked his eyes and swished his tail but didn't take a step.

Jack whistled and yanked on the rope again, but the donkey wasn't moving. "Come on, buddy, it isn't time to call it quits yet."

Reasoning with the donkey wasn't working. Jack glanced over to find Hector and Sophie watching him. Hector was grinning, no doubt pleased to see Fred acting up for someone other than himself. Sophie looked amused, her lips slightly curved upward. At least she wasn't scowling.

"I think he's done," Jack said with an answering smile. "What do you think about making camp here?"

Sophie dropped her eyes, and Jack hoped he could smooth things out. While opening up to her about Heather's betrayal had been hard, it had also been freeing.

Hector looked around and nodded in approval. "*Sí*, the ground is flat, and we'd have to stop soon anyway."

Fred brayed his endorsement and moved toward Hector as if he knew he was going to have the load on his back removed. Jack shrugged his own pack off and stretched. He watched Sophie do the same.

"Do you want any help with your tent?" Jack asked her.

She didn't even glance his way and grunted something unintelligible as she rolled out her tent.

"What? I didn't hear you." He shouldn't antagonize her, not if he wanted to make things right. But how long was she going to keep this up?

"I said *no, thank you.*" Her words were clipped and terse, with just a touch of sarcasm.

Jack had never seen her this way and couldn't help it. He laughed outright. "Oh come on, are you still mad at me?"

Sophie spun around, meeting his gaze. "Why would *I* be mad at you?"

Jack met her icy glare and swallowed. She expected to get an admission of guilt. But he was sticking to his story— he had not kissed Elaina.

Ironically, it was the truth. After saying goodbye to Manuel, he had been waylaid by Elaina. Clutching his arm, Elaina had cried in desperation, weeping that her life was over if Jack walked away. Jack had tried reasoning with her, getting her to laugh. Elaina had blindsided him by throwing her arms around his neck and kissing him soundly on the mouth.

He eyed Sophie, who still waited for an answer, her toe tapping in agitation. Jack crossed his arms in front of his chest. "I don't know. Why are you so mad at me?"

She narrowed her eyes. "I never said I was mad. Remember, you asked me. And I quote, 'come on, are you still mad at me?'"

Shoot, she'd definitely been hanging out with him too long. Jack held up his hands in mock surrender. "Okay. You're right. From now on, just pretend like I'm not even here." He pulled out his own tent. "Kind of like you've been doing all day," he grumbled.

"What did you say?" Sophie asked indignantly.

Now she wanted to talk? "Nothing." Jack made the motion of zipping his mouth shut and throwing away the key.

The corner of her mouth twitched before she turned her head abruptly. He could tell she didn't want to stay mad at him, and she didn't seem like the type to hold a grudge.

It made him like her all the more, and, whether it was a good idea or not, Jack needed to figure out a way to talk to her.

They worked in silence, and as soon as Sophie had her tent assembled, she disappeared inside. While Hector put together a meal of white chili and fresh pineapple, Jack assembled Hector's tent for him. Afterward, he found a small pool of water and refilled their specialized water bottles.

He came back to camp, disappointed to find Sophie still holed up in her tent. An idea came to him, and he dug through his pack for the M&M's he'd been saving and placed them on top for easy access. What woman didn't like chocolate? He figured it would be an acceptable peace offering that would hopefully grant him a chance to make things right.

Soon, the once-dehydrated chili was bubbling, the scent drifting on the air. Hector ladled the soup into the tin cups. Jack was just about to call out for Sophie to come and eat, when she unzipped her tent and stepped out. He hoped she'd had enough time to let go of her anger.

"Mmm, something smells good," she said, moving to stand by Hector and completely ignoring Jack.

Nope. She was definitely still mad.

Hector winked at her. "It's not bad, just not as good as the fresh chili I make at home."

"I'll bet." She accepted the tin cup and sniffed the rising steam. "But right now, this looks wonderful. Thank you."

With her other hand, she took a plate of fruit, and then she turned back around, obviously going back to hide inside her tent.

"Sophie," Jack called. He wanted to talk to her, set the record straight about *the kiss*, and possibly let her know about his growing feelings.

She hesitated, looked over her shoulder and met his gaze. "What?"

"Come and sit by me," Jack said, watching the play of emotions cross her features. He could see the battle she was having, and when he thought she might not give in, he upped the ante. "Please."

Chapter Fifteen

Jack watched as Sophie's dark eyes softened, and she quietly moved back and took a seat beside him. She wasn't relaxed, though. Her back was rigid, and she still refused to look at him.

Hector watched the two of them, and Jack could tell he was trying not to laugh. He took his food and walked past them. "I think I'm going to sit by my tent and listen to some music." Before disappearing behind his tent, he made a show of pulling out his iPod, a signal to Jack he was giving them their privacy.

After a few seconds of uncomfortable silence, Jack waited for Sophie to look at him, but her focus remained on the cup of chili. "So, are you going to say grace or am I?" He knew he would get a reaction from her and wasn't disappointed.

Slowly, she looked at him and rendered a small smile. "I think it's your turn to pray," she said a little too sweetly.

Jack grinned. He could tell she didn't think he would do it, but he called her bluff. "Okay."

Her eyes remained locked on his and then fluttered closed.

The words came easy as Jack thanked God for the food, as well as their safety traveling today. Then just before ending the prayer, he added, "And, Lord, please bless Sophie not to be mad at me anymore."

When he finished, he looked over to find Sophie's brown eyes fixed on him, her lips slanted up into an extremely pleased smile. *Score.* He'd just made some major points.

She broke the connection, taking a sip of the chili.

"Hector is always so willing to make us our meals." Her gaze flickered back to Jack. "You're lucky to have such a good friend."

"I am lucky, especially since I dragged him away from his wife and seven kids."

"I saw pictures of his family. His wife is beautiful and so are his children. All seven of them."

Jack gave a low whistle. "I can tell you his house is always very busy and a little loud. Every once in a while, Hector likes to get away, but he's always anxious to get home to his wife. They actually like each other." He leaned over and whispered, "I mean, they do have seven kids, right?"

She laughed softly and shook her head as a pretty blush colored her cheeks. "He's a good husband and father. I think men who love their wives and families are special. I hope someday I'll have someone who will want to come home to me."

Jack wanted to laugh. Who wouldn't want to come home to her? But her contemplative tone made him stop and think. "So Peter isn't the type to come home?"

Sophie glanced at him, but took her time answering the question. "I guess it all depends on what you define as coming home. The way I mean it is someone who puts his family first and his career second—someone who wants to spend more time with his family than anything else. My dad's career always came first."

"Does Peter's career come first?"

She shrugged and took a bite of her chili. "It's not fair to judge him when he isn't even a husband yet."

Yet? As in *her* husband? Her words hit him squarely in the chest. Although she'd said she didn't love Peter enough to marry him, the man was certainly still in the running.

Again, Jack felt inadequate. While his career didn't come first, his family certainly didn't come first, either.

She finished off the chili and set the mug in one of the chair's built-in cup holders. "Peter's father is a dedicated family man. I assume since Peter's had such a great example, he'll be a good husband to whomever he marries."

Jack didn't know what to say. This conversation wasn't what he'd had in mind. He didn't want to talk about Peter Elliot and whether or not he'd make a good husband for Sophie.

Discouraged, he finished off his chili and reached for the plate of fresh pineapple Hector had picked up from *Por El Rio*. Before he could eat any of the pineapple, Sophie put a chunk of the yellow fruit in her mouth, chewed and then promptly spit it out. Frantically, she grabbed the nearest water bottle, which happened to be Jack's, and drank greedily.

"I guess I'll pass on the pineapple," Jack said, setting the plate down.

Sophie's cheeks were pink as she lowered the water bottle. "Sorry, it was really bad, as in fermented." She started to place the water bottle in the other cup holder of her chair when she realized her bottle was still sitting there. "Oh, no. I took your water."

"Don't worry about it." He reached out and snagged the bottle and then took a long drink. "It's filtered, so even if you left floaties, I wouldn't know."

She swatted at his arm and laughed. "I didn't leave floaties."

Jack shrugged and took another drink. "Even better."

Sophie gazed forlornly at the innocent looking fruit. "I was really looking forward to the pineapple. I wonder if Hector has any bananas."

"Wait right here," Jack said. "I have a surprise for you."
He jumped up and grabbed his pack, pulling out the package
of M&M's. Sophie was applying a thin layer of lip gloss
when Jack sat back down and showed her the bag.

"You've had chocolate all this time?" she asked.

He ripped open the package. "I have a sweet tooth, and
I like chocolate. Do you want some?"

"What do you think?" Sophie held out her hand, and the
lip gloss dropped to the ground.

Jack leaned down and picked up the pink-colored tube.
"Island Daiquiri," he read. His eyes zeroed in on her sparkly
lips. "I wonder how close it is to tasting like the real thing?"

"I don't drink, so I wouldn't know." She plucked the lip
gloss out of his fingers and slipped the tube into her pocket.

Whether or not it tasted the same, Jack bet kissing her
would be just as intoxicating as drinking a frozen daiquiri
served at a club.

"So," he said, dumping a handful of candy into her
palm, "I'm glad you're done ignoring me."

"I...uh, wasn't ignoring you." She chose a blue M&M
and popped it in her mouth.

"Sophie," Jack teased. "Lying is a sin."

"Okay." She ducked her head. "I was ignoring you."

He reached over and took a piece of candy from her
hand. "Is it fair to assume you weren't talking to me because
I was kissing someone else?"

She shot a look at him and pointed her finger. "See, you
just admitted that you were kissing her."

"That was the wrong choice of words," Jack said,
shaking his head. "You have to believe me when I say she
kissed me, but I didn't kiss her back." He stole another piece
of candy from her hand. "But out of curiosity, why does it
bother you?"

"Because I—" Sophie stared down at her hands and fingered the two remaining colorful pieces of candy. "I...think I like you, Jack."

Her admission was sweet, and he could tell by the faint blush she was embarrassed by her honesty. Playfully, he nudged her in the shoulder. "Why would you?" he asked wryly.

Sophie looked at him totally exasperated. "Honestly, I don't know. You are the most arrogant, annoying and obnoxious man I've ever met."

Jack snorted at her answer. "Don't hold back, Sophie. Tell me how you really feel."

Her mouth lifted into a smile. "Why do you always tease me?"

"Because," he said, reaching over to take her hand and intertwine their fingers together. "I think I like you, too."

"Oh." She kept her gaze averted and popped the last few candies in her mouth.

"Aren't you going to require that I list all of your endearing qualities?" he asked.

"No."

"Do I at least get a kiss?"

Jack waited, his heart thrumming with anticipation. She didn't answer him, but he heard her draw in another deep breath.

"Sophie?"

"Be quiet." She pulled her hand out of his. "I'm thinking about it."

After only a few seconds of hesitation, Jack hooked a finger under her jaw and made her look at him. Their eyes met, and the amusement died as something powerful passed between them.

"Sometimes you think too much," he murmured just before his mouth covered hers.

Making the kiss brief, he pulled back quickly. Sophie looked stunned. "Just so you know, that was me kissing you."

Then Jack curved his hand around the back of her neck and brought her mouth to his, kissing her again, slowly and deliberately. She responded to the kiss, leaning into him as his fingers wove through her hair. Her lips were incredibly soft, tasting like chocolate and the daiquiri flavored lip gloss she had on.

Reluctantly, he pulled away and whispered huskily, "That kiss—you kissed me back. Can you see the difference?"

"Just a second." Her breath was ragged as she put a hand to her head. "My synapses aren't quite working, yet."

Jack placed his fingertips on the inside of her wrist and felt for a pulse. "Hmm, you're heart rate is erratic, too. I had no idea I had that kind of effect on women."

She laughed and tipped her head to look at him through her thick lashes. "Are you fishing for another compliment?"

"Well…" He grinned and lifted his eyebrows. "…you have to admit that *was* a pretty good kiss."

"For someone who is so good looking, you sure are insecure."

"Just how good-looking am I?"

"Ha!" she said, bumping his shoulder with her own. "I am not feeding your ego anymore."

"Okay. How about another kiss, then?"

Giving him a flirty smile, she said, "Only if I get more chocolate."

Jack promptly handed over the bag of M&M's. "They're all yours."

The moment of levity transformed into something more as her smile faded and her eyes darkened with desire.

Slowly, she leaned toward him and pressed her lips to his. The way she delivered this kiss left no doubt in Jack's mind that she liked him. A lot.

He slid his hands along the side of her neck to cradle her face in his palms. His thumb stroked her jaw as he tilted her head to deepen the kiss. They took their time exploring, tasting; and Jack reeled with emotions he'd never felt before.

At length, Jack eased back to break off the kiss. Sophie trembled as she laid her head against his shoulder. He wrapped his arms around her and held her close, feeling her heart beating just as rapidly as his own.

Neither of them spoke, just held on as their breathing became even again. He wasn't sure what had just happened, but the intensity of it scared him.

"Jack," Hector said, coming around the tent. "Don't eat the pineapple. It's rotten."

Sophie pushed away and sat back in her chair. Her cheeks were a lovely shade of pink.

"Yeah," Jack said, standing up. "We figured that out. Didn't we, Sophie?"

She kept her face down and only nodded her head. Hector laughed. "That's not the only thing you figured out, ¿no?"

"You're right. Sophie finally kissed me."

Her head snapped up. "Jack! You kissed me."

He shrugged. "Okay, it was a joint effort."

Hector walked past them, still chuckling. "I'm going to check on Fred. I'll be back in a minute."

Sophie stood up and put her hands on her hips. "Is this what it's going to be like all the time?"

"Like what?" he said with a laugh.

Glowering at him, Sophie started to walk away. "I need to get some sleep."

"Sophie," Jack called, following behind her. He was glad when she paused and let him catch up to her.

He took her hand and she automatically looked up in to his eyes. "I'm sorry." He brought her hand up and placed a kiss to the back of it. "I'll try not to be such a tease."

The corners of her mouth lifted slightly. "I just never know when you're serious or not."

"I seriously like you."

Her smile widened. "I like you, too."

He raised an eyebrow and grinned. "I know."

A giggle escaped. "You are incorrigible."

"Yeah." He tapped her on the nose. "But remember you like me."

Then he kissed her again, and, to his satisfaction, she kissed him back.

Chapter Sixteen

Jack bolted upright, his heart pounding madly from the bad dream that had awakened him. He listened carefully, only to hear the typical sounds of the jungle. In his dream Sophie's screams had seemed so real. As his pulse rate slowed, he still felt disturbed by the haunting images and needed to reassure himself that Sophie was okay. He tugged on a shirt and crawled out of his tent.

"Sophie," he whispered as he approached her tent. When she didn't answer, he slowly unzipped the door and pulled back the flap, whispering her name again. Relief washed over him as he studied her beautiful face, soft and relaxed in sleep.

Knowing she was safe, he scooted back and pulled on the zipper.

Suddenly her eyes flew open and she gasped, "What's wrong?" She sat up and placed her hand over her heart. "Did I have a nightmare?"

"No. I did."

There was just enough light from the rising sun to see her eyes fill with concern. "I'm sorry. Are you okay?"

"Yeah. Now that I know you're safe."

An expression of wonder crossed her face. "You dreamed about me?"

He slanted her a glance. "Let's just say since I've met you, you've been invading my sleep."

"Jack, that is so sweet."

"It is not." He half laughed and half groaned as he scrubbed his face with his hands. "That was the worst dream I've ever had, or at least that I can remember."

"What happened?"

Jack studied her for a few seconds. "Someone took you from your tent. I could hear you crying, but I didn't want to get up if it was just another nightmare. I even heard you call out my name. But by the time I finally crawled out of my tent, a man was taking you away. I was too late and couldn't catch up, and I knew I would never see you again." He laughed dryly. "I know it doesn't sound like much, but it was so real."

Sophie let out a long breath. "You don't have to tell me how real a bad dream can be. I've been dealing with almost the same nightmare for over a month."

He reached for her hand. "If you get up now, I'll make you some hot cocoa."

"Deal," she said, squeezing his fingers.

He tugged on her hand, pulling her a little closer. "Is there any chance I get a kiss this morning?"

She backed away. "I think it's highly probable, but first I need to brush my teeth."

"Then let's get your teeth brushed." He moved out of the tent doorway, giving her a playful smile. "I'm feeling a little insecure this morning."

She laughed and shook her head. "Sure you are."

* * *

The muscles in Jack's arms strained as he slashed his machete through the thick foliage, cutting down the dense growth to clear a path for Sophie and Hector. Their destination was *Del Sol*, the village where they hoped to find Edward Kendrick, or at least find out his whereabouts. Behind him, he could hear Sophie humming. It made him smile—something he'd been doing all day long.

He was falling in love with her. He knew it. He just couldn't tell her. Not yet. The feelings were still too scary for a man who believed he'd never get married.

Furthermore, what if Sophie didn't feel the same way? Yeah, she liked him, but that didn't mean she loved him. He wasn't sure he could take that kind of rejection again.

Letting out a deep sigh, he glanced up, spotting an open area where they could make camp. He turned to see how far back Sophie was from him when the toe of his boot caught on a vine, making him stumble. Unable to regain his balance, he fell forward, feeling the sharp blade of the machete slice into his shin.

Jack yelled out, biting back a curse word as the searing pain shot up his leg. He looked down to see his pant leg soaked in bright red blood. *Oh, man. This can't be good.*

Sophie rushed to his side. "Jack, what hap—" She stopped when she saw the blood. "Oh, Jack. Hang on, I need to put some pressure to stop the bleeding." She rummaged through her daypack, trying to find what she needed.

Hector knelt down next to Jack. "*Amigo*, what have you done?"

"How bad is it?" Jack questioned through gritted teeth.

"I'm not sure," Sophie answered while tearing away his pant leg. "I need to get the bleeding stopped."

The burning pain made him dizzy. Still, he rose up on his elbows to survey the damage. Sophie ripped open a pink plastic package, pulling out a thick white pad. Jack choked on a laugh when he realized what it was. "Are you using a woman's sanitary pad on me?"

"Yes. They're always clean, absorbent and large enough that I probably won't have to add more to stop the bleeding." She looked up and said softly, "Now lie back down and rest. I need to apply pressure for about five minutes. Once the bleeding has stopped, then I can assess the damage."

Jack moaned, feeling the forest floor press into his back as he lay back down.

Something crawled across his arm and he twisted his head to make sure it wasn't anything deadly. A small yellow butterfly took flight as he moved his arm slightly.

The pain had localized to the area where the sharp blade of his machete had probably left considerable damage. How was he going to manage not fainting if Sophie had to sew him up?

After some time had passed, he felt Sophie lift the pad. He watched her lean over to inspect the wound. Grimacing, she replaced the pad. "What's wrong?" he asked, feeling a little alarmed.

Her features relaxed into a forced smile. "We just need to keep the pressure on for a little while longer." She looked at him with concern. "How's your pain?"

Jack closed his eyes and grunted, "It hurts."

"Just keep taking deep breaths," she soothed, pressing firmly on the wound. "The bleeding has slowed down, but not enough so that I can treat you."

What did she mean by that? Jack swallowed hard, hating how much he detested needles. His worst fears were confirmed when Sophie said, "Hector, can you come over here and apply pressure while I get what I need to stitch it up?"

Jack sat up abruptly. "Does it really need stitches?"

Sophie switched places with Hector, grabbing her medical bag. "I'm afraid so. Don't worry, I'll numb the area first and give you something for pain. All you should feel is a little pressure."

Don't worry? Shoot, he was just about to hand over his man card to the woman he was falling in love with. "How exactly are you going to numb it?"

"I'll inject a small amount of two percent lidocaine," she answered, seemingly unaware of the panic racing through his veins.

Inject. Just thinking about what that meant made him feel as if all the blood had drained from his face. Sophie looked alarmed as she moved near his shoulder. "Jack, you're as white as a sheet. Please lie back down." She placed her cool hand to his forehead, smoothing her fingers through his hair. "Do you feel nauseated?"

"No, just a little dizzy." If he was lucky, maybe he'd die and save face.

* * *

Sophie brushed her fingers along Jack's forehead again, concerned with how pale he looked. She wanted to press a kiss to his furrowed brow, hating the pain he must be in. "Are you allergic to any meds?" she questioned, grabbing her medical bag and removing various vials of medication.

Jack opened his eyes and shook his head. "Not that I know of." When she pulled out a few hypodermic needles, his blue eyes popped open with shock. "What are you doing with those?"

"I need to give you a shot of Penicillin and probably a little morphine to help with the pain."

"No shots," he stated firmly. "I hate shots."

She smiled. "Most people do, Jack." Finding the morphine, she tore open an alcohol wipe to clean off the vial. "You have to have the antibiotic. And believe me, after the lidocaine wears off, you'll thank me for the morphine."

"Why can't I just take some pills?" He looked at her intently. "Please, Sophie. I really hate needles."

"You can take oral pain meds if you want, but I insist on the Penicillin shot."

The look he gave her reminded her of some of the little boys she'd taken care of over the years. "Will the antibiotic be the only shot you have to give me?" he asked, almost pleading.

She couldn't help laughing. "Well, remember I have to use a small needle to numb your leg. If you're up to date on your tetanus, then those will be the only ones."

He glowered at her. "I don't need a tetanus shot."

"Jack, I need you to be truthful. As much as I'd like to shut you up sometimes, lockjaw would not be the way to go."

"Very funny. I had to get one two years ago after an incident while fishing." He closed his eyes again. "So...how many shots are we actually talking about?"

"No more than three."

His eyes flew open in alarm, and he grumbled, "Just knock me out."

"Honestly, Jack," Sophie said on a laugh. "You're worse than a four-year-old."

He flung his arm over his eyes. "Laugh all you want, but I have a serious aversion to needles." Then he peeked out from under his arm. "Where exactly are you giving me the Penicillin shot?"

"Well, since you're so ripped, I can give it in the deltoid."

"Dumb it down, Sophie."

A giggle escaped as she placed her hand on his well-developed bicep. "The deltoid muscle is right here." She skimmed her fingers up his arm and underneath his sleeve.

Jack smiled sheepishly. "Oh, yeah. I knew that."

Hector snickered, but didn't make a comment. Sophie gave Jack's arm a gentle squeeze. "Of course you did. Now just try to relax and trust me. I promise to take good care of you."

Jack's gaze locked on hers. "I think I like having you take care of me. It's been a long time since..." He gave her a crooked smile. "Well, let's just say *I* usually take care of Jack."

She couldn't help the intense feelings washing over her. It probably wasn't the best time to confess she was falling in love with him. Leaning down, she gently brushed her lips against his mouth. He placed his hand on the back of her head, preventing her from pulling away, and prolonged the kiss. Heady emotions swirled, and she could hardly think straight.

She pulled away and Jack stroked her cheek with his thumb. "I hope you don't do that with all your patients," he muttered dryly.

"Never," she said breathlessly. "I'm in pediatrics, remember?"

"That's pretty good, *amigo*," Hector teased. "You even managed another kiss today while injured and complaining about a needle."

Jack dropped his hand and smiled weakly. "Yeah, what can I say? The doctor finds me irresistible."

Sophie laughed softly and scooted away from Jack. The truth was she *did* find him irresistible. A fact that had her wondering what would happen when she had to return to Colorado.

Pushing the questions from her mind, Sophie reconstituted the powdered Penicillin with saline water. She rolled the vial between her palms until it was completely mixed. Getting a new syringe, she drew up the medication and then moved toward Jack.

"That is a very big needle," Jack said, eyeing her with a leery expression.

Sophie replaced the cap. "Jack, it's the exact same size I used on those children the other day." She set the syringe aside and pulled out a bottle of Lortab tablets. "Are you sure you don't want the shot of morphine?"

He shook his head. "Pills, Sophie. Give me the pills."

Chuckling, she shook out two of the tablets and helped support his head as he took both pills and washed them down with a drink of water. "You should start to feel the effects of the medicine within twenty to thirty minutes."

He gave her an impish look. "I don't think I should be held accountable for anything I say while under the influence."

She patted him on his chest. "Don't worry. I never take anything you say seriously."

"Ha ha," he said as she pushed up his sleeve and prepped his arm with an alcohol wipe.

Feeling him tense his impressive muscle, she massaged his arm beneath her target. "Hey, try to relax. I promise it won't be that bad. I'm good at this."

He kept his eyes shut tight. "Just tell me when you're going to do it."

Sophie talked to him softly, and then as she injected the needle, she said, "Okay. Now." Grateful he didn't pull away or tighten his muscle, she withdrew the needle. "See, that wasn't so bad."

He looked at her with disbelief. "You already did it?"

"Yep, all done."

He raised an eyebrow. "Wow, you are good."

"I have lots of practice on children."

The corners of his mouth tipped up. "Are you saying I'm not a man?"

She leaned over and kissed him quickly. "That is something I could never say." She ran her hand across the dark stubble on his jaw. "You are definitely all man."

A look of pure satisfaction sparked in his eyes.

Sophie turned away and moved down toward his leg. Hector was still at his post, keeping pressure on the wound. He had the biggest smile on his face.

She had completely forgotten she and Jack weren't alone. "I'm just trying to help him remain calm," she said, trying to defend her actions.

"It seems to be working," Hector said, moving over for Sophie to take his place.

"Smart aleck." She removed the pad and noted the bleeding had slowed enough for her to suture it closed. She glanced over at Hector. "I'd like to move him into his tent as soon as I'm done with the stitches. Could you please set it up for me?"

"*Sí.* I'll get your tent up as well. But if you need anything, just let me know."

"Thank you," she said, removing a disposable razor from her bag. "Jack, after I numb your leg, I'm going to shave around the laceration."

He groaned again. "Now you're shaving my legs?"

She bit back a smile. "Don't worry. We've already established you're a man. I promise not to do more than I have to."

Jack grunted and waved his hand for her to continue.

Sophie injected the lidocaine, and he only flinched a little, even though she knew the medication burned. She moved the needle and injected several different parts, trying to be thorough. Testing the skin around the wound with the tip of the needle, she determined he was sufficiently numb. She quickly shaved the area and then prepped it for stitches.

The laceration was deep, but hadn't gone through the muscle. If she could avoid infection, Jack should heal okay. She irrigated the wound with sterile saline, then sutured the deep tissue with absorbable stitches that would dissolve over time. By the time she closed the top layer of skin with non-absorbable sutures, the pain medicine already seemed to be taking effect.

Groggily, Jack said, "I hardly felt a thing. Are you all done?"

She moved up to sit next to his shoulder again. "Yes. You were a very good patient."

"Thanks." He turned his head, staring at her with those sky blue eyes.

As she returned his gaze, her stomach tightened with emotion. She had to face reality. Sophie more than liked him—she was in love with him.

Right then, she felt sorry for Peter. Unrequited love was not an optimistic prospect. Sure, Jack said he liked her, but given his views on marriage, he would probably run the other way if he knew she had fallen in love with him.

Looking away, she stood and called for Hector to help her move Jack. He had just finished setting up the tents, and together they managed to get Jack moved inside his. The scent that always clung to Jack teased her senses as she helped situate him in the small confines of the shelter. Her overwhelming feelings seemed to crowd around her, stealing her breath. She needed fresh air and a chance to sort out her thoughts.

"Don't leave me," Jack said, capturing her hand and preventing her escape.

The warmth from his hand edged up her arm. "Okay," she said softly. "I'll stay here until you fall asleep."

"Thanks," he murmured without opening his eyes.

When his breathing became even and slow, Sophie started to untangle her hand, but Jack's grip tightened. "I'm not asleep yet."

She squeezed his fingers. "Okay, I won't leave, but you need to rest."

Just when she thought he had finally fallen asleep, he stirred and opened one eye. "Hey, Sophie?"

"Hmm?"

"Do you really think I'm ripped?"

Oh, this man. "Yes," she said giggling. "Now go to sleep."

Chapter Seventeen

Jack woke up sometime during the night, acutely aware of the throbbing pain that radiated from his lower leg all the way up to his chest. He ran his tongue across his parched lips, wishing he had a drink. Moving slightly, he eyed his tent door, wondering if he had the strength to unzip it to get help. The pain in his leg was bad enough to request a shot of morphine. He still didn't like needles, but Sophie had eased his fear considerably.

Sophie. Just thinking about her and the loving way she cared for him took his breath away. The longing he felt to be with her nearly surpassed the pain from his wound. He never realized the desire to be with someone could be so intense, and it wasn't just in a physical way either. It was as if he had been living in a cold world, void of light, and Sophie was like the sun, warming him and lighting up his soul.

He needed her. He wanted her. He might even love her.

Another electric shock of pain reminded him that *right now*, he needed more pain medicine.

Gritting his teeth together, he struggled to sit up. His head swam, and he felt beads of perspiration dot his forehead. He drew in a slow, deep breath and waited for the dizziness to pass. Before he could start to move toward the tent door, it opened up and Sophie slipped inside, holding a small LED lantern.

"Hey, I thought I heard you wake up." She knelt beside him. "How's the pain?"

"Bad enough I might consider a shot of morphine."

She gave him a small smile. "At this point, oral meds would be much better. They last longer and will give you better pain control."

She placed two pain pills in his palm. "You should take these now," she said, offering him a water bottle.

"Thanks." He swallowed the pills and watched as she leaned over to check his leg. The soft glow from the lantern silhouetted the curve of her cheek, her full lips and the gentle slope of her perfect small nose. She was so beautiful.

Her fingers lightly brushed his leg as she checked the sutures. Her touch did more to combat the pain than any pill did. She replaced the bandage and glanced over to catch him staring at her.

"What's wrong? Did I hurt you?"

"No." Jack gave her a sheepish smile. "I was just admiring my pretty doctor."

He watched the slow curve of her mouth lift into a radiant smile. "I think I like you this way."

"And what way would that be?"

She moved to sit beside him. "All sweet and saying nice things."

"I've said you were pretty before."

"If I remember correctly, you said, 'I have no desire to take a beautiful woman into the jungle.'"

Yeah, he had said that. "But I also told you how pretty you looked in the dress I bought you."

"True." She gave him a level look. "Then you sat with another girl and let her feed you fresh fruit."

He rolled his eyes. "Don't remind me."

Sophie gave a soft giggle and pulled out a protein bar from the pocket of the Texas A&M sweat pants she had on. "I brought you something to eat." She opened the package and broke of a piece. "Would you like me to feed it to you?" she teased.

Jack grinned. "Yes, please."

Shaking her head, Sophie slanted forward and placed the chocolate morsel between his lips.

The soft touch of her fingers against his mouth made his heart skip, then take off at a rapid pace.

A faint blush colored Sophie's cheeks as she eased away from him. Their eyes held, and Jack knew he had been wrong. Having a woman feed him did do something for him.

He swallowed, and Sophie anticipated his need for a drink, offering him the water bottle. "Thank you." His voice came out low and soft, intimating the eddy of emotions rushing through him. He was falling more and more in love with her by the minute and wasn't sure how long he could hold back from telling her.

"You're welcome." She moistened her lips and handed him the rest of the protein bar. "You need to finish this so the pain meds won't upset your stomach."

Feeling slightly dizzy, whether from her touch or his injury, he took the bar and bit into it. The sooner he ate it, the sooner he could lie back down.

Sophie brought her knees to her chest, wrapped her arms around them and rested her chin on top, watching Jack with a soft look. "We won't be able to travel for the next few days."

"I'm sorry." He grimaced, feeling guilty for holding up their journey. "But we're only a day or so away from *Del Sol*. I'm sure if I rest tomorrow, I'll be up for the travel the next day."

He took another bite of the protein bar as Sophie sat up and shook her head. "No you won't." She pointed to his leg. "You need at least forty-eight hours with your leg elevated or lying flat to prevent swelling. After two days, we'll evaluate things and go from there."

"I'm a fast healer," he said, finishing off his meal. When he saw she was ready to protest again, he said, "But, like you said…we'll see."

"Yes we will." She took the empty wrapper and stuck it in her pocket. "Now you need to lie back down and go to sleep."

Jack's stomach tightened with anxiety as she moved toward the door. He wasn't ready for her to leave. Even though he knew it was selfish, he reached out and took a hold of her hand. "Please don't go."

"What is it?" she questioned, her brown eyes filled with concern.

"I...I don't want to be alone." The words were so literal to him—he didn't want to be alone anymore. Discovering Sophie after all these years had been a gift from God, and Jack was going to do everything he could to make things right and accept it.

"Okay." She settled next to him, once again hugging her knees to her chest and resting her chin on top. "I'll stay here until you fall asleep."

"Thanks." He licked his lips. "Maybe you could answer a few questions for me."

"Sure." She eyed him curiously. "That is, if I know the answers."

Part of him didn't want to talk about those days following the betrayal by his fiancée, his brother, and even his parents, but he knew in order to find his way back to God, he had to talk about what had happened.

"When Heather told me she was pregnant." Jack's voice faltered, and he cleared his throat. "I was hurt and very angry, not only with her and Adam, but with my parents and...with God."

"That's understandable." Her eyes softened. "I can't imagine how painful that time was for you."

He clenched and unclenched his hands.

"When Adam came to talk to me, his idea of an apology was to tell me it was my own fault for leaving Heather alone so I could go and build houses for poor people and preach to them about Jesus."

"What a jerk," Sophie said, surprising him and making him laugh.

"Yeah, well I hit the jerk in the face and broke his nose." He smiled. "It really messed up the wedding pictures."

"That must have been hard for you," she said quietly. "To have to attend their wedding."

"It was." He swallowed and met her gaze. "But I don't recall one person ever acknowledging my feelings. My parents were angry with me for hitting Adam. They were even angrier when I'd made it clear I had no intention of attending the marriage ceremony."

"How soon was the wedding?"

He gave a humorless laugh. "Believe it or not, since the church was reserved and paid for, they kept it on the same day Heather and I were supposed to be married."

"You're kidding!"

"I wish I were." He loved the indignant look on her face. "It was like my parents and Heather's parents thought everyone would think Adam had always been the groom and there had just been a mistake on the wedding announcements. I was messing up their plan by not yielding to their wishes to get over my anger and support my brother." He laughed again. "My parents even had our pastor talk to me about how my sin was greater by not forgiving Heather and Adam. In the end, I was made out to be the bad guy because I wasn't doing what God wanted."

"That's ridiculous. You didn't even have time to process everything. Even God knows you needed time to work through all your emotions."

Was that really true? Had God been willing to let Jack forgive when he was ready? Still, Jack had a hard time with all that had happened, especially since he had been doing God's work.

"Even if you're right, why would God have allowed that to happen to me in the first place? I was out doing exactly what the Bible teaches, and the thanks I got was my fiancée pregnant with another man's baby—my brother's baby."

Jack hated how harsh his voice sounded. He wanted to get rid of this bitterness once and for all. He just didn't know how to.

Sophie's eyes remained soft and understanding, without a hint of condemnation. "God didn't make Heather and Adam betray you. They made a choice, and as much as it pained both you and God, it was still their choice. The hard part is what *you* choose to do. You can choose to turn your back on God and remain unhappy and angry, or you can choose to forgive and see what else God has in store for you."

Her simple words were exactly what Jack needed to hear. He'd had a choice. Like it or not, how he'd handled everything had been his choice. Even now, he had a choice. Since hanging onto his anger hadn't brought him any peace, maybe it was time to pick the other option.

Suddenly, there in a small tent in the middle of the jungle, Jack knew what he wanted more than anything. He shut his eyes and prayed in his mind for God to forgive him. He prayed for strength to forgive his parents and to forgive Heather and Adam.

An intense pressure of warmth squeezed his chest and spread through his limbs, and his eyes burned with emotion.

"Jack," Sophie whispered. "Are you okay?" Her fingers were feather light as they wiped away a tear that had seeped out from under his eyelid.

He opened his eyes to find her face close to his own. "Yeah." He cupped her cheek with his palm and met her gaze. Could it be that this woman was what God had in store for him? His heart slammed against his chest as he finally acknowledged the extent of his feelings.

"I…love you, Sophie," he said in a shaky voice.

Her eyes widened, and she sucked in a sharp breath. He could tell she was shocked. *Shoot.* The stupid pain meds were making his tongue loose. He was about to make some wise crack about his premature declaration but stopped when Sophie's mouth curved up into the most radiant smile.

"Oh, Jack." She hiccupped a light laugh. "I love you, too."

He relaxed and ran his thumb across her bottom lip. "I think I knew that."

Sophie smiled. "Are you sure this isn't the pain medicine talking? You told me I shouldn't take you seriously."

"I'm feeling pretty cloudy, but not enough to make me say something I don't mean." He took a deep breath. "I'm not good enough for you, though."

"Jack—"

He stopped her with another intense look. "I'm not. But I'll do everything I can to be worthy of you."

Tears shimmered in her eyes. "I think I'd like that." She turned her face and pressed a kiss to his palm.

His head felt fuzzy as the pain medicine kicked in. "You better go back to your own tent. I'll call if I need you."

He smiled playfully and amended his words. "Well, I know I
need you, so I'll call if I need more pain medicine."

She traced the curve of his mouth with her fingertip.
"Okay. Good night, Jack."

He kissed her finger. "Good night." She started to pull
away again and Jack stopped her one last time. "Hey,
Sophie…I really do love you."

She grinned. "I know."

He gave a low chuckle. "Oh no, you're starting to sound
too much like me." He could feel his eyelids growing heavy.

Just before letting go, he felt Sophie press a kiss to his
forehead and whisper, "I really love you too, Jack."

* * *

Jack sat on a log, pouting like a spoiled little boy, his
arms crossed over his chest in defiance. "I can walk, so I
don't see why we can't leave."

Sophie bit her lip and mentally counted to ten. Talk
about a non-compliant patient. His idea of feeling better
meant he could do everything he had done before, including
leaving their campsite. She met his scowl. "Don't look at me
like that. If you rip open your stitches, we have to start all
over again."

"I won't rip out the stitches," he growled.

She marched over and stood in front of him, placing her
hands on her hips. "You are so grouchy this morning."

His mouth tilted up slightly. "Yeah, well, you're really
bossy this morning."

This coming from the man she'd taken care of for the
past twenty-four hours. "I am not bossy. I just expect my
patient to follow my orders."

"Sophie, we can't stay here forever," he moaned, trying
a different tactic.

She snorted unladylike. "One day is not forever, Jack."

She knelt down to check his leg. "It actually looks pretty good. Maybe if we take it slow, we can leave tomorrow."

Jack reached for her hand as she stood up. "What difference will it make to wait another day?"

He twined their fingers together, and Sophie's autonomic nervous system immediately responded to his touch, increasing her pulse rate and making her brain foggy. "The rest will aid in the healing process. Please, just trust me, okay?"

"Okay."

"Really?" She eyed him warily. "You're going to listen to me?"

"Yep." Jack tugged on her hand, pulling her down onto his lap. "So, are you going to stay by me and entertain me all day?"

"Sure. But I don't sing or dance. If I had a few balloons, I could make you a dog or a giraffe."

"Well," he said, giving her a mischievous smile. "Since we don't have any balloons and you can't entertain me otherwise, I'd like to hear just what it was that made you fall in love with me."

"I'd have to say it was the charming way you consented to take me along with you the first day I met you," she said dryly.

"Hey, I want to hear my good qualities. Come on, remember I'm injured."

"Right." The playful look in his eyes gave her an answer. "You make me laugh, even if I don't want to."

He winked. "Now that's what I'm talkin' about." He pulled her close to him. "What else?"

She may as well go along with this. After all, it was going to be a long day. "Hmm, you are very attractive."

He raised an eyebrow and flexed. "Don't forget ripped."

Bulging muscles had never been her thing—until now. Her mouth went dry. "Well, there is that."

Jack gave her a smug smile. "Keep going."

She twisted their joined hands so his was on top. "I like your hands," she said tracing the veins on his very masculine hand with her finger.

Then she trailed her fingers up his arm and across his chest. "And you have a good heart." Through her flattened palm, she could feel his rapid pulse beating beneath his shirt. Looks like Jack's autonomic nervous system reacted just like hers.

Her hand moved from his chest to his face, his whiskers rough beneath her palm. Once again, she gazed into pools of blue and noticed the smug look was no longer there. "But I think the thing I love the most are your eyes."

Jack took a ragged breath. "Okay. That was good. But maybe you should tell me what you don't like about me." He sat back, releasing her hand. "Good grief, woman, you can't say stuff like that when Hector isn't around."

She lifted one shoulder up. "I can always go get my journal and read everything I don't like about you."

"Ouch."

She laughed. "Ready for more flattery?"

"Please."

Pressing close to him, she slid her arms around his neck and whispered, "I also love the way you kiss me."

Jack proceeded to prove her point and kissed her long and slow.

She wasn't sure how much time had passed when Hector cleared his throat and said, "When you two come up for air, I'll have lunch ready."

* * *

Jack gritted his teeth, determined not to complain.

They'd been traveling all day, and his leg throbbed as he slowly followed Hector and Sophie. In spite of the pain, there was no way he was going to let his doctor know about it—they were so close to *Del Sol*.

Sweat trickled down his back as he paused to take a drink of water. He probably needed another pain pill, but he hated how loopy they made him feel. A wave of dizziness hit him, and Jack gripped the walking stick tighter, hoping he didn't pass out.

Sophie looked over her shoulder and immediately rushed to his side. "Are you okay?"

No, and he didn't want to talk about it. "I'm fine. Let's keep moving," he said sharply.

A hurt look flashed in her eyes. "Do you need more pain medicine?"

I am such a jerk. Sophie had been nothing but kind and caring toward him. "Sorry I snapped at you." He was getting good at apologies, especially since he meant them. "Maybe I should rest for a few minutes. I probably need something for pain too."

And just like that, Sophie was by his side, offering her assistance. Crouching down, she lifted his pant leg. Her fingers felt cool as she probed the injured area. "Wow, Jack, that leg is very swollen. It must be throbbing." She looked up at him, censure written all over her face. "Why didn't you say something earlier?"

"Well, you can just add stubborn to your journal entries."

She narrowed her eyes. "I'll be sure and write that one next to hard headed."

That made him smile, hopefully hiding just how much pain he actually was in. "Sorry I'm such a non-compliant patient. If you want to fire me, I'll understand."

The corner of her mouth lifted, and she sighed. "I won't fire you." She stood up, placing her hands at the small of her back and stretched. "Are you sure you can't ride on the donkey? Sometimes the two of you seem so similar. I swear his name should be Jack instead of Fred."

Jack chortled. "I can't believe you just said that. Now I *know* I'm getting on your nerves. Was that an intentional pun? You know as in jack—"

Sophie clapped her hand over his mouth. "Don't you dare say it."

Expelling a puff of laughter through her fingers, Jack moved her hand away. "Okay, but that was very clever."

She looked at him, totally exasperated. "You are impossible! I never meant it that way. I just—"

"Compared me to a donkey."

He could tell she was trying not to laugh, but Jack caught the grin on her face before she turned away.

"I'll get your pain medicine." She slipped her backpack off and searched for the bottle of Lortab.

"Thank you," Jack said when she gave him one pain pill.

Her lips twitched. "When we reach *Del Sol*, you are elevating that leg for a least four hours, understand?"

"Yes, ma'am."

A smile creased her pretty face as she put on her backpack again. "Do you need any help?"

Jack wasn't about to pass up an opportunity to have her close. He'd already declined previously and regretted it. "Yes." He held out his arm and Sophie slipped next to him, wrapping her arm around his waist. He looked down and squeezed her shoulders. "Now why didn't we do this earlier?"

She tipped her face up and squinted. "Because you wouldn't let me."

Jack flashed a self-depreciating smile. "Oh yeah." Then mimicking Forest Gump, he said, "I am not a smart man."

* * *

Sophie was relieved when they entered the outskirts of *Del Sol*. Although Jack was doing his best to hide the pain he was in, she knew he couldn't go much further. On their last break, Hector had made Jack a walking stick, and she could tell he was relying heavily on the device to keep moving forward.

The village was close. As they drew nearer, her heart fluttered with apprehension. She'd been so preoccupied with Jack's injury, it had been easy to set aside her worry about her father's wellbeing. But now that she was almost to their destination, her mind raced with the possible outcomes.

Knowing her father, the scenario she hoped to find was that he'd simply become so engrossed in his work that he'd forgotten to come up for air long enough to contact the university or his daughter. The other possibilities were much more difficult to dwell on.

Jack cast a sympathetic look toward her. "You doing okay?"

"Yes."

His eyes skimmed over her and focused on the left side of her head. "At least it's dried now."

Sophie wrinkled her nose. "Ugh. I'm not sure that's any better."

About an hour ago, she'd walked under a low canopy of trees where a variety of birds had perched. Sophie had stopped, wanting to get a few pictures of the colorful display. It had been just her luck—good luck, according to Hector—to have one of the birds poop on her head.

It didn't feel lucky. It felt disgusting, especially when it had also dripped onto her shoulder.

"I just hope it all comes out."

Jack lifted a brow. "It should."

That didn't sound very promising. "Do you think Hector is there yet?"

Since Jack couldn't travel as quickly as before, Hector had gone on ahead of them. He'd promised to find out any information he could about her father and then procure accommodations for Sophie to take a bath. Although she wasn't sure about her dad's living arrangements, it would be nice if she could get cleaned up where he was staying. In the past, if something was available, he would be housed in one of the village huts. Other times, it was just a tent.

"Yeah," Jack said. "He's making much better time with Fred than you are with me."

"That's okay. You're much better company than a donkey."

"But just as stubborn?"

He was teasing her, and it helped to ease the mounting anxiety each step brought. "Probably."

Jack smiled, but she could see the tightening of his jaw and knew he was in pain. Sophie was worried about him and hoped that rest and elevating his leg would reduce the inflammation.

A few minutes later, they entered *Del Sol*. Right away, Sophie could tell the village was larger than *Por El Rio*. The hum of several generators could be heard above the laughter and chatter of the local people as they studied the strangers with curiosity.

In one covered pavilion, a television was on with a large crowd watching a soccer game. Sophie scanned the faces, hoping to see her father among them. Anxiety lodged like a rock against Sophie's throat when she spotted Hector coming their way and her father wasn't with him.

"I was just about to come looking for you," Hector said, appearing to be relieved to see them. "I've arranged for hot baths and a meal." Hector glanced at Sophie and pointed to her bird-poop-encrusted hair. "You can go first, *chica*. Jack and I will get things unpacked."

"But what about my father? Did you find out anything?"

Hector hesitated. "The people here are very cautious of strangers, and it's been hard to track down the right person to talk to." His gaze shifted to Jack. "Didn't you say you have the name of the village leader here?"

Jack nodded his head. "If my information is correct, I think his name is Carlos."

"Then let's go find him," Sophie said.

Jack and Hector exchanged a look Sophie couldn't decipher. Then Jack placed his hand on the small of her back. "Since it might take a few minutes to locate Carlos, why don't you go with Hector, and I'll see what I can find out while you wash your hair."

"That's a good idea." Hector gestured behind him. "The bathhouse is just over there. The owner said if you hurry, the water will definitely be hot. Jack can talk to Carlos and come and find us after."

Sophie was reluctant to agree. She knew her father wouldn't care if she was cleaned up or not, but already a crowd of villagers had gathered around them, and several of them were pointing to her hair. "Okay, but I won't be long." If she was quick, Hector could take her to find Jack.

"I'll see you soon," Jack said before he turned and headed in the direction of the group of men watching the soccer game.

Fingers of worry gripped her stomach as Sophie followed him with her eyes. What would Jack find out about her father?

Part of her wanted to run after him and insist on going with him, but another part of her wanted to delay knowing the outcome. Deep inside, Sophie had a sinking feeling her father wasn't here.

Chapter Eighteen

I t only took Jack a few minutes to confirm that Carlos was the village leader and where he could find him. He pivoted on the walking stick and sucked in a quick breath at the sharp pain that jolted up his leg. A wave of nausea hit him, and he stood still until the world stopped spinning. At least Sophie was no longer watching him. She wouldn't let him take one more step if she knew how bad he felt.

It was so stupid to be this incapacitated, unable to simply walk without assistance. His hand tightened its hold on the stick, and he forced himself to ignore the pain the movement caused and to keep going forward. As he slowly made his way south, Jack detected an ache in his back that made his skin feel prickly. In fact, his body ached all over, making him wish he'd taken two pain pills instead of one.

Many of the locals watched Jack as he limped along the path. Several children followed alongside him. Their curiosity at the stranger was evident by their comments to one another as they speculated about what had happened to the gringo to make him walk so funny. Despite feeling so bad, he offered a smile to the kids and reassured them he had not been attacked by a puma.

When he spoke in their native tongue, the group of children started pummeling him with questions, wanting to know where he was from, why he was here, and if he had seen a puma. Apparently, the large cat had been sighted outside the village a few nights ago and had killed a goat.

Already slowed by his injury, Jack's progress was heeded even more by the growing masses of brown skinned boys and girls.

He finally had to stop moving and leaned heavily on the walking stick. Then, to his relief, a loud voice instructed the children to leave the man alone.

The kids scattered like cockroaches, and Jack found himself standing eye to eye with an older gruff looking man that had to be Carlos.

"*Hola*," Jack said, offering his hand. "Are you Carlos?"

The man took his hand, shaking it briefly. "*Sí*." He studied Jack with somber brown eyes. "You have come to find Dr. Edward?"

"Yes," Jack said hopefully. "Is he here?"

Carlos slowly shook his head. "I'm sorry, *amigo*, but he is not here."

Jack didn't want to ask the next question. He was sure he wouldn't like the answer.

"Do you know where he is?"

The man lowered his eyes as an uncomfortable silence followed. Jack waited and could feel his pulse throbbing in his aching head. Finally, Carlos met his gaze and said, "You have brought Dr. Edward's daughter, ¿*no*?"

When Jack nodded his head, he immediately regretted the movement. The mounting headache was making him dizzy.

Carlos pointed to a hut a few yards away. "Dr. Edward's bungalow is over there. He hoped his daughter would come looking for him if anything ever happened to him."

Jack knew right then the news wasn't good. He was aware of how much this was going to hurt Sophie and a band of sorrow tightened around his chest, making it hard to draw a deep breath.

"Dr. Edward died nearly six weeks ago," Carlos said somberly. "Come, I will show you the things he left for his *niña*."

Six weeks? They had missed him by a lousy six weeks. Silently, Jack followed the man to Edward's humble home. Carlos held open the door, and Jack entered, surprised to find the hut so well furnished. It almost looked like someone still lived here. On one end, Jack noted two cots and a small dresser. A bookcase, filled with a variety of books, stood next to a rocking chair. A small table with two chairs sat near the middle of the room with a basket sitting on top.

Carlos walked to the table, pointing to the basket. "Dr. Edward wanted his daughter to have these things."

Jack felt another wave of dizziness hit as he walked next to the table. Leaning heavily on the make-shift cane, he wiped the back of his hand across his forehead. Despite the warm humid air, Jack actually felt chilled.

Fingering the items in the basket, Jack picked up a photo of Sophie and smiled at the younger version of her. She was just as beautiful.

He thumbed through a few more photos as he listened to Carlos explain Edward's death; a death which had been no accident and had not been due to natural causes. Jack reeled at the news, trying to figure out how to soften the blow to Sophie. He hated to be the one to have to tell her and felt completely inadequate to offer her comfort. He had told Sophie he loved her—and he did—he just didn't know if he would be enough.

* * *

Sophie pulled on a yellow tee, her last remaining clean shirt. She would need to see about getting her laundry done. Jack would know who to ask. The khaki pants were mud-stained, but unless she put on the dress Jack bought her, the pants were her only option.

The trivial thought about dirty clothing helped to keep the nagging fear about her father's whereabouts from overwhelming her.

There was a tiny flicker of hope left inside her that he was still alive, and she held onto to it as tight as she could.

She ran a comb through her damp hair, grateful the bird droppings had washed out. Although she'd planned on bathing quickly, her bath had been delayed when the proprietor found out she was a doctor. He had a granddaughter with a splinter imbedded in her foot that was starting to get infected. Sophie had used some of the hot water to soak the little girl's foot in before she extracted the sliver of wood.

Anxious to meet up with Jack, she exited the small bathhouse. Hector wasn't waiting for her, but Jack was. He sat on a rudimentary bench, hewn from a log, leaning over with his head in his hands.

"Jack?"

He lifted his face and squinted, watching her come toward him. "You look nice," he said, his voice gravely and low. He cleared his throat. "Do you feel better?"

Sophie stood in front of him and studied his face. His blue eyes were clouded and dull. The skin beneath the dark stubble covering his jaw appeared to be pale. "I think the question is do you feel worse?"

He licked his lips and tried to shrug. "Maybe a little."

Taking a seat beside him, Sophie touched his forehead with the back of her hand. "Jack, you're burning up. It has to be your leg."

She started to rise up from the bench, but Jack took her hand and held her back. "It can wait."

"Jack—"

"Please, Sophie. We need to talk first."

A knot of dread twisted her stomach. She didn't want to talk. She just wanted to focus on getting Jack well. Being a doctor was automatic. Caring for someone else meant she didn't have to think about herself.

Ignoring the plea, she moved and knelt down to raise his pant leg. "This won't take long to assess." She met his gaze, and he must have read the desperation in her eyes because he didn't protest any further.

Heat radiated from the reddened skin around the wound, and the stitches strained against the swelling tissue. "I don't think the antibiotics you're taking are doing the trick. It's definitely infected."

"Okay. What do we do?"

She tried to think of the supplies she had available. Treating Mario had depleted her options. "I need to give you a stronger antibiotic called Rocephin. It should cover whatever is causing the infection, but it has to be given through an IV or as an injection."

Jack licked his lips again. "Either way it involves a needle, right?"

"Yes."

"I don't want an IV."

"Ok. But that means you need to drink plenty of water, and you have to keep that leg elevated for the next twenty-four hours. No exceptions."

"Yes, ma'am," he said, obviously too weak to argue. "By the way, Hector already took your backpack and medical stuff to the hut you'll be sleeping in tonight."

Sophie wanted to take Jack there and get the new medicine in him as soon as possible. The odds Jack would let her do it right now were about as good as her father walking around the corner.

Slowly, she moved back to sit next to him. Jack took her hand in his. The warmth from his palm was a stark contrast to her cool skin. Bracing herself, she bravely met his gaze.

"Sophie, I don't know how—" He drew in a shallow breath and tightened his grip on her hand. "I found out—"

No. No. No. She swallowed hard as moisture gathered in her eyes. But deep down she knew what he was going to say.

"Jack, I think I know." Her voice cracked, and she lowered her lashes. "I think I've known all along."

"I'm so sorry, Sophie." His arms came around her, pulling her close. "I'm so sorry."

Clutching his shirt, she buried her face in his chest and wept. Her dad was never coming home again, and it was too late to tell him how much she loved him.

Jack let her cry. He didn't say anything, just held her and rubbed one hand soothingly on her back. As her tears subsided, the need to know everything made her edge back so she could see his face. "When? How? Did Carlos say?"

A shadow of grief flickered across his face as Jack reclaimed her hand. "A couple of months ago, your dad had been out doing fieldwork in an area about twelve miles away. He was only supposed to be gone for three or four days, but when he hadn't returned after a week had passed, Carlos and some men went to look for him." Jack gave her fingers a gentle squeeze. "Apparently a puma had been sighted in the area, and they were afraid Edward had been attacked. They found him a few miles out, critically injured from a gunshot wound to the chest."

Sophie gasped and sat back. "Somebody shot him?"

"Yeah." She clutched her stomach, listening as Jack explained about her father's crusade against illegal bird trading and that he most likely knew too much or came across them unexpectedly.

"Illegal bird trading?" she questioned. "I would have thought it would have been illegal drugs."

"It's probably both. Most of the exotic birds that reside here in the Costa Rican jungles are popular as pets in the United States. It can be a very profitable business to export the birds illegally, and usually, drug dealing goes hand in hand."

"Did he die right away?"

"No. Carlos said he never did regain consciousness and was too unstable to move. One of the village healers stayed with him day and night, hoping he would improve enough so they could try and get him better medical care, but he worsened and passed away about a week after they found him."

Sophie concentrated and tried to do the math in her head. "So that was what, like five or six weeks ago?"

Fresh tears stung her eyes when Jack nodded his head. She couldn't believe her father was dead, and she'd missed him by a little more than a month.

"If only I'd come sooner, I might have been able to save him." She sniffed, unable to think of him broken, bleeding, and alone. "I should've known. How did I not know?"

"They had no way of contacting you, and you came as soon as you could."

She knew Jack was right, but it didn't stop the guilt from pressing down on her, weighing her down. "Where did they bury him?"

Jack studied her for a moment. "Here in the jungle it's not a good idea to bury the dead. His body was cremated, and his ashes were spread in the river not far from here."

She swallowed back another sob, wishing she could've talked to him one last time.

Jack grasped onto his walking stick and stood up. "Come on, I want to show you something."

"Are you sure you can make it?"

He smiled. "Yeah, I'm okay." He circled one arm around her shoulders. "But it wouldn't hurt to have you help me out a little."

They walked in silence, Sophie's grief battling against her growing concern for Jack. Heat radiated from his body, and his movements were slow and stiff. The risk of sepsis worried her. In any case, the systemic infection wasn't a good situation. Out here in the remote jungle, without the proper medical supplies, it could be fatal.

"This is where your dad lived," Jack said as he came to a stop in front of a hut.

Sophie stared at the simple dwelling and knew once she stepped inside, her father's death would become a reality. His belongings might still be in there, but he would be absent.

Jack opened the door for her. "Carlos said your father left some things for you."

Unable to speak, she nodded her head and entered the bungalow. She expected the place to feel desolate, as if it knew the owner would never return. Instead, she found the living space to be warm and cozy—peaceful.

"Nobody has moved in here yet?"

"No," Jack said. "I think the way your father was killed has people a little scared. Carlos said he hopes that with you staying here, the people will know it's safe."

"Is it safe?"

"I wouldn't let you stay here if I didn't think so."

Sophie nodded her head and looked around again. She smiled when she saw the rocking chair positioned by a well-stocked bookcase. In her mind, she could see her father sitting in the chair pouring over books about the eco-system just like he'd always done at home.

She made her way to the bookcase and traced her finger down the spine of a book she had given her dad one Christmas. Withdrawing the volume, she opened the page to see the inscription she'd written. A lone tear escaped and marred the white paper as she read the small note.

Dear Dad, I saw this book and instantly knew you would love it. I'm sorry we can't be together for Christmas this year. Maybe when I'm through with residency we can get together. Merry Christmas Dad, and remember I love you. Sophie

She closed the book and replaced it on the shelf, feeling a small measure of peace that she had told him she loved him. They hadn't been able to spend very many holidays together, but after she and David had broken up, Sophie had made an effort to do what she could. Last year, she'd been able to take off the week before Christmas to make a visit to her dad's home in Texas. It had been a good week, and her father had actually been interested in an article Sophie had written that had been published in an upcoming pediatric medical journal. It was the first time he'd shown interest in her medical career.

This year she had planned on inviting her dad to spend Christmas with her. It hurt to know there wouldn't ever be another opportunity. Like most people, Sophie had always believed there would be plenty of time to spend with her father once her practice had been established and once he had finished with his latest research. Both of them had squandered their time, and it was something they could never get back.

Turning away from the bookcase, Sophie noticed the basket centered on the small table. She met Jack's gaze. "Is this what he left for me?"

"Yes." He moved behind her. "Apparently your father had once told Carlos he wanted the items in the basket to be returned to you if there was ever a time he couldn't do it himself."

She scooted the basket closer and peered inside. The photograph on top had been taken her first year in college when she had only been sixteen. She looked so young and happy, her face filled with an excitement that belied how insecure and scared she had felt.

The basket held several more pictures she didn't remember sending him, encompassing her years in med school, residency and even one with David. It wasn't too long after the picture with David that she'd moved to Colorado, and Sophie hadn't taken the time to send her father anymore pictures.

Beneath the photographs were a few of the letters she'd sent from time to time when she knew emailing her father hadn't been an option. Her breath caught when she saw what lay on the bottom of the basket. It was a journal very similar to the one she kept. Picking up the book, she opened the pages, thrilled to see her father had actually written in it. How could she not know her father had kept a journal?

Randomly, she thumbed through the pages. Her father's handwriting was small, and his journal entries were usually only four or five sentences. But the dates indicated he wrote in it almost every day, spanning over four years. She closed the book, pulling it in to her chest. Perhaps her father had other journals back in Texas.

"Now I know where you got your journal writing gene from," Jack said softly.

Meeting his gaze, her lower lip trembled. "I didn't even know my dad wrote in a journal. There are a lot of things I didn't know about him." Her voice quivered with emotion.

"I don't even know if he was proud of me."

Jack touched her arm. "How could he not be proud of you?"

Feeling the heat from his hand, she remembered the fever and infection he was suffering from. "You're still burning up." She replaced the journal in the basket and tugged on Jack's hand, leading him to one of the cots. "The first thing we need to do is get your leg elevated."

Taking care of someone was something she was good at. It felt good to focus on something else besides the pain she felt from the loss of her father.

Chapter Nineteen

Jack smiled with relief as he lay down on the cot.
"Really? Just elevate my leg? I thought for sure you said something about another injection."

She patted him on the chest. "That too."

He groaned as she placed a pillow under his injured leg. Then Sophie retrieved her medical bag Hector had brought inside earlier. Before doing anything else, she found the ibuprofen and a bottle of water. The medication would hopefully reduce the fever as well as the swelling.

"Thanks," he said after swallowing the pills.

Sophie drew up the antibiotic in the syringe. She paused when she saw the alarming look on Jack's face. "Are you okay?"

"I feel like a wimp," Jack said, grimacing, "but I have to ask…is the shot really necessary?"

"Yes." A smile tugged at her mouth. "And my man is not a wimp."

Jack grinned. "Thanks for that."

After she finished giving him the shot, Sophie took a seat in the rocking chair, and Jack turned his gaze on her. "How are you doing?"

She took one of his hands, needing to draw strength from his touch. "I guess okay. Like I said, I think deep down I knew my dad was gone. It's not something you really want to accept until you have to." She took a stuttering breath. "Thank you for being here for me."

Jack squeezed her fingers. "I wish I could do more. I don't like to see you unhappy."

She gazed into his eyes, and her heart swelled with love.

It was hard to believe how different he was. Giving him a soft smile, she leaned in close. "Where is the grumpy man I've been taking care of for the past two days?"

Chuckling, he said, "I'm sure he'll be back."

"Yeah, you're probably right."

Jack raised an eyebrow indignantly. "Hey, I'm sick. The least you can do is keep flattering me."

She did something better—she kissed him. His mouth was hot, most likely from his fever, but Jack responded like an extremely healthy man. It was hard ending the kiss. Sophie craved the comfort the physical contact gave her.

"Wow," Jack said a little breathlessly. "That was a great kiss."

"I shouldn't take advantage of you, though."

"Sophie, you don't hear me complaining."

Out of nowhere, tears welled up in her eyes again. "Why didn't I spend more time with him?"

An expression of concern crossed his face. "You didn't know this would happen. If I remember right, it was your dad who was always away, not you."

"I know. I just wish I could've told him that I love him one last time." She wiped away a tear with the back of her hand. "And that I'm sorry I never learned Spanish."

"He knew you loved him." Jack's mouth lifted into a crooked smile. "I'm pretty sure your rebellion about taking Spanish wasn't a big deal to him. In your cute, little, teenager mind it just seemed that way. You're a brilliant doctor, and I'm certain your father was very proud of you."

"Thank you." She smiled sadly. "But what about the dreams I've been having? Why did I feel like I needed to come here so urgently?"

"I'm not sure, but I believe God wanted to you to come here, Sophie."

He brought her hand to his mouth and kissed her fingertips. "I'd like to think it was just so you could rescue me."

"Well," she sniffed, "you are the silver lining in the cloud."

"I am?"

She laid her head on his chest. "Definitely."

He stroked her hair for a few minutes, neither of them speaking. His fingers slowed and then stopped, his chest rising and falling with slow, deep breaths.

With Jack asleep, she gently moved away and took a seat at the table. Once again, she picked up the journal and opened the book to the first page. She ran a finger over her dad's handwriting, following the small swirling letters.

As Sophie read the words, the sounds of the frogs and cicadas faded, making her father's voice nearly audible. Jack was right—her dad had been very proud of her. She savored the words of praise and felt her heart overflow with love as her father described the pride he felt over having a daughter in medical school. While she read, Hector brought her in some food and told her he had his tent set up outside the door. His dark brows drew together when he looked at Jack. "Is he going to be all right?"

"I plan on doing everything I can to make sure of that." She didn't want to think about losing Jack. "But a few prayers in his behalf wouldn't hurt."

"I'll pray for you too, *chica*." Hector gently patted her on the shoulder. "I'm sorry about your papa. But now he is with your mama, *¿no?*"

In the midst of everything, how had Sophie failed to think about her mother and father being reunited? "Thank you, Hector," she said, reaching up and touching his hand. "I needed to be reminded of that."

He gave her hand a gentle squeeze and instructed her to awaken him at any time if she needed help. After he left and she finished eating, the fatigue sapped what little energy she had left.

Unable to read anymore, Sophie tucked the journal back inside the basket and checked on Jack one last time. As he slept, she studied his face and resisted the temptation to caress his strong jaw. The last thing she ever expected from this journey was to fall in love with Jack.

Anxiety about her future—their future—tightened like a tourniquet around her chest. What would happen now? She had no idea if Jack would really follow her back to Colorado. And even if he did, would he want to marry her?

* * *

Sunlight streamed in the room, making Jack squint. Lifting his hand to block out the light, he was startled to find it attached to an IV bag. *What in the world?* He turned his head, trying to get his bearings. *Where am I?*

The door swung open, and in stepped Sophie. "Well, look who's finally awake." She glided to his bedside, feeling his forehead with her hand. "No fever today. That's a good sign, Mr. Mathison."

Jack tried to move, but his body felt stiff and sore. Especially his back. He gripped the edge of the bed, feeling the thin metal frame of a cot. The memory of entering Edward Kendrick's hut flooded his mind. He looked over at Sophie. "If it's a good sign, how come I feel like crap?"

"Really?" Her eyebrows drew together with concern. "Tell me what's wrong."

"You tell me." He looked down at the needle in his hand. "I don't recall you putting that in me."

"That's because you were out of it." She leaned over to check the IV site, the clean scent of her hair drifting past him. "Does it hurt?"

"No, but my back is killing me. Just how long have I been sleeping here?"

"Two and half days."

Jack groaned. "Are you serious? What happened to me?"

She patted his face. "The laceration on your leg festered."

Her fingers felt smooth against his jaw. Jack reached up with his free hand, running his palm against a whisker-free face. "So you had to shave my face in order for me to get better?"

"Nope. That just kind of happened."

"I can't wait to hear this."

A corner of Sophie's mouth curled into a wry smile. "Well, Hector hired someone to give you a sponge bath, and Vinita took it upon herself to shave you." Sophie's eyes gleamed. "I had Vinita shave you again this morning."

"Sheesh, can't a man have a little dignity? I don't even want to ask who Vinita is."

Sophie leaned in close. "She was old enough to be your grandmother." She kissed his cheek. "Don't worry, she was practically blind."

Jack's eyebrows rose. "And you let her shave me?"

Sophie sniggered. "She wasn't *that* blind."

Jack liked her laugh. After finding out about her father, he'd wondered if it would be absent for a long time. He captured her hand. "Hey, how are *you* doing?"

A serene look lit her eyes. "I miss my dad and have regrets, but reading his journal is helping me." She gave him a soft smile. "Oh, and you were right—my dad was proud of me and loved me a great deal."

"That's awesome. I'm happy for you." He loved how peaceful she appeared.

"I'm going to check out your wound." Releasing his hand, Sophie stood up and moved to his leg. Her fingers were soft and cool against his skin. The tenderness around the wound had lessened, which hopefully meant he would be able to travel soon.

"It looks good." She lifted her eyes, meeting his gaze. "The stitches can come out tomorrow."

"When can we leave?" Now that their quest to find her father had ended, it was time to go home. A twinge of anxiety crept in alongside doubt. Sophie would be going back to Colorado to resume her medical practice, but what about Jack? His life—his livelihood—was in Costa Rica.

"If you feel up to it, probably in a couple of days."

He licked his lips, his mouth suddenly dry. "Any chance I can have a drink of water?"

"Sure." Sophie jumped up and got his water bottle off of the table. "Sorry, I should've thought of this before you had to ask."

"I think you've had your hands full." Jack raised up on his forearm, and the tubing from the IV pinched his skin. He took a few gulps of the tepid water before handing the bottle back to Sophie. "Thanks."

"Anything else?"

He ran his tongue across the top of his teeth, wishing he had a toothbrush. "How about a piece of gum?"

She smiled and dug into one of her pockets and withdrew a stick of gum. Opening it up, she gave Jack half and kept the other half for herself. "Better?"

"Much. Thank you." He lay back down and became aware of an uncomfortable pressure that would necessitate a trip to the outhouse. "Can we take this thing out?" He held up his hand with the IV. "I'd like to get up now."

He hoped Hector had been the one who took care of his bodily functions while he was out of it, and not Vinita.

"Okay." Sophie grabbed her medical bag. "It'll only take a couple of minutes but if it's…urgent, I can get Hector to help you first."

"I can wait."

"Removing the tape might hurt a little," she warned. "But I'll be as gentle as I can."

He winced as the adhesive pulled at the hair on his arm. "Just do it fast."

Sophie did as he asked, making him draw in a sharp breath. "Sorry." She applied pressure to the exit site with a small gauze pad. Her brown eyes flickered up, and a tiny smile curved her lips. "Do you want me to kiss it better?"

The flirty tone of her voice sent a rush of heat through Jack's body, and the anxiety about the future fled as quickly as the tape had come off. He smiled and crooked his finger, beckoning her closer. "They say laughter is the best medicine, but I'd have to disagree." He cupped his hand around the back of her head and brought her mouth down to his and kissed her.

Yeah, the experts had it all wrong, because suddenly Jack felt much, much better.

* * *

The next day, Jack dressed in a clean shirt and pants, and all without feeling dizzy. He rubbed his clean-shaven jaw and stepped outside to find Sophie watching a group of children chasing a chicken, a small smile playing at her full lips.

She turned to see him, and Jack saw the approval evident in her gaze. While Sophie had liked his rugged look before, the new clean-cut-Jack seemed to please her even more.

"Is that lunch?" He pointed at the chicken and took a seat beside her.

"I hope not." She studied his features. "You look like you're feeling much better." She leaned over and kissed him on the cheek. "Oops," she said, and rubbed at his cheek. "Lip gloss print."

Jack could smell the fruity concoction and recognized it was the same stuff she'd used the first time he'd kissed her. "I missed out on Island Daiquiri?"

Her eyebrows shot up. "You know what flavor I'm wearing?"

He grinned and lowered his head, giving her a slow kiss. "Yeah, that is definitely Island Daiquiri," he murmured against her lips.

"How did you know?" Sophie said as she pulled back and ended the kiss way too soon.

"Let's just say that first kiss was pretty memorable."

"Huh." Two little lines dented her forehead. "I'm impressed."

"Then why are you frowning?"

Her gaze skittered away, and she didn't answer him.

Jack sighed. "Does this have anything to do with Peter?"

"Sort of," she hedged.

Taking her hand, he led her back to the hut and sat her down on the doorstep. Joining her, he asked, "So what does *sort of* mean?"

"It's just that Peter would sometimes try to guess what flavor my lip gloss was and could never get it right. Ever."

Jack didn't exactly like hearing about how often Peter had kissed her, but the fact that he'd gotten it right on the first guess made him feel a little better. "Well, you can write that one down on your "like" column."

"My what?"

"You know, from your journal. I figured since you have a list of things you don't like about me, there has to be one about what you do like."

"I, uh, haven't started one yet."

"Really? Nothing?"

She lifted one of her shoulders up and captured her bottom lip with her teeth. "Sorry, no."

While he was kidding around, part of him wanted to ask if she had a list of things she did or didn't like about Peter. "There are things you like, though, right?" He suddenly felt territorial, if not a little insecure.

"Didn't we already establish what made me fall in love with you?" She nudged him in the shoulder with her arm. "Remember, I love your sense of humor, your awesome physique and your eyes?" Sophie placed her palm against his smooth jaw. "And I love your new look."

"You forgot kissing."

She laughed. "I might not have mentioned it, but I didn't forget."

Following Sophie to Colorado seemed daunting to Jack, and he had no idea how it was all going to work, but the thought of never seeing her again was even scarier. Then there was Peter Elliot. The muscles in Jack's stomach went taut when he imagined Peter trying to figure out what flavor of lip gloss Sophie had on.

"Yeah, about kissing." Jack hooked his arm around her neck and pulled her close. "I think I have exclusive rights since I nailed Island Daiquiri the first guess."

"I think that sounds reasonable." Sophie looked up at him and smiled. "Maybe later on this evening I'll introduce you to Pure Paradise."

Jack lifted a brow and grinned. "That sounds very intriguing, but do we have to wait until this evening?"

"Just so you don't get any ideas, that's the name of my newest lip gloss."

"I'm looking forward to it," Jack said before sampling Island Daiquiri one more time.

Chapter Twenty

Sophie trudged behind Hector and Fred, more exhausted than she'd ever been after pulling a forty-eight hour shift straight during residency. It had rained all day, and she was wet, tired and a little irritable. The enormous leaf Jack had called a poor man's umbrella had been the only thing that had saved her from total misery. The rain had let up about an hour ago, and Jack and Hector were both scouting out places to set up camp as they went along.

They were skirting around *Por El Rio*, and as much as Sophie hated the idea of stopping there, she longed for a bath and a dry hut the little village could offer. But when Jack had made the suggestion, Sophie had adamantly refused. The last thing she wanted to do was give Elaina another shot at seducing Jack. To his credit, Jack had seemed relieved by her refusal.

She nearly jumped out of her wet clothes when Jack tapped her on the shoulder.

"Sorry," Jack said, looking as if he were holding back a laugh. "Just wanted to see if you'd changed your mind about going on to *Por El Rio*?"

"No. I'm not in the mood for drama," she snapped. "Let's just make camp now. I'm wet, tired and hungry."

"Don't forget grumpy," Jack added dryly.

Like he had room to judge! She put her hands on her hips. "I have the right to be grumpy too, you know."

Jack held up his hands in mock defense. "Hey, I never said you didn't."

Hector snorted. "Jack, quit while you're behind."

Sophie didn't like being so cranky, but she felt frustrated with Jack.

Ever since leaving *Del Sol* three days earlier, he'd said very little about what would happen when their journey came to an end. If she tried bringing up the subject of whether or not Jack was moving back to Colorado, he'd effectively shut her down by changing the subject. The closer they got to home, the more uneasy Sophie became.

Turning away from Jack, she said, "Hector, I'd like to help with dinner. Would you like me to cut up the fruit?"

"*Sí.*" He smiled and patted her on the shoulder. "Jack will take care of Fred for me."

Chuckling, Jack took the donkey's reins. "I know when I'm not wanted."

Not wanted? That was the whole problem. Sophie wanted him so much it hurt. She touched Jack's arm, meeting his pale blue eyes. "I'm sorry for snapping at you."

His eyes crinkled. "I know."

A smile crept across her face. "Go take care of Fred."

"Yes, ma'am."

Watching him walk away, Sophie wondered if Jack had even considered seeing her after she returned home. Sure, he'd said he loved her, and he certainly enjoyed kissing her, but she shouldn't have assumed that meant he was looking for a serious relationship.

What if Jack just wanted to date for an indefinite amount of time, like as in a long-distance relationship? What if he never wanted to commit to marriage? For heaven sakes, Sophie didn't even know if Jack wanted to have children. He knew she wanted a large family, but he'd never voiced his opinion one way or the other. Although, now that she thought of it, he had asked her what she would do if her husband only wanted a couple of kids. Did that mean he only wanted two kids?

To be fair, she hadn't come right out and asked him any of this. She'd simply hinted at different things, hoping he'd take the ball and run with it, which he hadn't.

She watched Jack disappear with Fred and knew she had to be honest with him. Turning away, she followed Hector to the clearing where they'd make camp. Somehow, she and Jack needed to have a talk.

After changing into clean clothing, Sophie sliced a couple of mangos while Hector fixed beef stew from their dwindling selection of MRE's and dehydrated food pouches. After finishing the task, she washed her hands, then took a seat on a log.

"The stew smells good," Sophie said, pulling her journal out from her backpack. "I'm starving."

"Me too." Hector lowered the flame on the butane burner and stirred the stew with a spoon a couple of times. "I'll go down to the river to wash up and send Jack back to camp."

"Good. I'm beginning to think he fell in or something." Jack had been gone for a while now. Sophie wondered if she'd been so grumpy that he was now avoiding her.

Laughing, Hector took off for the riverbank. "I'll call if I need a doctor."

Sophie hoped Jack would come back quickly. She didn't like being alone, especially with all the sounds of the jungle. As the sky darkened, the sounds of the animals and insects seemed creepy. Trying to keep her mind occupied, she opened her journal and found the page she was looking for.

Her eyes quickly scanned the paper, and she was unable to suppress a smile. She'd decided to create a what-she-liked-about Jack list. If the man ever got a chance to read it, his head would swell bigger than his bulging muscles.

Reading over the glowing attributes she'd listed, Sophie knew she was hopelessly, head-over-heels in love with Jack. She'd even written her name coupled with his last name. *Sophie Mathison.* She hadn't tested her name with the last name of a boy she liked since high school, and if Jack was ever to see this she, would be mortified. Even though she had been tempted, at least she hadn't written down the names of her children—their children—with his last name. That really would be embarrassing, especially if Jack didn't want her or a family.

An almost desperate, panicky feeling enveloped her when she considered the possibility of things ending with Jack. She wanted to get married, and she wanted babies. Sophie was still young, but in three years, she would be thirty-five—the age which the medical professionals considered to be advanced maternal age. She knew Peter was eager to start a family right away, although he only wanted three or four children since both of them had their careers to think about.

However, Sophie had always wanted to be a stay-at-home mother and maybe work one or two days a week as a pediatrician without doing any surgeries. If she got in with a big enough group, she would only have to take weekend call every six weeks or so.

Again, she wished she could talk openly with Jack. She sighed, turned the page, and read last night's entry that clearly reflected her frustrations with Jack and his lack of communication.

A twig snapped, and she gasped, jerking her head up. "Oh, I'm glad it's you."

"Sorry. I didn't mean to scare you," Jack said. He had an impish glint in his eyes which meant he'd had every intention of sneaking up on her.

"Somehow I don't believe you." His hair looked damp, and he had on a clean shirt. "Did you take a bath?"

"Not intentionally. Let's just say Fred doesn't like me as well as Hector." He sat down beside her and leaned over, making an obvious attempt to sneak a peek at her journal. "What're you writing about?"

She closed the journal and placed her hands on top of it. "I wasn't writing. I was reading."

The corner of his mouth lifted. "Okay. What're you reading about?"

"Stuff."

He narrowed his eyes. "What kind of stuff?"

This was the perfect opening to talk to him about her concerns, but it wasn't really the best time. Hector could come back at any moment.

When she didn't answer right away, he tapped his finger on her journal. "Maybe you should just let me read it myself."

"No way." She pulled the book close to her chest and glanced toward the river. "Hector's coming back any minute now, so it can wait until we're alone."

"Before I was curious, but now you've got me worried."

This was not going how she had wanted it to, and now Jack did look concerned. She was being ridiculous and making it much worse. "Okay." She moistened her lips. "What's going to happen to us when I go home, Jack?"

His eyes appeared even more troubled than before as he sucked in a breath and exhaled slowly. "I don't know."

"What do you want to happen to us, then?" she questioned softly.

After a few seconds of contemplative silence, he shifted on his seat. "I know I want to see you again, Sophie. I just don't know all the logistics."

Meaning, he wasn't planning on moving back to Colorado anytime soon. Honestly, It wasn't fair for him to have to be the one to move, but unless she got a good attorney and paid a steep fine, she wouldn't be able to get out of the four year contract she'd signed with the hospital two years earlier.

"Me either, but I'm glad you want to see me again." She looked up at him through her lashes and gave him a tentative smile. "I should've talked to you sooner. Maybe then I wouldn't have been such a witch today."

"A witch?" Jack laughed and winked at her. "You've been slightly crabby today, but I figured that had more to do with the rain and the bugs."

"That probably added to my misery, but, to be honest, I thought you were avoiding talking about the future because you weren't interested in seeing me again." She shrugged. "It made me cranky."

He reached over and took her hand. "Actually, I *was* avoiding the subject, but not because of what you thought." He held her gaze as he slowly circled his thumb in the center of her palm. "The thing is, Sophie...I'm scared, and don't feel worthy to date you, let alone marry you."

Jack wanted to marry her! Sophie's heart soared with his words, but she forced herself to sit still and let him finish.

"I'm trying to make things right with God, and I'm working on figuring out a way to contact my family, but I can't guarantee I'll be able to reconcile with them." His eyebrows bunched together, and he dropped his head to focus on their hands. "I only have one brother. I don't know if he's still married to Heather, or how many kids they have. I can't promise you big family get-togethers for holidays and special occasions, or that those get-togethers will be pleasant. I'm willing to share my parents, but I don't know if they're interested in sharing my life."

Sophie felt her bottom lip quiver with pent up emotion. Jack remembered everything about their conversation. Well, almost everything. They still hadn't discussed children.

He lifted his face and pierced her with his eyes. "I want kids, too. I don't know how many, but I'm willing to negotiate."

The obvious love in his eyes nearly took Sophie's breath away. All her life she'd dreamed about this moment—discussing her future with the man she'd fallen in love with—talking about the possibility of starting a family and what they wanted out of life. No wonder she could never return Peter's affection. Everything she felt at this moment went beyond what she had ever thought possible.

She could feel her heart and respiratory rate increase. There was a warm current flowing from Jack's hand throughout Sophie's entire body, settling in her stomach. When she got back to Colorado, she planned on studying the autonomic and sympathetic nervous system in depth as well as the physiology of a person experiencing love. The medical doctor in her was fascinated by the way her body reacted to this one man.

"While having a large extended family would be great," Sophie said, clutching his hand tighter. "It's you I want, Jack. You, and eventually our children, will be enough."

Sophie leaned over and kissed him. The moment their mouths touched, the soft kiss she'd intended exploded into something much more passionate. That certainly hadn't been her intention, since Hector could walk in on them at any moment.

Jack returned the kiss with equal vigor and circled his arms around her, pulling her close. Sophie gave herself over to the kiss with abandon and was vaguely aware of her journal falling to the ground.

The warmth of Jack's palms against her back heightened her awareness. As he deepened the kiss, Sophie became lost to everything around her.

The incredible love she felt proved beyond any doubt that God *had* created a man and a woman to be together. Never before had she felt this way about anyone. Not even David.

Needing to take a breath, Sophie pulled away. "Well," she said, her voice trembling, "that was very enlightening."

Jack's blue eyes blazed with passion. "Are you going to share your enlightenment?" His voice was low and intimate.

"I think I need more research before I share my findings."

"More research?" Jack asked, his eyes dipping down to her mouth.

He leaned forward to kiss her again, but Sophie pressed her hand against his chest to stop him. "Not now. Hector will be back any second."

"He's actually here now," Hector said coming back into camp.

"Ah, Hector," Jack teased. "You're timing is terrible. A few more minutes alone with Dr. Kendrick and I could have persuaded her to talk."

"*Amigo*, it looks like you were doing more than just talking."

Sophie's face flooded with heat as Jack said, "That, my friend, would've been part of the persuasion."

* * *

Sophie awakened sometime during the night and immediately sensed someone was watching her. As her eyes adjusted to the dark, she saw a man crouched down by her sleeping bag. Thinking she was hallucinating, she blinked several times, but he was still there.

Terror filled every part of her when he pulled out a knife and flashed it before her eyes.

Is this just another nightmare? The apparition violently grabbed her wrist, making her cognizant of how real he was.

God, please help me! She scrambled for the door and started to scream. A dirty hand covered her mouth, muffling her cry for help. She struggled to free herself and felt bile rising in her throat, making her nauseous. The man moved his hand away and jumped back as Sophie emptied her stomach onto the sleeping bag. The evil man spoke angrily in Spanish.

She had a split second before he would cover her mouth again. She screamed Jack's name and barely got out, "Help me!" When a fist slammed in the side of her face. The impact snapped her head back, and she fought to stay conscious.

Fear clawed at her throat as the man grabbed her by the hair. He flung the soiled bag out of the way and pulled her to his body. His hand cupped her mouth again, and he spoke in a low, angry voice. She couldn't understand anything he said, but instinct told her he'd kill her if she screamed again.

Had Jack heard her? She prayed that he had.

In an instant, her life seemed to flash in front of her. Sophie knew if this man took her away, she would never see Jack again. Just like in Jack's dream.

Her muscles tensed again as she fought to free herself. Over the pounding of her heart, she heard a quiet voice—as if God was speaking to her—tell her to stop struggling. She relaxed her body, and the man loosened his grip.

"Doctor. Come," he said in broken English, his breath hot and smelling like stale cigarettes.

How did they know she was a doctor? Afraid to speak, she mutely nodded her head.

The man held up her shoes, motioning for her to put them on. When she finished tying them, he jerked her arm and roughly pulled her out of the tent. Sophie's body shook intensely, making her legs feel unsteady. The side of her face throbbed where the man had hit her.

Frantically, she shifted her eyes to Jack and Hector's tents. They were silent. How could they sleep through this? Then she had a horrible thought: What if they'd already been killed?

Thick fingers gripped her arm. "Stay," the man said as he released his hold.

Her abductor put a dirty cloth in her mouth to gag her. The problem was it literally gagged her. The full moon provided enough light for Sophie to see his dark eyes narrow with anger when she started to retch. Using the back of his hand, the man slapped her face again, and Sophie swallowed down the acid from her stomach as he finished securing the rag over her mouth to silence her.

Forcefully, he jerked her arms in front of her, binding her hands together with thick twine. Every defense course she'd ever taken, stressed the importance of never allowing the abductor to take you to another location. The man came around behind her, and Sophie desperately tried to come up with a plan.

"Go," the man whispered harshly. He shoved her in the back, and Sophie stumbled, falling to her knees. *God, I don't know what to do. Please help me*, she silently pleaded as she struggled to stand back up.

Her prayer was immediately answered when Jack suddenly appeared out of his tent. "Please," he begged softly. "Don't hurt her." Then he shook his head slightly and spoke in Spanish, "*Por favor, no le haga daño a ella.*"

The man held the knife to Sophie's throat and replied in a harsh voice. Whatever he had said made Jack's eyes go wild with fear, and she felt the tip of the knife bite into her skin.

Chapter Twenty-One

Every instinct Jack had was screaming for him to attack and then rescue Sophie, but watching the knife cut into her skin made him stand down. His hands clenched into tight fists as a small bead of blood appeared at the tip of the blade.

"If you kill the doctor, she won't be able to help your friend," Jack said in Spanish. "The knife is cutting her."

To his relief, the madman holding Sophie captive moved the blade away from her throat. "Stay out of this," he growled.

"She doesn't speak Spanish. I'm her interpreter, as well as her assistant, so I'll need to come with you." Jack hoped his voice came off calmer than he felt. His mind raced with desperation, trying to think of way out of this. The gun he'd brought along for protection was packed deep inside his gear.

Behind him, Jack heard the sound of someone walking through the brush. If it was Hector, Jack wished he could warn him. Sophie's eyes reflected panic as Jack heard the distinct sound of a gun being cocked right behind his ear. It was a good guess this wasn't his friend.

Feeling the barrel of the gun at the base of his skull, Jack asked for heavenly help. The man holding Sophie hostage spoke, "Don't kill him. He speaks for the doctor."

The man behind him grunted, still pressing the gun to his head. "We don't need him, Alberto."

"But Cruz does," Alberto said. "We can kill him later."

Jack wondered who would win the argument. He also wondered where Hector was and if he was alive.

The gun pressed harder. "Put your hands behind your back, *hombre*."

Jack obeyed and tried not to wince as the rope dug into his flesh. The dream he'd had unfolded before his eyes, but this time Jack had listened to Sophie's cry for help. When he'd heard her scream out his name, he had awakened immediately. Quietly, he'd tied on his shoes all the while praying to God for guidance.

The man moved the gun and pressed it into Jack's back. In a low menacing voice, he said, "Try anything and I will kill you." He circled around and got in Jack's face. "Where is the other man?" he asked through clenched teeth.

Hector was gone? If they didn't know where he was, Jack still had hope. The man aimed the gun at Jack's heart and repeated the question.

"He's in his tent," Jack answered.

Sliding the gun up under Jack's chin, he said, "No, *hombre*. He is not there."

This guy was itching to pull the trigger. Jack swallowed, willing his heart to slow down. "I don't know. He probably ran away when he heard you were here."

The donkey brayed, pulling his captor's attention away. The other man holding Sophie said, "Forget it. We need to get the doctor to Cruz."

Jack felt temporary relief when the man agreed. He pointed the gun at Jack one last time. "You will not try anything. If you do, you will die, and then after the doctor is done—we will kill her." The man leaned close to Jack's ear. "But first I will have her."

Hot anger surged through Jack. If anyone touched Sophie in such a vile way, he would die trying to save her. Tightening his jaw, Jack kept his gaze even and nodded his head briefly. He knew this was not the time or the place to rescue Sophie.

Alberto, the man holding Sophie, pulled on her tied hands, making her press forward. Jack was shoved from behind, and he staggered to regain his balance. His captor trailed after him, bringing Fred and most of their supplies.

With each footstep, Jack prayed for help. Although the situation seemed hopeless, he refused to give into his fears. He hadn't found Sophie just to have her taken away.

The full moon peeked through the heavy foliage, allowing him to see Sophie stumbling up ahead of him. She wore her cut off sweats and a dark T-shirt. The clothes wouldn't provide any protection for her against the vegetation and bugs.

Without his compass, Jack had no idea which direction they were heading. It was impossible to make any notations of the landmarks they passed. The jungle looked pretty much the same. He could only keep praying that somehow Hector had escaped and would bring help.

Eyeing the man up ahead, Jack tried to logically think about the motivation behind the abduction. From what he could gather, it seemed to simply be that they needed a doctor to help their fallen comrade. While it would keep Sophie temporarily safe, Jack wasn't stupid and knew once she'd completed her task, nothing would stop these ruthless men from hurting her in the worst way imaginable. He had to save her before that happened.

After traveling by foot for more than a couple of hours, they stopped near some water. Disoriented, Jack couldn't be sure about the river or where it led. Alberto, the man holding Sophie, dragged her with him to uncover a canoe.

Jack's captor pushed the cold steel in his back. "Get down on the ground," he ordered angrily.

Jack obeyed without question. Moisture from the wet grass seeped into his pants at the knees. The twigs and rocks dug into his flesh as he awkwardly lay on his stomach.

Raul, as Jack had learned his name, ground his boot into Jack's back. "You move and I will shoot you, understand?" he asked menacingly.

"*Sí*," Jack replied.

Raul unloaded the donkey and then jerked Jack to his feet, pushing him forward. Sophie already sat in the canoe. The gag had been removed, and by the soft moonlight, Jack could see her dirty, tear streaked face was red and swollen on one side. The scumbag had hit her! He curled his fingers into his palms, wishing he could take a swing at either man.

Sophie looked at him with desperation, her mouth opening as if to warn him. A deafening sound exploded in Jack's ear. He stared numbly at Sophie again, waiting for the pain of the bullet to register in his brain.

Raul brushed past him, and it took a second for Jack to comprehend he hadn't been shot. Glancing to his side, he saw the donkey lying prostrate, clearly dead. At least he hadn't suffered. Jack could see that the bullet had killed the animal instantly.

The ringing in Jack's ears muffled the sounds all around him, although he didn't miss Raul's dark chuckle, nor his chilling words. "Next time, *amigo*, it will be you."

Swallowing hard, Jack silently thanked God he was still alive.

With a hard shove, Raul pushed Jack to the canoe, ordering him to sit in the middle. Jack awkwardly sat down and met Sophie's gaze. Shocked and pale, he knew Raul had succeeded in terrifying her. She was still staring where Fred had been gunned down, and Jack wished he could comfort her.

They traveled up stream for what seemed like an hour or so, but Jack couldn't be sure. The further they went, the more desperate he felt.

Right now, it was just the two men. When they reached their destination, how many more would there be?

A chilling human-like scream rent the air, making Sophie jerk her head in the direction of the sound. Jack recognized the cry of a puma and the frenzied screeches of the monkeys. Ironically, Jack felt his and Sophie's chance of survival would be better if they were to face the big cat rather than these ruthless men.

By the time the men glided the canoe to one side of the river, the first fingers of light were piercing the dark sky. "Take the doctor to Cruz right away, " Raul said as the canoe scraped along the bottom.

Alberto banked the boat on the shore. He jumped out and pointed to Jack. "What about him? She needs him."

"Soon. I'll bring him soon," Raul said, his voice low and menacing.

Anxiety curdled Jack's stomach. He didn't want to be left alone with Raul, and he certainly didn't want to be separated from Sophie. Since his hands were tied, he didn't have much of a choice.

Alberto jerked Sophie to her feet and helped her out of the unsteady watercraft. As he untied her hands, he spoke to Jack. "Tell her I'm taking her to Cruz."

Jack climbed out and looked into Sophie's eyes "He's taking you to the injured man, Cruz." He swallowed and hoped what he said next was true. "I'll come along to help translate in a few minutes."

Sophie nodded her head. He wanted to say so much more to her but didn't want to risk making Raul mad. The guy was itching to get rid of Jack and probably wouldn't use any restraint.

"I need my medical bag," Sophie said.

As quick as lightening, Alberto backhanded her in the face. "*Cállate!*"

"Hey!" Jack shouted. He twisted out of Raul's grasp and moved toward Sophie. "Don't hit her—"

Raul came at Jack from behind and punched him in the kidney. "Take one more step and I'll kill you right now."

Anger ripped through Jack's body, overriding the pain from the sucker punch to the side of his lower back. "She needs her medical bag," Jack spit out before Raul hit him in the same spot again.

"Tell her to get her bag, *hombre*," Raul hissed into Jack's ear. "Then do not speak again until you are asked to."

"You can get your bag," Jack rasped. The pain in his side took his breath away.

He could see Sophie's lower lip trembling, and her large eyes shimmered with unshed tears. She nodded her head slightly and retrieved her bag from the ground. Unable to do anything else, Jack watched her walk away with Alberto.

Please, God. Don't let anything happen to her. I'll do anything you want. Please, don't let them hurt her, Jack pleaded silently.

Another man came to take the confiscated supplies. Left alone with Raul, Jack waited as the man circled in front of him like a sleek panther taunting his prey. He met his menacing gaze and Raul spit in his face, cursing him. Then, without provocation, Raul slammed his fist into Jack's stomach. As he started to double over, Jack received another blow to his face. He staggered, trying to regain his balance. With his hands tied, he had no way to defend himself.

"When we no longer require your services, I will kill you." Raul leaned in close enough for Jack to feel his hot breath on his face. "But first, *amigo*, I think I will make you watch me enjoy the woman."

Jack ground his teeth together and kept his eyes forward.

Raul wanted a reaction—an excuse to kill him. He didn't acknowledge the man's words, although they turned his stomach inside out. Right now, remaining calm was the only thing he had control over.

A feral grin stretched across Raul's face as he raised his fist to strike Jack again. "Bring the doctor's assistant," a man called out, sparing Jack for now.

Narrowing his dark eyes into thin slits, Raul laughed contemptuously. "I will finish this later."

Jack had no doubt about that, but what mattered most was getting to Sophie. Tasting blood from his split lip, Jack concentrated on slowing his heart rate down and walked alongside Raul. A drop of sweat rolled down the side of his face, stinging a cut below his eye. Jack's muscles ached from his arms straining behind him. His face throbbed, and his lip felt swollen. But he was alive, and so was Sophie.

Entering the good sized hut, Jack saw Sophie examining a large man laid out on a cot. His abdomen was covered in blood. He looked like a corpse, but Jack caught the barely discernible rise and fall of his chest.

Scanning the room, he saw at least a half-dozen men watching Sophie with interest. Renewed anxiety clenched his gut. The chances for them to escape unscathed seemed pretty slim right now.

Raul shoved him from behind. "Ask her if he will live."

Jack lurched forward, stopping next to Sophie. "They want to know if he'll live." He wished he could say something to comfort her, tell her he had a plan of escape.

Sophie's gaze flickered to his, and he noted her gloved hands were covered in dark red blood. "I'll do everything I can to save him, but I need your help." She bent over, preparing to start an IV. "Will they allow your hands to be free?"

Jack directed the question to Alberto, not really expecting him to accommodate him.

Alberto's nostril's flared, and he eyed him menacingly. "We will kill you if you try to do anything stupid."

"I understand," Jack said as Alberto pulled out a large knife. He moved behind Jack, yanking tight on the ropes before cutting him loose.

Rubbing his sore wrists, Jack stood beside Sophie and watched as she skillfully inserted the IV catheter. She instructed him to tear off a couple of pieces of tape that she used to secure the IV tubing. All the while, Jack continued to ask God for a miracle, because that was the only way he and Sophie were going to get out of this alive.

* * *

Sophie focused on the critically injured man and tried not think about the odds of him living, which weren't very good. The IV would give her a little more time. But, in the end, she didn't believe it would matter.

Without her asking him, Jack figured out a way to hang the IV bag from the low ceiling. It was a miracle these thugs had stolen a large cargo of medical supplies. She had used the last of the IV fluids when Jack had been sick. The minute she had walked in and saw the condition Cruz was in, she knew without the lifesaving fluids she wouldn't be able to prolong his life for another five minutes, let alone long enough for her and Jack to get out of this situation.

"What else can I do?" Jack asked, standing close beside her.

"He's lost a tremendous amount of blood. I need to try and get his fluid volume back up."

She concentrated on the mechanics of sustaining the man's life, trying not to think about what would happen to them after this was all done; when this man died.

Removing the extra-large surgical pad from its packaging, Sophie lifted the mass of soiled rags covering the mangled tissue and tossed them on the floor. The wound continued to seep blood, making her question how Cruz still lived.

Placing the pad on top, she said, "Jack, you'll have to apply pressure to the wound, but first I need you to get a syringe and the vial of medication labeled epinephrine."

Sophie had already examined the man and couldn't find an exit wound. She had no choice but to leave the bullet in, focusing on treating the symptoms. The epi would hopefully elevate his blood pressure.

"Is this right?" Jack asked, holding out the small glass vial and needle."

Their eyes met briefly. Sophie hoped she didn't look as hopeless as Jack. "Yes, thank you." She gave him an encouraging smile. "Just apply gentle pressure to the wound."

Behind her, she heard the group of men murmuring and she involuntarily shuddered. When she'd first walked in, the stench of blood and body odor had overwhelmed her. One man had stepped in front of her, groping at her body and leering at her with brown stained teeth. Alberto had shoved him out of the way and escorted Sophie to Cruz. At least his desire for her to attend to their leader remained in the forefront. For now.

Drawing up the medication, Sophie once again focused her attention on her patient. If she didn't get his volume and pressure up, Cruz would go into hypovolemic shock. Realistically, she guessed he was already there. After all, his blood pressure had barely registered.

Her hand shook slightly as she injected the bolus of medicine through the IV port.

Then she opened up the roller clamp and squeezed the
IV bag gently, so it dripped continuously. She needed to get
as much fluid in as quickly as possible.

Mentally, she thought about everything she didn't have:
Oxygen, whole blood and an operating room where she
could repair the internal damage left from the bullet ripping
apart his gut.

Placing her fingers against Cruz's throat, she found his
thready and rapid pulse, a sure sign of hypovolemic shock
and eventual death. Cruz hadn't stirred, and his respiratory
rate remained shallow. Without a miracle, there was no way
he'd last an hour.

"Jack, I need you to leave that for a minute. Come over
here and gently apply pressure to the IV bag. Just do it like
this," she said, placing her hands around the bag and
demonstrating for him. Then she gathered what she needed
to suture what was left or recognizable. All she was doing
now was buying time. The longer he lived, the better chance
she and Jack had of finding a way to escape.

Blood oozed out of the wound, making her task even
more difficult. Without the help of lighting or the ability to
cauterize the blood vessels, she sutured what she could. It
was a mess, but Sophie continued to sew up the mangled
tissue.

The men in the room relaxed when they saw both of
their prisoners were actually doing the job they'd been
hijacked to do. Except for the occasional grunt or sporadic
word, she could almost ignore them.

While Jack kept steady pressure on the IV bag, Sophie
alternately blotted the seeping blood and sutured until her
fingers ached.

"The bag's almost empty," Jack said.

She looked up and met his eyes. "Do you think you can hang another one?"

"Sure."

He picked up the bag and ripped open the package. "I guess I pull this tab, right?"

"Yes. Then remove the empty bag and push the spike into the new one."

It was such a relief to be able to talk to him freely. She needed to keep him occupied so there would be no reason to dispose of her assistant.

"You don't happen to know how to take a blood pressure do you?" she asked him after a few minutes.

"I've learned before, I just don't know if I'll remember how to do it correctly."

"Give it a try in a minute, but first I need you to get about six or seven 4x4's. Open them and hand them to me one at a time."

Sophie took each gauze pad and did her best to pack the wound. The materials weren't optimal and, of course, nothing was sterile.

Removing her soiled gloves, she went ahead and took the man's vital signs herself. While his pulse remained rapid, she could detect a slight improvement. His blood pressure was even up a little. At least enough to keep him alive for a few more hours. Beyond that, it would be up to God.

Chapter Twenty-Two

Jack's heart nearly stopped when Sophie removed her gloves, like she was done. He glanced at the patient, who didn't look any better. Was the guy even breathing? Heck, Jack couldn't even tell if *he* was still breathing. He watched, and when Cruz took a shallow breath, Jack felt his own lungs expand with relief.

Alberto stood. "Cruz is better?" he asked, looking hopeful.

Sweat trickled down Jack's back as he glanced at Sophie. "He wants to know if he's better."

Sophie answered diplomatically, without the slightest hesitation. "Yes. His blood pressure has improved, and his heartbeat is more regular. I'll need to continue to monitor him throughout the night, and he'll need more IV fluids."

How could she continue to be so cool and collected? If they survived, it would be because of Sophie. Jack repeated the prognosis. The men were jovial with the news. Jack hated to think about what the men's reaction would be when Cruz died.

Jack noticed Sophie swaying slightly. Alberto must have noticed too because suddenly he turned into Mr. Nice Guy. He smiled and pulled out a chair for Sophie. "Sit, *señorita*." Then he offered her a drink from his flask.

Sophie wrinkled her nose slightly. "I don't drink alcohol."

Alcohol? Jack briefly scanned the room. Just great. It looked like they were all drinking. Before he knew it, there would be a room full of intoxicated men. In Spanish, Jack tactfully said, "The doctor needs a clear head to continue taking care of Cruz."

Shrugging his shoulders, Alberto took another drink. Jack felt hopeless at ever getting out of this alive. He could see the way all of the men lustfully eyed Sophie. Even with a bruised and dirty face, she was still beautiful.

Alberto must have already been feeling the buzz. Grinning at Jack, he said, "*Amigo*, have a seat next to the doctor." Then he held out his flask. "Would you like a drink?"

Jack would need more than one drink to feel better. "*Sí*," Jack replied. "*Agua* would be good for both the doctor and me."

Raul sniggered. "He isn't man enough for your whiskey."

The other men laughed, and Alberto pointed to the floor where some of their supplies had been rifled through and dumped. "Give Jack some *agua*," Alberto said, using his first name. "He can share with the doctor."

A skinny man with horrible acne, and who was wearing a dirty white T-shirt, tossed a bottle of water to Jack. Instinctively he caught it. Unscrewing the lid, Jack offered the bottle to Sophie.

She hesitated and then took a long drink. Wordlessly, Sophie handed the bottle back to him. Their fingers brushed slightly, and Jack treasured the contact, however limited. Taking a drink from the same bottle somehow made him feel closer to her.

While the rest of the men became loud and boisterous, Raul's face darkened. *Awesome.* It looked like the guy was also a mean drunk. Raul kept his eyes solely on Sophie, the lustful look making Jack shake inside with anger.

Desperate to figure a way out of this, Jack shifted his eyes to look at Cruz. He hadn't stirred, but he could still see his chest rising. How much longer would he hold on?

Even though Sophie's report had been optimistic, it didn't take a brain surgeon to figure out the guy was not going to make it. When Cruz died, so would they.

Sophie shifted in her seat uncomfortably, drawing attention to herself. Raul's gaze intensified as he took another drink. Wiping his mouth with the back of hand, he stood and walked in their direction, stopping in front of Sophie.

He challenged Jack with his eyes before taking his filthy hand and slowly caressing Sophie's bruised cheek. "*Eres una mujer hermosa.*"

You are a beautiful woman, Jack translated in his head. He clenched his jaw and fought back the urge to strike the man.

To her credit, Sophie didn't draw back at his touch. The move would only incite the menacing man. Raul dropped his hand and took another swig from his flask. Shifting his eyes again, Raul glared at Jack, one corner of his lip curling into a sneer. "Soon, *mi amigo*. Soon she will be mine."

Jack clutched his hands to the chair and, using great restraint, lowered his eyes. Raul chuckled darkly, almost daring Jack to give him a reaction. Praying for strength, Jack was able to remain silent. His taut muscles only relaxed marginally when Raul walked away and took a seat in the corner of the room.

It didn't take long for the men's attention to return to Sophie. The crude remarks made him glad she didn't speak Spanish. With each passing minute, he grew more and more desperate, as did his prayers.

The door swung open. An older woman, dressed in a yellow shirt and denim skirt, burst into the hut ranting in Spanish. "Get out! Get out!" She pointed a finger in Alberto's face. "The food is ready, and it is too early to be drinking."

Alberto chuckled. "But we are celebrating. The doctor has done well. Cruz will live."

The petite woman, with salt and pepper colored hair, looked to be in her sixties. She clucked her tongue and shook her head at the group of men. "No celebrating. Go eat before the food grows cold. There will be time for a *fiesta* tonight."

Alberto reluctantly stood. He stumbled drunkenly, and the men roared with laughter. Jack prayed fervently that the woman could actually succeed in vacating the room.

Alberto pointed his finger and barked, "Raul, bind them to the chairs." Then he glowered at Jack. "Tell the doctor if Cruz needs her help she is to tell Maria. We will always have a man nearby."

Taking the rope from his belt, Raul tied their hands behind them. He wound the rope through the slats of the chair, and Jack felt him yank on the bindings tightly. Circling in front, Raul brought his face within inches of Jack's. "I will be back," he warned in a low, threatening voice.

Maria patted Raul on the arm. "Leave me with my Cruz. Go. Go."

Reluctantly, Raul moved to the doorway, with Maria still clutching his arm. Tears coursed down the older woman's cheeks. "*Por favor,*" she pleaded softly.

Casting Jack one last dark look, Raul left them alone.

Who is this woman? Jack stared at the door, still amazed the men were gone. He didn't know how, but this had to be the chance he and Sophie needed to getaway.

Maria moved to Cruz's bedside, taking his hand. "*Mi hijo,*" she moaned softly. With her other hand, she crossed herself and prayed out loud for her son.

Not knowing how long they had, Jack turned his gaze on Sophie. "Are you okay?" he mouthed.

Her eyes filled with tears. "Yes," she whispered softly.

"I love you," he said quietly, unable to help himself.

A tear slipped down Sophie's bruised, swollen face. "I love you, too."

Jack tugged on his bound arms in vain. The effort caused his chair to scrape against the dirt floor. Jack froze as Maria turned to look at him. Their eyes remained locked, and Jack desperately wished he could read her thoughts. Could he trust her? "*Por favor*. Help us escape."

Her lips pinched together, and Jack held his breath, praying she would help them. Quietly, she turned and placed her son's hand across his chest. Then she went to the door and partially stepped outside. Cautiously, Maria scanned the area.

Neither he or Sophie spoke as they watched her come back inside.

"The men will get drunk and sleep. They cannot stop themselves," she said, looking at Jack.

Hope filled Jack's heart. "Will you help us, Maria?"

She nodded her head. "*Sí.*" She ran a hand through her salt and pepper hair with agitation. "But Raul, he will not sleep. He will only become more cruel. I must help you escape before he returns."

"*Muchas gracias*," Jack said. He turned to Sophie. "She says she'll help us escape once the men pass out."

Sophie started to weep, and Jack pulled at the ropes again, wanting to hold her close.

"We must wait a little longer," Maria said, looking at Sophie with compassion. She pulled out a cigarette from her pocket and lit it. After taking a long drag, she cast Jack a somber look. "If Raul comes before then, you will have to kill him."

As much he hated the man, Jack wasn't sure he could actually take his life.

He glanced at Sophie, saw the bruises marring her face and knew he would do whatever it would take to keep her safe. "I can't do anything tied up to this chair."

"*Sí*, I know." Maria blew out a circle of smoke. "I will release you, but you have to take me with you. My Cruz will not live much longer. Then his *mamá* will no longer be welcome here."

"Of course we'll take you," Jack assured her. "Please, untie my hands."

Maria held the cigarette between her lips and moved behind Jack. The rope bit into his skin as she tugged at the knots.

"What did she say?" Sophie asked, her voice quivering with emotion.

Although Jack wanted to spare Sophie the details, he felt impressed to reveal everything to her, including Maria's directive to kill Raul if he returned.

Sophie wrinkled up her brow. "But you don't have a weapon."

The observant comment was the truth, something Jack was fully aware of. "Then I'm going to have to get creative."

He looked around the room, trying to find anything that could work. Aside from the basic medical supplies, there were a few bamboo chairs and the rope Maria was loosening. If he had time, he could break apart a chair and try to sharpen the end. What he'd use to make a sharp point was one drawback to that plan. Right now he'd settle for a reasonable length of the bamboo to create a makeshift Billy Club.

"Jack," Sophie said, bringing his gaze back to hers. "I know how to take care of Raul."

"I'm open to suggestions." While the guy was despicable, Jack didn't actually want to kill anyone.

Sophie's idea most likely didn't involve brutality.

"Ketamine. I have a few vials of ketamine. The drug is very fast acting and will impair his motor function, making him virtually paralyzed."

"I'll need to inject it in him?" he asked uneasily. His aversion to needles seemed to be lessening day by day. But he could do it—heck, it would beat trying to take the man down with his bare hands.

"Yes, but don't worry. I can do it," Sophie volunteered.

Jack scowled. "Absolutely not. I'll do it. I don't want him to touch you ever again."

"Thank you." Tears filled Sophie's eyes, and her lips trembled as she gave him a soft smile.

He had to force his muscles to relax as Maria worked at the knots in the rope. Finally, the tension slackened, and Jack was able to wiggle free from his bonds.

"*Gracias*," Jack said, standing up. He moved behind Sophie, immediately working on her bindings. They weren't nearly as tight as Jack's. Within thirty seconds, she was free. Jack swept her into his arms, hugging her close. "I thought I'd lost you," he murmured, pressing a kiss to her hair.

"I know." Sophie's grip tightened around his back. "Thank you for saving me."

He pulled back, studying her bruised face. Softly, he trailed his fingertips over the discolored skin. "I can't believe they hit you."

She sniffed and blinked back her tears. "I'm okay."

"Shh." Maria glanced nervously at the door. She took one last drag of her cigarette and dropped it to the ground, crushing it with the heel of her shoe.

Right. There would be time for this later. Jack released his hold on Sophie. "So, you really think this ketamine will work?"

"Yes. It's commonly used on large animals like horses." Sophie quickly moved to pick up her medical bag. "I'll get it ready while you round up a few of our supplies."

Maria stood guard while Sophie drew up the medication, and Jack gathered what goods he could carry, shoving them into his backpack the thugs had taken. Among the mess, he found the compass Hector had given him for his birthday a few years back. Slipping the compass in his pocket, Jack didn't allow himself to think about his friend. Deep down, he felt Hector was still alive—he had to be.

"Raul," Maria said fearfully, "I think he is coming."

Jack's gut clenched tight with apprehension. "She said Raul's coming."

Sophie's face paled as she handed him a syringe. He noticed she retained an identical one for herself. "Where should I try to inject it?" Jack asked, his hands shaking slightly from the adrenaline rush.

"He has lightweight pants on. Aim for the thigh muscle."

Jack looked pointedly at the syringe in her hand. "I see you have back up ready."

She gave him a wobbly smile. "Just in case."

Maria crossed herself and prayed softly, moving away from the entrance.

Jack mentally prepared himself for what he needed to do. He was counting on Raul's reflexes being impaired by his alcohol consumption. Hopefully it would give Jack the upper hand.

"Sophie, you need to get over there by Maria," Jack instructed tightly. The last thing he needed to worry about was her getting hurt.

"Jack, please be careful." She backed up, fear evident on her face.

"I will," he said, his voice gruff. "Don't stop praying."

Outside, Jack heard heavy footsteps and Raul muttering to himself. They all took a collective deep breath, waiting for him to enter. Adrenaline surged through his bloodstream as the door swung open and Raul stepped inside.

Jack did the first thing that came into his mind. He stuck out his foot and tripped the drunken man. Raul fell to the floor with a thud, but he unexpectedly rolled away and was on his feet with agility Jack assumed he would be lacking.

Raul pulled out a knife. "You are a dead man," he threatened through clenched teeth.

Not if Jack could help it.

The two of them measured each other, waiting for someone to make the first move. The needle Jack wielded wasn't much of a weapon compared to the sharp knife the evil man brandished. But at least the guy didn't have a gun.

From his peripheral vision, Jack could see Sophie and Maria back further into the corner. He took a step backward, hoping to lure Raul further away from the women.

In disbelief, Jack was horrified when Raul suddenly turned and lunged for the women. He shoved Maria down, thrusting the knife into her chest. Sophie screamed as he pulled the bloody knife out. Raul had gripped Sophie by her arm, impeding her escape.

Before Jack could even process what had just happened, Raul had his arm around Sophie's neck in a choke hold. The knife, dripping with Maria's blood, was pressed against her throat.

"First, I will slit her throat. Then you, *amigo*, will die," Raul hissed.

Sophie's eyes went large with fear. Jack didn't know how to reason with this mad man. He did the only thing possible.

"You want to kill someone—take me." Jack held his hands up and dropped the needle. "I'll do anything, but don't hurt her. Please," Jack begged, kneeling down on the floor.

The silence was deafening as Raul slowly grinned. He kept his eyes on Jack as he moved his mouth to Sophie's ear, his tongue flicking out like a serpent. "Perhaps I won't kill her first." He planted a slow kiss where his tongue had been.

Jack felt his blood boil as the rage mounted inside him. He prayed for some way to get Sophie away from the filthy man. Suddenly, Cruz let out a long moan. It almost sounded like he called for his mother. Honestly, Jack was surprised the man was still alive.

Raul's face paled as he lowered the knife to look at the man laid out on the bed. Then his eyes went wide with shock as Sophie jabbed the needle in Raul's thigh.

Stunned, he released her from the choke hold and looked down. The needle protruded out of his leg. Sophie tried to push him away and screamed out in pain when Raul sliced into her arm with the knife. He bellowed loudly and grasped the needle, pulling it out of his leg.

Sophie scrambled away, and Jack rushed to her, shielding her body with his own. Raul, full of rage, held up the knife and moved menacingly toward them.

"How long until the medication takes effect?" Jack questioned, pushing Sophie back.

"One to two minutes. But I'm hoping his alcohol consumption will hasten the effect."

Jack prayed for a miracle. Right now, two minutes seemed like an eternity. Raul's steps faltered, and he put a hand to his head. Growling, he shook his head like a wounded animal. He cursed and stumbled forward.

Jack kept pressing Sophie back toward the door. He could deal with Raul if he knew she was out safely.

Raul swayed like a drunken sailor, his eyes glazed with confusion. He took one more step before collapsing to the floor.

"Finally," Jack said, letting out the breath he'd been holding.

Gripping her injured arm, Sophie moved to Maria and checked for a pulse. It was clear the woman was dead. Next, she moved to the fallen man and pressed her fingers to his throat. Jack hated that she was even touching the man.

"Sophie, you're hurt. Leave him alone."

She glanced up at Jack. "I don't remember the half life of ketamine, but I suggest we leave immediately."

"I completely agree." He reached down and helped her to her feet. "Let's go."

Nodding her head, she looked one more time at the fallen woman. "She saved us, Jack. I hate leaving her here."

"Sophie, she's with Cruz now." The man's chest was no longer moving and his lips were tinged blue. "We have to leave or she will have died in vain."

"I know."

Keeping Sophie behind him, Jack stuck his head out of the door and scanned the area for any men. Other than the low hum of a generator and the chirping of birds, the camp was eerily quiet. Jack figured by now the men would be passed out or too wasted to do anything to stop them. He had a suspicion Raul hadn't been drinking the same thing as the other men.

Almost as if they were protected in a bubble, Jack and Sophie made their way to the riverbank. Quickly cutting the lines on the two other canoes, Jack pushed them downstream. Taking the third canoe, they made their getaway.

* * *

Sophie's eyes flew open as the canoe rocked to the side. A small moan escaped her lips, and Jack whipped his head around. "Are you okay?"

"Yes." She grimaced as a sharp pain shot up her shoulder. "Well, I guess I'm in a little pain." They'd been traveling on the river for over an hour now, hoping to come across a village. After taking some pain medication, Sophie had fallen asleep.

Jack squinted, a hint of a smile on his lips. "I'll bet it hurts more than a little. Come on, Sophie, you're making me look bad."

A grin tugged at her mouth. "Okay. I'm in a lot of pain."

All traces of humor left his eyes. "What can I do for you?"

Moving her sore arm slightly, Sophie confirmed no muscle or tendons had been damaged. If the laceration required stitches, would Jack be up for the task? She also needed a shot of Penicillin, but she could do that herself.

"First, I need the vial of Penicillin and one of the syringes."

She tried not to laugh when all the color drained from Jack's face. "I…you need me to give you a shot?"

"What happened to my brave assistant?" she teased.

"He, uh…works better under duress."

"Don't worry." She chuckled. "I can give myself the shot."

He gave her a skeptical glance before setting aside the paddle, allowing the current to pull the canoe downstream, and rummaging through her bag. When he had the requested items, she instructed him how to reconstitute the powder medicine with normal saline, and then had him roll it in his hands to completely mix it together.

"I'll do this if you really need me to," Jack offered as he handed her the syringe.

"Thank you, but I got it." She moistened her lips. "I may need your help later on with something I can't do for myself."

He raised an eyebrow. "Oh?"

"Let me do this, and then we can talk."

Jack smiled grimly as if he might have guessed what it was she was going to ask of him. The poor guy hated needles, but suturing her wound by herself wasn't possible. His troubled gaze remained locked on her, waiting for her to proceed.

"Jack, I need to give the injection in my leg—and not through my dirty clothing."

One side of his mouth lifted in a wry grin, a mischievous glint lighting his eyes. "On second thought, I think I better give you the shot after all."

She couldn't help laughing. "Jack Mathison, you are shameless. Now turn around like a gentleman, and let me do this."

Chuckling, he did as she asked.

Sophie struggled with the sweats, grunting with the effort.

"Sure you don't need help?" Jack asked as he paddled down the river.

"Nope. I've almost got it."

After a few moments of silence, he said, "You do realize how hard this is for me not to turn around?"

Actually, she did. "I know, but thank you for using restraint."

"You're welcome," he said with a chuckle.

After giving herself the injection, she pulled her sweatpants back up. "Okay, Jack. You can turn around."

He still wore a grin. "I didn't even hear you make a noise. Either I'm a wimp or your pain threshold is much higher than mine."

"Yes—well, we'll see about that." She gripped her wounded shoulder and could feel the gauze bandage was already soaked with blood again. "I think I might need stitches."

The lines in Jack's forehead creased as he swallowed. "I'm guessing this is what you can't do for yourself, right?"

"Yes."

"Sophie," Jack said, running a hand over his short hair, "how on earth am I supposed to stitch up your arm?" He sighed heavily. "The only time I've even attempted to sew anything was to put a button back on a shirt, and that was in college."

Whether Jack attempted to sew the wound closed or they used the steri-strips tucked into the front of the backpack, Sophie would need to see a plastic surgeon once she was back home. The important thing now was to stop the bleeding

"Let's try using butterfly bandages first. If it works, then you're off the hook."

Relief flooded his handsome face. "Okay, but if it doesn't, I promise I'll do what I have to do."

She couldn't resist touching his face and lightly brushed her fingers over his whiskers. The cut below his eye had started to turn purple, but at least he wouldn't have a full blown black eye. "I believe you would do anything for me," she whispered, recalling the crazed look in his eyes while pleading for her captor not to hurt her.

"Yeah," he said gruffly. "You have me totally wrapped around your finger."

"Do I now?" She wondered if that meant he would be willing to move to Colorado until her contract was up.

"Oh, yeah." He bent his head and covered her mouth with his. The kiss was gentle, but just as powerful as every other time their lips met. The heady sensation, mixed with the effects of the narcotic she'd taken earlier, eased the pain considerably. Love was a potent pain reliever.

They both jerked apart when they heard an unfamiliar noise. Jack put a finger to his lips, and they listened to the sound of a diesel engine chugging in the distance, drawing closer.

Shaking, Sophie clutched Jack's arm. "What is that?"

Chapter Twenty-Three

Fear seized Jack, squeezing him around the middle. How could he protect Sophie without a weapon? "It sounds like a boat. Get down on the floor and lie flat."

She didn't listen to him, instead pressing her body closer. Jack scanned the bank, looking for a place to hide. Since their uneventful escape, part of him had been expecting Raul and his men to come up on them any second.

"What if it's Alberto?" Sophie whispered, her voice quivering as bad as her trembling body.

Using the paddle, Jack maneuvered the boat to the side. "It can't be him. Listen, you can tell the sound is coming from up ahead." He tried convincing himself as much as her.

The underside of the canoe scraped along the bottom as Jack hid the watercraft behind the foliage lining the river. He wrapped his arm around Sophie's shoulders, careful not to touch her injury.

"Please don't let them take me again," she said, burying her face against his chest.

"Shh. I won't let anyone hurt you, Sophie." His stomach knotted with fear. How could he keep that promise?

The noise grew louder, and the smell of diesel fuel permeated the humid air. Jack's muscles tensed as the flat boat came into view. Several men wearing the uniform of the Costa Rican federal agents stood on deck. If they were authentic, he and Sophie would be safe.

But if they weren't, this could be the end.

Still hesitant to believe the men might not be criminals, Jack wavered about revealing their location. Slowly, the watercraft moved closer, and he knew their time was almost up before they were discovered.

Sophie made a tiny gasp and pulled away from Jack. "Hector?" she whispered. Then more loudly, "Hector! Hector! Over here."

Their tiny vessel rocked, and Jack's first reaction was to cover up her mouth with his hand. He thought she'd lost her mind, especially when the armed soldiers swiveled around and pointed their guns directly at them.

Over the thunder of his bounding pulse and the chugging of the boat motor, Jack heard his name being called along with Sophie's. He couldn't believe it! Hector was alive and apparently bringing the cavalry into rescue them.

Guiding the canoe to the bank, Jack helped Sophie out of the boat. The moment Hector disembarked, Sophie threw her uninjured arm around him and kissed him on the cheek. "You're alive!"

Hector's face flushed with pleasure, and he raised his eyebrows comically at Jack. "I think she is happy to see me, ¿*no*?"

Jack laughed as Sophie let go and stepped away. "She's not the only one happy to see you." He reached out and gave Hector a bear hug, patting him on the back.

"I'm glad to see you too, Jack, but please don't kiss me."

With another laugh, Jack let go. He blinked back the tears blurring his vision, so grateful he didn't have to tell Hector's wife she was a widow. "Where have you been?"

Before Hector could answer , a couple of the federal agents stepped in between them and started asking questions. Jack did his best to recount their ordeal as accurately as possible. When he got to the part about the men drinking until they passed out, the agents were eager to go up the river and make the arrests before Alberto, Raul and the other criminals sobered up and moved out.

The day before, one of their comrades had been shot and killed in a gun battle with Cruz.

Jack didn't even get to the part about Maria's death or how they had escaped. Apparently, having heard enough, the captain of the small brigade was shouting for his men to get back aboard their vessel so they could move forward.

It was impressive how quickly the men acted, and within a minute, they were on their way. As soon as the flat boat was out of sight, Jack wanted to get back into the canoe and leave immediately. The captain had told Hector about *Paraiso,* a small village that was only a couple of hours away downstream.

One look at Sophie's pale, drawn face made Jack change his mind. "How's your arm?"

She had her hand pressed against her wound, and when she moved it so he could check the site, Jack saw her palm was covered with fresh blood.

Hector gave a low whistle. "*Chica,* what have you done?"

"I'll let Jack tell you the story." She started to sway. "Maybe I better sit down."

Jack steadied her before he placed one hand under her knees and lifted her up to cradle her in his arms. He directed Hector to get the backpack from the canoe while he found a fallen log for them to sit on.

"You don't know how to do stitches, do you?" Jack asked Hector when he returned carrying the backpack.

"No, *amigo.*" He drew his dark eyebrows together. "It is bad, then?"

"*Sí,*" Jack said. "That scum Raul cut her with a knife."

Sophie winced as Jack removed the bloodied bandages. "The steri-strips should work just fine, Jack."

With Sophie instructing them as to what to do, Jack and Hector managed to close the laceration with the strips of the long bandages. It wasn't pretty, but the wound was closed and appeared to have stopped bleeding.

Jack finished up by winding a clean stretchy-gauze around Sophie's upper arm to cover the bandages, while Hector fiddled with the GPS. "Did you get the map?" Jack asked.

"*Sí.*" Hector showed the coordinates to Jack. "*Paraíso* is here, and from there *San Benito* is only about two or three days out, depending on how fast we travel."

"We'll have to reimburse them for Fred," Jack said as he tied the gauze into a soft knot.

"Poor Fred," Sophie said, scratching at one of the many mosquito bites they'd both acquired on their night-time boat ride with Alberto and Raul. "He didn't deserve to die."

"No, he didn't." Hector scowled. "But when I heard the gunshot, I thought for sure they had killed one of you."

Jack stood up to stretch his legs. "By the way, how did you avoid being captured in the first place?"

"The stew we had for dinner did not sit well on my stomach." Hector shrugged. "After using the latrine, I started back to camp when I heard the two men arguing about whether or not to kill you. I kept hidden, silently tracking the both of you. After you got into the canoe, I knew I couldn't rescue you by myself."

Sophie stood up and moved next to Jack. "But how did you enlist federal agents to help you?"

They all headed for the canoe as Hector finished his story. "I was on my way to *Por El Rio* to get Manuel's help when I came across the federal agents."

"What a miracle," Sophie said, stepping into the boat and taking the middle seat.

Hector snorted as he held onto the canoe so Jack could take the back seat. "No, the miracle was that they didn't shoot first and ask questions later." He rubbed the back of his head with one of his hands. "Lucky for me, I didn't lose consciousness when one of the agents hit me over the head with his assault rifle."

"Are you okay?" Sophie asked.

"No worries." He winked at Sophie. "Besides, they were very apologetic once I explained two men named Alberto and Raul had kidnapped my friends to save the life of their leader."

"I didn't save his life."

"No, she saved both of our lives," Jack said.

"Well," Hector said as he climbed into the front of the canoe. "Since we've got the time, I'd like to hear all about your escape and how Sophie got that nasty knife wound."

* * *

Jack wished they had about six more hours of daylight, but despite how hard they'd pushed it the past two days, they were not going to make it to *San Benito* until tomorrow. Ahead of him, Sophie stumbled and barely kept herself upright. Jack hurried forward and grasped her by the elbow.

"Hey, I think we better start making camp before it gets too dark."

She looked up at him, gratitude evident in her eyes. "Okay, but I can keep going if we need to."

One thing he'd learned about Sophie was how little she complained, even when he knew she didn't feel good. Since leaving the small village of *Paraíso* a couple of days ago, she had suffered from a persistent headache, nausea and what she called a low-grade fever.

"I'd rather stop now. We still have about five or six hours to travel tomorrow just to reach *San Benito*, and then another three hours to reach the Jeep."

He had a feeling she was going to need all the rest she could get in order to make it tomorrow.

"Sounds good." She gave him a smile, and shrugged her backpack from her shoulders. Jack took the bag and decided that no matter how much she protested, he was going to insist on carrying her backpack for the rest of the journey. It wasn't very heavy, but he figured she would need to use all of her energy just to walk.

Hector came up behind her, his brown face glistening from perspiration. He'd at least been successful in getting Sophie to allow him to carry her tent. Since they hadn't been able to retrieve any of their camping gear, they'd been lucky enough to have purchased two beat up tents in *Paraíso*, along with a few blankets and mosquito netting.

"Jack and I will get your tent up first, Sophie." Hector slipped the straps of his backpack off and pulled out a water bottle. "Drink this, and we'll have everything set up in a few minutes."

"Thank you." She reached out for the water bottle, and Jack noticed her hand was as shaky as the aged man who had sold them the tents a few days before.

He and Hector worked quickly to set up camp. Once the tents were erected, Jack motioned toward the smaller one Sophie had used the past few nights. "Why don't you lay down and rest while Hector and I make dinner."

Sophie only nodded and quietly slipped inside the tent. The fact that she didn't even protest increased Jack's concern for her.

"I wish we'd made better time," Jack said as he met Hector's worried gaze. "Sophie isn't a complainer, and I'm afraid she won't let me know how sick she really is."

"She's been through a lot, *amigo*. Perhaps she is just tired, *no*?" The tone in Hector's voice implied he didn't believe Sophie was only "tired" any more than Jack did.

"I hope that's all it is, because we've got a long day of travel tomorrow."

"Yes," Hector said as he opened the last three packets of their dehydrated meals they had left, "but then we will be home and my Isabelle will take good care of her." He dumped the contents of the packages into an aluminum pan and slowly added boiling water.

Home. Just thinking about it sent an unexpected rush of anxiety through Jack that nearly stole his breath. Once they left the jungle, he would be forced to make some life-changing decisions. As much as he loved Sophie, what if she decided he wasn't good enough for her? Jack still had no idea how to go about reconciling with his brother and parents. He had no idea if they would even want to see him.

Sophie might believe she would be happy without the extended family she'd always wanted, but that could all change once she returned to Colorado. After all, Peter was still waiting there for her, and he had all the advantages Jack sorely lacked, like a secure job, a house, and a close-knit family.

Pushing back his apprehension, Jack glanced toward the tent. "I think I'll go see if Sophie is okay."

Without waiting for a reply from Hector, Jack quickly made his way to her tent. The zipper to the canvas door was only partially done up. He crouched down and pulled the zipper down the rest of the way. He peered into the open door and saw Sophie was already asleep.

Renewed concern for her well-being warred with the anxiety about their future as he studied the delicate features of her face. She was so beautiful, and Jack really did love her.

Deciding to let her rest, he started to pull the zipper closed. Sophie's eyes flew open and she sat up with a gasp. "Oh." She drew in a deep breath. "You scared me."

"Sorry. I just wanted to see how you're doing."

"I think I feel better." She raised a hand to her head. "But I must have gotten up too fast. I feel a little lightheaded."

"Will food help?"

"Maybe." Her hand moved to her abdomen. "Although, I'm not sure I feel like eating right now. "

"Dinner's done," Hector hollered. "Come and get it while it's hot."

Jack held out his hand and smiled. "You better not pass up your last backpacking meal. Tomorrow it'll just be protein bars."

She scooted toward him and placed her palm against his. "That sounds even less appetizing."

Jack laughed, grateful she was acting more like herself. He tugged her close and leaned down to give her a kiss. Sophie melted against him, and her soft sigh of pleasure made Jack's pulse surge. Being near her like this made it easy to suppress the anxious thoughts. Right now, anything seemed possible.

* * *

Sophie awoke the next morning and knew she was in trouble. Her body ached at every joint, and her head felt like it weighed two hundred pounds. It hurt to move, and she found it difficult just to sit up. Would she be able to even walk today?

A wave of nausea rolled over her as she grabbed the toiletry bag next to her sleeping bag. She took a few slow breaths until the feeling subsided and then reached inside the bag for the digital thermometer she'd brought along.

She already knew she was running a fever, she just didn't know how high. Placing the end of the thermometer under her tongue, she waited until she heard the low-pitched beeping sound to let her know it was done.

Her hands shook as she read the numbers. No wonder she felt so bad. Her temperature was nearly a hundred and three. She put the thermometer back and found a single dose package of Extra Strength Tylenol. She hoped and prayed it would be effective enough to get her out of the jungle.

Once she swallowed the tablets, she had to lie back down again. Closing her eyes, she offered a prayer, asking for guidance about her illness. Since she was taking a broad spectrum antibiotic to prevent any infection from the knife wound to her arm, she knew she was probably dealing with a virus. And since she had just spent the past two weeks in a jungle with mosquitos, she had an idea about what virus was making her sick.

Another wave of nausea hit her, and she had to concentrate hard not to throw up the medication she'd just taken. It subsided a few minutes later, and that's when she heard Jack and Hector breaking camp. She had hoped to have at least enough time for the Tylenol to kick in before getting up.

"Sophie?" Jack asked through the tent. "Are you awake?"

"Yes." Her voice cracked, and she gently cleared her throat. "Yes, I'm awake."

There was a long pause before Jack said, "Can I come in?"

She hated just lying there and knew she looked awful, but she didn't have the energy to do anything about it, let alone sit back up.

"Sure."

Jack opened the tent door and crouched down at the foot of her sleeping bag. "Hey," he said, watching her with an intense gaze. Two deep creases appeared between his eyebrows. "You look terrible…er, like you don't feel very good."

"Nice save," she said, giving him a small smile.

The corner of his mouth quirked up. "You're still beautiful. It's just obvious you're sick."

Without a warning, her eyes filled up with tears. "I'm sorry."

"Hey now, don't cry."

His voice was so tender and so unlike the first time she'd met him that it made her even more emotional.

"And you don't need to apologize for being sick." He moved far enough inside the tent to take her hand. The second he touched her skin, his blue eyes widened. "Sophie, you're burning up."

"I know." Her bottom lip quivered as the tears spilled over and trickled down the side of her face into her hairline. "If I have what I think I have, I'll probably get worse before I get better."

A look of concern etched creases across his forehead. "What do you think you have?"

Even though she was taking antimalarial medication, there was a small chance she'd contracted the disease, but she didn't think so.

"Have you heard of dengue fever?"

"Yeah," he said, sitting back on his heels. "Then you probably feel as crappy as you look."

She tried not to laugh at his blunt observation. "Thanks for sparing my feelings."

"You know what I mean." He shook his head and gave a low whistle. "One of the doctors in a group I guided a few years back came down with dengue. He was pretty sick."

"I remember when I was in pre-med my dad had the same thing. I researched it fairly thoroughly, and from what I can remember, people are usually sick for about three to five days." She was modulating the duration a little, but she was trying to be optimistic.

"We need to get your fever down." Jack gave her hand a gentle squeeze before releasing it. "Tylenol or ibuprofen?"

"Your medical skills are getting more impressive day by day."

"Yeah," he said with a wry grin. "Hanging out with a doctor tends to do that to you."

She smiled. "I already took some Tylenol. If you can give me a few minutes, I'll be ready to leave."

He looked at her skeptically. "I don't think you'll be up for travel today."

She didn't want to alarm him, but she felt an urgency to get back to San José. "Jack, I'm in the first few days of the virus, so we should leave while I can."

"Okay," he said rising. "We'll leave as soon as you feel like you're ready."

* * *

Jack wasn't sure how much longer Sophie could go. She was almost too weak to travel anymore. Her steps faltered, but Jack kept her upright, holding onto her elbow. "Do we need to stop and rest for a minute?"

She looked up at him, confusion written all over her face. "I need to find my dad." She tightly gripped his arm. "Please help me find my daddy."

Jack and Hector exchanged worried expressions. Sophie had been acting a little out of it for the past couple of hours. "How much longer?" Jack mouthed to Hector.

"Maybe thirty to forty-five minutes."

Jack shook his head. He didn't think she would make it another five minutes. "Let's keep moving."

"Peter," Sophie said, looking up at Jack. "I have to go by myself."

"Okay," Jack said going along with her. "But why don't you take another drink of water." He handed the bottle to her, growing more and more concerned.

"Thank you." She took a sip and made a face. "Do you have anything colder?"

"Not right now." Jack looked sidelong at Hector. "We need to get her to a hospital."

Hector solemnly nodded his head in agreement. "*Sí,* let's go."

It didn't bother Jack that Sophie had called him Peter. She'd also called him Camille. What bothered him was the delirium itself. He knew it wasn't normal. Taking the bottle of water from Sophie, Jack noted fresh bruises on her arms. For the life of him, he couldn't figure out where the bruises had come from.

"Come on, Sophie. We're almost there," Jack said, taking her arm and pressing forward. Each step brought them closer to *San Benito*—closer to getting Sophie help.

Under Jack's fingers, her skin felt clammy and cold. The fever had broken earlier, but her bizarre behavior had him more worried than the high temperature. Looking down at Sophie, he wished she could at least clue him into what was going on with her.

He kept his arm firmly around her waist, practically dragging her. *Only thirty more minutes,* he repeated over and over in his head.

Her steps faltered, and she started to sink to the ground. "Jack?" she asked, her voice cracking with emotion as he kept her from falling.

"What, honey?" She seemed to know who he was, but her eyes were clouded with confusion.

"What's wrong with me?" Her words slurred together like she'd been drinking.

"I don't know, but we're almost home." He met Hector's concerned gaze. Neither one of them knew what to do for her.

Sophie moaned in pain and pressed a hand to her stomach. "I don't feel very good."

Jack was afraid she was going to throw up. Instead, her knees buckled and her body went limp. He gripped her arm, catching her before she hit the ground.

Chapter Twenty-Four

"Sophie," Jack said as he eased her body to the ground. "Come on, Sophie," he said again, grasping her by the shoulders and gently shaking her. "Wake up, honey."

She remained deathly still, her face without any color. Trying to recall basic first-aid, Jack made sure she was breathing. Then he placed his fingers against her throat and felt for a pulse. It seemed a little too fast. *Please, God, help me know what to do.*

Hector rushed over. "What's wrong?"

"I don't know." Jack felt utterly helpless and knew she needed immediate medical care. He discarded his backpack and scooped her up in his arms. She weighed practically nothing. "Let's just go. She needs to be in a hospital."

The terrain was difficult and seemed to slope uphill the entire time. Although she wasn't heavy, his arms and legs burned. With each step, Jack prayed for a miracle—prayed for her to wake up, but Sophie remained unconscious.

Perspiration dampened his T-shirt, and his lungs heaved from the exertion. Several times he had to pause and readjust his hold on her. Finally, after what seemed like hours, they reached *San Benito*.

A small group of children were playing soccer and grew very quiet when they saw the strangers enter their village. Jack heard some of the children whisper, "*Es muerta.*" He didn't have time to reassure them Sophie wasn't dead.

When they came to a grassy area, Hector turned around. "Wait right here. I'll go find help and get the canoe ready."

Jack had no idea who could help, but at this point, he would welcome the village shaman. Carefully, Jack laid Sophie's limp body on the grass.

Alarm swept through him when he noticed a small trickle of blood seeping from one nostril. Had he inadvertently injured her somehow?

He wiped at the blood with his thumb, fighting the feelings of despair and frustration. "Please," he begged God in a broken voice. "Please, let her be okay." Silently, Jack prayed for help and promised God he would do whatever he could to make Sophie happy, even if that meant moving to Colorado without knowing how he would support a wife.

A crowd had gathered around him, some murmuring prayers of their own. Jack pinched the bridge of his nose, the tips of his fingers growing moist from his desperate tears. Suddenly, the group parted, and Jack looked up to see a tall, balding man walking toward them. Hector was right behind him.

"What do we have here?" the man asked in perfect English as he knelt down next to Sophie. He was an American, probably in his early sixties, wearing khakis and a loose fitted, white cotton shirt and had a stethoscope hanging around his neck.

"Please tell me you're a doctor," Jack said, hardly able to believe his luck—no, an answer to his prayers.

"That I am, son." He placed his fingers at Sophie's throat to feel for a pulse and introduced himself. "I'm Mark Webster."

"Jack Mathison." Jack gazed at Sophie. "This is Sophie."

"Tell me about the onset of the illness and what the symptoms have been?" Dr. Webster asked as he opened Sophie's eyelids and shone a small penlight in each eye.

"Sophie's a doctor and suspected she had dengue fever." Jack told him about her elevated temperature and the delirium and then pointed out the bruises on her arm.

The doctor saw the faded bruises on her cheek and raised a questioning eyebrow. "It looks like someone hit her in the face."

Jack read the accusation, but couldn't blame the man. "Someone did hit her. A few days ago we were both abducted by some men so Sophie could try to save their injured comrade." Jack pointed to the bruises on his own face. "That's where I got these from."

"I heard about that from the villagers." The doctor offered Jack a friendly smile. "You've evaded one kind of tragedy. How about we see if we can avoid another one?"

Jack exhaled heavily. "That's what I've been praying for."

The doctor unwound his stethoscope. "Is she your wife?"

"Not yet."

Dr. Webster smiled. "Well, we better get this young lady better so you can make that happen." Dr. Webster put the stethoscope tips in his ears and concentrated on Sophie.

As the man listened to her lungs and heart, Jack looked up to see Hector. "Do you have the canoe ready?"

"*Sí.* Everything is all set to go."

Winding the stethoscope around his neck again, the doctor asked, "Has she had any fluids or medication today?"

"I've tried to get her to drink water and this morning she had some Tylenol."

Dr. Webster nodded his head, continuing his examination. "And the bruises on her arm appeared this morning?"

"I actually noticed them this afternoon," Jack answered.

The doctor lifted Sophie's shirt slightly, and Jack couldn't even appreciate her toned stomach. It was covered with tiny red spots. "Is that a rash?"

"Although that's what it looks like, it's not actually a rash." Mark palpitated her abdomen and Sophie groaned slightly. "The tiny pin-point spots are caused by blood leaking out of the capillaries under the skin."

That didn't sound very good to Jack. Before he could ask more questions, he heard a commotion. Jack raised his eyes to see a trim American woman with long, silvery hair, rushing toward them. She wore jeans and a colorful T-shirt with the logo of a Christian humanitarian organization.

"Mark, what do I need to get?" she questioned, kneeling down.

"Honey, we need to get an IV started as soon as possible," Mark said, pulling Sophie's shirt down.

He looked up at Jack. "This is my wife Jane. She's also my nurse." Mark stood up. "Jack, can you carry Sophie to the bungalow?"

"Sure." Adrenalin coursed through his body as Jack scooped Sophie up. He followed Mark and Jane, thanking God for putting them in this village.

While Jane started the IV, Mark pulled Jack aside. "She's very sick, and I need to get her to the hospital in San José."

Jack raked his hand through his hair in agitation. "My Jeep is in *Del Cielo*, about a half an hour from here by canoe." He swallowed back the fear he felt. "Do you know what's wrong?"

Mark rubbed his balding head. "My guess is dengue hemorrhagic fever. I won't know for sure until I can get some blood work done, but from what I can tell by examination and her history, I'm almost 99% sure that's what we're dealing with."

Jack had never heard about the hemorrhagic part of dengue fever.

He listened as the doctor explained the potential complications and possible mortality if they didn't get her to a medical facility soon.

"It's rare, but she may need a platelet blood transfusion. Unfortunately, I won't know that without getting a CBC." Mark pulled out a satellite phone from his pant pocket. "I'm calling a friend of mine who happens to be a helicopter pilot. He'll be waiting for us in *Del Cielo*."

Jack wanted to hug the man. "I—" His voice cracked with emotion. "Thank you so much. I can't believe you and your wife were here."

Dr. Webster looked at his wife and smiled. "Sweetie, tell him about this morning."

Jane nodded her head. "We're here with a Christian humanitarian aid organization, and this morning after we met for prayer, I had the feeling that Mark and I needed to remain behind." Her eyes filled with tears. "Now we know why God wanted us to stay."

Jack felt his throat tighten with emotion. God had heard his prayers. "Thanks for listening."

Mark patted him on the arm. "Let's get your young lady to the hospital."

* * *

Mark and his wife climbed aboard the helicopter with Sophie. "We'll take good care of her, son," Dr. Webster said over the whir of the helicopter blades.

"I'll be there as soon as I can." There wasn't any room for Jack, forcing him to make the journey home by his Jeep.

Before backing away, Jack took one last look at Sophie. Her dark lashes brushed against her pale cheeks, making her look like a sleeping princess. Snow White was it? If only his kiss would awaken her.

The helicopter revved its engines in preparation for flight, and Jack and Hector moved to stand by the Jeep. Both men shielded their eyes from the flying debris as the chopper ascended above the trees and hovered there for a few seconds. The pilot transitioned the helicopter from vertical to forward motion, and gracefully, the big machine flew away for San José.

Jack turned to Hector. "Do you mind if I take shotgun?" Consumed with worry, Jack figured he wouldn't be able to concentrate on driving down the mountain.

"*Sí, amigo.*" Hector climbed in behind the wheel. "Let's go."

As Hector pulled away, Jack unlocked the glove compartment to retrieve his cell phone. Within twenty minutes he should have service. His phone powered up briefly, flashing low battery. After a few seconds, it shut off. "Great!" he shouted in frustration. "My phone is dead."

Leaving in such a hurry, he had forgotten his charger. Dr. Webster needed Jack to call Sophie's family to get her medical records. Her friend Camille was the closest thing to family Sophie had. Well, besides Peter, but Jack wasn't calling him. "I need to get a hold of Tyson so he can tell his sister to call me."

Tempted to throw his phone out in frustration, he put it back in the glove box. Then Jack noticed Sophie's iPhone. It would most certainly have Camille's number programmed in it. Powering up the device, he felt relief she didn't have a passcode and that her battery was almost fully charged.

Scrolling through her recent calls, he noted Peter Elliot's name. Camille's number was listed right above. Impatiently, Jack waited until the bars appeared, indicating he had cell phone service. Jack quickly scrolled through the list again and tapped on Camille's name.

"Sophie! Are you back yet?" a man asked before Jack could say a word. It must be Camille's husband.

"Uh, no. Could I please talk to Camille?"

"*What?* Who is this?" an angry male voice demanded.

"Who are you?" Jack snapped. He didn't have the patience to deal with a suspicious or jealous husband.

"I asked first, and why are you using my fiancée's phone?"

"*Fiancée?*" Jack rubbed his head. "I obviously have the wrong number."

"This is Peter Elliot, and I want to know where Sophie is!"

Shoot. He had pushed the wrong number. But why was the guy referring to Sophie as his fiancée?

"Look, Mr. Elliot, this is Jack Mathison, and I didn't mean to call you—"

The man cut him off before he could end the call. "Mathison? Aren't you the guy Sophie hired to help find her father?"

"Yeah, and I'm sorry to bother you, but I really need to talk to Camille."

"I want to talk to Sophie this instant."

Jack ground his teeth together. "Mr. Elliot, Sophie is sick, and I need to talk to Camille immediately. I don't have time to explain anymore right now."

"That is unacceptable. I want answers immediately!"

"Sorry, but I can't talk right now. I'm hanging up."

Jack pushed end, cutting off a very angry Peter Elliot. Finding Camille's number, Jack was careful and made sure to press the correct line. Almost as soon as it started to ring, an annoying beep cut in. Jack took a quick glance at the screen to see Elliot was trying to call him back.

Not that he blamed him, but Jack couldn't deal with him until he had Sophie's medical records. He pushed the ignore button and prayed Camille would answer.

"Sophie!" a woman squealed in delight. "I'm so glad you called—"

"Hey, Camille, this is Jack. My phone is dead so I'm using…look, Sophie is really sick, and I need your help."

"Oh no. How can I help?"

Jack explained the chain of events leading up until Sophie boarded the helicopter. "The doctor here needs her medical records. Do you think you can get those?"

"I'll get right on it," Camille said. "As soon as I have the information, should I call you back on Sophie's phone?"

"Yeah." The annoying beep started again. Jack pushed ignore, wishing Elliot would just go away.

"Do you need to get that?" Camille asked.

"No," Jack said. "I accidentally called Elliot first, and now he won't leave me alone."

"Elliot? As in Peter Elliot?"

"Yeah. I guess you know him."

"I know him all right." Camille sighed. "I can't believe you called him. He'll be beside himself with worry."

"I didn't mean to call him!" Jack blew out a big breath. "I said I couldn't talk to him now, but he obviously didn't believe me."

"One thing you should know about Peter is that he doesn't give up."

Jack snorted. "I kind of got that. The idiot kept referring to Sophie as his fiancée."

"He bought her a ring. So in his mind, Sophie is his fiancée."

Jack glowered and held onto the dash with one hand as Hector took a sharp corner. The beeping started up again.

"He obviously has a hard time with people telling him no."

Camille snickered. "Yep, that's Peter."

The beeping ended without Jack pushing the ignore button. "So you'll get her medical records?"

"Yes. Sophie and I go to the same doctor, and I'm sure she'll help me get her records."

Jack leaned his head back against the seat of the Jeep. "Thank you. I'll text you as soon as I get to the hospital."

"Okay—" Camille's voice cut out. Then she said, "Crap, Peter's trying to call me now. I guess I better answer it."

"Good luck."

"Thanks." She cleared her throat. "Out of curiosity, why does it bug you that Peter refers to Sophie as his fiancée?"

"Because," Jack said in a tight voice. "I'm the one who is going to marry her."

A loud, girly-squeal pierced Jack's ear, making him smile. "I knew it!" Camille said with a triumphant laugh. "Please tell me Sophie fell in love with you too."

Jack let out a slow breath. "Believe it or not, she did."

Camille squealed again. "This is so great. I need to talk to Peter, and then I'll get started on the medical records. Talk to you later!"

"Thanks," Jack said before he ended the call.

"Congratulations, *amigo*," Hector said.

Jack cast him a sidelong look. "For what?"

"You're getting married."

Yeah, he'd actually announced that out loud. As unprepared and as unworthy as he felt, he'd meant every word.

"She still has to say yes." Jack pictured Sophie the last time he'd seen her—pale and lifeless. "But first she needs to get better."

The urgency to see her again made his gut clench. *Please, God, just let her be okay.*

* * *

Leaning over with his head in his hands, Jack sat in the hard plastic chair and waited for word from Dr. Webster. He was tempted to look at his watch again, but guessed only five minutes had passed since the last time he'd checked the time.

Although Jack had been at the hospital for nearly two hours, all he knew was Dr. Webster's diagnosis had been correct. The update on whether or not Sophie needed a platelet transfusion would be determined by the lab results. In the mean time, Sophie was being treated with IV therapy, and Jack wasn't allowed to see her yet.

Sophie's phone alerted him of an incoming text. He sat back and looked at the screen and saw it was from Camille. Tyson's sister was as funny as her brother. Since Jack had been forbidden visiting rights, Camille had been encouraging him to break the rules and sneak in to see Sophie. Her latest idea was to pose as a doctor.

Despite the severity of the situation, Camille's message made him smile. He would need a shower, a change of clothes and probably need to shave before passing as a doctor. Hector had gone home to see his family, but had promised to return to the hospital with Jack's razor and a change of clothes for him. He made a quick reply, telling Camille that he'd just spent the past two weeks in the jungle and that that was exactly what he looked like.

Jack liked Camille, mainly because she liked *him* better than Peter. It was nice having someone on his side, especially since Peter was supposedly coming to Costa Rica to rescue Sophie and take her home to Colorado.

Another text came in, asking about an update on Sophie. Jack quickly typed in that he was still waiting and would let her know something as soon as he could. Then he asked about an update on Peter.

Peter hasn't left Colorado yet. Don't get too excited. He's still trying to make arrangements, and is probably leaving within the next 24 hours. Do you think you and Sophie could elope by then? They have hospital chaplains there, right?

Jack couldn't help laughing at Camille's message. At least she'd provided comic relief for him over the past two hours. Plus, she'd managed to get Sophie's medical history to Dr. Webster in record time. She would definitely be a good ally in the war for Sophie's affection.

Slipping the phone back in his pocket, Jack stood up and stretched. He couldn't sit any longer and was determined to hunt down someone to give him a report. Just as he was about to start his campaign to track down Mark, the doctor's wife Jane came into view.

Chapter Twenty-Five

Jack rushed to meet her. "How is she? Can I see her?"
Jane took his hand and patted it gently. "She's
actually doing a lot better. Mark is holding off on the blood
transfusion for now." She dropped his hand. "And yes, you
can see her."

"Now?"

"Yes." She smiled. "I know how anxious you must be."

"You have no idea." Jack let out a shaky laugh. "Is she
awake yet?"

"She's still sleeping." Jane winked at him. "But she's
mumbled your name more than once."

"That's good, right?"

"I don't know," she said wryly. "Did you want her to
ask for anyone else?"

Jack thought about Peter and scowled. "No."

"That's what I thought."

Jack trailed alongside Jane through a brightly lit
hallway to the ICU. They passed by a busy nurses' station
where several of the healthcare workers were talking on
telephones in such rapid Spanish even Jack had a hard time
following.

As they approached Sophie's room, Jack heard
machines beeping steadily, making him realize how serious
the situation was.

Jane paused outside the door, and placed her hand on
Jack's arm. "Don't be alarmed by all of the equipment. Most
of the monitoring is standard for the ICU."

"Okay." He nodded his head, more than ready to see
Sophie.

Jane crossed the threshold, and Jack followed right behind her. He felt his breath catch at the sight before him. Sophie looked so fragile lying in the hospital bed, her skin so pale in comparison to the deep blue hospital gown she was wearing.

A nasal cannula provided oxygen, and Jane pointed out the machine that flashed the percentage of Sophie's oxygen saturation. The other numbers on the screen monitored her respiratory rate and heart rate. The IV tubing was connected to an electronic pump that delivered an intermittent drop of fluid every few seconds.

Jack sat down next to Sophie's bed, his eyes scanning over her again just to make sure she was really okay. He stretched out his hand, wanting to stroke her face, but pulled back. Would touching her be okay?

Jane stepped up beside him. "You can talk to her quietly, and I think it would be all right if you held her hand."

"Okay. Thanks." Taking Sophie's small hand in his, he gently circled his thumb across her palm, basking in the warmth of her skin. She no longer felt cold and clammy.

"Hey, Sophie. I'm here with you. Mark and Jane are taking good care of you. You're going to get better now, baby." His voice broke. "I promise."

Sophie's hand twitched faintly, and the beeping sound from the heart monitor sped up slightly. The reassuring sound of her vital signs responding to his touch buoyed him up. "Camille said to tell you hi. She's funny and has been trying to give me ideas about how to sneak in to see you."

Jack felt it was wise not to mention anything about Peter. Instead, he told her all about Hector's family, especially his wife who was eager to meet her.

Too soon, Jane placed a hand on his shoulder. "Jack, I promised the nurses we'd keep your visit short."

Reluctantly, he let go of Sophie's hand and leaned over to brush a kiss across her forehead. "I'll be back, love," he whispered softly.

* * *

A sore muscle in Jack's neck prevented him from sleeping very soundly—that and the nurse who kept coming in every hour to check on Sophie. He adjusted his body, trying to find a more comfortable position in the small recliner that was positioned next to Sophie's bed. The chair groaned in protest, and Jack was afraid it would disturb Sophie. He watched her carefully, and tried not to worry when she didn't make the tiniest indication she'd heard anything.

Although she had only roused briefly over the past forty-eight hours, her prognosis was good. Mark assured Jack her deep sleep provided her body time to heal. After her blood work had showed an improvement in her platelet count, Mark had changed her medical status from critical to serious, but stable. She'd been moved out of ICU, and Jack had been allowed to stay in her room.

Jack shifted in the chair again and thought about getting up and returning to the hotel to take a quick shower. He glanced toward the window and saw the first fingers of dawn lighting the darkened sky. If he hurried, he could go and be back within a half an hour. But in that thirty minutes, Peter might show up.

His eyes moved to the clock on the wall, and he mentally calculated the time. Peter had left Colorado nine hours ago. Depending on layovers, he could show up any minute, and Jack wanted to be here when he did.

Not wanting to risk missing his arrival, Jack leaned back and closed his eyes. Just as he felt himself start to relax, he heard a male voice using horrible Spanish, demanding to see Sophie.

Perfect. Peter Elliot had just arrived.

Before Peter could barge into the room, Jack got up and quickly crossed the floor. Making his way out to the nurses' station, Jack paused to study the frustrated American. Dressed in gray dress pants, a white button-down shirt and conservative tie, Peter stood toe to toe with Yolanda—the grumpy nurse who liked to protect her patients. Jack had just barely gotten the heavy set nurse to warm up to him.

Watching Peter struggle with the language, Jack took a moment to size up the competition. He came to the conclusion he was at least an inch taller and broader in the shoulders than the well dressed, dark-haired attorney. But Peter had come armed with something Jack couldn't even hope to compete with. Family. Or at least pictures of family.

Yolanda lost her grouchy look as Peter held up the large poster board covered with pictures of what Jack assumed was Peter's family. There were messages written on every inch of white space. Peter pointed to several of the pictures and tried explaining in Spanish they were Sophie's family.

Jack's gut tightened with jealousy at the one thing he could never give Sophie. Even if he did make amends with his brother and parents, it would never amount to this large family.

Yolanda, who spoke both English and Spanish, grinned and said in a perfect American accent, "Such a lovely family. The *señorita* will be pleased when she awakes."

"You speak English?" The relief in Peter's face, and his wide grin, made Yolanda's face light up even more. "Thank you, I know my Spanish is horrible."

A giggle of delight bubbled out of Yolanda's mouth. "*Sí*, it was very bad."

Peter had just effectively taken one of Jack's allies away in a matter of seconds. What if he was successful in winning over Sophie just as quickly?

Yolanda spotted Jack and motioned for him to come over. "*Señor* Jack, this man is Sophie's family." She beamed. "Isn't it wonderful?"

Yeah, fantastic.

Peter's eyes narrowed as Jack approached. "You must be Mr. Mathison."

"It's Jack."

"Peter Elliot." He stuck out his hand.

Jack held his gaze as he grasped the man's hand and gave it a firm shake. "Right." He dropped his hand and crossed his arms over his chest. "It wasn't necessary for you to come."

"Since I'm marrying Sophie, I think it's entirely necessary."

The smile on Yolanda's face was replaced with a shocked look. "But I thought *Señor* Jack was marrying her?"

"I am—"

"No he's not—"

The men spoke at the exact same time, their voices clearly reflecting their stance.

Yolanda stepped forward, her don't-you-dare-mess-with-my-patient look back on her face. "I'm warning both of you right now that there will be no fighting." She put her hands on her ample hips and gave each of them an evil eye. "Do I make myself clear?"

Peter turned on the charm and scored a point in his favor. "Of course, ma'am. The most important thing here is Sophie's wellbeing." He shifted his eyes to Jack. "Isn't that right?"

"*Sí.*" Jack gave him a hard look. "Sophie's welfare has always been the most important thing."

Yolanda eyed both of them like she was trying to see if they were telling the truth—which they were.

Sophie's happiness *was* most important. The hard decisions could come later when she felt better.

"Good." The stern nurse looked like she wanted to say more but had to answer the telephone.

"I'd like to see Sophie," Peter said once he and Jack were alone.

A churning of unease made Jack want to find a way to prevent Peter from visiting Sophie. Ever. Too bad that wasn't a realistic goal.

"First, we need to talk."

"Not until I see Sophie."

Jack ground his teeth and stepped closer. "Look, Sophie is sleeping right now. We need to get a few things straight, like the fact that you and Sophie are not engaged."

The muscle in Peter's jaw jumped. "Not officially."

"I believe you asked, and Sophie turned you down."

The tips of Peter's ears went red. "And how do you know that, Mr. Mathison?" His tone had risen in both volume and irritation.

Yolanda cleared her throat. When he and Peter turned to look at her, she held up one finger. "This is your only warning. The next time I will call security."

"Elliot, you and I need to take this outside before we both get thrown out of here."

Peter's eyebrows rose. "Outside? Are you planning on a fist fight?"

Not a bad idea, but probably not the wisest thing to do. "No. I told you we need to talk."

Peter stared at Jack for a few seconds. Finally, he nodded and turned toward the nurses' station. "Ma'am," he said holding up the poster board. "Could you please hold on to this for me? Mr. Mathison and I are going to go outside for a moment."

"*Sí.*" Yolanda took the oversized get-well card and narrowed her eyes. "I hope you both can come to a reasonable understanding."

"Thank you, I do too." Peter flashed his perfect white teeth, and Jack noticed a dimple crease the man's cheek.

Yolanda must have noticed it too. A blush colored her plump cheeks, and the smile she gave the man as she waved them both away indicated she liked Peter—probably more than Jack.

Neither man spoke as Peter followed Jack outside to a small courtyard. The cloudless sky glowed a deep purple as dawn approached, promising a beautiful day.

"Now," Peter said evenly. "Since you seem to know so much about my relationship with Sophie, I'd like to ask you a few questions."

The guy was all lawyer now. Cocky and so sure of himself. Jack didn't like it. "Go ahead."

"Am I to believe that *you've* fallen in love with Sophie?"

"Yes."

"And how does Sophie feel about you?"

"She loves me," Jack answered confidently. "I plan on asking her to marry me."

One of Peter's eyebrows rose up. "If she says yes, how do you plan to support her? Sophie doesn't want to work full time once she starts a family."

Jack hated the arrogant tone reflected in Peter's words. "I know. We've discussed that already."

A flash of uncertainty darkened Peter's eyes. "You didn't answer my question."

"I don't know why I would have to answer to you."

"Because," Peter said, his voice low and steady. "I do care about Sophie, and I'm her friend."

Lousy lawyer had a point. "Sophie and I don't know how everything will work out, but I assure you I can support a wife." Jack ignored the knot in his stomach. He could provide for a wife, couldn't he?

"Assuming that's true," Peter said with a hint of sarcasm, "I did a little digging and discovered you're estranged from your family. Is Sophie aware of this?"

The guy had done some kind of background check on him? "Yes." Jack inched forward. "She and I talked about it extensively."

"The private investigator I hired was able to track down several of your previous clients. With a few pointed questions, it was fairly simple to conclude you aren't exactly on good terms with God. If you truly know Sophie like you claim to, you'll know how important her faith is."

Jack clenched his hands into fists and kept them firmly at his side. "My stance with God is none of your business."

Peter lifted his brow again. "Mr. Mathison, I'm in love with Sophie. I've been in love with her for nearly a year. I've wanted to marry for just as long. Believe it or not, I do want her to be happy. If that means marrying you, then so be it." He took a step toward Jack. "But I won't go without first seeing Sophie, and I won't step away from her unless *she* tells me to go."

They stared at each other for a few intense seconds. Peter stuck his hands in his pockets and lifted one shoulder. "Besides, if you're so confident in her feelings for you, then it shouldn't make a difference if I stay."

How could Jack argue with that? "Sophie's been through a lot the past two weeks. I don't want her hurt or upset."

"I would never do anything to hurt Sophie."

"Neither would I," Jack said. But what if he wasn't what Sophie needed?

Despite how much he detested Peter Elliot, he also respected him. And it was obvious the guy was completely in love with her.

Peter nodded his head, and, without saying a word to each other, they made their way back inside the hospital. They stopped at the desk where Peter retrieved the poster board. "Would you please show me to Sophie's room?" he asked Jack.

Jack couldn't say no. "Sure." He acknowledged Yolanda with a smile. "We worked out a deal, so you don't have to worry."

"I am very happy to hear that."

Jack glanced at Peter. "Let's go. I don't want Sophie to wake up and be all alone."

* * *

Sophie heard the murmured voices in the room, and she struggled to open her heavy eyelids. She'd been dreaming about Jack and Peter. Together. She didn't remember what they were saying, but they'd both seemed so real.

"Sophie, how are you feeling?" The male voice was unfamiliar.

"Okay," she croaked. "I think." Her mouth felt dry, and she longed for a cool drink of water. Fighting the intense grogginess, she forced her eyelids open. The bright light blinded her, and she squinted, unable to move her arms to block out the light.

A woman laughed softly. "That's better than what you said yesterday."

Sophie tried to focus on the person hovering above her. The woman had long silvery hair and a pretty face. "I talked to you yesterday?"

"Yes, and you said you felt like the one and only time you've ever had a hangover."

Another face came into focus. The man was balding, his skin tanned with deep laugh lines around his eyes and mouth. "And to answer the same question you asked yesterday, no, you haven't been drinking."

"Then what happened to me? Am I in a hospital?"

"Yes. I'm Dr. Mark Webster." The man winked at her and pointed at the woman. "This is my beautiful wife Jane."

"Hello." She licked her dry lips. "So what's wrong with me?"

"You've had a pretty bad case of dengue hemorrhagic fever." He offered her a smile. "But you're out of the woods now and should start to feel a lot better."

Her mind was suddenly flooded with memories of getting sick the last leg of their trip. An image of Jack flashed in her mind. "Where's Jack?"

"I'm right here, baby." The sound of his voice made her feel warm inside. She searched the room until her gaze centered on his handsome face.

"I hope this means we made it out of the jungle."

"Yes," he said with a laugh. "A few days ago."

"Really? I don't remember anything."

"Not even the helicopter ride?" Jack took her hand, and an electrifying pulse skidded up her arm.

"A helicopter? Just how sick have I been?"

He brought her hand to his mouth, his warm lips caressing her skin. "Sweetheart, you had me very worried."

The tenderness in Jack's words, and the look of love in his light blue eyes, stole her breath. She wished they were alone.

"You had us all worried." Dr. Webster patted her on the shoulder. "More of your memory will come back, so don't be too concerned." He smiled and winked at her again. "Jane and I will be by later on tonight."

"You boys behave, all right?" Jane said before walking out the door with her husband.

Boys? Before she could ask, another person stepped forward. "Hello, darling."

The male face before her made her gasp. "Peter?"

A frown wrinkled his forehead. "You don't remember talking to me yesterday?"

"No." She continued to stare at her former boyfriend. He looked like he'd just gotten off work, wearing a blue dress shirt and tie. Was she still in Costa Rica? "What are you doing here?"

"Jack called me."

Now that didn't make any sense at all. She turned questioning eyes to Jack. "You called Peter?"

The muscle in his jaw tightened. "Not on purpose."

"Sophie," Peter said, making her shift her eyes back to him. "It was by divine intervention that I received the phone call about your illness."

"No," Jack snorted. "It was a mistake." He looked into Sophie's eyes. "My phone was dead, so I used yours. I accidentally selected Peter's number instead of Camille's."

Sophie blinked, wishing the cobwebs would clear from her mind. "So I'm still in Costa Rica, right?"

Jack brushed back a wisp of hair away from her face. "Yes."

"And Peter's really here?" Her voice broke again, and she coughed a little, trying to clear her throat.

"Yes, sweetheart, I'm really here."

"Where is—" She couldn't finish her question due to her dry throat.

Peter stepped closer. "Would you like something to drink?"

She settled her gaze on Peter, noting his grim smile and that his dimple was absent. Sophie's head swam, her brain still a little slow. Maybe this was all a dream.

"I don't know what I want."

This comment made Peter smile widely, and just like that his dimple appeared.

Jack tightened his grip on her hand. "Sophie, you don't have to choose now."

Huh? What did these two guys think she was talking about? She tried to moisten her lips. "Well, it's between water or apple juice. Either one would be nice."

Jack started to laugh and leaned over, kissing her right on the mouth. It was only a peck, and she felt strangely cheated.

Peter frowned. "Certainly, honey. Just say the word, and I'll be happy to get you a drink."

"Thanks, Peter. Apple juice really does sound delicious."

Peter leaned over and kissed her on the cheek. "I'll be right back."

"Hey, Pete? Can you make that two? I'm a little thirsty," Jack said with a grin.

Peter's scowl deepened before he swiftly left the room.

"I get the feeling the two of you don't like each other that much," Sophie said understatedly.

"Pete's an alright guy. He just isn't that happy about you falling in love with me."

"Pete?" She shook her head. "Jack, I know he hates being called Pete. Are you playing nice?"

The impish grin on Jack's face said it all. Without answering, he leaned in and whispered in her ear. "I'm dying to kiss you."

Inhaling the familiar scent of his tangy aftershave, Sophie's lips tilted up into a smile. She couldn't help it. "Me too. But until I use a toothbrush, you'll have to wait."

"Or," Jack said, pulling out a stick of gum, "I have gum." He raised both of his eyebrows triumphantly.

"I'll take the gum."

Jack removed the wrapper, placing the gum between Sophie's parted lips. She slowly chewed, never taking her eyes from Jack's face.

"Better?" he asked in a low voice.

"Yes."

He leaned over and kissed her softly, caressing her lips with skilled deliberation. She wanted to put her arms around him to pull him closer, but her muscles were too weak and refused to cooperate. The kiss was achingly sweet, and she never wanted it to end.

"I have your juice," a voice interrupted angrily.

Chapter Twenty-Six

Sophie's brain registered Peter's voice at the same time Jack released her mouth. Red in the face, Peter brought the juice can close to her bedside.

"Where's mine?" Jack asked with amusement.

He didn't need to be so mean. "Jack," Sophie reprimanded. "You can get your own juice."

He didn't look at all bothered by her reproof. "I'm not that thirsty anyway."

A nurse came into the room. "*Buenos días*," she said, giving Sophie a big smile. Then in perfect English, said, "It is good to see you are wide awake, *señorita*. How do you feel?"

Sophie's eyes darted between the two men. They were complete opposites. Jack, his light-brown hair with sun kissed highlights, pale-blue eyes and dressed in casual shorts, T-shirt and flip-flops. Peter with his curly, dark hair, brown eyes and dressed for a business meeting. Sophie looked back at the nurse and answered, "I feel a little out of it."

The nurse checked Sophie's IV and catheter. "That's normal. But you know this. You are a doctor, *¿no?*"

"Yes. But my expertise is in children." Her eyes flickered back to the two men who both probably needed a timeout. Well, at least Jack.

The nurse patted her on the arm. "I'm going to empty your catheter. Hopefully we can take it out sometime today."

Sophie noticed both men look at each other nervously. Jack started to back up. "We'll just leave you alone for a minute."

Sophie watched them leave together, too tired to think about what to do. She loved Jack, but she cared about Peter and didn't like to see him hurting. Jack could be insensitive, and it wasn't necessary to hurt Peter any more than he already was.

Outside her room, Sophie could hear the low sound of two male voices conversing with each other. How would things work out?

* * *

"You don't need to be so overbearing," Peter said tightly once they were outside of the room.

"Kissing Sophie isn't overbearing," Jack defended. He did feel a little guilty, though. Especially since Sophie seemed upset with him. "Besides, I asked her first."

"I should've never left you alone with her." Peter skewered Jack with a look. "And I hate when you call me Pete. I believe I've asked you several times not to address me that way."

Jack's male ego was running rampant this morning. Sophie wouldn't be very pleased with him. Thinking of her, Jack apologized, "I'm sorry, Peter. I wasn't being very nice, and I was doing it on purpose."

His honest admission seemed to disarm Peter. He exhaled heavily. "I can see I probably don't stand a chance." He looked at Jack imploringly. "Please, just give me some time alone with her to say goodbye. I'm scheduled to fly out of here in a few days, but I can always get an earlier flight."

Wow, Jack wasn't expecting that. Peter had just accepted he'd lost. The least Jack could do was give him time to say goodbye. "Uh, sure. I'll go to my hotel and do a load of laundry and answer my email."

Relief crossed the man's features. "Thank you."

Yolanda came out of Sophie's room. "You can both go back in there, but I expect you to continue being good." She narrowed her gaze at Jack. "Especially you, *Señor* Jack."

Jack felt even guiltier for his immature behavior. "I will."

Peter opened the door and allowed Jack to go in first. Sophie eyed both of them warily. "Everything okay?" she asked hesitantly.

"Sure," Jack said, moving to her side. "Peter is going to stay and keep you company while I run to my hotel room to answer emails."

Her eyes clouded with worry. "How long will you be gone?"

"Not long. I'll be back in an hour or so."

Peter looked surprised Jack was giving him that much time. "I'll take good care of her."

Jack nodded and bent down, brushing his lips against Sophie's forehead. "I'll see you soon."

On the drive to the hotel, Jack started to feel nervous. He'd won the girl, and he'd made the statement several times that he was going to marry Sophie, which meant he would be relocating to Colorado. His stomach felt queasy as he thought about everything he needed to do in order to make that happen.

He would have to sell his house, or he could turn it into a rental property. That way he and Sophie would have a place to stay when they came for a visit. Jack rebuffed the idea that it would also be security if things didn't work out with Sophie.

The night before, he and Peter had talked. Peter had suggested that Jack and Sophie's feelings for each other were mainly based on the bond they'd shared when Sophie learned of her father's death and then again when they'd been kidnapped and escaped together.

While that might be true, Jack knew his attraction to Sophie had been strong from the moment he'd first met her. Still, chemistry was a fickle thing. What if he moved to Colorado and his or Sophie's feelings changed?

Then there was the whole issue with his family. He still had no idea how to go about mending those relationships. Jack's hands gripped the steering wheel hard. If things didn't work out with his family, would Sophie ever be able to be truly happy with just Jack and eventually their children if they had any?

Peter's family was close, and they did love Sophie. He'd read all the personal messages on the poster board to her. They already considered her a part of their family. Some of the notes mentioned seeing her at Thanksgiving, which was only a couple of weeks away.

It was a holiday that typically brought families together, and it would probably be the perfect time to reunite with his brother and parents. Still, it scared him to think about facing his family again. Seeing Heather and Adam together would hurt. Even after all these years, he knew it would hurt. Could Jack really forgive them for all the pain they'd caused?

By the time Jack pulled into the parking lot, he wasn't sure what to do. The only thing he knew for certain was that he loved Sophie.

* * *

Sophie didn't know what to say to Peter. They both listened silently to Jack's retreating footsteps. With her heart monitor no longer needed, the room seemed awfully quiet.

"I'm sorry about your dad," Peter said, his brown eyes filled with tenderness.

"Thank you." Her voice quavered, and she bit her lip to control her emotions. "At least now I know what happened to him."

"My family sends their love." He smiled and picked up a white poster board that was leaning against the wall. "They all got together and made this for you. I showed it to you yesterday, but I'm guessing you don't remember that either."

He turned it over and her breath caught. Pictures of Peter's parents, his siblings and their spouses and children covered the board, with messages for Sophie written in between them.

"That is the sweetest thing in the world." She held out her hands and Peter handed it to her. "I can't believe they did this for me." Her eyes skimmed over the familiar faces. She read a few of the messages and couldn't help smiling.

"They love you Sophie." Peter's voice was so soft and sad at the same time. "So do I."

Her vision blurred as tears filled her eyes. Part of her still loved Peter. It was nothing compared to the way Jack made her feel, but she still cared about him. "I know you do."

Peter reached into his pocket and withdrew the velvet pouch containing the ring he'd given her. "I brought this with me, hoping you'd decide to accept my proposal." He took a seat in the chair next to her bed and emptied the bag, letting the engagement ring fall into the center of his palm.

Sophie stared at the glittering diamond, seeing her dream of becoming a wife and mother packed into such a small package. A lump lodged in her throat. She had decided not to accept the ring, even before she'd met Jack. It was the right decision, but deep down she had this fear that this might be her only chance to get married. Jack still hadn't said anything more about marriage. Of course she'd been too sick for them to have any kind of a serious discussion, but what if he didn't want to marry her?

Peter picked up the ring and held it between his long fingers. The vulnerability she read in his eyes pierced her heart. Before he said anything, the nurse named Yolanda came into the room.

She spotted the ring in Peter's fingers and clapped a hand over her heart and said something in Spanish. Peter knew a little of the language and Sophie saw he liked what Yolanda had said.

"*Sí*," he said, winking at the nurse.

Yolanda smiled at Sophie. "He is a good man, *Señorita*. I can tell." Then she turned around and left the room as fast as she'd appeared.

Sophie wasn't sure what to think about the woman's statement. For some reason, the nurse didn't seem to like Jack. Trying not to be bothered, she focused on Peter and found him watching her closely.

"I want to marry you, Sophie." He leaned forward, and the diamond sparkled under the lights. "I know you have feelings for Jack, but I believe you still care about me."

"Yes." She shook her head. "I mean, yes I still care about you, but I fell in love with Jack."

Peter tipped his head in acknowledgement. "I can understand that." He twisted the ring so it caught the light again. "But have you considered your feelings for him are based off of the bond you two shared when you learned about your father's death? You two also went through a lot together with the abduction by those ruthless men and then your illness."

"It's more than that, Peter. I don't know how to explain it."

He palmed the ring and closed his fist around it. "I'm not trying to undermine your feelings."

Sophie frowned. That was exactly what he was trying to do.

Peter let out a big breath. "Okay, I guess I am, but I want you to be sure you know what you're doing." He sat back, his lips pressed flat. "We've been together for a long time, Sophie. You know me, both my good and my bad. You know where I stand with God. You know my family."

He pinned her with a solemn look. "How well do you really know Jack? What about his family?"

Her throat was tight, and she felt like she couldn't breathe. She'd known Jack for two weeks, but it's not like they were getting married next week. But when would they get married? Neither of them had a plan. Was Jack staying in Costa Rica, or would he try to move to Colorado?

She swallowed, wishing Jack would come back now. She felt so unsure about everything. When he was with her, it was easier to imagine them together.

"I...I don't know." Sophie dropped her eyes and stared at the poster board once again. A few of Peter's older nieces had referred to her as Aunt Sophie and asked if they could have another princess movie night at her condo over the Thanksgiving holiday. They'd done it before, and Sophie had relished every second of the time spent with the sweet little girls.

Suddenly she felt so tired. She really didn't know how to answer Peter. Any argument about her feelings for Jack—which appeared to be based solely on physical attraction—seemed hollow.

"Sweetheart," Peter said, reaching over and taking one of her hands. "I'm sorry if what I've said has upset you." His hand, so smooth and warm, tightened around hers. His touch wasn't electric like Jack's, but it was comforting. "You don't have to make any decisions right now. I just want you to think about it, okay?"

"Okay." Her voice was barely audible. Tired, like how she felt.

Peter must have sensed that. "Go to sleep, honey. I'm right here." He stroked her palm with his thumb. "I'm not going anywhere unless you tell me to."

* * *

The scene before him was not what Jack had expected to find. He leaned against the doorjamb and fought to control his emotions. Both Sophie and Peter were asleep, and they were holding hands.

He tried to tell himself it meant nothing, but after what Yolanda had just said, he wasn't so sure. Had Peter really proposed again, and with a diamond ring? Sophie's left hand was tucked underneath Peter's, so he couldn't see if she was wearing a ring or not.

Feelings of betrayal and jealousy gripped him around the middle. What had happened in the hour and half it had taken him to answer his emails and do a load of laundry? He'd been so confident about Sophie's feelings for him that he hadn't been in any hurry to return.

As if sensing she was being watched, Sophie's eyes fluttered open, and when she saw Jack, her face lit up. "Hey," she said softly. She pulled her hand out from Peter's and stretched.

"Hey, yourself." Jack didn't see a ring and felt a measure of relief ease the tension in his chest. "Did you have a good nap?"

"Yes." She glanced over at Peter. "I guess we fell asleep."

The innocent remark struck a nerve. "Yeah, I could see that."

Sophie's pale cheeks flushed pink. She dropped her gaze as if she felt guilty. "I'm glad you're back," she said, her eyes darting back up at him.

"Are you?" Jack hated the bitter sound in his voice, but it was as if he was reliving those days when Heather had told him she was pregnant with Adam's baby.

"Of course." The confused, hurt look that crossed Sophie's face made him feel bad. He started to apologize, but right then Peter jerked awake and stood up. Something dropped on the tiled floor and pinged twice before coming to a rest.

Jack looked at what had fallen and felt his skin grow cold. A gold wedding ring with at least a two carat diamond sparkled under the lights. "You dropped something," he said evenly.

The tips of Peter's ears were red as he shuffled forward and picked up the ring. Jack's breath felt trapped in his lungs, and he wasn't sure he wanted to wait around to see what would happen. He drew in a shallow breath of relief when Peter dropped the ring into a black velvet pouch and slipped the bag inside his pocket. While Peter hadn't put it on Sophie's finger, it looked like he had been a busy boy doing something other than saying his goodbyes as he'd led Jack to believe.

"Did you two have a nice visit?" The tone of Jack's voice oozed with irony as he kept his gaze firmly centered on Peter.

"We did." Peter narrowed his eyes. "Were you able to get any work done?"

"Yeah." His eyes flickered to Sophie. "A group of doctors out of Utah and Idaho want me to guide them on a two week humanitarian mission a couple of weeks before Christmas." Jack hadn't responded yet because he wasn't sure what he was doing with his business or where he'd be living. Now he wanted to pull out his phone and confirm the reservation.

"Are you going to take them?" Sophie asked in a soft voice.

Jack felt his wall of self-protection going back up, and he shrugged. "I haven't decided yet." The tension in the room was as tight as a coiled spring. No one spoke for several heartbeats. Then a buzzing sound ended the awkward silence.

Peter reached inside his pocket and pulled out his cell. He glanced at the screen and heaved a sigh. "Excuse me, but I need to take this."

Peter left Sophie's room to talk on his phone. When he was gone, Jack looked at Sophie and felt bad about the wounded look in her eyes.

"Why are you so angry?" she asked.

Jack shoved his hands in his pockets. "What did you and Peter talk about while I was gone?"

Sophie twisted her hands together and stared at him for a few drawn-out seconds. The white poster board on her lap started to slide down the blanket, and she grasped onto it before it could fall. "We talked about my dad." She moistened her lips. "And about us—that is you and me—and our relationship."

"Oh? And what did Peter have to say about our relationship? I'm sure it was very insightful."

"Jack, stop acting like this." Her voice quavered. "I don't care what Peter said. I love you, and it doesn't matter that we've only known each other for a short time."

Nice. Not only had Peter lied about his intentions, he'd also used his time to plant seeds of doubt in her mind. The problem was Jack already had those same doubts swimming around in his head. What if he moved to Colorado and Sophie realized she wasn't really in love with him after all?

"Did he propose to you?"

"Not exactly." She let out a big breath. "He brought the ring, hoping I'd changed my mind."

"You were holding hands."

"I was feeling insecure and tired. He was trying to comfort me."

Jack snorted. "You were feeling insecure because of what he said."

"Yes and no." She lifted one shoulder up. "Truthfully, I'm feeling insecure because I don't know what is going to happen to us."

Jack wanted to say something to reassure her, but his tongue felt thick. He looked away from her and swallowed hard. "I...don't either."

The sharp intake of her breath brought his gaze back to hers. The moment their eyes connected, all the powerful feelings he felt for her slammed into him. *Oh, man.* He loved her so much. She wasn't anything like Heather. Logically, he knew that, so why was he feeling this out-of-control insecurity?

Needing to be near her, he crossed the floor and sat down on the edge of her bed. "But we'll figure it out, okay?"

A look of relief flickered in her eyes. "Okay."

The giant card Peter had given her started to slip off of her lap again. Jack took it from her and studied the pictures and messages. Compared to this, the family Jack had to offer Sophie was so inadequate. "Wow, I got to hand it to him. He really does have a nice family."

"Yes, he does."

"They already consider you a part of their family."

"That's true." Sophie took the card and propped it in between her mattress and side rail. "But I'm not marrying Peter just so I can have his family."

Jack's eyes widened, and she laughed. "Sorry, that came out wrong."

She reached out and laid her hand on top of his. "I'm not marrying Peter at all. For any reason."

Jack turned his hand over so their palms were pressed together. He knew he loved her, but no matter how much he loved her, he could never give her what Peter could—a large, loving family. Plus, it's not like Jack was that great of a catch. He thought about how easily the anger and bitterness toward Heather and his brother had returned so quickly only moments before.

Part of him had to be realistic. Was it really possible he would reconcile with his family? Sophie had only known him for two weeks, and Jack had only been humble enough to ask God's forgiveness for half that time. What if he couldn't stay recommitted to his faith? How would Sophie feel about him then?

"Please don't be mad at me," Sophie said in a soft voice.

"I'm not mad at you." He was scared. If Heather had the power to hurt him, Sophie had the power to completely destroy him.

One of her perfect brows lifted up in disbelief. "You sure seemed like you were."

"I know." He threaded their fingers together. "I'm sorry I was such a jerk."

Someone outside the door laughed. Then Hector walked into the room. "Jack, she's only been awake for a few hours and you're already apologizing for being a jerk?"

Chapter Twenty-Seven

Sophie had never been so relieved to see someone in her life. "Hector! What are you doing here?"

"Well, I came to see you." He pointed his thumb in Jack's directions. "But maybe I should take this idiot outside and knock some sense into him"

Jack rolled his eyes. "How about just knocking out Sophie's boyfriend?"

"I thought that was you."

So did Sophie. She frowned and wanted to throw something at Jack for acting so stupid.

"Stick around," Jack said sarcastically. "Peter should be back any minute now."

As if on cue, Peter came rushing back in. Sophie watched Jack's face and saw the flash of anger mar his features. He was angry because he was jealous. That realization made her feel a little better.

Peter ignored Jack and smiled at Hector. "Hello."

Hector grinned. "*Hola.*"

Peter held out his hand and said something in Spanish. Sophie thought Hector looked mildly disappointed he couldn't pull the same trick he'd pulled on her. The two men shook hands.

"How are you related to Sophie?" Hector asked in English.

Peter's jaw dropped, and Jack laughed out loud. Hector knew very well Sophie didn't have any living relatives.

"We're not related. I'm her…" He glanced at Jack, then Sophie, and back to Hector. "I'm Peter Elliot, and Sophie and I have been dating for the past year."

"Ah, I see," Hector said with a wide grin. He looked around Peter and spoke directly to Sophie. "Maybe I should take care of both of them, *¿no*?"

Sophie tried to suppress a giggle that came out sounding more like a hiccup. Peter's forehead creased as he glared at Hector. "And you are…?"

"Here to see Sophie," Hector quipped.

Peter didn't find it as funny as Jack or Sophie. "Peter, this is Hector Garcia," Sophie said. "He traveled with us and did most of the cooking. He also helped rescue Jack and me."

The lines in Peter's forehead softened. "Thank you, Mr. Garcia, for being there for Sophie."

Hector shrugged. "Sophie was the real hero that day, right Jack?"

"We wouldn't have gotten away without her."

Peter's scowl was back again. Apparently, he hadn't heard all of the details of their escape.

"What—" He started to question her, but just then, a beautiful, dark-haired woman came into the room carrying a bouquet of colorful flowers.

Hector gave the woman a quick kiss and then introduced her to Sophie. "This is my wife Isabelle." He grinned widely and winked. "Now you know why I'm always so happy."

Hector was teasing again, but it was the sweetest thing Sophie had ever heard.

Isabelle's caramel colored skin was as radiant as her smile. "Hello, Sophie." She walked over and handed the flowers to her. "I'm so happy I finally get to meet Jack's bride to be."

The comment was innocent, but it proved to be too much for Peter.

He turned toward Sophie, his face red. "You're engaged to Mathison?"

Sophie had never heard Peter sound so angry. "No." She wanted to be, but Jack hadn't asked.

Jack sauntered forward, a cocky smirk tipping his lips. "Not officially."

"Have you proposed to her?" Peter demanded.

This time Jack's face flushed red. "Uh, no."

Sophie waited to hear Jack follow up with some kind of explanation like there hadn't been the right moment, but Jack just stood there without saying another word.

A crushing fear pressed down on Sophie, making it hard to take a breath. She thought about pushing the nurse call light to ask for something for pain when Yolanda came in holding a lunch tray.

"I'll bet you're hungry, ¿no?" Yolanda said, placing the tray on the bedside table.

Actually, Sophie felt sick to her stomach. Yolanda must have noticed and shooed everyone out of the room, saying Sophie needed to rest.

Although Sophie was exhausted, the fear that she was losing Jack made it hard to go to sleep. She would probably be discharged the next day, but she had no idea what would happen after that.

* * *

Sophie glanced at the clock, wondering where Jack or even Peter was. She had eventually fallen asleep after Yolanda kicked everyone out of her room and had slept for nearly two hours. The rest must have done her some good, because she had just gotten out of bed and, with the help of her new nurse, had walked to the sink to brush her teeth and wash her face.

There was a brief knock on the door, and Dr. Webster walked in. His wife wasn't with him, but Jack and Peter were.

"Well, you look much better, young lady," the doctor said.

"I feel much better." Especially now that Jack was here. "When can I go home?" Sophie asked, anxious to leave the hospital.

"I'd like to run another CBC, and if your platelet count is the same, you can go home in the morning."

"Home as in Colorado?" Peter questioned.

Dr. Webster looked at her pointedly. "I think you would be okay, but you need to listen to your body."

"I can upgrade her flight to first class," Peter offered.

A stormy look crossed Jack's features. "Let's get her out of the hospital before we start making solid plans."

Dr. Webster stepped forward, cutting off the two men. "Jane and I are leaving in the morning to meet up with our group. I'll talk with the doctor who is also following your care and if everything looks good, we'll write the order for your discharge."

Sophie shifted in her bed. "Thank you. Will you please make sure to leave an address where I can keep in contact with you?"

He reached inside his pocket and pulled out a business card. "Here's our email address. We check it as often as we can."

Sophie accepted the card. "I can't thank you enough for your help."

"Yes, thank you, Mark," Jack said, shaking the man's hand. "You were an answer to my prayers."

Peter shook the doctor's hand as well. "Thank you, sir. For everything. I don't know what I would've done if I'd lost Sophie."

"It was my pleasure." He smiled and turned to Sophie. "Since your nurse reported how well you did ambulating, I wrote the order for your catheter to be discontinued."

Sophie grinned. "What about the IV?"

"As long as you're drinking enough fluids, the IV can be DC'd as well."

"Thank you. I can't wait to take a shower."

Dr. Webster laughed and walked toward the door. "I'll let the nurse know, and we'll see you in the morning."

After the doctor left, Peter pulled out his cell phone. "I've got a room at the Marriott, and I can reserve another one for Sophie."

"That's not necessary," Jack said, crossing his arms in front of his chest. "She can come to my house."

Peter lowered his phone, his eyes narrowing with irritation. "I don't think that's appropriate."

"What you think doesn't really matter to me."

"Hey, you two," Sophie said, interrupting them before it turned into a fight.

"What?" the two men said at the same time.

"Do I have a say in this?"

"Of course," Peter said.

"No," Jack snapped.

She closed her eyes, laying her head back on the pillow. The two men couldn't be more opposite.

"Sophie," Jack said, moving next to her bedside. "I'm not about to put you in some hotel when I have a home that will be much more comfortable. Plus, I don't think you should be alone, in case you have a relapse or something."

Peter stepped next to the bed as well. "And I don't think it would be appropriate for you to be alone in his house."

"Give me some credit, Elliot," Jack said sharply. "I'm not going to take advantage of her. Besides, Isabelle and her two oldest daughters are coming to stay."

Peter looked only slightly mollified. "How far away is your house?"

"About two hours."

"Two hours!" Peter's voice was louder than his usual volume.

Before another argument erupted, the nurse walked in. "The doctor say I remove the catheter." Her English wasn't as good as Yolanda's, but she wasn't as grumpy.

"I would appreciate it," Sophie said, glad for the excuse to kick Jack and Peter out.

"I'll be outside," Peter said, leaving first.

Jack paused for a second, his look hard. "I'm not going to argue about this anymore, Sophie. You're coming to my house." He turned to leave but stopped, looking back at her over his shoulder. "You know, if you'd just tell one of us to take a hike, this would all be a lot easier."

He left the room before Sophie could even come up with a response. What was going on with Jack? She thought it was obvious she was in love with him and not Peter. Did he expect her to yell at Peter and tell him to leave and that she never wanted to see him again? Peter was scheduled to fly out the day after tomorrow, so she assumed telling him to leave wouldn't be necessary.

Closing her eyes, Sophie forced herself to remain calm and told herself it would all work out. Jack was just uptight because of Peter. At least she was being released tomorrow. Once Peter left for home and she was convalescing at Jack's house, they would have an opportunity to really communicate and make some tentative plans without Peter hovering around.

* * *

The minute Jack stepped out of Sophie's room, he zeroed in on Peter.

He stood at the end of the hallway, apparently waiting for Jack. He started forward and the urge to deck the guy was so strong Jack thought it might be better if he just kept on walking.

"Jack," Peter said. "Could we talk for a minute?"

"Sophie is coming to my house, Peter. End of story."

"Right." Peter's lips flattened. "So you can just string her along a little longer before you decide what you want to do?"

"What's that supposed to mean?"

"I think you know exactly what I mean." He leaned forward, his eyes hard. "Sophie has no idea what is going to happen between the two of you. Obviously, you don't either."

The accusation stung, mainly because it was true. "Our relationship is none of your business."

"You better believe it is!"

A nurse hushed them and pointed to a door that led to a small patio outside. Jack wasn't sure he wanted to finish this conversation, but he followed Peter out anyway.

"You know," Jack said, once they were outside. "If you were going to make a play for Sophie, you should've said so instead of giving me all that crap about needing time to say goodbye."

"I was saying goodbye, but I also intended on letting Sophie know that I love her and I still want to marry her."

"Yeah, you also threw in your two cents about how we haven't known each other that long and that her feelings for me are fleeting."

"I believe that's true."

"You just keep telling yourself that, counselor."

Peter's eyes flashed with irritation. "Okay, Jack, for the sake of argument, let's assume Sophie is really in love with you, but are you really in love with her?"

"Yes." Jack didn't even have to think about the answer. He did love her.

"Then what was that back in Sophie's room earlier? You haven't talked to her about any future plans or when you'll see each other again. Thanksgiving and Christmas are two holidays where families and loved ones get together, yet you haven't once made any plans to spend time with Sophie. In fact, you insinuated you might be taking a group of doctors into the jungle."

"Sophie was obviously upset about that," Peter continued. "It was almost like you wanted to let her know you probably won't be moving to Colorado any time soon. To be honest, I got the impression you wanted to hurt her before she hurt you."

Ouch. Jack squirmed under Peter's direct gaze, his gut knotted with guilt and remorse. He wished he could deny it, but he knew on some subconscious level the allegation was true.

"She's just lost her father, Jack. What she needs right now is to be surrounded by friends and family. People who love her and can help her get through the lonely days ahead as well as the holidays. What about you and your family? Are you prepared to give her that support?"

Jack felt trapped. Peter knew very well Jack hadn't spoken to his family for over a decade. The feelings of betrayal were still pretty raw, or he wouldn't have reacted the way he had when he saw Sophie and Peter holding hands. Even now, with so much on the line, Jack couldn't see himself seeking out his brother and his parents. Would they expect an apology from him?

Jack's throat tightened, and he looked away. He was so messed up. Did he really think saying a few prayers and deciding he wasn't mad at God anymore had fixed him?

He had years of bitterness and anger stuffed into every part of him. He talked about forgiving his brother and his parents, but at the same time, he doubted it would actually happen.

How fair was it to ask Sophie to give up her chance to have a guy like Peter and his remarkable family for a screw up like Jack? Worse, she would probably do it without having any guarantees Jack would be the kind of man she deserved.

"I think it's safe to say we're both in love with her," Peter said, gaining Jack's attention. "So let's do what is best for her."

"And what would that be?" Jack clenched and unclenched his hand. "Have her fly home with you and live happily ever after?"

"Frankly, yes." Peter held up his hands to stop Jack's protest. "Just listen to me for a second."

The muscles in Jack's arms tensed, and his jaw ached from gritting his teeth. Rather than try and talk, he just nodded his head.

"Look, I'm man enough to admit Sophie is crazy about you." Peter puffed a wry laugh. "It's obvious by the way her face lights up every time you walk in the room."

Jack felt panicked by how much she loved him. He wasn't worthy of it.

"Sophie's already turned me down, and she made it clear she wasn't changing her mind," Peter said, his voice reflecting how hard that had been to admit. "So what I'm suggesting isn't some lame effort to have you give her up so I can have her. It doesn't work that way."

"What exactly are you suggesting?"

"Let Sophie fly home with me. Give her a chance to have some time to think about her choices without all this conflict." Peter's eyes grew more serious. "It will also give you a chance to figure out what you want."

The band of guilt around Jack's middle tightened. Peter's suggestion might be self-serving, but the reasons behind it were valid. The weight of his thoughts made the muscles in Jack's shoulders tense. A desire to escape made him take a step backward.

"I need time to think about it."

"All right." If Peter was surprised by Jack's compliance, he didn't let on. "I won't say anything to Sophie."

Jack didn't trust the guy and wanted to say something sarcastic. Peter must have sensed that. He held out his hand for Jack to shake. "I give you my word, Jack. I won't say anything to her."

After a few seconds of battling his pride, Jack grasped the other man's hand. "I hope you mean that." He gave it a firm shake, then quickly dropped his hand and took another step back. What he needed right now was a good workout. His hotel wasn't the Marriott, but it had a nice fitness room. Hopefully it would be available when he returned to his hotel room.

They went back inside to wait for the nurse to come out of Sophie's room. Jack paced the hallway, his mind preoccupied by Peter's observation. He felt unworthy to pray but did it anyway. If there was ever a time in his life when he needed divine guidance, it was now.

Finally, the nurse came out and said it was okay for them to go back into the room.

Sophie was sitting up in bed, her face a shade paler than her normal color, but otherwise, she looked so much better.

The tension was still in the room, although not as thick. Jack was pensive and distracted, but tried not to let Sophie see that. Peter did a good job keeping her engaged in conversation until an hour passed and the nurse came in to tell them visiting hours were over.

Peter said goodbye first, kissing Sophie on the cheek. He didn't make eye contact as he walked by Jack, leaving him alone with Sophie.

"Are you okay?" she asked.

Jack rolled his shoulders back and took a seat on the edge of her bed. "Yeah, I just have a lot on my mind." He couldn't resist touching her, taking her hand in his. Warmth from her skin rushed through him, the chemistry between them still so potent. "I want you to know I'm praying about us and what happens next." He gave her hand a gentle squeeze. "Will you pray too?"

A soft smile curved her lips. "I haven't ever stopped."

Jack swallowed, his love for her so strong it nearly crushed him. "You have a good night and I'll see you first thing in the morning."

He slanted forward and kissed her. Her mouth was soft and warm and tasted minty. She must have just brushed her teeth. Jack held back, even though he wanted to lengthen the kiss indefinitely. With great effort, he broke the connection and rested his forehead against hers. "I love you, Sophie. Don't ever forget that."

Peter wasn't waiting in the hall, and Jack was tempted to go back into Sophie's room and sleep in the uncomfortable recliner. But he had a lot of thinking to do and needed to make a decision by morning.

Once back in his hotel room, Jack changed into running shorts and a white tee. He found the fitness room and started a series of reps, working his arms and chest first. The workout cleared his mind and helped him to focus. By the time he finished, he knew what he needed to do. He just prayed it was the right choice.

* * *

Sophie removed the tag from the pink T-shirt and pulled the soft tee over her head, thankful the simple task of getting dressed wasn't too draining. She unfolded the black, drawstring yoga pants Peter had purchased from the hotel gift shop for her, and slipped them on. It felt good to be dressed in something other than the unattractive hospital gown.

She sat on the edge of the bed and glanced at the door. Dr. Webster and his wife had come by early this morning to say goodbye. Her discharge order had been written and she was ready to leave. But she couldn't leave until Jack and Peter returned from the cafeteria. The two men were not friends, but they'd obviously learned to get along for her sake. Although she'd only seen them briefly this morning, they weren't at each other's throats like the night before.

It still wasn't clear to her what was going to happen today. As far as she knew, Jack was driving her to his house and Peter was going to follow them. His flight wasn't scheduled until the next day so she assumed once he was satisfied Hector's wife and girls were in Jack's residence, he would say his goodbyes and go back to his hotel.

There was a short knock on her door. "Sophie, are you dressed?" Jack asked.

Just hearing his voice made her heart take off. "Yes. Come on in."

The door creaked and Jack stepped inside, then closed the door behind him. A smile edged up one side of his mouth as he made a slow perusal of her. "You definitely look pretty in pink."

"Thank you." She started to get up but Jack stopped her.

"I asked Peter to give us a few moments alone so we can talk." He crossed the floor in a few long strides and sat down on the bed with her.

A nervous tremor started in her belly and worked its way through her. Was Jack going to ask her to marry him?

Jack drew in a deep breath and ran a hand through his hair. It had grown out over the past two weeks and she liked how thick and wavy it was. The desire to run her own fingers through his hair was tempered by Jack's nervousness.

"I've done a lot of praying." He cleared his throat and finally met her gaze, his blue eyes looking so serious. "Sophie, I love you more than anything." He fumbled for her hand and she was surprised by how cold his fingers were. "I want to marry you. I do."

An icy feeling spread through her limbs. Why didn't this sound right?

He swallowed hard and continued, "The thing is I can't marry you, not until I get my life straightened out."

A high pitched ringing buzzed in her ears as she tried to comprehend what he was saying. Jack wasn't proposing, he was breaking things off with her. She snatched her hand back and covered her mouth with her palm. *No. No. No. Don't do this to me.* A sob broke through and she felt the sting of tears blur her vision.

Anguish filled Jack's eyes. "Please don't cry. I need you to try and understand what I'm saying."

Sophie stood up abruptly, her legs so shaky she thought she would fall. She grasped the railing for support.

"I understand perfectly, Jack." She hated the pitiful sound of her voice. "You don't want to marry me."

"What I want and what I should do are two completely different things."

Jack stood up, but she didn't want him to touch her. She took a step backward, still clutching the bedside railing. "Don't, Jack. Don't make excuses."

He groaned and rubbed his hands over his face. "I'm not making excuses, Sophie." He looked at her, begging her with those blue eyes of his to understand. "If I married you like I want to, I'd make you a lousy husband. Within months you'd be regretting your decision and grow to hate me."

She shook her head. "That's not true. I could never hate you."

"I'm screwed up, Sophie." He tapped his head. "Here." He tapped his chest. "And here." His voice faltered, and she watched the color of his eyes intensify as they filled with tears. "I have to work through some things before I can even hope to be good enough to marry you."

Slowly, his words sunk in, and Sophie felt a tiny flutter of hope. "I don't care how screwed up you think you are. I can help you work things out. We can even go to counseling together if you want."

A faint smile touched his mouth. "As much as I'd like to take you up on that offer, I know this is something I have to do on my own."

A few tears rolled down Sophie's cheeks as he closed the distance between them. She didn't move away. Couldn't move away.

"I'm not asking you to wait for me," he said softly, "but I'm selfish enough to ask you to not give up on me."

Amidst all the anguish encompassing her, she felt a comforting peace settle over her.

Sophie lunged forward and wrapped her arms around him, pressing her face against his chest. Jack's arms enfolded her, holding her in a tight embrace. His breath was ragged, and his heart thumped wildly as she clung to him.

"I won't give up," she mumbled into his shirt. "And I will wait for you."

Chapter Twenty-Eight

A knock on the door startled Sophie awake. She blinked a few times and sat up. There was another round of tapping, then the door cracked open. "Sophie, are you awake?" Camille asked, peeking inside the room. "Nope. You were sleeping."

"I'm awake now." Sophie swung her feet over the edge of the bed and glanced at the digital clock. "I slept through my alarm again, didn't I?"

"Afraid so." Camille stepped into the room and flipped on the light. "You told me if you did it again, I was supposed to dump a glass of water on you." She held up a glass and grinned wickedly.

"I was kidding," Sophie said, shading her eyes with one hand.

"Were you?" Camille walked toward her.

Sophie quickly scrambled back up against the wall. "If you do it, you'll just add another load of laundry to your list."

"It might be worth it."

"I'll move back to my condo and there goes your built-in nanny."

"Okay, you win." Camille laughed and took a drink from the glass.

Sophie laughed with her, although some days she felt too hollow to even smile. Four weeks had gone by since she'd left Jack in Costa Rica and flown home with Peter. Camille had invited her to stay at her house until she felt better, and Sophie wondered if she would ever be able to move back home.

"I can't believe I overslept." Sophie got out of bed and automatically turned to make her bed. "Am I ever going to be normal again?"

Camille sighed and sat down on the bed, impeding Sophie's work. "Hey, I can't finish with you there."

Her friend patted the bed. "Come sit by me. We need to have a little chat."

"You do realize that's how Jack dumped me?"

"He didn't dump you." Her mouth puckered. "At least not technically."

Sophie sank down on the bed and laid her head on Camille's shoulder. "He hasn't emailed me for over two weeks now. I guess he ended up taking that group of doctors after all."

"At least he's keeping in touch with you. When you first came home, you were convinced you'd never hear from him again."

"True." Although their correspondence wasn't very satisfying, at least Jack had emailed twice the first week she was home and once a week later. They were pretty much the same, asking her how she was feeling and then he'd tell her some cute story about one of Hector's kids. He never talked about himself, or them, and Sophie had never asked.

Camille nudged her in the shoulder. "It's time to snap you out of your funk. You're leave from work is almost up, and we're going shopping today to buy a sexy dress for you to wear to the hospital Christmas party. Next, we'll have lunch, and then I made appointments for hair and nails afterward."

"I don't want a sexy dress. The party is for the kids, remember?"

"Well, I want a sexy dress then. Mine and Scott's anniversary is coming up this weekend, and I want to knock the socks off of my husband."

Sophie giggled. "You seem to do that any time he sees you." Camille had an amazing marriage. Living with them for the past four weeks had proven that to Sophie. It was embarrassing how many times she had caught the married couple making out. "I'm volunteering my nanny services as an anniversary gift."

"Thank you, but Peter won't be very happy with you." Camille stood up and pulled Sophie to her feet. "He's still looking for a date to his fancy party at the country club this weekend."

"I've already told him no." Sophie sighed. "He still believes my feelings for Jack are shallow and will eventually go away."

"Peter needs a girlfriend. Let's sign him up for one of those online Christian dating services. I'll bet he'd be a big hit."

"You can't do that, can you?"

Camille shrugged. "I have no idea, but it would be worth the try." She motioned for Sophie to follow her. "The twins just went down for a nap, and the girls are at a play date. I've got homemade hot cocoa warming on the stove and cinnamon rolls ready to be iced."

"If you keep feeding me like this, I won't be able to fit into any sexy dress." Sophie eyed her friend's slim figure. "In fact, how do you stay so thin when you eat like you do?"

"Because I'm chasing kids all day long. And I'm not that thin, my clothes hide what giving birth to two kids and a set of twins can do to your body." She glanced over at Sophie and smiled. "Speaking of thin, you need fattening up. Your ten pound weight loss isn't a good look for you."

"Hey," Sophie protested. "It's not like I did it on purpose." She just hadn't had an appetite since returning home.

Because of her illness and the death of her father, the hospital had granted her a six week leave of absence. She was scheduled to go back to work right after Christmas.

Camille poured them each a steaming cup of chocolate and topped them off with a dollop of whipped cream. "So, did you get your dad's house on the market?"

Sophie scooted the mug toward her and nodded her head. "Yes, I emailed the real estate agent the contract yesterday."

Not all of her time had been spent wallowing in despair. She'd flown to Texas twice. The first time had been to make arrangements to sell her dad's condo. Since he'd spent the majority of his time traveling to Central and South America, the contents of his house had been pretty sparse. She'd taken home a box full of mementos that had a special meaning to her and a dozen journals she'd found inside his closet. The rest of the furnishings had been donated to charity.

The second trip, a week later, had been to attend a memorial service for him that the university had put together. It had provided the closure Sophie needed, giving her the sense of peace she was desperately looking for.

"I know that must be a relief," Camille said, placing the pan of homemade cinnamon rolls on the countertop. "I'm glad everything worked out."

"Me too." Sophie lifted the mug and took a sip of the cocoa. Now if only her relationship would work out with Jack. She couldn't bear to think about never seeing him again.

Camille started icing the cinnamon rolls. "What about the hospital party? Is everything lined up for that night?"

Although Sophie wasn't working, she'd still agreed to help with the annual Christmas party for the children who were in the hospital, as well as their families.

It was a big event where a lot of businesses donated wonderful gifts for those kids too sick to celebrate Christmas at home. Peter's law firm was one of the biggest contributors. Sophie wondered if he would attend the party this year and if he would bring a date.

"I thought I had everything done, but I got an email from Santa last night. He has a conflict with the date and can't do it. I've tried other agencies, but everyone is booked."

"What about the guy you used last year?" Camille asked as she spread thick cream cheese frosting on the roll.

"Don't you remember he showed up intoxicated? I was trying to pump coffee in him as fast as I could before the kids started coming."

Camille started to laugh. "Oh, right. I forgot about that. The twins were only six weeks old, and I was a little crazy from lack of sleep." She slid an iced cinnamon roll over to Sophie. "You know, there was a guy the church used a couple of years ago who was really good. His beard was even the real thing. I could call around to see if I can get a name if that would help you."

"Thank you!" Sophie said with relief. "I don't know what I'd do without you." Her eyes filled up with tears. "I really mean that. You and Scott, and your adorable kids, have kept me sane."

Camille took a seat beside Sophie. "We love you, Sophie." She nudged her in the shoulder again. "And I'm glad my kids haven't driven you crazy." She took a sip of her cocoa. "Things will work out, and pretty soon you'll have your own children to make you about as nuts as you can be without being admitted to a mental hospital."

"I can't wait."

"May I quote you on that when you've been up all night breastfeeding and changing poopy diapers?"

Right then, the baby monitor in the kitchen transmitted the sound of one, or both, of the twins crying.

One of Camille's eyebrows rose up and she grinned. "It's good thing they're so stinking cute." She scooted away from the bar and stood up. "And the way they light up when they see me makes being crazy totally worth it."

Sophie watched Camille run up the stairs. A few moments later, she heard the sound of Camille cooing to the babies, and the crying stopped. Longing for a family of her own shot through her, and she wondered if her turn would ever come.

* * *

Sophie listened to the cheery Christmas music and glanced at the clock for what seemed like the hundredth time tonight. Not only was Camille's family late to the party, so was her Santa. The jolly fellow was supposed to make an appearance fifteen minutes ago. The man Camille wanted to get had moved out of the state, but luckily one of Scott's golfing buddies had a brother-in-law who dressed up as Santa Claus each year and was free for the evening.

Sophie adjusted the antlers on her head, grateful the children were having fun decorating the sugar cookies to leave out for Santa tomorrow night. But most of them would tire out quickly, so she wanted to get Santa here before that happened.

Saying a quick prayer, Sophie fiddled with the zipper on her brown velour hoodie, wondering what she would do if Santa was a no-show. If she'd gone with last year's costume and dressed as an elf, she could probably improvise and pass out the gifts herself. But this year, she decided to be a reindeer, dressing in a comfortable brown velour jogging suit with a cream colored camisole underneath.

Completing the ensemble, she wore a headband with antlers and had painted her nose black. If it came right down to it, the kids would be okay with getting gifts from a reindeer. At least she hoped they would.

The doors opened and several more families joined the party. Camille and her children trailed behind the group. Scott's parents were with her, each holding a twin. Scott wasn't with them, which hopefully meant Santa had arrived and he was staging his entrance.

Camille crossed the room, holding her youngest daughter's hand. "Sorry we're late." She grinned and eyed Sophie's outfit. "Don't you look adorable. Santa will be happy to see one of his reindeer."

Brooklyn tugged on her mother's hand. "I need to go to potty before Santa comes."

Sophie leaned over and whispered, "Speaking of Santa, where is he?"

Camille's eyes sparkled. "Don't worry, he'll be here." She looked around. "In fact, Scott should be coming in any second to announce his arrival."

"Good." She peered behind Camille, seeing her oldest daughter Taylee already seated at the table to decorate cookies. "When did Scott's parents arrive?"

"About an hour after you left. I'm so glad they decided to forgo their cruise until after the holidays. They adore the boys and vice versa."

"Are you sure you want me to stay with you through Christmas?" Sophie asked, feeling very much like an orphan. "With Scott's parents here, your house is going to be full."

Camille scowled while Brooklyn jumped up and down. "Of course we want you. You're not moving out until after Christmas, and that's final."

"*Mooommmy!*" Brooklyn whined. "I need to go to the bathroom."

"Go," Sophie said, laughing.

"I'll be right back. Scott and his guest should be arriving any moment."

Linda, the HR director caught Sophie's eye. She tapped on her watch, a look of alarm on her face.

Just as Sophie reached her, Scott rushed through the door. "We're here."

Sophie looked around. "Where's Santa?"

Scott pointed to the entrance. "Just right outside the doors."

Linda rushed over to the microphone, announcing Santa's arrival. The song *Here Comes Santa Claus* played over the speakers, lighting up the pale faces of those children who were hospitalized for various illnesses and injuries. Tonight, they smiled just as brightly as their healthy siblings.

Sophie heard the distinct sound of Christmas bells as Scott opened the door to allow the man of the hour inside.

Sophie sighed with relief as the man playing Santa took his seat and gave a hearty ho-ho-ho. The last Santa had staggered in smelling like a brewery and sounding more like a pirate, as in yo-ho-ho.

Linda sidled up next to her. "He's good, and he's not drunk."

"Thank goodness," Sophie said, watching the volunteers help Santa distribute the appropriate gift to each child. Those children who were patients at the hospital received more expensive gifts than those of their siblings.

Linda hugged Sophie briefly. "This has been a great party. Thanks for all your hard work."

"You know I enjoy it."

Linda gave her another smile. "I'm glad you're feeling better. It'll be good to have you back at work."

"Thank you. I'm looking forward to it." Linda wandered off, leaving Sophie by herself.

At that moment, Santa looked in Sophie's direction and grinned. Sophie returned the smile and moved to speak to some of the other guests as they waited in line.

The joy she experienced as the sick children received their presents, which included iPod's, portable DVD players and mini game systems, made all her effort worth it. Even though the children were usually exhausted by the end of the night, she loved watching them return to their rooms happy.

She made a mental note to make sure Peter got a personal thank you from her for his contributions. He'd come at the beginning of the party—with a beautiful woman at his side—but hadn't been able to stay. It turned out that Peter had recently connected with Melanie Spencer, an old girlfriend from his sophomore year in college, when they'd both attended the same wedding a few days earlier. Melanie's cousin had happened to marry an acquaintance of Peter. Apparently the renewed friendship must be going well because Peter was flying out to California to spend Christmas with Melanie and her family.

Seeing Peter happy and totally smitten with someone else had helped ease Sophie's conscience. It also made her miss Jack even more. When he returned from his latest outing in the jungle, she was going to be more assertive and tell him it was time for them to talk again.

For now, Sophie was going to enjoy this moment and the smiling countenances on the children's faces.

Things continued to go smoothly, but throughout the evening Sophie caught Santa staring at her. It made her feel mildly uncomfortable, so she tried not to look at him very often. Unfortunately, she was going to have to stand near the man since the Campbell children had moved up in line and Sophie wanted to get a picture of the kids on Santa's lap.

As she took a few steps toward them, Santa glanced her way and winked at her. Sophie quickly shifted her eyes and hoped he'd get the message that she wasn't interested.

Brooklyn was first, and Sophie couldn't help moving even closer so she could hear what the little girl had to say. After asking for all of the Disney Princess's dresses, Brooklyn threw her arms around the man's neck and posed for Scott's camera. Sophie took her own shot with her cell phone. When she lowered her phone to wait for the twins, she found the oversized elf staring at her again. He grinned and had the nerve to wink once more.

Wonderful. This one wasn't drunk—he was flirting with her.

Once they took a picture of Santa holding the twins, it was Taylee's turn. Santa asked her if she'd been good and what she wanted for Christmas. In between, he continued to make eyes at Sophie. It was getting a little embarrassing.

After Taylee climbed down, Santa used his gloved finger to beckon Sophie to come to him.

She scowled and spun around, giving her back to him. It was so annoying to have to deal with this. Wanting to avoid him further, she searched the room for someone to talk to. She spotted another coworker across the floor and started toward her.

Before she got very far, Taylee skipped in front of her, holding a piece of paper. "Aunt Sophie, this is from Santa." She handed her the note.

Stunned, Sophie took the note and glared at the man. He had the audacity to wave at her. Ignoring him, Sophie turned away and unfolded the note.

Hey, Reindeer Girl, come see Santa and tell him what you want for Christmas.

Sophie felt her face burn with embarrassment.

"What does it say?" Camille asked, coming up to stand by Taylee.

Sophie showed her the note and spoke in a low voice so Taylee couldn't hear her. "Who is this guy? I thought he was married."

Camille shrugged. "I never said that."

"Well, I can't believe he's hitting on me," Sophie whispered indignantly. "I'm tempted to give him a piece of my mind."

Camille placed her hand on her arm to stop her, barely concealing her laughter. "You can't cause a scene."

"Do you have a pen then?" Sophie asked.

Camille handed her a thin black sharpie. "Be nice, Reindeer Girl."

Sophie wrote something on the paper and folded it back up. "Taylee, honey, can you give this to Santa?"

"Sure." She grabbed the note and skipped off.

Sophie watched her deliver the note. The Santa dissolved into laughter as he read the message.

"What did you say?" Camille questioned.

Sophie adjusted her antlers. "I told him I wasn't that kind of reindeer and that he needed to find someone who liked chubby, near-sighted, white haired men."

Camille put her hand over her mouth. "You go, girl."

Sophie looked up to see the jolly man heading her way. "Oh my gosh. He's actually coming over here." Sophie looked around for an escape. "I, uh, need to find a bathroom."

"Wait," Camille shouted.

Sophie was not in the mood to fight off Santa's advances in front of the kids that remained. She practically jogged across the room and pushed on the doors, escaping into the hallway.

The hospital corridor was pretty quiet as Sophie rushed to the women's restroom. Santa entered the hallway just as Sophie slipped inside the bathroom.

After a few minutes, Sophie pulled out her cell phone from her pocket and called Camille. "I'm in the bathroom. Did he come back inside?"

Camille snorted. "Don't worry, the coast is clear."

Feeling relieved, Sophie looked in the mirror and applied some lip gloss. Next year, she was finding a nice, unassuming Santa without flirting or drinking tendencies.

She opened the bathroom door and stepped out to the quiet hallway. Having only taken a few steps, Sophie nearly screamed out loud when she heard, "Hey, Reindeer Girl."

Clutching her chest, Sophie stared at Santa Claus, secreted in a small waiting area. The guy was stalking her. Feeling annoyed, she decided to confront him. "What do you want?"

"You," he said simply.

She marched forward, ready to tell him off, when her brain registered the familiar voice. She stood in front of him and peered into his eyes. His really, *really* blue eyes. "Jack?"

He laughed. "Jack, who?"

It *was* Jack. Sophie was so stunned she could barely breathe. "I don't…What're you doing here?"

"Well," he said in a deep voice. "I don't dress up like a chubby, white haired man for just anyone, ya know."

A tremor started deep in Sophie's tummy. Jack was really here. She began to shake and felt her knees start to buckle.

Chapter Twenty-Nine

Whoa," Jack said, grabbing a hold of Sophie before she went down. "Don't faint on me." He had only wanted to surprise her, not make her go into shock.

He watched her beautiful dark eyes shimmer with moisture. *Great.* Now he was making her cry as well.

"You're here," she said as if she couldn't quite believe it. She put a hand to her head and swayed to the side.

Jack acted quickly and put his hand under her knees, swooping her up in his arms. "Maybe we should sit down for a minute."

He carried her to a big leather chair and sat down, holding her on his lap. "See, this isn't so bad."

Sophie's lower lip trembled, and he could feel her entire body shaking. Oh man, this wasn't going like he'd thought. He probably should've never asked Camille for help. After she'd called him stupid more than once, she'd agreed to assist him. This whole thing had been her idea, and she was convinced Sophie would forget what an idiot Jack was and give him the second chance he wanted.

"So," he said, winking at her. "Are you ready to tell Santa what you want for Christmas?"

A tiny smile curved her tantalizing mouth, and she slowly nodded her head. Then she wrapped her arms around his neck and kissed him.

Jack had wondered if he'd only imagined the powerful effect she had on him, but the moment their lips touched, the fiery passion ignited inside him. Wishing he didn't have a foam stomach between them, he pulled her as close as he could and kissed her slowly, tasting the fruity lip gloss he'd craved for a month.

"Aunt Sophie, why are you kissing Santa Claus?" a little voice interrupted them.

Sophie gasped and broke the connection. Jack took a ragged breath, and they both turned to see Camille and her youngest daughter watching them.

"Well, Brooklyn," Camille said wryly, "Sophie has either been naughty or nice. I'm just not sure which one it is, though."

"Nice, Brooklyn," Sophie said breathlessly. "I've been very nice."

Camille sniggered as she pulled her daughter toward the bathroom. "Go back to being…nice."

Jack laughed. "Yes, Reindeer Girl. I think I'd like that." He kissed her again, but the fake beard was seriously hampering the experience.

He eased away and grinned when Sophie grabbed the front of his suit and pulled him back to her. After a few more kisses, Jack moved his mouth to her cheek. "I have so much to say to you, but I'd really like to change clothes."

Sophie looked up at him through her dark lashes, her fists still holding firmly to the front of his suit. "I can't believe you're here."

"I can't believe you wouldn't sit on my lap."

"I thought you were someone else. What happened to that guy, anyway?"

"He's home drooling over his courtside tickets to the next Nuggets home game I had to bribe him with."

"Are you serious?" Sophie let go of the material and smoothed her hands down the front of his chest. "We already cut him a check for three hundred dollars."

"He really wanted this gig. I guess Scott's friend told him how hot you are, and he was very interested."

She smiled at that. "So you bought him tickets to take his place?"

"He drove a hard bargain, but it was worth every dime."

Sophie's eyes darkened. "I love you, Jack Mathison."

Jack was glad he was sitting down. Although her voice was barely above a whisper, the force of those powerful words would have toppled him.

"I love you too." His throat felt thick, and his voice was low and gravelly. The weeks of separation had been so painful. There were days when he had missed her so much that he'd been tempted to make the trip to her house and beg her to marry him, screw-up and all.

He couldn't resist giving her one more kiss. When Sophie's fingers got tangled up in the beard, Jack decided it would be worth it to take the time to change out of his costume.

"Wait right here, okay? Technically, Santa is supposed to be returning to the North Pole." He helped Sophie stand and then made her sit in the chair. "Don't move and I'll be back in five minutes."

Jack ducked inside the bathroom where Scott had hung his clothes. He removed the hat, wig and beard, then changed out of the velvet, padded suit into a pair of dark wash jeans and a red button-down shirt. The new clothes weren't as comfortable as a pair of cargo shorts and tee, but with two feet of snow on the ground, he had needed a new wardrobe.

He slipped on the new shoes and thought about the shopping trip he'd gone on two weeks earlier. It had been monumental because he'd gone with his mother and his fifteen year old niece Julia.

The first day after Sophie had gone home to Colorado, Jack had been miserable and knew he couldn't live without her. It had killed him to fly into Denver only a week and half later and make the two hour drive to his parents' house without so much as calling her.

Once he'd contacted his parents, he had decided not to email Sophie until he and his family worked through the years of hurt, anger and mistakes.

It hadn't been easy, but the effort had been well worth it.

Jack combed his hair and then brushed his teeth. He hung the bag with the costume in it on the bathroom stall and texted Camille's husband to come and get it. He liked Scott and Camille and was grateful they'd let Sophie stay with them while he got his head screwed on straight.

The first step had been seeing his parents, which had gone so well Jack wondered why he'd let it take so long. The hardest part had been confronting Adam. His brother's life hadn't been easy. Heather had run off with another man and left Adam to raise their four-year-old daughter, Julia, by himself. Adam had started drinking and their parents had taken custody of Julia.

His brother's life had changed the day Adam had been driving drunk and survived wrapping his car around a tree trunk. By the grace of God, no one else had been involved in the accident, and it had been a wakeup call for his brother. He had turned his life around and later met and married a widow with two children. Julia still lived with Jack's parents, but Adam and his family were only a few miles away and had a close relationship with his oldest daughter.

Jack exited the bathroom and hurried back to Sophie. Forgiving his family—really forgiving them—had freed him in a way he never thought possible. Jack still couldn't believe that God hadn't ever given up on him, and then He'd sent him Sophie.

She stood in front of the chair, watching him walk toward her. Her antlers were gone, and she'd cleaned the black makeup off of her nose. She was beautiful, even more so than he'd remembered.

Jack stopped only inches from her. "Thanks for waiting for me." He hooked his hands around her waist and tugged her close. "And thank you for giving me a second chance."

Sophie slid her arms around his back, the warmth from her palms seeping through his shirt. She lifted her chin to look up at him, her eyes shining with love. "I told you I'd never give up on you."

A group of people exited the main ballroom, and Jack led Sophie further into the alcove where they were hidden by the shadow. With her back pressed against the wall, he breathed in her scent as he skimmed his fingers along the side of her jaw to cup her face. "I missed you," he said as he lowered his mouth to hers and kissed her soft and slow.

This kiss was different, more binding, as if they were joining their souls together. Sophie sighed, and Jack deepened the kiss. In that moment, he knew they belonged together. If he had his way, Sophie would be his wife the day after Christmas.

A large crowd began exiting the ballroom, the party coming to an end. "I guess we need to go help with the cleanup," Jack murmured against Sophie's mouth.

"I suppose so." She pressed her face in the hollow of his neck. "I think this is the most perfect moment in my life."

"I think I know how to make it a little better, at least for me."

She edged back and looked up at him wide-eyed. "How?"

Jack grinned and untangled his arms from around her to reach one hand into his pocket. He withdrew a small package, wrapped in red and silver foil paper. "I have an early Christmas present for you."

Sophie moistened her lips and took the gift. Jack could see her hands were shaking as she tore the paper off.

The small red box had a hinge, and Sophie's eyes flickered up to Jack's. "Should I open it?"

"I'd like that very much."

Her focus returned to the box. She lifted the lid to reveal a diamond ring his niece Julia had claimed would make any girl say yes.

"Oh, my," Sophie said, her eyes darting back up to meet his. "The answer is yes."

"Hey," he said with a laugh. "You didn't even give me a chance to ask you."

"Then ask me." She bit her bottom lip. "Please. I'm dying to put the ring on."

Jack grinned and took the box from her. He removed the wide, platinum band with a large emerald cut diamond in the center, flanked by a row of tapered baguette diamonds.

"Sophie Kendrick, I think I fell in love with you the moment I first saw you. You were the most beautiful girl I'd ever seen, and that terrified me. I was a jerk, and an idiot and I can't believe you still found me loveable." He reached for her left hand and slid the ring on her slim finger. "Will you marry me? Soon? Like in three days?"

Her eyes shimmered in the dim light, and the smile curving her lips was something Jack would always remember. "Yes! Yes, I'll marry you."

She held out the ring so it caught the low light and flashed.

"It's beautiful, Jack. I love it." Then her eyes snapped up to his. "Wait, did you say in three days?"

"I know it's short notice, but I'm a little—"

Sophie placed a finger against his lips to quiet him. "Three days seems like an eternity, but since tomorrow is Christmas Eve, I guess I'll have to accept it."

Jack smiled when she dropped her finger. "We can always elope. Vegas isn't that far away."

Her eyes lit up. "When can we leave?"

This time Jack laughed out loud. "Camille and my mother would kill me if I spoiled their wedding plans."

"Did you just say your mother?"

"Yes." Jack tugged on her hand and started to lead her out of the waiting area. "It's a great story and one I plan on sharing with you, but right now my family is here, and they're anxious to meet you."

She pulled him to a stop. "Jack, that's wonderful. I'm so happy for you."

"I couldn't have done it without you."

He kissed her then, but kept it short since there were a lot of people waiting back inside the party to know if she had said yes. "Ready to meet my family?"

"Yes, but what if they don't like me?"

"They already adore you, especially since I told them I wasn't good enough for you, but for some reason, you seem to love me anyway."

"There are a lot of reasons why I love you."

"I know, and I expect you to tell them every single one."

"Wow." She wound her arms around his neck again. "We're getting married."

"Yeah." Jack settled his hands on her waist. "Thanks for saying yes, by the way."

She laughed. "Before you even asked."

Camille suddenly appeared, one hand on her hip and an indignant look on her face. "Everyone sent me out here to find out what the verdict is."

"We're coming in right now. But first—" Jack lowered his head and gazed into Sophie's eyes. "—I believe my fiancée was just about to kiss me again."

A beguiling smile curved Sophie's lips before she pressed her mouth to his, kissing him in a way that staked her claim. Jack surrendered easily and decided to take his time. He was vaguely aware of Camille's fading footsteps and the sound of a door opening.

"They won't be coming in anytime soon," Camille announced loudly. "But in case you're wondering, she said yes."

Epilogue: One year later

Sophie had just barely closed her eyes when the crying started again. She moved to climb out of bed when Jack pulled her back down. "I'll get him, honey."

She didn't argue. Their two and half month old son, Carson, had cut his first tooth and hadn't been very happy about it. The tooth had finally emerged a few days ago, but Carson had grown used to having either his mom or dad hold him all the time, and now he didn't like being left in his crib.

"He shouldn't be hungry, but he might need a diaper change."

"I got this," Jack said as he leaned over and kissed her. "Now go to sleep."

Her eyes were shut before Jack got up. As soon as the crying stopped, she let herself start to relax. Jack had the magic touch when it came to getting Carson to sleep. Just before she let go and gave into the fatigue, something else grabbed her attention.

She rose up on one elbow and listened to the baby monitor. Jack was singing a Christmas song to the baby.

She listened to the melody of *Santa Claus Is Coming to Town* and decided she needed to see this for herself. There were times when she thought she'd heard him singing to Carson, but when she'd asked him, Jack would always smile and say she must have been dreaming.

Climbing out of bed, she tiptoed across the floor and down the hallway to the nursery. Staying as quiet as possible she peeked inside the room and felt her breath catch at the sight before her.

In the soft glow from the miniature Christmas tree sitting on the dresser, Jack stood with the baby pressed snuggly against his white tee, gently jostling him and singing the Christmas song. Carson didn't make a sound as his father lulled him back to sleep.

Leaning against the doorjamb, she continued to watch her husband sing softly to their son. It was hard to believe that in a few days, she and Jack would celebrate their first wedding anniversary, and they would be celebrating it with a new baby.

When they'd gotten married last year, she and Jack had decided not to use anything to prevent pregnancy. Sophie was sure it would take her a while since she was older and hadn't always had a regular cycle. The baby had been a honeymoon surprise, but both she and Jack had been thrilled with the prospect of becoming parents.

The singing stopped, and Jack stared down into their son's face, watching the tiny little boy with an expression of awe and tenderness. After a few moments, he pressed a kiss against the baby's downy hair and then carefully laid him back down in the crib.

Carson immediately started whimpering, and Jack leaned over and gently picked him up.

"Okay, little guy. You and me need to have a talk man to man." He cradled the baby in one of his impressive arms and held out his pinkie finger for Carson to wrap his tiny hand around. "I know you love Mommy. So do I, but she needs her sleep or she'll get real cranky."

Sophie's mouth dropped open, but she kept quiet, interested in what else Jack might say.

"She's not cranky very often, and that's the way we want to keep it." Jack pressed a kiss to the baby's forehead.

"So how about you try to be a good boy and sleep for a few hours? Then maybe Mommy will be a good girl and go to sleep right now like she's supposed to be."

Busted.

Jack turned and winked at her, making her knees go weak. She smiled and walked across the room, still as madly in love with her husband as the day she had married him.

"Why aren't you asleep?" Jack whispered.

"I heard singing."

He grinned. "So now you know my secret."

"Yes I do." She slipped her arms around him, resting the side of her face against his bicep so she could stare at their baby. "He's so incredible."

"Yeah, we make pretty cute babies."

"We sure do." Carson was a combination of both of them. He had Sophie's nose and dark hair, but his eyes were the same color of blue as Jack's.

The heat of Jack's body warmed Sophie, and she found herself struggling to stay awake. The frequent middle of the night feedings was taking their toll. She wasn't sure how she'd survived all those sleepless nights during her residency. Despite being exhausted, she was blissfully happy. Being a wife and mother was all she had dreamed about and more.

As soon as she'd found out she was pregnant, Sophie had negotiated her contract with the hospital to reduce her hours by half once she had the baby. After her three month maternity leave, she only had another year commitment, and then she planned to join a large pediatric practice where she would work one to two days a week and take weekend call every eight weeks.

On the days she worked, Jack would be taking care of Carson. Over the year, he'd expanded his business of guiding medical professionals and other humanitarian organizations through the jungle by making Hector a partner and hiring a couple of other men Hector had recommended. Jack didn't actually lead any more expeditions, leaving that to Hector.

He mainly focused on marketing and finding and coordinating the groups. He'd also turned his house into a rental property. That had been so successful Jack had purchased two other homes and was looking for another one. Hector's wife, Isabelle, had turned out to be a great property manager.

"Let's see if this little guy will stay asleep," Jack said, gently laying the baby down. Carson squirmed a little but didn't open his eyes or start to cry. Jack put his arm around Sophie, and she leaned close, taking in his familiar scent.

They watched the baby for several minutes, and Sophie had to fight the urge to reach out and stroke his soft cheek.

"I think you did it," Sophie whispered.

"For now." Jack guided Sophie out of the nursery. "You need to go back to bed and this time stay there."

"I will, but if I have a hard time falling asleep, will you sing to me too?" Sophie teased.

A mischievous grin spread across Jack's handsome face. "If you can't fall asleep, I won't be singing to you."

Sophie's laugh was cut off by Jack's kiss. A few minutes later, Jack eased back and looked into her eyes. "Now, are you going to go to sleep?"

"Yes." She could barely keep her eyes open.

"Good." Jack took her hand and led her back to their bedroom. "There's plenty of milk in the freezer, so I'll get up with him for the next feeding."

He kissed Sophie on the forehead. "You need to get as much rest as possible. My family will be here tomorrow, and then I doubt either of us will get much down time."

"Oh, it might be crazy and busy, but I have a feeling your mom and sister-in-law are going to spoil me." Sophie climbed into bed, and Jack slid in next to her. "They're insisting on doing all the cooking, and Julia has called dibs on Carson."

Sophie snuggled up to Jack, and he tucked an arm around her. "Does that mean I can sneak off with you for a night to celebrate our anniversary?"

"I'll sneak off with you anywhere, Jack Mathison," Sophie said on a yawn.

He chuckled and tightened his hold on her. "I love you, Sophie."

"I love you too." Sophie snuggled closer and tried to go to sleep. After a few minutes, she said, "Jack, are you awake?"

"Yeah."

"I think you need to sing me to sleep."

Jack laughed and kissed her instead.

About the Author

Cindy Roland Anderson has always had a penchant for chocolate and reading romance novels. Naturally, romance is what she loves to write—usually with chocolate. Cindy has won several awards for her writing, including first place with her bestselling novel *Fair Catch*. She hones her writing skills by attending workshops and conferences, and is active in a critique group with some awesome ladies. Cindy is a registered nurse and works in the newborn intensive care unit. She loves to bake, not cook (there is a difference!) and enjoys spending time with her family. Cindy and her husband John reside in Farmington, UT. They are parents to five incredible children. Over the past few years their family has expanded by adding a son-in-law, a daughter-in-law and two adorable grandchildren. To contact Cindy or to see other projects she is working on go to www.cindyrolandanderson.com

Acknowledgments

I have learned that writing wouldn't be possible without the love and support of my family. So let me first give a huge thank you to my husband John and my two boys living at home, Jason and Matthew, for allowing me to write instead of doing other things like laundry, dishes and cooking. I guess I should also thank Little Caesars for feeding my neglected family.

A special thanks to my talented editor Sadie Anderson. Every revision she suggests always reflects my voice and I truly appreciate that! She also does an incredible job on the typesetting and formatting.

I also want to thank my son Tyler Anderson for being willing to read my romance manuscripts so I can have a male perspective.

Thank you to my beta readers Elise May, Stephanie Fuhriman, Lisa Ferguson, and Valerie Bybee. I am always so impressed by the different things each of them point out to help shape the story. I also want to express my gratitude to my critique group, Cindy Hogan, Jennifer Moore, Susan Tietjen, and Angela Woiwode. I'm lucky they let me into their talented circle and I value their friendship.

Thank you to my daughter Nicole Harbertson for once again being the cover model, and for looking great in a pair of heels. I think I'm having just as much fun buying the shoes for the book covers as she is wearing them.

I also want to thank Casey Harbertson for the incredible cover artwork. Seriously, words cannot express how grateful I am for his artistic ability. He is simply amazing and so gifted.

A special thanks to Dr. Matthew Feil, an emergency room doctor at Lakeview Hospital. He took the time to answer my questions about medications, lacerations and bullet wounds, all of which were greatly appreciated while writing this book. Any medical errors are completely mine.

Lastly, I want to thank my mom and dad for sharing their love of Costa Rica with me, and for answering my questions about such a beautiful place. I am blessed.

Fair Catch

By
Cindy Roland Anderson

Chapter One

Ellie Garrett's feet pounded rhythmically against the pavement, her anger growing with each step as her mind replayed the frustrating phone call she had received thirty minutes ago. Sweat trickled down her back as she made another loop around the jogging trail. She wiped her hand across her forehead and slowed her tempo. She needed to cool down—in more ways than one.

Thomas Garrett, her ex-husband, had done it again. He'd managed to make her angry, disappoint their son Cade, and place the blame on Ellie's shoulders. She already had too much weight on her shoulders. Raising her four-year-old son by herself was more than enough.

Decreasing her pace down to a brisk walk, Ellie slowly blew out her breath and looked around the affluent area where she now resided. She was definitely the little fish in the big pond. Six months ago her dad, a professor of ancient history at the University of Colorado, fulfilled a life-long dream by taking a position in England for the next two years, teaching at Cambridge.

When her parents left, Ellie and Cade moved from their tiny condo in Boulder, Colorado to her parents' house in Pleasant Wood, a suburb of Denver, allowing her to quit her part-time job.

So now, according to Thomas, she was rolling in the money and could take Cade to Disneyland herself. She added delusional to his list of defective qualities.

Glancing at her watch, she noted it was almost time to pick up Cade from preschool. Inevitably, he would ask about going to Disneyland with his dad. How was she supposed to explain to her little boy that his father had another pressing obligation and wouldn't be coming?

"Father. Right," Ellie muttered. She wished for once in his life Thomas would try to be a father. Currently, he lived in Australia, enjoying the life he'd always dreamed about. Translation: Single with zero responsibilities.

A derisive puff of air escaped between her lips when she thought about his lame excuses. Ellie couldn't relate. Cade—their son—was her only obligation. More than likely, Thomas's urgent business involved a woman.

Pulling the band from her ponytail, she finger combed a few blonde strands of her long curly hair away from her face. The mild breeze sifted through her curls and cooled her off. A young couple, pushing a toddler in a stroller, walked in front of her. When Cade had been that size, Ellie had been all alone.

Twisting the band back around her hair, she set off at a slow jog toward home. She needed a shower. And chocolate.

Coming up behind her neighbor's house, tiny branches and pebbles crunched beneath her shoes as she veered off the paved trail. As she entered the secluded cul-de-sac, Ellie saw a large moving truck parked at the enormous two-story house across the street from her parents' home. She stopped running and stared at the gorgeous French Country manor. Made of gray stone, it resembled a small castle, complete with a stone turret bordering the left side. On the market for nearly two years, everyone was anxious to meet the new owner, especially since the sale was confidential.

Ellie squinted against the bright May sun, looking for

any kind of evidence the new owners had children. She couldn't tell, but maybe her friend would know something.

Betsy Stewart stood on the sidewalk, no doubt trying to be the first one to welcome the mystery home-owners before anyone else. Her husband, Owen, was the pastor of Pleasant Wood Community Church, and knew the identity of the anonymous buyer. He wasn't allowed to say anything to anyone—including his wife. The suspense was killing Betsy.

Cutting across the road, Ellie headed toward her neighbor. Betsy's short, auburn hair swayed as she whirled around, a wide smile stretched across her tanned face. "Ellie, can you believe we'll finally get to meet the new owners?"

Ellie wasn't as intrigued as Betsy. She just hoped the new neighbor wouldn't mind a precocious four-year-old who, on occasion, wandered into houses without his mother's knowledge.

"It'll be nice to meet them. If I'm lucky, Cade will get a playmate."

While she watched the movers carry in an entertainment center, Ellie pulled at the front of her sweat-dampened T-shirt, allowing cool air to pass through. Sure, having the empty house occupied would be a good thing, but as far as Ellie was concerned, the cul-de-sac she lived in was perfect just the way it was. The Stewarts lived on one side. The Colemans, a nice jet-setting retired couple, lived on the other.

The gorgeous house across the street was flanked by a huge yard. The entire property actually consisted of the other three lots that had been available when her parents had built their home. The asking price was astronomical, and she felt a little intimidated by the kind of people who could afford such a home.

Images of Thomas flitted through her mind. He loved

money and expensive things. He also hated parting with that money to pay alimony and child support. At twenty-seven, the last thing Ellie had ever dreamed about was being a divorced, single mother. She'd married Thomas right after her twenty-first birthday. Eighteen months later, she gave birth to Cade. When Cade was only three weeks old, Thomas told her he had a girlfriend and wanted a divorce.

Betsy nudged her with her arm, cutting into the dark memories. "I'm baking bread right now, and then I'm planning on taking over a welcome basket. Do you want to come with me?"

Ellie's mouth watered just thinking about the fresh-baked bread. "I can't. After I pick Cade up from preschool, I'm taking him into Denver to the children's museum." She gave a deep sigh when she remembered what she had to do. The forty-five minute drive to the city would probably be a good time to tell Cade about the canceled trip to Disneyland. "We won't be home until this evening."

"Hey, you sound like you're a little upset. Is everything okay?" Betsy asked. Although Betsy was twice her age, she was Ellie's best friend.

Shaking her head, Ellie heaved another defeated sigh. "No. Thomas called this morning—he's not coming to take Cade to California."

"What?" Betsy's naturally happy face clouded with anger. "You know, if I ever meet that man face to face …well, maybe the next time he's here, I'll sic all four of my boys on him."

Ellie grinned. The Stewart boys were as mild mannered as the pastor. "Don't worry, my brothers told me to call them the next time he pulled something like this. They'd like a little time alone with him, and I don't think it's just to talk." Really, her big brothers wanted a chance to knock some sense into him. Too bad both boys lived out of state and were never around when Thomas did make a visit.

Betsy chuckled. "Your brothers are just looking out for their little sister." She patted Ellie on the back. "Honey, we just need to find you a man."

Ellie grimaced. "Please don't! The last thing I need is a man." Having been thrown back into the dating world, Ellie hated being back on the market, so to speak. She hated how everyone seemed to think she needed help dating and finding another husband. She didn't want anyone else—not after what Thomas had done to her. It would be a struggle to trust a man ever again. The wounds he'd inflicted still hadn't completely healed.

Betsy smiled at her knowingly. "Ellie Garrett, you are a beautiful woman, and I know the Lord is preparing someone special for you."

Why did everyone think that? She'd already had a husband, thank you very much. As for her beauty…it wasn't enough to keep him from leaving.

"Hey, I'd better go inside to shower." She avoided Betsy's eyes by looking at her watch. "Cade's class is out in thirty minutes."

Betsy laughed and nudged her in the shoulder again. "I get it. You don't want to talk about it right now."

Ellie took a couple of steps backward. "That's why I like you so much."

"Yeah," Betsy said with another laugh. "I said right now. You and I need to have another talk, young lady."

"Did I just say I liked you?"

Betsy grinned and waggled her finger. "You *love* me. By the way, I made an extra loaf of bread for you and Cade."

"You're right. I do love you."

Ellie decided to leave while she had the chance. She

turned toward her house and waved goodbye. "Have fun today."

Fifteen minutes later, Ellie left to get Cade. As she drove out of the cul-de-sac, she passed a white Denali. At the stop sign, she glanced in her rearview mirror. The SUV turned into the driveway next to the moving truck. It was probably the new owners.

Ellie paused as she debated about whether or not to wait and see who the new neighbors were. When they didn't immediately get out of the vehicle, she pressed on the gas and made a left turn.

Her curiosity could wait. Cade couldn't.

* * *

Nick Coulter grinned as he made the last turn toward his new home, and the GPS declared he made it to his destination. His phone buzzed just as he pulled in beside the moving truck. Grabbing the phone from its cradle, he saw the name on the screen and thought about declining the call. His manager, Alec Lawson, would put a damper on his good mood.

Nick's thumb hovered over the decline button. He probably should answer it, especially since he had promised to return the call a couple of hours ago. He pressed to accept. "Hey, Alec. Sorry I didn't call you back."

Alec snorted. "Yeah, right."

Nick leaned back in his seat and stretched out his legs. "No really. I've been busy driving. And thank you for asking, but yes, I made it safely."

"Wonderful. How is Pleasure Garden?"

Nick rolled his eyes. "*Pleasant Wood*."

"Whatever."

He glanced out the window at the tall maple shading the driveway. "It's beautiful. Retirement is going to be awesome."

Alec let out another sarcastic laugh. "Don't get too relaxed. You've got a packed schedule and a few proposals to look over. Incidentally, I still think we should do a press release right away about your move to Colorado. The news would get your name out there and boost your revenue."

Nick thought about having a few days without the media knowing about his new location. That would be better than the Colorado Smashburger he hoped to have for dinner. "Nah, let's keep it until next week like we planned."

Alec let out a deep breath. "I still can't believe you opted for Podunkville instead of L.A. Do you know what you're missing?"

Yeah. Life in the fast lane. At thirty-four, Nick, a recently retired pro-football player was ready to settle down. The rural community outside of Denver had been home to his best friend and college roommate, Jared Huntsman. Whenever Nick had needed a break from his crazy life in California, Jared's house had been like a refuge.

Then, six years ago, Jared and his wife had been killed by a drunk driver. Their deaths had changed Nick. Suddenly, he hadn't felt as invincible. He had taken a good, hard look at his life, and didn't like what he had found. All the money and fame he'd gained over the years had filled every part of him, leaving no room for his Christian faith.

Days after the funeral, Nick had gone home to stay with his parents for a few weeks. There he'd found the solace he was seeking, and had come away with a renewed commitment to his faith.

Although Nick loved his parents, when it had come time for him to retire, Pleasant Wood, Colorado had sounded more appealing to him than staying in California. Plus, it was where he was supposed to be. A decision confirmed by prayer.

"I won't be missing anything, Alec."

"I really don't get you."

"Yeah, I know."

"Nick, ABC sent over another request. Are you sure—"

"I'm not doing it. I can find a wife on my own." ABC wanted Nick to be their next bachelor. Having seen previous episodes of *The Bachelor*, Nick had declined the offer. Despite what everyone thought, sitting in a hot tub with more than a dozen scantily clad women vying for a rose was not his idea of having a good time. No amount of whining on Alec's part was going to change Nick's mind.

"You're kidding?" Alec said sharply. "Do you have any idea how much money this could get you?"

"We've already talked about this. I'm not doing it."

"Fine. Make sure you read the email with your schedule for the next month. Call me if anything comes up."

The phone went silent. It wasn't the first time Alec had hung up on him, so it didn't offend Nick. His relationship with his manager wasn't exactly symbiotic, but Alec did play a valuable part in Nick's life. He had saved Nick's reputation a few years ago, making him forever in his manager's debt.

Nick slanted forward and propped his hands and chin atop the steering wheel, his eyes sliding over the beautiful home. He purchased the house sight unseen because it fit the needs he'd requested. In all honesty, it was too large a house for a single man. However, he needed the square footage to host the mandatory parties required to maintain his charity foundation which helped underprivileged kids throughout the United States.

Anxious to be out of the car, he climbed out of the Denali and made his way to the front door. He stepped into the large entryway and looked around. It was a beautiful home—sparsely decorated, though. Why hadn't he listened to his mother and hired a decorator before moving in? He made a mental note to call his mom later. She'd said something about having a friend who could help him.

The two men from the moving company came down the stairs. Larry grinned and stuck out his hand. "All done, Mr. Coulter."

"Thanks." Nick gave him a firm handshake. "You guys were fast."

He pulled his check book out of his back pocket and had the men follow him into the kitchen where he wrote out the check. As he handed it to Larry, he reminded both men about the bonuses they'd receive if his move wasn't leaked to the press.

Offering the men the extra money was one way to ensure his privacy until his new location was revealed. His realtor valued word-of-mouth references and wouldn't dare to jeopardize his reputation. The only other person who knew his identity was Pastor Stewart. He happened to live across the street and, like everyone else, vowed to keep Nick's confidentiality.

After thanking them again, he stood on the sidewalk and waved goodbye as the truck turned the corner, disappearing from his sight. With his hands on his hips, he glanced around and took in his surroundings. The neighborhood was beautiful and secluded. Just what he'd wanted.

It appeared to be empty right now. Really empty. And quiet. Despite what he'd just told his manager, part of him had kind of hoped for a welcome-to-Colorado party.

As the former quarterback for the Sacramento Defenders, he was used to the media and the fans. He hated to admit if he'd gone ahead with the press conference, he'd definitely have a welcoming committee. But that was not why he'd moved here. Instead, he wanted peace and quiet. Normal.

He looked around again and felt...*lonely?* No. He was just a little tired. As he turned to go back inside his house, he heard a door slam. Looking across the street, he saw a woman coming toward him. She wore a big smile and carried a basket on her arm. As she drew closer, he could see she was probably about his mother's age. He wondered if this was the pastor's wife.

"Hello!" She waved with enthusiasm, crossing the street.

Nick raised his hand to wave at her. At least somebody was going to welcome him to the neighborhood.

"Hello," she said again as she drew closer.

"Hi. I'm Nick, your new neighbor."

"Well, I'll be." The woman stopped dead in her tracks. "Owen is in so much trouble."

17731340R00208

Made in the USA
San Bernardino, CA
16 December 2014